LAST OF
THE APRIL TEN

Carl A. Posey

LAST OF
THE APRIL TEN

ISBN: 978-0-9965177-0-6

AUTHOR'S NOTE

Although actual venues, historical figures, and borrowed names now and then appear in its pages, *Last of the April Ten* is entirely a work of fiction, populated by imaginary people.

To my trusted sidekicks, great and small.

I

Krylov reached the airstrip on the Maragheh highway before the morning sun had quite cleared Mount Sahand, whose high frozen rim floated like a ribbon of incandescent smoke upon the rising day. Inside the clay-stained stucco box that served as a terminal, a sleepy policeman glanced at Krylov's credentials, pulled at a dyed mustache for a moment, then nodded him toward the deserted tarmac. And there, in the company of his single leather bag and an aluminum instrument case, Krylov waited for the ride Churches had promised.

"Nice chaps," the Englishman had exclaimed over dinner the night before. "Bulgarians, I think. Offered us transport to Tehran."

"Bulgarians?"

"I think."

At forty-three, Churches was not much larger than a boy, with a British lad's rosy cheeks and quick enthusiasms. He was always excited, always exclaiming, always sweeping a hand through thin blonde hair for emphasis, his blue eyes popping with the moment's agitation. And, like a boy, he did not always tell the whole truth, a flaw for which he was generally forgiven by those he had, in seeming innocence, deceived. Churches could be as irritating as a fly to Krylov, who was still big and fit enough to make other men nervous, and who, when things got interesting, remained as calm as stone. He had no idea why they got on, but they did.

"Too soon for me to leave, Viktor. I want to do a few more days' cat and mouse here. Make the argument for Bonab going under Safeguards, reactor or no reactor. So I told them, the Bulgarians I mean, I couldn't. But then I thought, here's this ride, and here's old Viktor heading back to Tabriz to catch the Tehran plane, thence Iran Air back to Vienna. Ordeal by narrow seats, crushed knees. So I thought, do your Russian chum a favor. Slip him the ticket. Well, no ticket, really. But you see what I mean. I told them you'd be at the highway strip at dawn. They'll get you to Khomeini before noon. You can shop. Buy a rug. Dried fruit. You know."

"What is this ride *on*?"

Churches had shrugged. "An airplane, Viktor. An airplane. Of course. Silly boy."

Trained to a sharp wariness of gifts that seemed to come flapping out of nowhere, Krylov hesitated. Then, as he considered the two-hour drive in some smoking wreck of a taxi to the airport at Tabriz, the packed Antonov to Tehran, the endless eddying in the Khomeini terminal, the anonymous Bulgarians began to look more presentable. We share an alphabet, after all, he thought. We freed them from the Yoke of Turkish Oppression; they must still feel some gratitude. And the offer of a ride had been filtered through an English colleague and friend. What could go wrong? "I think I'll do it."

"Jolly good." A bashful glance, entirely feigned. "Can you take the gear?"

"You don't need it?"

Churches shook his head. "I just have some interviews." A faint pulse had flitted across the face of this British boy, but Krylov couldn't say whether it was a tremor of mendacity or just a ripple in the ambient light.

Now he stood in the mountain's cold shadow, his leather jacket zipped against the autumnal cold. On the far side of the field a flock of sheep flowed like a rusty fog across the barren ground. Beyond them he could just discern the rooftops of Bonab, five kilometers west of the field, the buildings spread like scattered rubble, pierced here and there by the odd grove of struggling trees and minarets rising to the light.

He thought a column of illuminated dust must be his taxi, heading home; the glowing plume spun to nothing as the sun stirred up the day's first winds. The contours of nearby villages appeared in faint relief and the rough shadows of the surrounding land greened into fruit orchards. The lavender haze lifted from the southeastern finger of the lake, a sapphire promise of water in this high, arid land. It was an empty promise, like one of Churches', for Lake Urmia was only a few meters deep and more saline than the sea.

Iran was a veritable bazaar of such contrary stuff, Krylov had decided, all beauty until the mask came off, tranquil until the self-lacerating frenzies began, brilliant until you got to God, modern until you realized those fancy levers were being yanked by a medieval hand. As with this vast blue lake, you always arrived at the salt. "It could wear you out," he murmured to himself, knowing as he heard his words that it was not Iran that exhausted him. It was the job. No....the mission.

There had been a time when Krylov believed Safeguards inspectors might really stem the spread of nuclear weapons. Not at the beginning, of course. At the beginning, he hadn't cared one way or another, for he was just a technical Russian without much belief in anything, and, like most of his compatriots, he had come to Vienna as a spy. But by the time his spying days had ended, he believed his work made a difference in the world. In that frame of mind, Krylov would have gladly spent his life crawling through the nuclear community's littered cable runs and tunnels and domed containments, its invisible mists of radioactivity. He'd been proud to be one of those atomic people who took risks to save civilization. He became a true believer.

But in the past few years, his faith had begun to evaporate, leaking away like love escaping from a cracked marriage. As though suddenly, his old beliefs acquired the gauzy texture of half-remembered dreams. He wasn't sure what had cut him loose from his former certitude. It wasn't just Pakistan's going nuclear and selling her knowledge everywhere, or North Korea's brandishing catastrophe, or the presumed weapons program in Iran. It wasn't just those former Iraqi colleagues who'd looked you in the eye and said the boys at home had no dirty secrets.

It was the hard fact that there were too many people in too many countries working on too many clandestine bombs—the sense that, behind all the obliquity, all the lies, all the smoke and all the mirrors, there was a universal willingness to render the world a more dangerous place. Those wonderful atomic people had merely delayed the inevitable. As Simon Bolívar famously said of his own efforts, they had merely plowed the sea.

One day, Krylov now believed, all but the poorest nations would have the bomb. No submarine-launched multiple warheads or thermonuclear devices in suitcases—those were for the very rich. The rest of the world would have a kind of atomic Kalashnikov, a small, jury-rigged fission bomb with just enough kilotonnage and fallout to win a seat at the big table—or, if it came down to it, to take a large bite out of some great city. The future, which had once seemed almost promising to Krylov, had become a monster crabbing toward him through time, bringing all that everyone had feared—except extinction.

In a way, that was the horror of it. The world would become inured to occasional nuclear exchanges, tolerating them as it did the occasional genocides by machine gun and machete. When word came that a hundred thousand Nubians had been vaporized in the Sudan, no one would even look up. The world would become that little bit hotter. Like the inhabitants of the forbidden villages around Chernobyl, everybody would eat radioactive food and worry less about infant mortality and life span. Tourists would visit the planet's grounds zero with digital cameras at the ready. Humanity would cease caring about the minutiae of survival.

In the old days, Krylov would have stayed with Churches, trying to discover whether, as rumor had it, the cyclotron at the Bonab Research Center was being rigged to produce plutonium. Now he didn't care. Everyone wanted a bomb. Everyone would eventually have one. Uranium-235 and plutonium-239, it turned out, were as addictive as uncut heroin, and Krylov, like a worn-out veteran of the drug wars, carried the certainty of failure like a planet on his shoulders. It was the weight of that, not the contradictions of Iran, which had exhausted him. He could hardly wait to get back to Vienna, his soft, sweet home from home.

Krylov shivered, either from the cold or some premonition. You had to care about very little to be out on this forlorn airstrip at dawn, waiting for some Bulgarians to do you a favor.

THE HELICOPTER SEEMED TO MATERIALIZE OUT OF THE GLARE, a mere dot at first, low and slow, creeping down the solar rays like a hunting spider on a web of light. Soon Krylov could hear the thump of its rotor, the hiss of turbines. Vortices of dust spun up around the machine as it stalked toward him, the bug-like greenhouse nose down, as though following a scent.

Yes, he thought, here it comes, like the atomic future, ugly and inevitable, this Mil Mi-8 transport that NATO, in its disparaging way, had codenamed Hip all those decades ago. Krylov had passed some of the best and worst moments of his life in these machines, flying over just this kind of ground in Afghanistan. This one was white with maroon piping on the side, wearing the rusty patina acquired by all machinery in the desert. A Persian inscription in bright yellow flowed along the upper fuselage like a string of bright rags blowing in the wind.

Krylov couldn't read the legend, but he smelled the affiliation. The aircraft would be from one of the tramp fleets operated by Globair, Flightline, or some other western contractor, and flown by a crew drawn from the world's vast pool of idle helicopter pilots. You saw these old Soviet choppers everywhere these days, secretly doing God knew what American mischief in what had once been Persia.

Of course there wouldn't be any Americans aboard today, just Churches' Bulgarians, dressed in blue coveralls like Sofia street sweepers, to fly the thing. There might also be a bad boy or two on board, drawn from the world's vast pool of idle bad boys. It was not the combination of equipment and crew Krylov would have chosen. He wondered how he might recall his taxi and have it take him up to Tabriz for the Tehran plane. He wondered how he might repay Churches for this favor.

The Mi-8 crept to within ten meters of where Krylov stood, pivoted in hover to present its port side to him, and settled heavily upon its wheels. The five-bladed rotor spun down as the turbines were brought back to idle. Now the portside hatch slid open and a short, broad man in a blue flight suit leaned out, his wild black hair writhing like Medusa's in the downwash. "Krylov?" he yelled.

Krylov nodded.

The man hopped to the tarmac, then trotted over and shook his hand. "Panov," he said a trifle breathlessly. He picked up the instrument case and turned back toward the idling helicopter. "Come, come," he urged in English, nodding toward the machine. "Come."

Krylov followed his aluminum case into the vibrating hull. Panov shut the hatch and strapped himself into the left seat in the cockpit. The pilot, a younger man with a great bush of blonde hair framed in a green Dave Clark headset, leaned into the aisle and nodded a greeting. Krylov, seeing no bad boys aboard, felt the muscles in his back relax; without realizing it, he had gathered himself to spring. He took the first window seat behind the pilot and began to think this wasn't such a bad way to get to Tehran after all.

The sleepy policeman and a stern-looking fellow in a grey suit and open-collared white shirt had emerged to watch the helicopter. When Panov waved to them, they waved back. No doubt they saw a good deal of one another, these Bulgarian nomads and officials at the rural airports of Iran.

The pilot added power and the great screaming beast wrenched itself from the tarmac, producing a metallic clamor that had always sounded to Krylov like a giant washing machine tearing itself apart. Then, nose down, it swung toward Bonab and the lake, climbing slowly in the thin air, following the mile and a half of runway 26. Krylov thought it was a lot of runway for such an idle field, and then remembered it was none of his business.

He stretched his long legs into the aisle, dropped the seat back as far as it would go, and shut his eyes. This was so much better than the taxi ride to Tabriz. The gentle, noisy rocking of the rickety old ship eased him into sleep.

Krylov awakened with a start, as though fleeing some anxious, now-forgotten dream. But, no, it had just been one of his alarms going off. His body had waited for the centrifugal tug of the helicopter's eastward turn toward Tehran. Instead, the machine marched steadily westward, clattering upward along the axis of the runway.

Bonab fell away behind them. Off to his right, the southern thumb of Lake Urmia wheeled past, its cluster of dun islands rising from water of a molten cobalt blue. "The most beautiful blue in the world," his driver had boasted earlier. Beautiful, but sterile; its water was too saline for any but the more rudimentary forms of life. It had the infertile beauty of the jeweled settling ponds near copper mines. To Krylov it looked toxic and dead.

He saw the pilots' windscreen fill with the rough, ruddy flanks of the Zagros, the high snows of the sierra rising to four thousand meters. He unbuckled his seat belt and knelt behind the open cockpit door. "Panov," he called, giving the copilot a hard tap on the shoulder with an index finger.

Panov turned, eyebrows raised, all innocence.

"Do you know where you are?" Krylov nodded toward the mountains.

Holding up a chart, Panov pointed to a spot just south of Lake Urmia. "Here."

Krylov jabbed a finger at a spot well to the east. "We should be here."

Panov shrugged and tapped his headset. "Air traffic control. A little more west. Then we turn."

"Liar."

A quick motion of the pilot's hand brought the helicopter's nose up suddenly, sending Krylov reeling back toward his seat, off balance long enough for Panov, with the quickness of a cat, to shut and lock the cockpit door.

Krylov thought about giving it a good bang with his hand, so that the Bulgarians would know they had a problem back in the passenger compartment. Then he thought he would conserve his hands, but kick the door open, drag Panov out of his seat, and shake him like a rat. But at that point, the pilot would have pulled a gun, and no one would be flying the aircraft, and they would all wind up in the shallow grave an Mi-8 dug when it crashed and burned on this sand planet. Krylov sat down and hitched his seat belt. He could shake his Bulgarian rat after he learned what was going on.

They had been skirting the southern tip of the salt lake, with terrain something like Mars to their south. Now they entered the Zagros foothills, following a narrow valley between the highest peaks. Winter had already visited these highlands, leaving scoops of white snow on every northern slope. This rough ground had been part of the front in the Iran-Iraq war, a region where armor, artillery, and close-air support would have been almost useless, where battles would have been fought as they had been a century before, with men running madly into fire from the enemy's machine guns.

With sudden, wonderful grace, an American F-16 drifted down into his window, nose high, flaps out, landing gear extended, struggling to be slow. Another appeared on the far side of the helicopter. For a moment the fighters mushed along near the stall in formation with the slower Mi-8. Then, apparently satisfied by some communication from the Bulgarians, the pilots put on power, pulled in their flaps and undercarriage, and lifted the fighters swiftly out of sight. Krylov whispered, "Well, Viktor, welcome to Iraq."

The cliff walls pressed closer to the helicopter, which clattered along, never more than a hundred meters off the rough ground, following the thin mountain streams and animal tracks that threaded like veins through the narrow canyons. Now and then Krylov spied the clustered structures of what passed for a village in these mountains, mudbrick ruins raised on patches of level ground between the mountainside and running water.

He saw no life, no humans, no donkeys, no dogs, and a mere stubble of vegetation, although he knew there were whole families down there, scratching out their lives. No one came out to wave at their machine; helicopters could only mean trouble, of which these people had already experienced more than their share.

With the highest peaks behind them, the Mi-8 turned to the southwest, and slowed. The canyon opened into a broad valley, where streams of blue water had spawned stunted trees and grasses, a meager Eden cupped between the sere wrinkles of these western foothills. On the far side of this empty place, the cliff face wore a purple scar that, as they approached, became a deep, enshadowed cleft in the rocks and shale, marked by a dark fan of charred ground, like the brand of an old brush fire.

A quartet of vehicles parked nearby resolved into a black Suburban with blinded windows, and two white Range Rovers, one marked with large letters made of yellow tape: *TV*. An ivory Toyota pickup with what looked like a storage tank in its truck bed backed up to the cleft. A crowd of armed men stood among them, waiting, it seemed—waiting, perhaps, for Viktor Krylov. Sinking to within a meter of the ground, the big machine crabbed toward them, hovered, and settled awkwardly to earth.

Krylov thought the cockpit door might open, allowing him to grab Panov by the throat. But the Bulgarians stayed where they were. On the port side, there was the sound of someone fiddling with a latch, and then the hatch slid suddenly open, the sunlight intruding like a bomb. Krylov stood up, stretched, thought tactically for a moment, as possible courses of action were discarded one by one, like a bad hand of cards. Then he strode to the door and hopped lightly to the ground.

The four Americans were built like big cats, three white, one black, wearing mirror-finish sunglasses, tee-shirts, black vests, cargo pants, desert boots, tattoos. Krylov could feel their latent restless agility; one expected them to pace, like tigers in a cage, but they did not. They were all nearing or just past forty, which meant their military service was behind them. This was their retirement, standing around in the desert cradling one of the new Special Ops assault rifles, like extras in a post-apocalyptic film. Their faces opaque as lead-lined boxes, they looked around the desolate place as if it teemed with enemies only they could see. Their heads moved like birds'. Krylov found their single-mindedness a little scary.

Behind these contractors stood four more, in line abreast. They were also armed, also in sunglasses and tattoos, but fatter and darker than the first lot. No military service among them, Krylov decided, and nothing scary. Definitely not first-team material. He thought they must be king-sized Polynesians, from Fiji perhaps, here for the money, and not very sensitive about being less valuable than their American comrades.

In the center of all this protection stood a solitary figure dressed like a university student, desert boots and denim jeans below, blue blazer, white shirt, and scarlet bow tie above. Dressed for television, Krylov decided, remembering the markings on the Range Rover.

Behind the amber lenses of aviator glasses, the man's narrow eyes were the color of river stones, capable of looking upon any horror without blinking. His hair, where it still grew on the sides of his head, was shoulder length and white; above the hairline, a pink, freckled dome gleamed in the morning sun.

He was of medium height, medium weight, average everything, somewhere in his sixties. In the old days he would have kept himself invisible; now he was the one you would pick out in a crowd. Krylov could smell the decades of war, cold and otherwise, upon him, the odor of a secret man who, like so many secret men, had come to relish a life of endless conflict. Combat aged the very young; but for men like this one, war was the fountain of youth.

Krylov realized then that he was not just recognizing a familiar type. He had seen this particular fellow somewhere before. He hadn't time to think where, for the man had come close enough to extend the small, spade-shaped hand of an American aristocrat. "Emerson," he said.

Krylov nodded.

Emerson put his scorned hand into a pants pocket and grinned, his cold eyes gleaming. "Sorry about the unexpected stop. That's the Middle East for you. Always surprises." He nodded toward the helicopter, where the Bulgarians were unloading Krylov's aluminum case, and one of the islanders hurried to pick it up. For a moment, Emerson poised, his head cocked, as if listening to the vast emptiness around them, whose silence was broken only by their voices and the wind. "God, what a place! Walk with me, Viktor."

Sharply aware of the squad of armed robots behind them, Krylov fell in beside Emerson as he strolled toward the mountain.

"In our line of work," Emerson began in a voice so soft Krylov had trouble hearing it, "we sometimes need a little technical help. Churches said you'd be glad to give it."

"You talked to Churches?"

Emerson grinned, baring teeth the color of old ivory. "Our Bulgarians did. We only found this place a couple of days ago, and we ran into some unforeseen measurement problems. Would've taken eons to solve them through normal channels. But then we learned you and Churches were just across the line in Bonab and thought, let's cut a few corners. So we offered you a ride."

"To Tehran."

"With one stop.

"Churches forgot to mention a stop."

"He didn't know about it." Emerson turned, his face uncomfortably close to Krylov's "Look, just donate an hour to a good cause. We'll get you to Khomeini in plenty of time for the Vienna plane."

"What if I just say no?"

Emerson shrugged. "We'll send you off to Tehran on the Hip."

"That simple?"

"Yep."

"So, okay. I say no. Now send me off to Tehran."

"In a minute."

They reached the cleft Krylov had seen from the helicopter, a tapering natural corridor several meters wide at the mouth extending perhaps twenty meters into the steep side of the mountain. The dark scar, he saw now, had not been made by ordinary fire; the surrounding rocks had been transformed into something like black glass and a glittering fan of molten sand spread outward for fifty meters. At the far end of the shadowed passageway he discerned a rough aperture cut into the mountain. It would have acted like a rocket nozzle, accelerating the escaping gases into a natural blowtorch. Krylov scooped up a handful of molten pebbles. "What happened?"

"We hope you'll help us find out."

Beyond the opening a light moved, then was suddenly eclipsed. A small hooded figure stepped through the portal, its face hidden by a goggled mask, its body swathed in a white antiradiation suit. It carried a powerful flashlight in one hand and what Krylov recognized as a recording dosimeter in the other. He felt something sigh within: Beyond this door lies ionizing radiation. His skin tingled, remembering the faint burn of gamma rays.

The newcomer pulled off the mask and hood to reveal a sweaty, freckled porcelain face, framed by a haze of strawberry blonde hair, light and translucent as a swirl of cotton candy. The woman looked to be in her early forties, although life in Iraq, and perhaps life in the world's radiation fields, had brushed her with antiquity, crazing her skin like old china, a kind of scrimshaw almost too finely etched to see. She was not exactly beautiful, and yet Krylov could not take his eyes off her.

"Liz, meet Viktor. He's a Safeguards guy from Vienna." Emerson looked at Krylov. "En route to Tehran."

"Hello, Viktor," Liz said.

Although most American English sounded about the same to him, Krylov thought she must be from the south. She removed a white glove and he took her small, long-fingered hand in his large paw. "Nice to meet you." Her eyes, he saw now, were the deep metallic blue of Lake Urmia, but there was nothing toxic or dead about them; they danced with sharp intelligence. He forced himself to look away.

"Liz is a Navy commander, Viktor. DTRA."

"Meaning?"

"Defense Threat Reduction Agency. One of their nuclear folk. For the moment also one of us."

"Did you kidnap her as well?"

Emerson laughed. "She volunteered. Hope you'll do the same."

"Did Ralph *kidnap* you, Viktor?" She laughed, evidently finding it funny for a big Russian to be shanghaied by Emerson's nameless "us."

"We're all first names and initials out here," said Emerson. "Let's move on."

"What's in the cave?"

She sent a questioning glance to Emerson, who nodded permission to talk. "We're not sure. It looks like something went really, really wrong." She nodded toward the blackened rocks outside the cave. "All we know is that this wasn't done with some hand grenade. Inside it's worse, plus there's all this radiation."

Krylov closed his eyes. Emerson had brought him here to explore a radioactive cave. In a moment, the American, for reasons Krylov could not yet fathom, would ask him to shave another year or two off the end of his life. A sane man would say no.

"We saw this fan of charred ground in some recon images," Emerson said. "Got some chat from local villagers about a secret facility. We expected some kind of lab. But then we got all this radioactivity." His shoulders flinched reflexively, as if he felt a faint caress of radiation.

"How long were you in there?" Krylov asked her.

"Ten minutes. I didn't get very far. I thought, every time you blink, that's another rad soaked up. Another head on your next baby."

"Are you…?"

"Pregnant? Lord, no. Probably never."

You would have to be a terrible coward, thought Krylov, not to go where this small, not exactly beautiful American girl had gone.

Liz nodded toward the instrument case, which the Polynesian guard had brought into the cleft. "Anything we can use?"

Krylov knelt and opened the case. "A portable multichannel analyzer."

"Good," she said.

"Good enough, anyway." Krylov took a small packet from the case and stuffed it into his jacket pocket.

"What's that?" Emerson wanted to know.

"Kleenex."

"For what?"

"I have a little cold."

"Really, what is it?"

Krylov held up the packet for the Americans to see. "Sampling kit. Cotton swipes. Baggies. Gloves. Pen."

"I don't know."

"We'll need those swipes, Ralph," said Liz.

Emerson turned to one of the bodyguards, a huge fellow with a tiny bald head and a powerful body blooming with tattoos. "Lamont, how about a suit for Viktor?"

Beckoning Krylov to follow, Lamont lumbered off toward the black Suburban. The Russian trailed after him, brushing the truck's hood as they walked by; it was still warm to the touch. Emerson's little caravan must have driven up just this morning, after he knew Krylov was in the helicopter and on his way.

Lamont opened the rear door and gestured for Krylov to step inside. From a cardboard carton the guard produced a plastic bag containing a neatly folded white costume and a mask. "Just leave your clothes here." His voice was high and soft; inside this giant's little, pear-shaped head, thought Krylov, there lived a little boy. "I'll be outside."

Krylov hefted the outfit and thought it looked a bit more substantial than the ones they gave the "interior expedition" at Chernobyl Number Four; inside the sarcophagus those suits offered about the same level of protection as a plastic raincoat.

He removed his leather jacket, shirt, and trousers, folding each carefully and placing it on the seat, like a fastidious suicide. He took off his shoes. For a time he sat in the sterile interior of the Suburban, nearly naked and growing cold in the autumn chill. Then, slowly and deliberately, he donned the white suit and booties, sealed the wrists and ankles, and slipped the respirator strap over his head, letting the mask hang loose below his chin.

And still he waited.

"Everything okay, Viktor?" It was Emerson, flicking the whip.

"Coming."

But Krylov stayed where he was.

No nuclear person would have come here without the right equipment, a Navy commander least of all. Had she done so, a snap of Emerson's fingers would have instantly produced a Chinook full of every instrument known to man. They didn't need his little MCA. They weren't keen on his taking environmental samples with his swipes. Krylov looked at the other vehicles, one labeled *TV*. Why the cameras? Why me? He felt no threat from the Americans, but it was vexing, to have been so easily snared.

"Viktor?"

A sane man would say no. A sane man would tell the liars to kiss his ass and fly him to Tehran. But Krylov, having heard about the cave, was no longer quite sane. Like the doomed members of the Chernobyl expedition, like all atomic people, he'd experienced the siren call of dangerous radiation; you entered the field, soaked up the rads, and then, worn out from looking Death in her empty eyes, you found yourself longing to go back for more. The prospect of entering this cave made his heart drum like a young lover's.

"Viktor?"

"Yes."

Krylov picked up the swipe kit and peeled it open. He took the baggies and 10-centimeter-square cotton swipes and stowed them in his suit's right hand pocket. The swipes would be contaminated by this rough handling, but they'd still be legible. If he was going to take this journey, he wanted a few souvenirs of his own.

He waited another minute to steady himself, to suppress the secret excitement, then stepped down from the Suburban. He ignored Emerson and walked over to the woman in white. "I am ready when you are." They would climb to the guillotine together.

Krylov picked up the MCA and switched it on. The pair adjusted their goggled masks and sealed the hoods around them. "Off we go," said Liz.

For an instant their eyes met. What they were about to do, thought Krylov, was in its way more intimate than sex. She nodded as if reading his mind, her eyes smiled. Then she stepped through the opening into the underworld. Like Orpheus, Krylov followed.

THE FEEBLE ILLUMINATION that spilled in from the outside was quickly swallowed by the deep well of darkness within. Krylov imagined he could feel the invisible hot rain of gamma radiation upon his skin, that he could hear the whisper of radioactive decay proceeding everywhere around him. The MCA readout showed a spike at the 661-Kev level. "I've got cesium," he said, and the awful term echoed through the cave: Cesium, Cesium, Cesium. Enough to render the cavern terribly hot.

People who worked with radioactive material were allowed about five rads' exposure spread over a year. In here they would be exposed to that dosage every five minutes. An hour here would wear them out. Two or three hours would send them shopping for new blood and bone marrow. Five or six hours would very likely kill. *"Job tvoju matj,"* he breathed through the mask. What have I done? *"Job tvoju matj."*

They had entered through a narrow passageway. Now, following the ochre beam of Liz's torch, they found themselves in a large, domed chamber, its flanks burned and blasted, sparkling where the light struck a vitreous face of molten rock.

Krylov noted the vestiges of an earlier civilization. What had once been low partitions had been reduced to charred stumps protruding from the cavern floor. A scatter of twisted metal might have once been office furniture. While Liz held the light, he took several swipes of dust from the cavern wall and floor, sealed them in a single baggie, wrote an arbitrary 01 on the label, and stuffed the sample into his left pocket.

They shuffled farther into the gloom, moving awkwardly in their stiff suits, sucking air through the filtered masks. Their booties stirred small vortices of pale dust and ash, which rose into the light, then settled quickly.

"This is as far as I got," she said, almost in a whisper.

From where they stood at the far end of that first open area, a curve of rough stairs had been cut in the rock. They followed these downward, past the remains of what must have been other rooms, of metal free-forms that might once have been beds, bizarre glass shapes that might once have been laboratory flasks and coils and beakers.

Below the stairs, another narrow passage shaped like a scorpion's tail curved into the darkness beyond the cavern. Here they paused, as if both sensed some greater evil waiting for them around this final bend. Krylov took swipes beside the portal, labeled the sample 02, and added it to the swipes in his left pocket. Then he let her torch lead him into the small antechamber that marked the far end of the cavern.

Before them lay a waist-high dune of fine pale ash, so delicately poised that just their proximity induced small avalanches. Then, as the light beam played across the ash, they saw a sudden smile of yellow teeth, a shard of femur, tail-like vertebrae, ragged ivory bowls that had once been skulls. It was a berm of the incinerated dead. Liz seemed to shrink. Krylov put an arm about her shoulders, comforting but also seeking some support himself.

The explosion must have begun back near the entrance, thought Krylov. You could read the progress of the blast wave that had leveled everything before it, raging outward from the zero point, then flowing back to feed the fireball that followed some tiny fraction of a second later. The people huddled in this antechamber would have been crushed by the overpressure, then devoured by the flames, all before the sound of the explosion reached them. But what had brought them here in the first place?

He pulled Liz around where he could see her eyes. "Did you know about them?"

She shook her head.

"Tell me the truth."

"I didn't know."

"The truth. What is this place?"

"Emerson told you. We heard there was some kind of lab here so we came to take a look. The radiation was a surprise. This," and she shuddered, looking away from the ash, "is a surprise."

"Why am I here?"

When she made no reply, Krylov gave her a jarring shake. "Why am I here?"

Almost inaudibly, "Emerson wanted an expert witness."

"Why me?"

"You're Agency. You're Russian. Outside the Coalition."

"But you could have staged all this."

"'You' being 'you Americans'?" She laughed and he felt her relax beneath his hand as her fear of him evaporated. "We're good, Viktor, but we ain't that good."

"Enough." Krylov shivered, the perspiration dripping down through the suit suddenly cold. "Let's start back, or they'll find our bones down here."

"Like Esmeralda and Quasimodo."

"No, like babies in the forest."

Liz drifted away into the darkness. Krylov let her go, taking a moment for swipes of ash, which he bagged, numbered 03, and pocketed. Then, as he followed her back toward the distant crack of light where they had entered, he took further samples, which he numbered and stuffed in with the others.

At the cavern's threshold she paused and turned toward Krylov. "Hope you're not camera-shy." A quick grin behind the mask and she stepped back into the world.

An Iraqi television cameraman was waiting for them with his light, blinding after the darkness of the cave. Krylov covered his eyes and turned away, ready to kill. Liz lowered her head and barged past the camera, past a young television reporter in khaki shirt and jeans, flak jacket, ponytail. Krylov thought he'd seen the man on CNN. An Iraqi soundman crouched nearby, holding a muffled microphone up to nothing, frowning at his box of electronics, as if some desperate resuscitation had failed. Krylov trailed after Liz, ripping away his mask, ripping off his gloves, banking his rage.

"Hey, Viktor," Emerson called, coming up behind the camera. "Let's wash you off."

Liz was already being sprayed by one of the islanders, who had uncoiled a hose from the tank in the pickup. She turned slowly, eyes closed, head back, as the chilled water swept away whatever radioactive dust she'd brought out of the cave. "Next," she said, moving away toward Emerson, shedding the white suit as she went. Krylov, standing in the spray of cold water, watched her go, a bit disappointed to see her step out of the radiation costume wearing a tan flight suit. He'd hoped for something less.

"Okay, man," the Polynesian said.

Krylov let himself be sprayed, then headed for the Suburban, where, after emptying his pockets, he shed the wet radiation suit and flung it and the mask out the door. Feeling lighter than air now he was back on his home planet, he put the unused swipes into their baggies and numbered them, 01, 02, 03. Turning to the MCA, he ejected its disk. He dressed and slipped on his leather jacket, putting the cavern swipes and the disk into a zipped inside pocket.

Then he waited, winding down, resisting the radiation-induced wish to sleep forever. He would not soon forget the cave, he thought. It would flow into his dreams, like Angola and Afghanistan. It would, as now, introduce a tremor to his hands he recognized from those old days, when, exhausted, he recalled the Russian boys broiled in their armor, the Afghan kids dismembered by a mine. Like a day's combat, it made him want a cigarette. "You quit," he told himself, and stepped back onto the charred ground.

One of the contractors had collected their suits for burning. Krylov saw the white material curling like plastic plates in a hot fire some distance away from the vehicles, but not so far one missed the acrid smoke. He took the MCA back to its aluminum case, inserting a fresh disk into the instrument as he packed it up, and stowed the unused swipes and baggies. He looked around for his abductors.

Emerson was over by the cleft, talking earnestly with the CNN reporter. The cameraman and sound technician hovered around them like jackals near someone else's kill.

Liz was nearby, talking to a small, wild-looking man with the hair and mad eyes of a marooned sailor. As she spoke he jotted notes with a stubby pencil, nodding now and then. They stopped as Krylov walked over.

"Viktor," Liz said, "this is Lou Bell. From the *Times*. Krylov gripped the man's leathery little hand. Even he had heard of Lou Bell, the *Times's* man in Baghdad. Churches once remarked that, had the Americans read Bell's reports, they might have taken their Forever War somewhere else. "Yes," Krylov said. "Good to meet you."

"Hope we can talk."

"I don't know. I'm going to Tehran." Krylov turned toward Emerson. "Right?"

"Right. In a minute." Emerson continued chatting earnestly with the CNN reporter.

"I was telling Lou what we saw," Liz said.

"What did we see?"

Bell stepped in, crazy eyes twinkling. "Liz described a cavern charred by what appeared to be a powerful explosion and fire, and highly radioactive." He glanced at his notebook. "Ashes and bones."

"And how did we explain what we saw?"

"I said it looked like an experiment had gone badly wrong." She gave Krylov a defiant glare. "We know it got hot enough to melt rock and that there's still a powerful radiation field in there. But we don't know where the radioactivity came from. Or," and her voice faltered, "the human remains."

"I do," Emerson announced, marching over with the other reporter.

Krylov thought he saw Bell roll his eyes.

"The Iraqis were building something they weren't supposed to be building. Maybe a rudimentary nuke. More likely a radiological device. Conventional explosive with a hot isotope. A filthy bomb. The remains? Human guinea pigs, staked out like sheep to demonstrate the effects of this thing." He shook his head in mock sympathy. "Turned out to be a damn sight more effective than their wildest dreams. They evidently got in a hurry, what with Shock and Awe thundering up the Basra road. A misstep, and Ka-boom!"

Emerson leaned closer to the two journalists. "They were building devices that, if you put them into the Paris Métro, or the Superbowl, or the streets of lower Manhattan, would produce massive casualties and contamination, yes, and that old mainstay, blind terror. A weapon of mass destruction. As we believed at the time. As we told the Congress and the American people. As we now know, looking at the evidence in this cave."

"But it's a dead issue," said Bell. "I mean, everybody's acknowledged there were no WMDs to be found. No programs. Not even evil intentions."

Emerson shrugged. "A lot of people want it to be a dead issue. But the gut feeling is a great divining rod, Lou. The President's gut feeling. The Vice President's. Mine."

Bell said, "They're gone, Ralph. And their 'gut feelings' were dead wrong."

"Not now, not with this," and Emerson waved a hand at the cave entrance. "The elusive smoking gun."

"That's your interpretation."

"No, it's what we have here. God, Lou, what else could it be? A fireball to melt rock? All that radiation? They sure God weren't working on a cure for cancer."

"I'd like to see it for myself."

The young CNN man averted his eyes, but nodded, willing but not eager to soak up some rads. The camera and sound men emanated nothing; they quietly went wherever their reporters took them, which, more often than they liked to think about, was to the grave.

Emerson shook his head. "That's not on, not right now."

"Then there's no story."

"No story! This is the story of the goddamned century. This is the story that explains why we went to war."

"Only if people think it's true. One hates to state the obvious, but this could just be more government stagecraft. Gulf of Tonkin meets Ali Baba's cave. My editors promoted those dire reports of yellowcake from Niger and centrifuge-caliber aluminum tubes. When it turned out to be shit, they were left a bit disenchanted. They no longer believe what you people say. But they still believe me, just. So, do I go in?"

Emerson turned to Krylov. "Viktor, tell the man what you saw."

Ah, enter the expert witness. Bell's pencil stub poised in mid-air, the CNN cameraman took aim. Krylov looked toward the portal. He imagined the spreading blast front, the fireball, the frightened people waiting in that anteroom. All that cesium. How else to explain what they had seen? "I saw what she described."

"A failed bomb experiment?"

"Who knows? Signs of a very hot fire. Strong radiation field. I don't know about bombs."

"A fission explosion?"

"No."

"A dirty bomb?"

"Maybe."

"There, you heard it from a Russian, Lou," crowed Emerson. "A Safeguards inspector."

Bell was studying Krylov. "I thought the Americans threw you chaps out of Iraq."

"I am here like you….by special invitation."

"Touché." Then, "Think this is the elusive smoking gun?"

Krylov shrugged. "If you want very much to have this smoking gun, of course. But people are always building something they should not."

"The cigar is just a cigar?"

"I don't follow."

"Never mind. You think they built a bunch of these things, whatever they are, before the accident?"

"An accident would come sooner rather than later. Like the first time you tried it."

"So you don't think what you saw in the cavern was consistent with Mr. Emerson's dirty-bomb hypothesis?"

"Consistent?" Krylov grinned. "Sure. Consistent with every kind of imagining. You should invent one yourself."

"Don't worry, I shall." Bell chuckled. "The Cold War must be truly over and done. Just by being here you've done the Americans a big favor."

"Sometimes being here can't be helped. Ask any journalist."

Bell chuckled. "We never learn, do we?"

"No, we never do."

Emerson quickly intruded between them. "Let's move on. We brought you in so you could begin reporting one very important story. It's not yours to tell just yet. Strict embargo. But after my people go on the air with it, and people stop calling my president a liar, it's all yours. Well, everybody's, but this thing today gives you a good head start."

Some distance away, the Mi-8 began to huff and puff, the rotors, drooping and still, slowly revived. Emerson said, "There's your Tehran flight, Viktor. Thanks for stopping by."

"So, it is over?"

Emerson grinned. "As you know better than I, Viktor, it's never over."

"*Job tvoju matj,* Ralph."

"Thank you, Viktor, your mother too." Emerson didn't bother to extend a hand this time. Krylov picked up the aluminum case and started for the helicopter.

Liz fell in beside him. "Sorry."

"I too."

"What do you think happened in the cave?"

"I am just wise enough to say I don't know." And, he thought, I am just smart enough to find out.

Panov stood in the open hatch of the Hip, holding on with one arm, beckoning eagerly with the other. "Come, come. We catch the Vienna plane."

"See you," she said.

"You never know."

Krylov boarded the helicopter and Panov closed the hatch behind him. The not exactly beautiful American Navy commander stood on the charred earth outside the machine, her heart, like his, deformed by the brief intimacy of this first contact. He was relieved when the helicopter, with a great howl and clatter, lifted off, and the woman vanished in the ecru whirlwind of its downwash.

As they climbed eastward, Krylov saw the vehicles begin to move, trailing plumes of pale dust as they headed back toward the lower desert and, perhaps, the airstrip at Bashur or Erbil. Far away to the southwest the Great Zab twisted like a thread of light toward its distant confluence with the Tigris. The helicopter eased into the narrow valleys of the Zagros foothills, climbing back the way it had come. Soon Krylov could just discern, in the distance, the strange blue sheen of Lake Urmia.

He pulled over the instrument case and opened it on his lap. The labeled baggies were gone and there was no disk in the MCA. As expected, one of Emerson's bad boys had stolen them. Krylov took the exposed swipes and disk out of his inside jacket pocket and stowed them with the analyzer, then closed and locked the case. He would like to be a fly on the wall when Emerson discovered that the stolen swipes were clean and there was nothing on the disk.

Panov stepped out of the cockpit, and, before Krylov could stir, held out a placating palm. "Is okay, is okay." Then, rummaging for a moment in a metal box attached to the fuselage, he brought forth a sandwich wrapped in aluminum foil and a bottle of Murree's Millennium beer, which he opened. "Here. Like Singapore Airlines, yes?"

The sandwich was stale brown bread wrapped around a limp fold of lettuce between a slice of lamb and a glob of sour cream. It might have been in the Mi-8 for weeks; Bulgarians were optimists when it came to food. Like the beer, it could have come all the way from Pakistan. But, by now a bit of an optimist himself, Krylov found the sandwich altogether delicious, and a deep draft of Murree's amplified his pleasure.

This was like an interlude in the Afghanistan war, when one took a moment to wolf something down with a little vodka while clattering along in one of these old machines. The memory was so vivid that, peering at the empty land wheeling below him, Krylov half expected to see the spiraling rise of a Stinger attracted by their thermal scent. It was then, straddling two epochs, that he remembered where he'd seen Emerson before.

It had been a lifetime ago, eighty-five, eighty-six, when there had still been a Soviet Union and the war in Afghanistan still seemed something one might win. Krylov had watched the American through the four-power sight on a Dragunov SVD sniper rifle, borrowed from a young *Spetsnaz* sergeant called Sasha.

The American was strutting around before a handful of mujahideen, rough young men in shalmar kameeze, turbans, chapans, squatting in the bright, dusty light of that northern desert, trying not to show how much they wanted the Stingers Emerson and his boys had brought in from Pakistan. Emerson had dark hair then, combed down slick as a British banker's. He wore khakis and a white dress shirt without a tie, the sleeves rolled up, civilian walking shoes. No fancy feathers yet. The veteran spy's invisibility was still intact.

"Go on," Sasha had urged in a whisper. "It's an easy shot from here."

"Here" was a concavity they'd scraped in the ochre ground the night before, and camouflaged, to wait for the Americans and their impassive audience. An easy shot, as Sasha said, not three hundred meters.

"Go on, take him. Take them all. You have ten shots. Kill ten of them. Then we walk over and take their Stingers and American Express cards, no problem." A reflective pause. "But don't try winging anybody. That just makes them angry. Go for the heart or the head. But do it, Viktor. You won't get another chance like this one."

Krylov had considered it, he was still that young. But then he'd thought, So I blow off this fellow's head and then everybody else comes running at us, Kalashnikovs and M-16s blazing. He had handed the Dragunov back to young Sasha. "You do it, but wait until I've gone."

Sasha had passed up the opportunity, and never had another. A few days later the Mi-8 hauling his squad to a new sector was brought down by a Stinger, perhaps one of those he and Krylov had watched the Americans demonstrate. Life was full of such evil symmetries.

Ah well, thought Krylov now, we all make mistakes. His had been to let the cave seduce him, and then, as the fellow from the *Times* had put it, to do the Americans a favor. He felt itchy and angry, a bit used, and yearned for a long, deep bath in his lovely old Vienna. Then, as the pendular motion of the old ship rocked him toward the sleep of an exhausted and thoroughly irradiated man, he produced one final thought: At least it's over.

Like an echo, his mind played back Emerson's sneering response: It's never over. But by then, Krylov was asleep, dreaming of a dune of human ash, from which skulls peered at him with lively golden eyes.

II

Often, when he slept, Peter Gayle dreamed of what he called his Captivity. At first, the dreams had driven him out of sleep, lathered and afraid, trying futilely to utter a desperate wordless cry. But the dreams had lost their ability to frighten. He thought they must be his mind's method of rinsing away hard memories and wished the process Godspeed. He was bloody tired of caring so much about a few weeks' hazing. New boys at Eton endured worse, he liked to tell himself, knowing it wasn't true.

In the dreams of his Captivity there was always the cave, although, as far as he could recall, there had been none. It seemed to him that he remembered every second of that cruel interlude, every beating, every moment lying in his own waste, every minute chained, every occasion of being trotted out for the general amusement of his Iraqi captors. But there had been no cave. Human sties, yes, prisons, yes, interrogation rooms, yes. Even the sweet solace of a hospital. But no cave. And yet his mind, as it bathed away the bad memories, kept showing him one. Ah, well, he thought now, it's just one of its tricks. The mind was a barrel of monkeys.

His ghost materialized in the narrow window, then hovered there, a tall, slender figure in one of the hotel's white dressing gowns, the pale aquiline face and scruff of platinum hair acquiring further definition as the night came down outside. Against the failing light, his reflection became almost another person in the room.

For a time Gayle studied this apparition of himself, this partial man who appeared in windows as darkness fell. He often felt that he was exactly like the reflected creature, not quite intact, almost transparent, spectral. But, no, not dead. The bastards hadn't killed him.

Don't think about the bastards. Think about this place you've always loved. The man in the window smiled. Remember where you are.

Gayle had often come here, to the Hotel Victoria in Glion, perched on a steep slope above Montreux, above the gunmetal glow of Lake Léman and the necklace of lights along its northern shore, Lausanne twinkling like hot ashes on a distant grate. As a boy, Gayle had thought it was Geneva, but, no, it had turned out to be Lausanne. Children were generally wrong about such things.

The first time Peter Gayle saw the Hotel Victoria he had been eight, trapped in a rattling 1962 Vauxhall estate the color of a rotting apple, sitting behind his mother; she wouldn't let him in the front seat while driving on the Continent. The Vauxhall had right-hand steering, and stood out like a cripple among the deft left-handers of Europe. Gayle hated the idea that people would think him the helpless little captive of this inferior vehicle and wonder why he was in the back seat.

Of course he kept such discomforts to himself. He would have run through the streets naked or robbed banks, if that was what it took to stay beside the most beautiful mother in the universe. She was nearly six feet tall, long-limbed, with a confident stride that said she owned the world, when, in fact, she owned very little. Her eyes were a sapphire blue and, like the gemstone, could be quite warm, or very cold. Her alabaster skin possessed an Oriental smoothness, her hair was the color of old gold, and, unfurled, reached to her narrow waist. The sight of her had always made Peter think of Vikings. He would have done anything for her, as she, it had always been clear, would have done anything for Peter.

They had come puffing and steaming up the switchback turns from the shoreline highway, the Vauxhall more or less throwing itself, exhausted, upon the level patch of gravel that was the hotel's small parking lot, as though the car had swum the lake and climbed a mountain to get there.

From that point onward, Peter remembered only magic. The hotel perched on the steep hillside as if carved from its rock, the cadmium yellow awnings over every window like the sails of a vessel setting out on a voyage of excitement and mystery. Gardens staked with tall trees ran from the main building down to a sharp edge, where the ground dropped ten stories to a narrow road, and then dropped again, and again, until it arrived at the vast slate desert of the lake.

Entering the hotel that first time had been like stepping into an earlier age, the lobby populated with antique figures and paintings, old plants, tapestries, Chinese carpets. Everyone seemed so graceful, and so unmodern. The wrinkles of crossing Europe in a nasty old Vauxhall were swiftly smoothed by the calm, pretty women at the reception desk, by the avuncular Theodore who, although not much taller than Peter, looked capable of carrying tons of luggage under his powerful, simian arms.

The rooms were what Mother had always had at the hotel, a suite on the upper corner of the building, with views over the lake from one wall, and from the other a vista of the treed hillside, still devoid of other structures, rising toward the sky. They had taken their meals in a sheltered corner of a terrace dining room, where, with utmost discretion, she taught him what to eat, and how. The tall, lovely woman and her slender blonde boy had become the English Couple, a name applied by their hosts without a trace of derision.

Gayle smiled, trapped in reverie. It had been magical indeed, to escape from the England of 1968, from that universe into this earlier one, where Victoria herself would have been at ease; to slip from a world where modernity devoured everything it touched into this secret reservoir of tradition.

His mother had been coming to the hotel since just after the war, with her mother; her father had been lost to the Blitz. They had come in the early autumn every year, as the hotel flickered nervously between epochs, enduring hard times, enjoying good ones, until it had finally settled for something like 1890 and a tolerable prosperity.

Peter wasn't sure whether his mother had come here with his father, a dimly remembered adult swept from the board of life by a broken heart. "Broken" had been Mother's way of dressing up a very ordinary sort of death, as she did a very ordinary sort of life by calling the lost father Mr. Gayle or the Guv. The boy didn't mind such stuff, although he never called his father anything, and never thought of the man when they visited the hotel. It had not seemed to Peter much of a place for fathers anyway.

The English Couple never stayed for very long; there wasn't money for that. But every year, well before winter took hold, she would withdraw enough from the small account she kept at the Union Bank in Montreux to support what she called, in her perfectly turned contralto, "Our Week at the Victoria." They did it in all the autumns left to her. Not even her cancer kept them away.

When, as cancers tend to do, hers finally won the contest, Peter brought her ashes to the Victoria and, late at night, straddling a windowsill with a crystal tumbler of whisky in one hand, secretly scattered them, handful by handful, into the moonlight. The beautiful woman became a pale cloud upon the night, a kind of ghost, haunting the air above the lake. That had been 1982, the year of the Falklands, the year Brezhnev died, the year Peter Gayle took seconds in English lit and history and went to see the RAF about becoming a pilot.

As he had his mother's ashes, Gayle had allowed the Week at the Victoria to drift out of his life. But he still returned now and then to this favorite place, often, as he had been trained from boyhood to be, in the company of a tall, beautiful woman. Now he cocked an ear toward the far room, where tonight's beautiful woman had begun to stir. She had the television going, he could hear the former American president on CNN, the flat drawl claiming some new discovery in Iraq.

Gayle heard the bathroom door click shut and wandered back toward their rumpled bed and the television glow. The president had been replaced on-screen by a masked pair, one large, one small, dressed in white radiation suits stepping out of a narrow portal in beige rock. A young reporter in flak vest and a khaki white-hunter shirt with pockets everywhere came on. His blonde hair was tied back in a queue. "What did you find in there?"

A big, angry-looking man appeared in close-up, hard blue eyes, a mane of disheveled black and silver hair, the hair of a middle-aged wolf. The screen legend said he was Nuclear Safeguards Inspector V. Krylov. A Russian, then. Gayle's interest rose. Cold War attitudes aside, he'd never met a Russian he hadn't liked.

"Signs of a very hot fire," the Russian was saying, "strong radiation field."

Cut to the reporter. "And human remains. Was it a fission explosion?"

"No."

"A radiological device, a dirty bomb?"

"Maybe." The Russian disappeared.

"What remains of the suspected bomb laboratory," the reporter said now, nodding toward a tumble of rocks behind him, "hides in a vast cavern behind these boulders." The camera zoomed past him to show the narrow passage from which the white-suited couple had emerged. "A cavern too radioactive for us to enter."

We're all thinking caves this afternoon, thought Gayle.

"Inside this cave," the correspondent entoned, "Saddam's scientists tried to build an arsenal of dirty bombs." He paused for effect; his smooth, fair face, now gone mock sad, filled the screen. "Tried and failed, horribly. I'm Biff Faraday somewhere in northern Iraq."

"Thank you very much for that, Biff," said the anchor in Atlanta. "A very important story. We're still waiting to hear from the White House, but let's play the former president's response again."

The ex-president reappeared, as always looking surprised to be there. "This discovery in Iraq is, I firmly believe, the first of many. Meanwhile, let me just say, probably not for the last time, that we misled nobody. That we did not skew intelligence. We have found what we always knew was there. I don't believe we need more evidence that Saddam Hussein was pursuing weapons of mass destruction. Everybody, including History, should've finally got it: the world is a better, safer place without that evil dictator in it."

Gayle had never liked the American president, not because he was dull, without affect, and a bully, but because he had once become a jet fighter pilot in order to avoid a fight, and then had abandoned flight. He had tasted and thrown away the rare, keenly felt life that Peter Gayle had lost and now missed like an amputated limb that never stopped hurting. There was nothing in the world like flying well and fighting hard at the same time.

He closed his eyes and for a moment felt the old adrenaline of strapping on a GR.1 Tornado, then booming out of what had once been RAF Muharraq, Gayle, called Whitey for his shock of pale hair, flying, Mickey Williams, called Mouse, in the back seat navigating, the Tornado flown by Jamey Trout, called Fish, on their wing.

It would be the desert's brilliant night with a bright smoke of stars, crowded with allied aircraft all lighted up, some to bomb, some to suppress antiaircraft, some to fly cover. Near the frontier, the Tornadoes, now two flights of four, found the huge VC-10 tankers orbiting as patiently as mother whales to feed the fighters.

Once topped off, the Tornadoes dropped toward the sand, wings in maximum sweep, afterburners lit up to 600 knots, then back to normal military power. Navigation lights out, they crossed the border 200 feet above the terrain, a pale wake of sand trembling behind them as they fanned out into two Card-Four formations, the airplanes several miles apart, then diverging further, each Tornado working up its own plan of attack.

All done on the quiet, no chit-chat on the radio, all hands-off as the autopilot followed the land, Mouse working them toward the target. A few minutes into their future, the air bases at Tallil or Rumaylah or Al Assad waited for these drab, quick British birds to fly into their nets. "Christ," Gayle whispered, weak with memory. "Christ."

One night, as, doors closed, they fled the arcing tracers and surface-to-air threats of Rumaylah, their thousand-pounders lighting up the world behind them, a missile detonated close enough to ignite the starboard wing and start the Tornado rolling madly. Gayle fought the airplane for a time, felt its mechanical vitality drain away to nothing, like a sparrow dying in his hand. "We're fucked, Mouse," he said into his mask. "Out we go."

"Roger, Boss," said Mickey.

They had ejected into the hammering slipstream of their doomed ship, into the wash of stars and the distant light of fires started by their bombs. Their seats released them to their parachutes, and the two men drifted down, several miles apart, toward the starlit desert floor and the platoon of waiting Iraqi soldiers. By the time the search and rescue boys had arrived, he and Mouse were trussed face down in the back of a Toyota pickup hurrying them toward their Captivity.

The odd thing was that one would do it again, and then again. The more you went in, the more you wanted to go, even knowing it would likely kill you or, if you did it long enough, break your spirit. It hadn't cracked Gayle, not the dangerous flying, not the shoot-down, not even Captivity. He would have liked to carry on. By now he would have moved on to the Typhoon. Ah, he could almost taste the Typhoon.

But The Powers thought he'd had enough. They thought they discerned some tremor, some crazing of his emotional surfaces, and had him stand down. Unfair, he thought, like everything. So he had left the flying to others, and then, finding military life without wings intolerable, he'd let The Powers invalid him out.

Cut off from flight, Gayle had begun writing about it, which he thought must be the next best thing. And finally, after rocking along as a freelancing war pensioner, he'd found a contract spot with Jane's that paid him to roam the aviation industry, doing work he would have done for nothing. Now and then there would be the odd flight in the back seat of a fighter, the chance to pull a few turns and effortless rolls. Some of the younger flying officers still called him squadron leader. Some of the older ones like Jamey Trout still called him Whitey, as he still called Mickey Williams Mouse. Such stuff wasn't everything he wanted, but it was better than a void.

THE SAME COULD BE SAID OF TODAY'S BEAUTIFUL GIRL, who now stepped into the room as though spun from the nimbus of steam that trailed her from the bath. She was almost as tall as Gayle, swan-necked and lithely built, draped in a white hotel bathrobe, absent-mindedly toweling a golden tangle of wet hair, but also wary. She came into the room like a wild creature entering an arena, like an amnesiac, wondering where she was, and why. But when she saw Gayle she relaxed, the blue eyes warmed, the broad mouth parted in a smile he thought must be friendly. He smiled back. For a time they poised that way, still a bit shy of each other, as if to ask, How did this happen and where do we go from here? Then, aware that they both heard the same unstated questions in the air, they laughed.

"Here," Gayle said, taking the towel away from her. "Let Anatole have a turn."

"Anatole?" she wondered, smiling.

"Of Toulouse."

"Ah. *That* Anatole."

Like all Gayle's beautiful women, today's was somewhere in her upper thirties—younger than that and they became extraterrestrial in their strangeness. She had what Gayle thought of as a smart face, which radiated clarity and something more, wisdom perhaps, or experience. She seemed to have seen and understood things. A serious face, then, as well as an attractive one, and strangely familiar. Where had he seen her before? He smiled. In a previous life. In a forgotten film. On a Paris street. Who knew?

She used almost no make-up, her vivid colors were her own. English skin, he thought, with a faint ivory sheen that whispered Asia. He thought she must be eastern European, even Russian. They hadn't got around to discussing origins in more than a general way. One didn't share much in the fast lane to intimacy, or during those delicious late afternoons spent in bed with a perfect stranger.

She would know he was British because she'd heard him speak and knew he had something to do with aviation because they'd met that morning in the Aerospatiale plant at Toulouse-Blagnac. They'd sat next to each other at a press conference on sales of the A380, "You know," Gayle had leaned over to whisper into the pearly shell of her ear, "the *Mumbo* Jumbo," adding light to her wise eyes, putting a smile on those rose lips.

Gayle had found himself at the poorly attended event only because he was at loose ends, having finished the interviews that had brought him to town, in which it was explained how production delays weren't really delays and weight gain had no effect on performance. On Monday he was supposed to be in Bern, pursuing a not quite solid offer to tour one of Switzerland's Hornet caverns, with the very slight possibility of some backseat time in an F-18. Then back to old Blighty to write everything up.

But meanwhile here it was Friday, and here he was not quite 500 miles from his favorite hotel, where he had, on impulse, booked his usual corner room for the weekend. He smiled and may have sighed, imagining how those yellow awnings would fill with a fair wind and sail him off into an earlier time. All he lacked was a suitable companion.

Just at that moment today's beautiful woman had appeared, striding through the sparsely populated rows of folding metal chairs. She wore a tan shearling coat of uncertain quality, the sort of thing you might pick up at an outside market in the east, and towed a cheap wheeled bag made of faux maroon leather. She looked like a moderately successful woman dressed to return to her humble origins. Her visitor's badge said she was Anna something; he couldn't make out the surname. He saw no wedding ring.

She had hovered barely a meter away, looking for a place to land. Then, as though noticing Gayle for the first time, she gave him a look of appraisal, half-smiled to herself, and took the adjacent chair. He had lifted his head like a retriever to the wind, drawing in her faint odor of soap and roses.

After the press conference everyone had shuffled around the breakfast buffet for a croissant and coffee, but she was suddenly not among them. Gayle languished by the bread tray, his fine weekend at the Hotel Victoria drifting away, leaving him with a lonely haul to Bern and a weekend throwing peanuts to the city's scruffy pit-bound bears. Then, just before the Victoria's brilliant awnings faded to nothing, there she was again, passing close abeam of him, so that they brushed and he, at least, felt a current of desire.

As she left the room, she caught his eye for just a moment, then turned away, as if to sever their brief contact. Gayle gathered his khaki raincoat and trailed her into the corridor. He waited with her for the elevator, and they rode down together, all in silence.

Outside, a passing front sprayed the glass and metal building with sheets of rain, borne on a chilling wind from a sky gone dark with ugly weather. A flock of newly minted Airbus planes huddled on the tarmac like birds afraid to fly.

"Ugh," she said, "How awful," and shivered.

"The rain will spoil your coat."

She turned toward him, as though suddenly reminded he was there. "I know, it's horrible."

"May a colleague offer you a ride?"

"But you don't know where I am going."

Gayle grinned. "Oh yes I do. Wait here. I'll bring the car."

The car was a Saab Viggen with a black soft top and a body the color of steel. Shaking himself like a dog after his trot through the rain, Gayle settled into the cockpit, cranked the engine, and let it idle, checking itself out. He would like to have done the check-out himself, flipping switches, reading instruments, frankly acknowledging that this machine was doing secret duty as a surrogate airplane. Viggen was a name borrowed from a Saab jet fighter, and meant thunderbolt, which Gayle found comfortably close to tornado. He'd bought the machine in 2002, the last year of the Viggen's production, and, remembering his boyhood shame of driving in Europe in the Vauxhall estate, he'd chosen left-hand steering. His much older Saab 900, arthritic and scrofulous with rust, had right-hand steering and stayed in Britain; the Viggen traveled the continent and stayed at the Hotel Victoria.

The woman, Anna, was still waiting by the door when Gayle roared in out of the rain. He popped the boot open, then scooped up her bag and stowed it next to his battered cloth and leather garment bag, which he'd bought with his first RAF paycheck. He paused long enough to see that her bag bore an old Lufthansa luggage tag: VIE. A Vienna girl, then. He had always liked Vienna girls.

As they eased out into the storm, Anna settled into the right hand seat, arranging herself so that her long legs could be crossed, and pulled her coat more closely about her before strapping herself in. One hand petted the soft grey leather facing of the seat. "A pretty car," she said. "Too bad I go only to the train."

"What about my great plan?"

She laughed. "I think you mean proposition."

"That comes later."

"So the plan is what, to kidnap me?"

"Lord, no. Transport, yes. Entertain. Feed. Admire. That sort of thing."

She leaned toward him and lifted his press badge. "Peter Gayle," she read. "Jane's." Her eyebrows lifted. "Your wife?" A broad grin. "Your mother?"

"My employer."

"Peter Gayle," she said, tasting the new identity. "Peter Gayle."

"And Anna something-or-other."

She held her badge where he could see it.

"Anna Nonperes," he read. "Of Air France. Hmm. Are you the captain of a *Mumbo* Jumbo?"

"Nothing so grand. A little p.r. for them."

"So now you take the TGV to....?"

"Back to Paris."

For a moment Gayle considered worrying about the difference between the VIE luggage tag and "back to Paris." Then he gave it up as not worth the trouble. They were circling a dirty weekend, not mating for life. "Would you like to hear my plan?"

"Do I have a choice?"

A mean thing to say, thought Gayle, but her voice was jolly enough. "Of course you have, but I'll tell you anyway. First we drive like maniacs up to Switzerland to a pretty old hotel above the lake."

"Where you take your kidnapped women?"

"Where I take people with whom I am willing to share my favorite place on this earth."

"Are you proposing?"

"Don't be silly. We stay there tonight and Saturday. Eat, drink. Be merry. Then on Sunday we drive up to Bern and I put you on the train to Paris."

"What do we do between eating and drinking in your favorite place on earth?"

"We fall in love."

Anna had turned away in silence. She watched Toulouse go by, the old rose city a mauve smear across the Garonne. She would be thinking about the alternative to his offer, Gayle decided, giving her a sidelong look. The train journey, alone, to wherever she was really going, which was probably not Paris but could be Vienna. Then a weekend on her own, or with her boyfriend, husband, child, maiden aunt...whomever. He could still call it off. The porte for the Gare Toulouse-Matabiau drifted toward them in the rain. She looked up to read the sign, then at him, then resumed her study of the grey world outside her window. They passed the porte. She said nothing about having to catch a train.

He stole another look at this Anna Nonperes, this woman with the smart, clear face that had seen things. There was nothing easy in that face, he thought, nothing that said she was readily available to men she didn't know, or even available at all. She kept silent until they were on the A61 heading for Montpelier, Toulouse drowning in the rain behind them. She spoke as if to herself, as if she were alone, as if she had just revived from a century of sleep. "I would like to fall in love."

Gayle's heart gave a small lurch of happiness. But when he glanced at her he saw an expression of utter joylessness—the face of a captive. His heart went stony until she, sensing this in him, rested a long hand upon his thigh. "Really."

He covered her hand with his own.

Anna left her hand where it was, but turned back to watch the weather stream past them. No talk of missed trains. No talk of Paris or of Wien. No talk of anything.

Gayle didn't mind the silence. He liked driving a fast car through a storm. It was a bit like flying, where the sounds you couldn't outrun were muffled by the helmet and the universe shrank to fit the cockpit.

All the exciting things that happened in a fighter happened within those close confines, bound by the hissing silence of the airplane.

He had never driven like a maniac—the maniacs were in those big Mercedes and Bimmers that ran up one's backside, high beams flashing angrily. Once on the autoroute Gayle set the Viggen at a respectable 175 kilometers per hour, about 95 knots as he liked to think of it, loafing along at a bit more than three thousand revs. The Saab ran steady as a Tornado heading in, the only sounds the rattle of rain on the soft top, the thump of wipers, tires sighing on the wet road, a bit of slipstream. The slower mid-day traffic parted magically ahead of them and magically closed in their wake. In the far lane, lorries trudged through the rain like lighted elephants. Now and then another maniac flew by.

The cockpit became their warm refuge in a cold universe, binding him and the girl intimately, but also insulating them against reality. By the time he'd made the northward turn past Montepelier, it was easy to pretend they had known each other for more than an hour, that they might find solace and pleasure in each other's arms, that they might fall in love in the Hotel Victoria.

THEY WENT DOWN TO DINNER AFTER EIGHT, ARM IN ARM, AS THOUGH they'd been going down to dinner together for years. Anna had put on a dress knit from a fine mauve wool, which draped gracefully upon the long, lovely body that, in the waning afternoon, she had allowed him to explore. Studying her now, Gayle hoped he had put those roses in her cheeks, although he made no claims. She possessed an unfathomable calm, a neutrality, that made her difficult to read. She evidently liked him well enough to share his bed and board for a day or two, he thought, but not enough to throw caution to the winds. There had been no window-shattering cries of joyous satisfaction; she remained cheerfully tranquil down to her toes. The rough edges he'd seen earlier had vanished. Now she had the confidence of an aristocrat before the revolution.

Somewhat awed by her transformation, Gayle had also dressed up, putting on his black cashmere blazer, a crisp cotton shirt of sky blue, a paisley tie. As they crossed the lobby, their reflections traversed a large mirror on a distant wall. He leaned close to Anna's ear. "What a handsome couple. Probably film stars."

She turned to look at the pair of strangers in the mirror, and Gayle felt a sudden tremor in her arm, like the flinching of a tethered wing. For an instant, the expression of the joyless captive flickered on her face, but only for an instant. She quickly shook that mask away to show him her smart, pretty smile, and tightened her grip on his arm.

Ordinarily, the people at the Victoria took some pains not to notice that Monsieur Peter had a new woman at his side. But upon their arrival the gentle simian Theodore had conveyed his approval with an almost imperceptible nod in Anna's direction. Mathilda, tall and rather pretty herself, and not too secretly fond of Peter, had given Anna a cold look up and down, and then surrendered to some quality she sensed there. Waiting to show them to their table, Roger, gaunt and serious as an undertaker, slightly lifted one pencil-thin eyebrow to acknowledge that M. Peter, in his estimation, had moved up-market. Gayle was by then grinning like a boy. He looked back at the reflected couple, who were about to vanish into the dining room. They seemed so comfortable together; they must have met a long, long time ago.

"It is a little cold for outside," Roger observed as he led them through the labyrinth of white-clothed tables. Gayle had always liked to take his meals on the terrace at one of the corner tables, from which only the lake and sky could be seen; one seemed to float in mid-air. But tonight Roger seated them in a far corner of the dining room, where the view and solitude were almost as good and they were protected from the autumn chill. Looking around, Gayle saw that, apart from a few couples and a family out for an evening in Glion, they had the room largely to themselves.

The weather they'd outrun just south of Geneva lay in purple folds beyond the mountains across the lake, with only a faint cirrus scrim upon the luminous sky. On the far shore, the grids of towns flickered like nebulae, linked by chains of tiny lights coalescing and vanishing in the darkness.

"Very beautiful," said Anna.

"Yes, very," Gayle replied. "The view isn't half bad either." She seemed to look everywhere but at him. Well, he thought, why wouldn't we still be a trifle shy?

"I'm sorry," she said, reading his mind. "I have never been kidnapped before."

"Ah."

"I thought all kidnappers were monsters."

"Not I. I'm a pussy cat."

She laughed.

Gayle blushed. "No, no, no. I meant a sweetie pie. Nice bloke. Harmless."

"You are a very nice bloke, Peter Gayle."

"So, no regrets."

"No."

"Good. Laugh and be happy. I don't want the staff to think I've made you sad. They like you."

"They don't know me."

"All one has to do, my dear, is look into those clear, intelligent eyes. And bingo, caught."

A young Italian waiter he'd never seen before came by with their Martinis. "Spent years training them," he told her. "Years."

"I've never had a Martini."

"Never kidnapped. Never had a Martini. You must live in a very quiet corner of Paris."

"Yes, very quiet."

"So, if I want to find you, I just find that quiet corner and there you will be."

She nodded. "There I will be."

Gayle suddenly regretted opening the Paris box, which he believed was stuffed with lies. His heart grew heavy. His mood declined. He felt a gathering in the atmosphere, like the coiling stillness before a storm. So she lies, so she disappears. Who gives a damn?

"What's wrong?"

"Nothing." It's only a weekend, Sunday and she's gone, he told himself, pushing depression away. Then, a fragile cheerfulness restored, he leaned toward her, holding his glass where she could give it a gentle clink with hers. "Here's looking at you, kid."

She laughed. "We'll always have Glion?"

Hearing their laughter, the other couples in the dining room looked up, smiling. What a handsome couple, they thought. Probably film stars.

"Squadron leader!"

The hissed sibilant and metallic trill of r's flicked at Gayle like a lash, returning him for a terrible moment to the fetid darkness of his former cell, Mickey Williams noting that "these boogers speak English like a focking snake" while they listened to approaching footsteps and Iraqi voices, and braced for the next humiliating surprise.

Gayle stood up, disoriented, moving like a diver two miles deep. His toppled chair crashed against the tiles, light years away. On the far side of the dining room, Roger and the Italian waiter hurried toward his table, like firemen smelling smoke. To him they were just a pair of menacing shadows. He turned toward the hated voice.

The newcomer was a stocky Arab in his fifties, wearing a mustache dyed black, a cosmetic smudge of grey at his temples, dressed like a London banker in slightly rumpled navy-blue pin stripe with a maroon and white school tie. Seeing the light in Gayle's eye, he put up a delicate little hand, almost a paw, as if he were confident that this simple gesture could deflect any threat. "My God, don't you remember me?"

Gayle stared at the man. His olive skin was sleek, seemingly poreless, flecked with black hairs. A patchy dark beard trimmed to a devilish point framed a pair of small, soft lips. Behind amber aviator glasses, his brown eyes were luminous and sad as a deer's on the surface, with something predatory moving in their depths. "I saved your life."

The person Gayle remembered had almost disappeared into this older man, but now he could just make out the younger fellow hiding in the camouflage of age. And now there came the sharp scent of his cologne. One day near the end of his Captivity Gayle had awakened to that sweetly anesthetic stink, much favored by his captors. He had opened his eyes, expecting more torment, and that younger face was looming over him like a sand-colored moon. "Is over," the moon told him. "Very sorry. But we take care of you. Then we send you home."

Roger insinuated himself between them, casting an inquiring look at Gayle, giving the Arab his back. The waiter righted the chair and checked its limbs for excess movement.

"Not to worry," Gayle said. "I know him." Then, to Anna, "This is Dr. Al-Rabiah, Anna. We met in Iraq." A shadow brushed her face as she nodded to their visitor. Gayle took it to mean she sensed and shared his apprehension, and was grateful to have her in his corner.

Al-Rabiah bowed toward Anna, watching Gayle warily as he did. He gestured toward a table across the room, where a big blonde waited uneasily, each of her thick arms clasping a girl of nine or ten, as if at any moment she would fly away with them under her wings. Now, cued by his silent command, she settled. "Sorry to intrude," the Arab said to Gayle. "I could not resist this chance to speak to you."

Gayle was still trying to crawl out of the past. He nodded toward an empty chair on Anna's side of the table. "Drink?"

"No thank you," said Al-Rabiah, sitting down. "Have you stayed here before?"

"Now and then."

"Silfer, my wife, who is Swedish. Anika and Sonya, my two angels. We heard of this place and decided to try it. Amazing how our paths crossed."

"Amazing."

To Anna, Al-Rabiah said, "The Squadron Leader and I have this history…."

Gayle toyed with his Martini, fishing out the olives, then drained the glass. The young waiter was watching him, wide-eyed, and Gayle signaled for another.

"It has been a long time," Al-Rabiah went on, leaning toward Anna, as if she were empowered to adjudicate the matter. "When the first Gulf War ended in 1991, prisoners were exchanged. Ten were repatriated on March fourth, thirty-five more a day later. Then we learned there were ten more being kept out of sight. I rescued them. I took them, what would you say? Under my wings. They were too weak to be moved. I sent them home immediately they were well enough to travel. It was like dropping them into the night sea. The April Ten, as they were called, vanished without a trace."

"Credit where it's due," said Gayle. "Without his intercession, all ten of us should have died." The young waiter brought his Martini, setting it down gingerly, like a vial of nitroglycerine. Gayle ate an olive, took a sip. He remembered very little of their rescue, beyond the fact that he and the others had become giddy with hope as they were plucked from their shit, cleaned up, and tucked between white muslin sheets in what looked like a proper hospital. He closed his eyes and there were the white walls of his room; pretty nurses drifted nearby, a weightless flock of ghosts.

"I see you are thriving, Squadron Leader. What about the others?"

"I don't know about the others."

"But you're all in the Forces…"

"Not I. You lot clipped my wings. No sacrifice too great, you see."

"You sound as if you think I was the enemy. I was not."

"No, you're my old Iraqi chum. Surprised to see you, though. I thought all you chaps went to Guantánamo ages ago."

"I have hardly seen Iraq since the first war ended. It exhausted and embarrassed me, and also I was blamed for taking care of *you* boys. Since 1992 I have had support for a modest immunology project. All theoretical and numerical. No mad science. We do not even dissect frogs."

"Hors de combat. Like me."

"Yes."

"Then that covers it. Thanks for stopping by. Good night. Safe journey. Regards to the family."

Al-Rabiah stood up, flustered. "I see my friendly visit was a mistake."

"You rescued me too late, doctor. They'd already filled me with poison."

Al-Rabiah studied the Englishman. To Anna he said, "Perhaps you can provide an antidote." Then, shaking his head sadly, a decent fellow reluctantly giving up on good works, he marched to his table and began gathering up his girls. Roger hurried over with his bill and ushered them toward the door. When they were gone, he turned back toward M. Peter and, with one of his rare grins, brushed the palms of his hands together. That was that.

Gayle drank down his Martini, smacked his lips. "Good stuff. Join me for another?"

"I still have mine."

"You don't mind if I…?" and he waved a hand at his empty glass. She shook her head and he ordered another.

"A squadron leader. Even better than the captain of the *mumbo* jumbo."

"Much better. Bloody marvelous."

"But you gave it up?"

"It was given up for me." Gayle grinned weakly, aware that the contact with the Iraqi had sucked out some of his spiritual marrow and left him feeling dirty and ashamed. He wanted to drink himself to sleep. He wanted to curl up in their soft, unmade bed, with this perfect stranger wrapped protectively around him. "Now I write about aviation. Drive a fast car…"

"Carry away innocent girls."

"From very quiet corners of Paris." Their eyes met, hers slid away. His Martini arrived and he pecked at it quickly. Then, willing himself to leave the evening's nasty surprise and all its mnemonic cargo, he forced a broad smile. "You must be starving. Let's order."

"Tomorrow," Gayle told her, "we take a long walk up the hill, up to the top, have lunch. Or we might drive over to Lausanne. Or we might visit the far side of the lake. Or we might go down to Sion and watch the Swiss Air Force practice touch and goes. Or…"

She put an index finger on his lips. "Or we might let tomorrow take care of itself."

They lay naked in the dark room, Anna cradled in one of his arms. The pale oval of her face, her smart face, hovered close by in the darkness. He thought he had never seen one he liked better. Their love-making had taken a long time, his body slowed by drink. Now, even in the night, he could see the roses in her cheeks. "I put them there," he murmured.

"What?"

"The roses in your cheeks."

"Ah, *those*."

Gayle ran his fingertips along the glowing curve of her face, moist, he saw now, with a faint sheen of tears. "Regrets?"

She shook her head.

"That's good." Then, after a quiet moment, "You know, I thought I was kidding."

"When?"

"When I said we'd fall in love."

"You *were* kidding."

"Are you sure?"

"I remember it clearly." She wiped at her cheeks. "You were definitely kidding."

"Tomorrow you'll tell me everything."

"Everything?"

"All there is to know about Anna Nonperes. Were you once a squadron leader?"

"Never."

"A prisoner of war?"

"No."

"Have you really not been kidnapped before?"

"Never."

"Was tonight really your first Martini?"

"Yes."

"Do you like me?"

"Very much."

"What if I wish to kidnap you again?"

"Then you come to my quiet corner of town."

"And there you will be?"

"There I will be." The lovely face glistened with new tears.

Gayle wondered what he could say that would dry those pretty eyes, lift her heart, and induce her to coil more closely about him. But the planet's gravity had become too much for him and now his limbs weighed tons, he could not lift his head. "There you will be," he mumbled to her through numbed lips. Far too much alcohol tonight, old Sunny Jim, far too much, he told himself. The dark room began to roll. The buggers must've hit a wing. "We're fucked, Mouse. Out we go." Gayle felt the slipstream take him in, gently this time, and then he was parachuting down and down, into the deep and everlasting slumber he'd yearned for since the encounter with his old Iraqi chum.

Near noon, the maid awakened Gayle enough for him to yell, "Later, please." Then he lay among the white tangle of sheets and tried to remember where he was, and how he had come to have a mouth like an ashtray, a tremor in his hands, a pulse that moved inside his skull like a trapped ferret. "Recalled to life," he finally announced to Anna's side of the bed.

Reaching over to touch her, he found the bedding empty and cool. He sat up, listening carefully for some sound, but there was nothing. No shower. No puttering about. Ah, well, then, thought Gayle, knowing he fed himself a lie, she must be having breakfast alone. But he knew she was gone. He got up and made an unsteady reconnaissance of the place. No shearling coat. No cheap wheeled bag. No Anna. Gone, gone, gone.

Nothing seemed to be missing, his wallet held the usual credit cards and currency, his proofs of identity were still there, along with his passport. She had given a lot, he thought, for precious little. Why had she bothered?

During a long, cold shower he checked himself for hidden damage, and found nothing beyond what looked and stung like an insect bite in his groin. He would have to ask Theodore about crabs, which would drive the amiable fellow crazy, the idea of lice in the Victoria. Gayle smiled.

When you thought about it, there was nothing remarkable in her leaving. The long slog from Friday night to Sunday had turned out to be more than she could do, so she'd taken herself off to Lausanne to catch the fast train. That had been the deal, after all. No promise of a life together. No promise of anything, except that they might like each other a little. Well, so they had, just not enough to carry her all the way to Sunday. Another bruise upon one's vanity, but nothing to cut off an ear about.

Besides, being on his own meant an easy day for him in the Victoria and an easy Sunday morning run up to Bern. He'd arrive at Switzerland's baby Pentagon on Monday rested and ready to fly. "All's well that ends well." Brave talk, when, rather unexpectedly, he felt his heart cracking within. "I thought I was kidding," he whispered to the empty room.

Theodore was behind the reception desk when he went down to forage for a late breakfast. The older man looked up, all mock surprise. "Why, Mister Peter!" he yelped, as though Gayle had returned from the dead; he was careful not to look the Englishman directly in the eye.

"Good morning, Mr. Theodore."

"Actually, it is good afternoon."

"Can I still get breakfast?"

"Of course." He scanned the lobby for Roger.

"I'll be eating alone."

"Ah." Theodore's eyebrows lifted, as if intending feigned surprise, then descended as he decided to be straight. "Miss Anna said she had urgent business in Paris."

"She didn't wake me. I don't know what time she left."

"Before dawn. With…" and, seeing the light in Gayle's eyes, Theodore ground to a halt, aware he had stepped into a mine field.

"With?"

"The Al-Rabiah party checked out about the same time. He saw her waiting for a taxi and offered a ride."

"To where?"

Theodore shrugged. "Montreux, probably. But who knows?" After a moment, he added, "We were sorry to see her go. She had a certain…." He raised his shoulders in tribute to life's many unexpected turns.

"You think she was The One?"

"Well, she certainly seemed an exceptional young woman."

"Probably looking for an exceptional young man."

"I can tell you she was not happy about leaving."

"Is that what she said?"

"No. But she could not stop crying."

III

Keeping his Paris-green Ford Focus always ten kilometers below the speed limit and always in the middle lane, Mohammad Al-Rabiah drove with the determined inattention of the unassimilated Third Worlder, hardly touching the helm with his plump little paws, oblivious to the road ahead and the vehicles that nervously coalesced and dispersed around him, like drops of mercury. The usual maniacs shot by, their flashing high beams glaring like the eyes of women scorned, horns yodeling a Doppler-shifted alarum, often punctuated by a raised fist or finger and a shouted expletive in one of the autoroute's many tongues. Silfer and the two little angels sat, crowded and sullen, in the narrow back seat. At the moment, they interested Al-Rabiah even less than the ambient traffic. His attention was fixed on Anna, who occupied the passenger seat.

"All these tears," he was saying. "And that stupid attempt to flee. The idea was to stay in the hotel with your squadron leader, go with him to the train, or wherever. Dull his suspicions. Instead, you come fluttering out before the dawn, going where? A good thing I came along."

Even as he chided her, Anna knew he thought their plot a grand success. The fatigued, impatient parental baritone of reason had become the giddy tenor of something big and clandestine achieved, and he grinned at her like a lad holding a snake. His eyes twinkled behind the amber glass. "And now we have these tears. I don't understand you, Anna."

"I don't understand myself," she replied in a whisper.

Straight as the runway it would become in wartime, the road pushed on toward the breaking day, past the glittering remnants of Lake Léman and into a neat matrix of vineyards and orchards, heading for Sion. Peter had said they might go there today to watch the Swiss Air Force practice touch and goes. She wondered what it meant. The term perfectly described what they had shared in the Hotel Victoria. Something transient. Something dangerous. The exit marked SION flashed by. Touch and go.

She had gone, but his touch lingered. Her body found it difficult to forget its gentle encounter with this odd, open man who fell so easily in and out of love. Touching and going. Well, she had touched, she had been touched, things had been touch-and-go for awhile, and now she was going. And in-between she had betrayed him.

We're fucked, Mouse. Out we go!

Even sleeping, Peter had anticipated her betrayal. The experience had left her numb, mere sad ballast in a hideous little green car, belted into a vinyl-covered seat that smelled of time, moisture, and the doctor's astringent cologne.

Anna looked at him, this stocky Arab just old enough to be her father, the sleek skin and soft lips, the moist deer eyes behind the aviator glasses. He wore the same pin-stripes he had the night before, rumpled now and without the striped tie. He seemed to feel her gaze. "What?"

"Why did you come to our table last night?"

He laughed and even tossed his head a little. "To deliver your equipment."

"Ah."

"And I wanted to see my old chum from Iraq." Another chuckle.

"Your old chum."

"His sarcasm, not mine."

"You didn't tell me you knew him."

"You never asked!" Al-Rabiah's voice still held that odd note of excited cheerfulness. "Anna, don't brood about this fellow. He's a standard Englishman. Troll a pretty blonde past his nose and everything falls into place. As predictable as a laboratory rat."

"How would you know?"

Al-Rabiah gave his boy-with-a-snake grin. "Because I have known thousands of laboratory rats." Of course, he understood what she'd meant.

"You treated him for a few weeks, years ago. You didn't know him before and haven't seen him since. How could you possibly know he would take me to the Victoria?"

"Well, of course, I could not. Someone must have studied your squadron leader closely enough to know what he would do. Someone must have been aware that he had booked a room."

"Someone?"

He shrugged. "People from the old days. Zealots. The Babylonian Jihad. Who knows? I do not." His voice sang with self-satisfaction. He turned to her. Vehicles on either side of them uttered startled honks and scattered while he settled the Focus back into its lane. "Listen, we both agreed to do an unsavory thing to help people we care about. I keep those people in mind, not some womanizing Englishman. Don't think about Peter Gayle." He glanced back at the road, humming to himself, then added, "Think of Sophie."

Think of Sophie. Ah, well, Anna had thought of little else since that Monday in September when her flatmate, Svetlana, had called to her come see, come see. And there, on the television, was Sophie, disheveled and dazed by the camera's bright light, wrapped in a black abaya, an opaque shadow with a bright face. In the background, out of focus and dreamlike, armed figures loomed in dark costumes and masks.

"My God," Svetlana whispered, her hands on her cheeks. "My God, Anna."

Deutsche Welle reporter Sophie Nieman, the Austrian news reader told them, had been on her way to interview a member of parliament in the Mansur district of Baghdad when two pickup trucks had cut them off in a narrow street. A surveillance tape showed the action at some distance, the five tiny figures in black converging on a blue van marked *TV* and *PRESS*, jumping from still frame to still frame, as they shot the translator-driver through his window, then the soundman, then the photographer, who had his camera up and running to the end. There followed what the cameraman had seen, the approaching men in masks, the shootings, and finally the fade to black.

Anna had not fainted; tending to the inmates of the medical intensive-care unit at Vienna's Allgemeines Krankenhaus had destroyed her ability to faint. Instead she had settled slowly to her knees, like a figure melting, her arms crossed tightly across her breasts, and watched the screen, where the story kept repeating, each time with some minor variation.

A group calling itself the Babylonian Jihad had claimed credit for the abduction. Deutsche Welle said it would do everything in its power to secure her release. The governments of Germany and Austria said the same. The British prime minister described it as the kind of appalling barbarity "we are fighting in the War on Terror." The American president said he would pray for Sophie's safe return. Al Quaeda in Iraq denied involvement. No one, Anna included, mentioned that this pretty journalist might be slaughtered on camera like a festival lamb or found headless in the sand beside a desert highway. Anna had not fainted, but she could not stop her tears once they began to fall. She could be such a crier.

Svetlana had brought a tray with a glass of orange juice, mug of black coffee, and buttered toast with jam, and set it down in front of Anna, followed by an awkward fumble of a hug. "Don't worry," she said in German, "they will let her go. How do I know this? Because they always let the women go."

Temperamentally the two flatmates were almost opposites. Anna's emotional skin was thinner; a beggar or stray dog could break her heart, although no physical injury was so ghastly as to make her look away.

Svetlana Maximovna Trulova had last cried in 1983, upon the sudden death of her father; since then no one but Anna had ever seen anything, least of all her heart, on her sleeve. Friends sometimes observed that this tall, big-boned woman had only to brush against a desperate situation to steady it. Svetlana was Cassandra before the curse: she always spoke the truth and people always believed her.

Anna thought that healing touch must come from an almost palpable aura of sorrows past, and the unshakeable seriousness she had seen in many Russians. Whatever the source, one could not look into that open, honest face, that pale, pretty moon framed in a sable braid, and not experience the relief that truth, even hard truth, brings. Svetlana's diffident hug and breakfast tray had immediately banished the horror of the moment, although it did not quite leave the room. Her gift was to ease pain, not to cure it.

"I wish I could stay with you," she told Anna. "But today is a special program at the Centre. I have to go in."

"Don't worry. I'm okay," said Anna. "It's as you say, they always let the women go." She had taken Svetlana's hands in hers, then, and held them against her cheek. "What would I do without you, Sveta?"

"Perhaps you would get ready for work."

When Anna was alone the telephone began to ring. Friends from the hospital calling to help, perhaps, but more likely the press, wanting one of those scenes in which the camera holds on a face until it crumples. Anna thought it must be like filming wild life, just standing there with the camera running while the mamba devours the precious speckled eggs.

She'd made a face at the telephone and left it ringing while she put on jeans and a mauve cotton sweat shirt found on holiday with Sophie in Greece, the only holiday they had ever shared (more tears). Then, the telephone still yelling at her, Anna grabbed her tote bag and set out for work, as if it were just another morning, as if Sophie were merely on assignment somewhere far away.

On that first terrible day, Sophie seemed merely to have been detained, albeit by desperate men. It had been possible for Anna to think that her abductors would soon realize their mistake and set Sophie free, and that Sophie, as she always had, would relish the perilous moment, write about it, become known for it.

A day later, release seemed less plausible. By the end of the first week, hope was drowning in the long silence; it was as if Sophie had been wrapped in chains and thrown into the ocean. Anna went about her life with grief perched on her shoulder like a dark bird only she could see. It was not so much that she missed Sophie; their paths rarely crossed from one year to the next. But the thought that Sophie might cease to exist chilled her to the core.

Dr. Mohammad Al-Rabiah had appeared at the hospital on the Thursday of the third week, a small man in a dark suit, faux school tie, scrubbed and perfumed, but with the émigré's inescapable aura of shabbiness. Masked by amber sunglasses, his soft brown gaze swept the nurses' station like a searchlight, then held on Anna, where she sat in her blue scrubs behind a low partition. She was far away, her grief percolating quietly within as she, numb with mourning and fatigue, fiddled with paperwork and tried not to think too much about the newcomers to her ring of the dying. When Al-Rabiah approached she had looked through him: just another Arab in a city that had begun to fill with them.

"Anna?"

"Ja."

"I am Dr. Al-Rabiah," he said in English. "Is there somewhere we can talk?"

"Go ahead."

"It is a delicate matter."

"Do you have someone here?"

He looked around to see that no one overheard him. "Sophie."

And still Anna did not faint. Instead, she got unsteadily to her feet, gathered herself as she would have to comfort an irreparably damaged child, and strode across the large room to an empty station, Al-Rabiah behind her. Once she had pulled the grey curtains together, isolating them, she turned to her visitor. "What about Sophie?"

Al-Rabiah removed his glasses, pretended to clean them with a handkerchief. "Early this morning, a man called me. He said he spoke for the Babylonian Jihad."

Anna believed she had stopped breathing.

"He said they would free Sophie. But first they want something from you."

Her mind ran a frantic search through all her worldly possessions, and found nothing there worth giving. "I have very little."

"Not money. An act."

"What is this....act?"

"They want a certain man given an injection without his knowing about it."

"Like Alexander Litvinenko?"

Al-Rabiah ignored the sarcasm. "They said it would not harm him."

"And if I do this?"

"They will give Sophie to the Americans."

"Are you one of them?"

"They want me to show proof. I am also trying to help someone."

"Another hostage?"

"More or less. These people hold all the cards, Anna. One must do a lot to obtain a little."

"Why couldn't they just grab this man the way they grabbed Sophie, knock him out, inject him. Why involve me?"

"Because you are a nurse. Because you leave no trail back to Iraq." He shrugged. "Because they have Sophie. If they had someone else, they might have gone elsewhere."

It had not occurred to Anna that she could say no. For Sophie, she would have murdered, she would have put on a suicide vest and walked into a school, she would have sold the mother from whose womb they had escaped not quite half an hour apart, Sophie, as always, in the vanguard. But she wasn't being asked to murder or blow up a school or sell their mother. They only wanted her to give a stranger a shot, which she did daily, flawlessly. Not even the children shrank from Anna's touch.

"An injection of what?"

The deer eyes went hard as slate. "I have no idea." Then, his expression softening a little, "But I have my suspicions."

"Tell me."

"This man was captured in the first Gulf war. This could be linked to his captivity. Perhaps to some lingering chemical evidence of abuse."

"But it's so long ago."

"The road to The Hague is paved with old evidence. People get nervous." He studied her a moment. "Tell me something."

"What?"

"Are you and your sister very much alike?"

Anna started to reply that they were twins, identical but also different. But some instinct warned her to keep something back. Let him think what he will. She gave a hopeless shrug. "Well, you know, we're sisters."

A day later, Al-Rabiah reappeared, this time bearing a Lufthansa ticket to Toulouse, a hundred-euro note, and an Air France press credential and French driver's license in the name of Anna Nonperes.

"Nonperes?"

"Nieman. Add a *d* and we have nobody in German. So we go to personne in French. And in personne we find Nonperes. Magic!"

"Anna Nobody. I think it suits me."

"Think of Sophie."

She had thought of her slightly older twin at each twist and turn of this business. She'd thought of Sophie when she let herself be carried off to the Hotel Victoria, numb with guilty apprehension, yet weirdly capable of jokes about being kidnapped, weirdly capable of being charmed. She'd thought of Sophie as she lay in Peter's arms in the late afternoon, trying not to be too happy, but also grateful to have been recalled to life.

Tucking him into bed last night, a little drunk but also very sweet, dropping him into an abyssal sleep, she'd thought of Sophie, and Sophie had been on her mind as she hefted the small syringe Al-Rabiah had passed her at dinner, watched the seiche of its cylinder of clear fluid. What could it be? Not polonium, it was cool to the touch; no apricot odor, no hemlock particulates. What could it be?

It doesn't matter.

Think of Sophie.

Then, her hand steady as a surgeon's, Anna had reached past Gayle's genitalia, found the pulse of the femoral artery, and gently inserted the needle, thumbed the plunger; she imagined the nameless fluid coiling away like white smoke into the dark, arterial blood.

Then she had waited for a time, seated on the bed beside him. Her free hand stroked the skin around the tiny puncture, causing a lazy stirring, which made her smile. She waited to see if she had killed Peter to save her sister. But the rhythm of his pulse continued unperturbed, the benthic tranquility of his slumber had not altered, bar a twitch or two, the sudden sprints of a dreaming dog, or possibly, she thought, a former prisoner of war. There were none of the signs, familiar ones to her, that Death had entered the room looking for him. In the end, Anna thought, she would have merely hurt Peter's feelings, and that only a little. In fact, the really injured feelings were probably her own, for she had given far more to this pleasant stranger than she'd intended.

Now Peter would awaken, wondering where love had flown, and why, and perhaps be a little sad they would miss another day together, watching the Swiss with their mysterious touching and going. She would return to her shared flat on Sternwartestrasse, telling Svetlana only that she had visited her ailing grandmother in Klagenfurt, which they both understood to be a fiction, code for a dirty weekend. She would forget the touches and focus on the goes.

On Monday she would resume her career in the Intensiv, where, by way of atonement she would care more intensively for the flock of ruined people brought there to wait for God. And in that way she would endure the interval before Sophie's return, which, by covering herself with shit, Anna had made possible.

ALONE, AL-RABIAH WOULD HAVE DRIVEN the thousand kilometers to Vienna stopping only for fuel, like a Bedouin crossing the Sahara on a camel, slow but steady. But from time to time, Silfer and the two angels broke their silence with agitated squeaks and grunts and enough fidgeting to rock the Focus. Finally noticing them, Al-Rabiah would roll his eyes in mock exasperation and begin looking for a place for them to pee. Near Salzburg they stopped briefly at an autobahn park to take on food and fuel. Anna didn't want to sit with the Al-Rabiah females, but bought a candy bar and bottle of mineral water and wandered out into the autumnal light of the waning afternoon.

Al-Rabiah was on the far side of the fueling area, talking earnestly into a mobile telephone, like a madman murmuring into his cupped hand. She could just hear him, speaking in an impossible tongue that she decided must be Arabic. The cheery boy of the past several hours had quite departed, replaced by a middle-aged man who moved, who gestured, who spoke with quiet authority, his voice rising now and then, but never shrill. Her supposed messenger was strutting around issuing orders like a general.

Anna felt suddenly hollow. For Sophie, she had done this strange and treacherous thing, and now the harmless little man who'd brought her into it looked like the little man in charge. It took her a moment to realize that Al-Rabiah had ceased his pacing and watched her, his eyes as cold as a serpent's, his soft mouth a hard line. Without taking his eyes off her, he closed the telephone and dropped it into a coat pocket.

"Good news," he said, drawing uncomfortably near. "Sophie goes to the Americans tonight."

"And that will be that."

He seemed not to hear her. "I told them your silence is assured, since what you did was criminal. In a good cause, but criminal." He smiled and lowered his gaze, mock shy. "Now, more magic. We make your Nonperes identity vanish into thin air. If you will give me those credentials?"

Anna rummaged in her handbag and handed over the i.d.s, wishing that the act would scrub away the stain of her Nonperes incarnation. Of course it did not.

"And the money?"

"What, your hundred euros?"

"We are a thrifty race."

Anna gave him the note.

"You won't hear from me again. But they will be watching. They have millions of eyes in Europe, and watch whomever they wish, whenever they wish. They know everything about you."

"I am as predictable as a laboratory rat?"

"Exactly. But my point, Anna, is that they intend to have your silence, one way or another. One way or another. You understand?"

Anna realized then that what she had believed to be a boyish excitement in the confines of the Ford was in fact an emanation of power, which now nearly crackled in the atmosphere around them. For a time she studied this new Al-Rabiah, this frightening, smug *success.* Her hands trembled, as they would upon that first close look at some appalling injury, then steadied as she took control. She put her fear into its mental box and, expecting the worst, said what was on her mind. "You're one of them."

"They are cogs."

"And you are the wheel?"

Al-Rabiah strode away toward the Focus.

"What did you make me do?" He kept walking. *"What did I do?"*

As if cued by Anna's cry, Silfer and the two little angels came out of the café. Preparing to reboard, he announced a change in seating. "Silfer, you come in front with me. And girls, give Anna some room back there."

Anna sat behind him, her head leaning on the window glass, afraid of him now, and ashamed of it. Oh, think of Sophie, think of Sophie, think of Sophie, she told herself. But all she could think of was that "they," meaning "we," meaning "he," intended to keep her quiet, one way or another. Now, whenever she looked into a Muslim face she would wonder if those dark eyes watched her. Should she speak of her time with Peter Gayle, one of those faces would hear and they—no, he, Al-Rabiah—would silence her forever.

To the east, night was settling over the low, wooded hills between them and lovely old Vienna, which Anna now missed with all her being—Vienna and Svetlana. God, how she missed Svetlana!

SVETLANA AND ANNA HAD BEEN FRIENDS FROM THE MOMENT THEY met at the Vienna International School in 1982, two twelve-year-olds who instantly recognized in the other the eternal outsider; they had bonded like binary stars.

Anna had been sent there six years earlier, when it was still the English School, by her father, a dull, dreamy man mired in personal disappointment. Until the day of his death near the end of 1999, Oscar Nieman had believed his destiny was to become a doctor. But there was destiny, as he often said, and there was reality. Waiting for medical lightning to strike, Oscar had made his career driving one of the little yellow ÖAMTC trucks that roam Austria's roads, looking for the disabled.

As he drove, he dreamed. There would be a chance encounter, a black Mercedes trapped precariously in the railing of a bridge, a red Ferrari sinking in a canal. He would intercede, at no small risk to himself, and rescue the man who would become his grateful benefactor, the dean of a famous medical school, perhaps, or a brain surgeon, someone who would immediately sense that this Samaritan in yellow auto-club coveralls had missed his true calling. And that would be that.

Herr Doktor Nieman would marry into the muted aristocracy of Vienna and waltz with his beautiful wife, whose name would be Sophie-Anna, at the Hofburg Palace on New Year's Eve. They would have a place in the Eighteenth, up by Türkenschantzpark, with well-to-do Viennese and United Nations officials for neighbors. On holidays they would go to Bali and Cape Town and Biarritz. All one needed was that crucial chance encounter.

While Oscar had waited for lightning to strike, reality had grown exponentially, like a metastasizing tumor. There was a random encounter on the A-1, but not with the dean of a famous medical school. Oscar had come upon Molly McCoy, whose ancient black Mini had expired three kilometers west of the Pressbau exit. She was English, blonde, plump, midway between plain and pretty. Like Oscar, she expected the momentary flowering of her destiny, although hers had not acquired any particular shape beyond a wish not to be always worried about making the rent, being treated as an inferior by others, and getting pregnant.

They had cleaved together without quite falling in love. Love, for Oscar, was what he felt for that Viennese aristocrat with whom, on the long stretches of the autobahns, he waltzed. For Molly, love was something remembered from a large screen long ago; beyond that, she had no idea what the term meant.

Because reality always trumps destiny, they had married. They acquired a two-bedroom leasehold flat in the Second District between

Wien Nord and the metallic cries of its trains, which seemed always in noisy motion, and the tattered gaiety of Prater Park. Oscar liked to tell people they lived between the great wheel and the indestructible flak towers that remained in the Augarten south of the railyard. Their neighbors were mostly railway and river folk, and contingents of Romanians, Turks, Arabs—the advance party, as Oscar called them, for the coming invasion from the east.

Holidays, when the Niemans could afford them, were spent in rented caravans parked near an Austrian See. Lightning never struck, destiny never flowered. They fretted over making the rent, were often treated as inferiors, and, in time, Molly became pregnant.

At the end of a long, angry confinement that left Molly and Oscar exhausted, the twins had arrived, first Sophie, then Anna, both named for Oscar's secretly imagined aristocrat. It had been the parents' first and only sighting of the bluebird of happiness.

One fine autumn morning, as they strolled along the Hauptallee in the shadow of the great wheel, the twins tucked into their pram and just enough Schillings in hand to buy a couple of Würstels from a kiosk, Oscar declared that they would send their girls to the English School. Molly, who had already begun to tire of motherhood, nodded and smiled. Believing her acquiescence marked one of their rare moments of concurrence, Oscar felt a quick tickle of the heart that he thought might be love for a difficult woman.

Anna never knew how her father had managed it, and never asked. But somehow, when the moment arrived, the parents, in a state of agitation, dressed the twins in their Sunday best, draped them with bookpacks, and took them off to Grinzingerstrasse 95 aboard one of the city's red and white trams.

Sophie had watched out the window, her excitement strategically damped except for a faint blush in her cheeks, her pale eyes cool and intelligent. Nothing scared her, ever, and she had not been known to cry. Anna thought she would suffocate with dread. Oscar and Molly sat erect and perfectly still, like aristos on their way to the guillotine.

Once the parents had vanished down the school's long steps, the twins exchanged one of their silent communiqués, and parted, Sophie on the scent of opportunity, Anna merely hoping to survive the day. Sophie had soon begun to make her English, with its odd Austrian nuances, perfectly English, and used her natural gravitation to draw in crowds of friends, attracted by her cool beauty and keen mind. No one could remember a more glorious child than Sophie.

Shy and never quite at ease, Anna had nearly disappeared in her sister's glare. She sometimes thought that, had they been fledglings, Sophie would have pushed her out of the nest. But Anna didn't take such stuff personally; it was just something birds and sisters did.

The years had crawled by, Sophie always ascending to some new plateau of popularity and achievement, Anna hanging on by her scholastic fingernails in the hope of pleasing her joyless father. And then, at last, along came Svetlana, providing a friendship that had been enough to see Anna through to adulthood.

Until then, Svetlana had spent her days at the Russian School in the Eighteenth District, which the children of Soviet families in Vienna were required to attend. But her father, who held a high, wonderfully ambiguous post at the Centre for Analytic Studies south of the city, had arranged her escape and placed her in what had by then become the Vienna International School.

Anna remembered Maxim Trulov as a large, powerful man with a black pompadour and a jolly round face, a man who emanated thunderclouds of affection for his daughter, and laughed a lot; but also a man who radiated something dangerous. A big, well-tailored, multilingual Russian with influence and enough money for the International School had to be KGB, which made Svetlana an interesting but not very popular anomaly in a school originally intended for the children of Empire.

Anna often envied Svetlana her dashing parent, with whom Oscar Nieman compared so unfavorably. She liked to imagine her father appearing in a tailored cocoon of grey Italian silk, as Maxim

Trulov did. She wished Oscar were more dangerous, but only until early 1983.

That winter, Maxim was dropped like a deer into the snow of the Hauptallee, the back of his head shot away by a sniper. His body had been found days later, drifting with the Danube ice. The faculty spoke in hushed tones of his having been executed by his own masters, but Svetlana, when her tears had dried up forever and she could speak, told Anna the Americans had killed him.

In 1985, the school had left the fine old manse in Grinzing and settled in a larger, California-style structure across the Danube in Kagran, near the towers of UNO City. That same year, Molly McCoy Nieman, whom everyone had thought to be the last of her line, had inherited a Hebridean stone cottage and a tiny income from a newly departed second cousin. Soon after, on a morning when Oscar was patrolling the A-1 in his yellow truck and the twins were at school, she had left for her new island home, without a note, without taking much of anything, without looking back.

The desertion had mystified and saddened Oscar and Anna, but Sophie, as always, had an explanation. "She didn't *have* us, Anna, she *found* us. Two big speckled eggs out in the Wienerwald. And she hatched us out. And here we are. We didn't mean a thing to her." Anna had leaned toward her sister, hoping to hear some faint note of regret; but there was none. Sophie's heart was even harder than her mother's.

Oscar continued to roam the autobahns for another decade and a half, looking for that chance encounter. He saw opportunities everywhere. Linz was the future, he must buy something there. No, it would be Graz. Carinthia, the Tyrol. Finally he became convinced that fulfillment waited somewhere in the mountain forests of Lower Austria. Oscar had gone so far as to put down a small deposit on an almost inaccessible hectare of rock and pine near Molzegg, southwest of Wiener Neustadt. He called it The Land.

Once he had taken Anna there in his yellow ÖAMTC van; Sophie had been busy with athletics that day. They had walked through the pines and sat upon the lichened boulders and discussed where this momentous acquisition would take them.

"With a little luck," he told her, using the phrase with which by then he opened almost every sentence, "we can improve the road to The Land. We can build a modest chalet and spend weekends there in the summer. We will plant a garden."

"We will learn Nordic skiing," said Anna, almost unable to breathe for excitement.

"Also, the investment. Something for you girls."

Of course, the little bit of luck never arrived. Oscar lost his deposit and The Land went to the bank. The modest chalet was never built, the garden never planted. They spent their summers as they always had, and no one ever learned to ski.

Anna had always accommodated her father's fantasies by voicing hope and optimism, while shielding herself from disappointment with the certain knowledge that his dreams never crossed into reality. But his putting down actual Schillings on an honest-to-Christ hectare of forest land that she had actually walked upon—well, that was something else again. It penetrated her defenses. The modest chalet, the garden, the skis, the investment had become so real and possible to Anna that her heart broke a little when the Molzegg fantasy spiraled down to nothing.

Oscar had always been blind to cracks in the hearts of others, but keenly aware of the empty spaces in his own. Now, as the hard line of life's horizon became more visible to him, he gave up trying to fill those hollows. His longings for a better life, for the chance encounter that would change the future, became secular prayers for his daughters, or, rather, for Sophie.

Bright and pretty and hard-edged, she would become a famous television journalist, rich and recognized. She might make a second career in a higher calling, like law or medicine or the arts. Her success would make him happy and fulfilled. And Anna? She would be a good nurse and marry a good man and raise a clutch of adequate sons; that was the best Oscar could conjure for his quiet twin.

His chance encounter with a noted physician finally happened, but not quite as he had hoped. Dreaming and drifting as he patrolled the A-3 down toward Mödling, his mind was on how he and his lovely Sophie-Anna, now in her sixties, would waltz at the millennial New Year's Ball. She had never been more real to him. After all these years, he could catch her scent, hear her calm, distinguished voice speak that fine, antique German, feel her as a physical presence in the cab. Were he to reach across with his hand, he would find hers, translucent and fine-boned, warm to the touch....

Oscar had reached out and grasped empty air, then turned toward the vacant seat to find himself alone. As he struggled with this troubling intrusion of reality, destiny took the wheel and steered his yellow truck into the passing lane.

Witnesses said the truck had been going no more than fifty kilometers per hour, the silver Mercedes saloon that struck it, more than two hundred. The two vehicles exploded in a shower of plastic and metal, yellow and steel-grey; their violently fused mass tumbled across the tarmac and exploded in flames. Hardly any of the Mercedes driver, a young dermatologist of some repute, was ever found. But Oscar had been thrown clear and lay in a border of Eidelweiss, where the medics recovered what remained of him.

When he awakened in the Allgemeine Krankenhaus, there was his daughter at his side, her eyes brimmed with tears.

"Sophie?" he asked, squeezing her hand.

"It's Anna, Papa."

"I want Sophie."

"She's away."

"Tell her to come."

"She will, as soon as she knows."

"Of course. As soon as she knows."

He watched Anna then, his old blue eyes above the oxygen mask moving with her as he tried to puzzle out what had happened and how he came to be here with his quiet twin, the one who would accomplish so little, yet was able to do *this*. "Are you a doctor?"

"A nurse, Papa."

"But, a medical person. A highly trained medical person."

"Yes, Papa."

Oscar had smiled, his body had relaxed. "I always believed I would be one of those."

"I know."

"Or Sophie."

"Shh."

"But it was you."

Having decrypted his situation, Oscar had settled down to wait for God. Anna told herself he would now understand that his medical dreams had led her to become a nurse—that she had hoped to fulfill at least some of his destiny for him. But Oscar was useless when it came to the imaginings of others. Whenever he awoke, he called her Sophie. Still, Anna believed her presence lifted his old, heavy heart as his life tapered to nothing.

Sophie hadn't come to Vienna after the accident, unable, as she put it on the telephone, to "simply drop" an assignment. Besides, she'd just be standing on the sidelines while Anna nursed him, and she wasn't a sidelines person, ha ha. Sophie had tried to keep it light, but Anna could hear her relief that Oscar's empty existence was finally ending, his litany of disappointment about to be stilled. Sophie had thought him tiresome and neurotic.

"You can't just wait for life to spring at you like a beast in the jungle," she'd told him (she had just read the James story) in a voice that reminded Anna of their mother. "You talk about reality and destiny as being different, but it is up to you to make them one and the same. Not God. *You.*"

Sophie called now and then to report a new assignment, a distant story, a new job opening up; to Anna, journalism was like a machine that manufactured excuses for being somewhere else. Sophie didn't reply to Anna's note about selling the leasehold flat in Vienna's Second District and splitting the proceeds, although Anna knew her sister would go crazy if their shares didn't match to a pfennig. Sophie had been "trapped, actually" in Amsterdam when Anna and Svetlana said goodbye to Oscar at the Zentralfriedhof crematorium. She was on assignment in Berlin the day they hired a car and drove down into Niederösterreich with Oscar's ashes, which they scattered over what he and Anna had once called The Land.

Sophie could not surprise Anna, who understood her sister through and through. She had known almost from birth that Oscar's imagined Sophie was just a father's wishful thinking. She knew Sophie had never felt the slightest affection for him, or for her. Sophie liked to introduce Anna to friends as her lesser twin. Nothing personal, of course, nothing evil. It was just how twins were. Sophie was Molly McCoy's child, unequipped for love in any of its more demanding forms. Anna often wondered whose child *she* was.

Now, crowded into the back seat of Al Rabiah's Ford with the two little angels, Anna wiped away her tears and managed a rueful smile. It was true that, for Sophie, she would have murdered, she would have sold old flint-hearted Molly into prostitution. She would have betrayed that pleasant man who'd put roses in her cheeks.

But she was not soft to the core. She had no illusions where her sister was concerned. She neither forgot nor forgave Sophie's behavior when their father died, yearning in vain for his favorite. So, there it was. Anna would do anything for Sophie except love her.

Al Rabiah half turned toward the back seat, causing the Focus to veer, briefly out of control. "Sophie should be on her way to the Americans."

Anna nodded. The ghostly twin reflected in the dark window nodded too.

IV

Anyone but Sophie Nieman would have gone mad with claustrophobia in the lightless subterranean hole, where the rough granular walls almost touched her arms, the ceiling was too low for her to stand, the air close as a tomb's. But she had never been afraid of what Fate doled out, or what the moment, the day, the week might hold. The future was unknowable. The present was all one ever had. She took what came with the fatalistic equanimity of an injured bird, and knelt or lay curled up in the darkness, unafraid.

The intruders had killed her three companions casually, just like that, shot through the head, one-two-three, and they had threatened to kill her. But she had sensed from the beginning that they would not, and when they had removed her blindfold and let her see their eyes, she knew she might suffer some indignities from them, but she would not die. Their eyes confirmed what she had known from birth: she was too beautiful and brave to be killed.

Now she smiled in the darkness. After making the video of her capture, the masked men had chattered for a time in low, excited voices, careful not to look at her, although it was clear she was the subject of their discussion. Finally one of them had led her out into the night and put her down this spider hole, with the millipedes and worms and the darkness. Sophie didn't mind. After a time another of the men, an older one, she believed, sent down water and dried dates and bread, and a thick wool chador to put between herself and the cold confines of this temporary grave.

Her captors took her out of the ground twice each day, and stood with their backs to her while she, behind a blanket pinned to a clothes line, shat and tried to squeeze a bath from a large pan of rusty water. Then they put her back in the hole, where she knelt or lay imperturbably in the darkness and let time stream by. She slept a febrile, unrefreshing sleep, descending as easily as an idle dog into shallow naps from which the slightest sound retrieved her.

Most of Sophie's waking moments went to organizing the story she would tell, the book she would write, the documentary she would produce, direct, and narrate, about her experience, no, her *ordeal* in the desert, no, her *captivity*. Her captivity. The inner editor liked that.

She would describe how she'd felt herself a luminous presence in the velvet darkness, still as a butterfly not quite ready to emerge, yet knowing she would finally fly free. She would describe the hole's loamy odor, no, its organic stink, no, its fleshy scent of a fresh-dug grave. She would describe her dreams of pistols darting through the windows of their van, and her three companions shot dead, one-two-three, just like that, the vehicle's interior sprayed with blood and brain. She would describe how one became so dirty, so filmed in grains of dust, that dirtiness no longer mattered. And she would tell the world that she had never felt a moment's fear, for she had seen her captors' eyes and knew they could not kill her.

Now she heard the faint cascade of sand and shale that told her they were preparing her evening exhumation, then the voice of the older one who was her shepherd: "Come up."

Sophie crawled to the vertical chimney of her hole and inched herself upward on the soft rungs cut into the walls. As she broke ground she was surprised to see that it was not the usual pale sky of early evening, but black night, with a bright wash of stars across the heavens, and cold. The man who tended to her crouched nearby, holding open the trap door that sealed the entrance to her hole. *Grave.* In her book she would call it her grave. "You're late," she said in English.

"We have many things. Not just you." He watched her as she stood and stretched, as she thought of it, beautifully, like a bird. No, like a swan. He was unmoved. "Come."

This time he led her not into the atrium where she had performed her rough toilet behind a draped blanket, but into the house, and to a doorless alcove with a WC, metal sink, and a hand-held shower. "Putting on the Ritz," she said.

"Clean yourself. Then we feed you."

"I need fresh clothing."

"Of course."

"Privacy?" she asked, nodding at the open door.

He must have smiled behind his mask, for his eyes twinkled. "Noor will keep an eye on you." Another masked figure, not much taller than a child with the awkward aura of early adolescence, emerged from the shadows. Serious eyes. No, miserable ones.

"While I shit?"

The older man shook his head.

"While I bathe?"

"Then, yes."

"But why?"

"To see what awaits him in Paradise." With that, he nodded to the boy and strode into the darkness.

Sophie regarded her new minder. "When do you leave for Paradise?"

The miserable eyes blinked slowly, but Noor gave no other sign. He looked away while she quickly used the toilet, but turned toward her as she peeled away her old garments, stained and stinking from her weeks of captivity. She could be angry or she could be impregnable, she decided, and opted for the latter.

For a long moment she stood naked before this masked boy, letting his unhappy gaze wander uncomfortably over her revealed body until, embarrassed or perhaps overloaded, he had to turn away. "You won't find anything like this in your Paradise, Noor." Then she walked under the tepid dribble of the shower and used the thin bar of brown soap to scrub herself, over and over, until she felt almost clean. By the end of her shower, her heart was light, for it had come to her: they were going to let her go; it was over.

Now the older man reappeared and, without looking in Sophie's direction, handed a brown paper package to Noor, with an Arabic comment she did not understand. The boy stepped close to her and bowed almost imperceptibly, his miserable eyes unable not to look her up and down one last time, then handed her the package.

Because of her good mood, Sophie treated the moment as a game, ripping away the paper as if it were Christmas wrappings and she a child. Some rough white undergarments. A red and purple pirhan with gold designs on the arms, a black doman to cover her down to her feet, a purple abaya with golden trim, and a beige headscarf. She put them on quickly, longing to see herself in a mirror, but pleased with the effect of this new costume. She would wear it home. She would bring it out for fancy-dress parties during Fasching. She would wear it for the jacket photograph of her book about Captivity.

The older man reappeared, looked her up and down, and nodded his approval. With a slight movement of his head he sent Noor off into the shadows from whence he had come. "Now we feed you," he told Sophie, leading her into another empty room where dishes had been laid upon a woven mat. This was where they'd made the video of her capture, but now the other masked figures were gone, she had only her minder. In other circumstances, this would be the moment to try an escape. But now, if her instincts were correct, there was no need to flee. In a moment, an hour, a night, her cocoon would part and she would fly free.

Sitting cross-legged on the edge of the mat, she broke off a crescent of the round loaf and scooped from a bowl of rice and nuts and raisins, and drank a tiny cup of sweet tea, but she could hardly swallow. She resisted the temptation to press her minder; it was important, from a narrative stand point, that the last act play out naturally.

At last the man said, "Tonight we give you to the Americans."

"What happened?"

"Our bargain was fulfilled."

"What bargain?"

"It does not matter."

"It does to me. Why did you take me?"

"You were there to be taken."

"Why kill my crew?"

"They were of no use to us."

"What did the Americans give you in return?"

He chuckled. "They will empty Guantánamo."

"No they won't."

"They will free all women prisoners held by the so-called Coalition."

She shook her head.

"They give us the atom bomb." He leaned toward her. "What do you like to hear?"

"The truth."

"The truth." His voice grew hard. "The truth is, with God's help, we will now drive a stake into the hearts of Jews and Crusaders."

"But how?"

He seemed to smile beneath his mask. "Ask your sister."

"Anna?" What could some little nurse in Vienna know about the abduction of a famous correspondent? It was insulting, impossible, and it totally fucked up the narrative line of the Captivity story.

"Yes, Anna. Ask Anna."

"My clever twin," she sneered

"Twin?"

Was that a note of agitation?

"You are twins?"

"Didn't you know?" She watched the eyes flutter, as the man regained his composure.

"Of course we knew."

Sophie thought: You're lying. But she kept quiet. Now all she wanted was to be free.

And, she could tell, the man was finished with her. "Now Noor gives you to the Americans." Such warmth as she'd heard in his voice was gone now. Sophie Nieman had ceased to exist. And what was this new sensation she felt along her spine? Fear?

He led her outside, into the chill darkness. She glanced quickly at the sky to find Polaris for north. Almost below the opposite horizon, an airport beacon pulsed green, green, white. If it was Baghdad International, she must be northwest of the city.

Noor waited at the wheel of an ancient Toyota sedan, once the color of cream, now brown from rust and a lifetime in the desert. He had removed his mask and Sophie saw that he was even younger than she'd thought, barely adolescent, a long way from discovering Paradise. He would not look at her, embarrassed, she decided, by their touchless intimacy. As she opened the passenger door, her minder slipped the obligatory black blindfold over her eyes. "Don't worry," she said, "I won't be coming back."

The man said nothing, but helped her find the front seat of the car. Noor cranked the starter and the engine came to clattering life. It would be a miracle if it made it all the way to Baghdad. "Good-bye," she told her minder. But he was already gone.

Then they were off, lurching for some minutes along a rutted track in the sand, then turning onto a paved road. She imagined the black land stretching out on either side of them. If they were northwest of the city, the Euphrates would be a silver ribbon off to their left, fringed with reeds, bounded by palms and eucalyptus trees and ranks of power poles, leaning every which way, like a file of drunks, wires madly crisscrossing the sky. She imagined the dark, leafy masses rising against the night. She imagined she was a Predator drone, watching from ten thousand feet as the little wreck of a car drummed south and east along the river, Lake Habbaniyah off to their right, Ramadi a thin cluster of lights behind them, Fallujah ahead, or perhaps they were closer than she thought and the lights ahead were Baghdad.

She told herself she must remember every detail of this final journey to freedom. And she would have to forget what her minder had said about asking Anna. Anna had nothing to bargain away. It had been another of the man's little side jokes, like Guantánamo and atom bombs. Besides, this was Sophie's story, not her twin's; she could tell it any way she chose.

She would say they fed her a samoon and kubba and a tiny glass of sweet tea before releasing her, that they believed they had driven a stake into the hearts of Jews and Crusaders, that they joked about what the Americans had done to secure her freedom. She would tell how she located her position from the stars, and traced their path, though blindfolded. The world would listen to her; the networks would make a path to her door. "This is Sophie Nieman, CNN," she whispered. "This is Sophie Nieman, BBC World." Her moving picture would flow out across the human universe, the fearless, beautiful correspondent who dared to open closed doors in dangerous places.

But wait, Noor was driving very fast now, she heard the engine straining as he squeezed all he could from a car near the end of its life....Ah, God, she thought then, an expendable car, driven by an expendable boy who didn't bother to wear a mask on his way to Paradise with an expendable girl. The eyes of her captors had lied; Noor was driving her to her death. Bastards. More angry than afraid, she ripped away the blindfold and head scarf, loosing her blonde hair to the wind.

The airport beacon was ahead of them and to the left, she'd got their position right. There was no traffic at this time of night, it was too dangerous to take the airport road alone, and here they were in this expendable car, the speedometer at a hundred thirty kilometers an hour.

"Noor, not so fast," she said, but he made no sign of having heard her. He stared fixedly at the pale ovals cast by the headlights and hunched himself over the wheel. Burned-out vehicles sprawled along the shoulder, and the headlights flicked across two dead men, stiff and bloated, prone in the sand. Now, ahead of them, she saw a few dots of light arrayed across the highway, a checkpoint. A light illuminated a large red and white octagon ordering them to stop. "Noor, slow down," and she pointed toward the lights. "Americans."

The boy turned to look once more at Sophie, his olive face ashen but serene. Then he relaxed his grip upon the wheel and leaned back in his seat, as though requited. But he did not slow down.

A line of tracers arced through the darkness ahead of the Toyota, like embers cast upon the night, trailed by the pop of small arms. A blinding light shattered the darkness. Noor drove toward it, the brave cosmonaut diving his ship into the Sun. More tracers. Something slammed against the car's bonnet, caromed singing off the roof. The checkpoint was no longer just a line of bright dots, but a lighted barrier with men and vehicles moving around, hurrying out of the Toyota's path, bringing weapons to bear.

Sophie could hear them yelling to one another. She thought she would have to jump, hit the rough ground rolling, arms over her face, a bone shattered perhaps, abrasions. But the hand she reached out toward the door seemed to go to the vanishing point without grasping anything; time had begun a mad dilation she was unable to traverse…

The windshield detonated, its shrapnel of glass rattling against the sedan's rear windows. The boy bit his lip, leaned toward the wheel, and managed to say, "Allah.." before his head exploded, splattering the car and Sophie with blood and brain, just like that. Something hit Sophie in the thorax with enough force to knock the wind out of her, so that her vision dimmed in a shower of sparks and black spots. Reviving, she felt wonderfully open to the night, the chrysalis unzipped, her bright wings spreading, and as she pondered what could have freed her so entirely another round raked her left cheek, creasing a lovely pale eye.

The *pompompom, pompompom,* of a heavy machine gun arrived amid this fresh rain of glowing tracers. The expendable car disintegrated, its tires peeled away like black rags, the screaming engine belched a plume of fire and clattered to stillness. Driverless and on its rims, the Toyota skittered off the right side of the road, dug into the sand along the shoulder, rolled once, and came to rest back on its wheels, fire flickering beneath the crumpled bonnet.

"Christ," Sophie whispered, "Christ," for pain had finally overtaken her wounds, horrible pain that made her want to scream, but she could not. She wanted to touch the crevice in her chest, but could not move. But she was alive, someone would come along and patch her up and she would get to tell her story, and there would be offers from CNN and the BBC and CBS.

Soldiers moved outside the Toyota. Sophie heard a cough of foam spewed at the fire, voices. A shadow in Noor's window, the sudden light of a handheld torch. "Driver here," a young American voice announced. "Ma Deuce in the head."

"Help me," Sophie murmured to the shadow behind the beam of light. "Help me."

The shadow leaned closer and she could see a young black face gleaming beneath the helmet. The light played over her. "We got a girl in here," he called over his shoulder. "Pretty white girl."

Pretty white girl. That perfectly described her, thought Sophie. A luminous entity, like a butterfly flying free.

"Ma Deuce in the chest," the young voice called. Then, the excited tone softening for her benefit, he said, "Not to worry, girl, you're gonna be okay, we'll get you outta this okay…."

The pain was like a great, universe-filling wail now, so that Sophie barely heard the soldier, and barely cared. But there, on the far side of her hurting, she could discern a comforting darkness, dense and velvet as the desert night, but starless, and cold, very cold. "I'm so cold," she whispered.

"We'll get you out, ma'am," another voice told her. There were several shadows in the window now, several lights. Another called out, "We're losing her."

Where the gathering darkness lapped against Sophie Nieman, it extinguished her pain, drained the fire of its light. That was the sort of detail she must remember. My pain, she would tell Sixty Minutes, dissolved in the desert night, which was cold, very cold…

"Fuck!" a young voice cried. "Fuck!"

But Sophie couldn't hear him.

V

Viktor Krylov's office occupied perhaps ten square meters on the sixteenth floor of the Vienna International Center tower in which the Agency had its headquarters. Because of his seniority, but also because he had sometimes been in trouble and was going nowhere, Krylov had the little room to himself.

He felt quite at home there. As seen from his window, the Danube might have been the Moskva; the low, steepled skyline of Vienna on the far bank, Moscow without the golden onions; the wrinkled green horizon of the Vienna Woods, the Sparrow Hills. On fine days he could just make out the white saddle of the Schneeberg more than sixty kilometers to the west.

His immediate supervisor, an intolerable Dane named Klaus Oldenburg, was fond of saying the room looked like a Moscow militsaya office circa 1928. It had the same worn lino floor, the same clutter of books and dossiers, loose papers everywhere.

Oldenburg had been junior to Krylov when, years earlier, they had gone off to monitor a refueling at the Angra-1 reactor south of

Rio. But then Krylov had embarked on an "unofficial" radiation assay in Bolivia, meaning only to do good. The Dane had recommended it to Krylov with the usual sneer: "Pays nothing. Profits no one. Sounds a perfect Soviet project. You know, one third-worlder helping another?"

The Beni Adventure, as Krylov thought of it afterward, had put him into such radiation fields as he had not seen again until he entered Emerson's cave. It would have killed him, except that the doctor at Embassy La Paz drained him of his pale, irradiated Russian blood and filled him up with the dark, oxygenated stuff of the Altiplano indians. He had returned to Vienna more Quechua than Soviet, only to discover that while he was away his homeland had ceased to exist.

Not exactly one of Stalin's leftover boys, Krylov wasn't entirely reconstructed, either. He missed his homeland, the crowded grey cities, the gleaming domes of empty churches, the smoky crawl of traffic, people who endured whatever came, winters out of Dante, the vast, unkemptness of the land, always in need of a haircut. He had fought for her, spied for her, defended her honor, and often even believed that what she did was as advertised. And then off she had gone, into oblivion. And here came America, like the paint in the Sherwin-Williams logo, oozing down over the world.

As jilted boys will do, Krylov had responded with a spate of bad behavior. He had turned up his natural surliness to the point where even Russian colleagues began to leave him alone. He consumed more vodka, sometimes shimmering like a desert horizon with its fumes on mornings after. The Safeguards director, an Argentine named Juan Carlos Imler, advised him to take things easy and kept him off the inspections roster, a good thing, for Krylov found it increasingly difficult to serve a world to which he was no longer attached.

On impulse, Krylov bought a used Lada, a small, red box that wheezed and farted down the streets of Vienna, trailed by a coil of black exhaust. It overheated in summer and produced no heat in winter. It regurgitated fuel and lubricants. He liked to say the Lada was his time machine back to the old days, causing his remaining Russian friends to roll their eyes, as Austrian mechanics did when they peeked under the hood.

But, in fact, the little wreck *had* been a kind of time machine for Krylov, a tether to a past that each day became fainter. It didn't matter if he spent hours waiting for the yellow ÖAMTC truck to find him on the road and restore the Lada to Arkady, its mechanic, a man as Russian and idiosyncratic as the car.

Krylov's odd behavior had lasted only a few months, although to him and everyone around him it seemed years. When the Lada had finally pulled up at death's door, he forbade heroic measures to resuscitate it. For weeks afterward, he had dreamed he floated slowly away from the little red car, like a loose cosmonaut.

Finally, one splendid autumn morning, he'd awakened feeling whole for the first time since Bolivia. He thought his Russian blood must have reconstituted itself, as though there had never been any gamma in his life, as though Mother Russia had never broken his heart. It was over.

In the spirit of a miraculously cured cripple tossing away his crutches, he had run out into the bright day and spent most of his savings on a Mercedes 300SL sedan, dark metallic grey with tan leather seats, in which he could cruise at two hundred kilometers, cooled by the air conditioner in summer, kept warm in deep winter, all in a hissing silence broken only by a sound system as rewarding as a night at the Bolshoi. He called it his capitalist tool.

Back in his good suits and silk ties, Krylov tidied up his life, paid delinquent bills, answered neglected letters. Someone had written asking whether the Krylov dacha, a rude one-storey cabin in the marshes north of St. Petersburg, might be for sale. This forgotten reminder that he still owned a tiny, mosquito-plagued piece of Russia Krylov took to be a favorable omen. He replied that the dacha was not for sale.

Then he began a note to old Axel, who lived in one of the cabins left from a failed commune several kilometers away from the dacha, but looked after it, more or less. Age had addled him a little, so that he was now and then cut adrift by a flickering memory and the simultaneous arrivals of democracy and greater poverty. Axel had never quite mustered out of the Soviet infantry and seemed disappointed if Krylov did not appear in polished boots and a grey overcoat and a chest festooned with ribboned gold, as happened once or twice in his KGB days. Axel rather liked playing the serf, bowing his head and touching his forelock in greeting, and calling Viktor Viktorivich "Master".

Krylov smiled, warm with memory. He finished his note with a reference to their long friendship and the good times they'd shared. Then he folded the paper and dropped it and two hundred euros into an envelope addressed to Axel's post box in Michurinskoye.

Then, nursing this moment of reverie, he wrote fatherly (but carefully undemanding) notes to his two grown children, to Andrei, who nowadays thought of little else but where he might take the next bite out of Moscow's money pie, and to Valentina, drained of youth and beauty by an older husband Krylov could not stand. Into each he slipped a hundred-euro note, contemptibly small change for the boy, perhaps, but a nice surprise for the girl, now that democracy had dropped her ageing rocket engineer into penury. Sealing the envelopes, Krylov felt like a man stepping into sunshine after months in a dark cell. Recalled to life, he thought. Recalled to life.

At work, Krylov made the necessary apologies, revved his professional engine, got himself back on the inspections roster. Belleville-1, Takahama-3, Three Mile Island, Sizewell-A, Leningrad-1, all the world's reactors, their echoing containments and cable runs and glowing pools, their alpha and beta and gamma, their fugitive neutrons, awaited him.

He managed to revive his belief in the Mission, although not very much or for very long. He chatted up old friends, went with them to the cafeteria for lunch and to the UNO City bar at day's end, although he drank very little, for a Russian. The word around the Agency was that the old Viktor had returned. "The bear is back on the unicycle," Krylov told the reflection he shaved each morning.

But by the time Krylov rebounded, Oldenburg had ascended to a vacancy above him. At first too mellow to care, Krylov had taken awhile to realize fully what had happened. He did what he could to stay out of Oldenburg's way, trying to avoid clashes. But a bear on a unicycle remains a bear, after all. Oldenburg liked to nag and needle, Krylov wanted mainly to be left alone. "Think of me as dead, Klaus," he growled.

"I thought you were."

"Fuck your mother."

Now Oldenburg poked his head through the door. "Christ, our militsaya station in the poor part of town. Where's your portrait of Stalin?" The usual insult. "Are you building a nest?"

Krylov said nothing, but raised his eyebrows, waiting.

"Have a minute?"

No response.

"Good." The visitor eased his long, supple self, done up in a charcoal woolen suit purchased for nothing at Shopping City Sud, over to the grey metal guest chair, where he pushed aside some loose-leaf volumes and sat down. For a time he studied his white fingers—he had the coloration of a rabbit in winter—which cupped one raised knee; then he opened the door to his displeasure.

"This Iraq business is a disgrace."

Krylov raised his eyebrows another notch.

"What in hell were you thinking?"

Up they went another notch.

"You owe us an explanation."

Ah, well, thought Krylov. Silence only takes you so far. "Us?"

"Me. Imler. The Director-General. We would like to know why you went into Iraq. Safeguards inspectors were thrown out of there years ago. We would also like to know why you went on international television. I know you enjoy playing the Russian cowboy, improvising. I don't forget Bolivia. But this new excursion is something else again."

"Talk to Churches."

"He was as mystified as we are."

"Indeed."

"Have you seen yourself on television?"

Krylov shook his head, although he had watched the clip over and over, trying to parse it, or, perhaps, trying to make it go away.

"You have real talent....as a clown."

"Thank you."

"What happened?"

"Look at the television."

"You must have taken samples."

Krylov shrugged; lying to this fellow was not really lying at all. "The Americans kept them."

"Did they also pay you?"

"Pay me?"

"For being their simple tool."

"Ah."

"Their Russian poodle."

Krylov got slowly to his feet. "A pretty big poodle."

Oldenburg remained seated, fingers clenched on his raised knee, pale cheeks going mauve as his blood rose. He forced a laugh. "I don't fear dogs."

"I see that." Krylov turned away from the Dane, watched the Danube for a moment, his arms folded tightly across his chest. "I think I have enough shit for now. Come back in January. Use the door. Or the window."

"The window doesn't open."

"We use force."

"I'm telling Imler."

"Telling him what? That I scare you?" Krylov walked past the Dane and opened the door to the hall. "I think he knows that already. Go tell Imler anything you want. But go."

Churches danced into the office not five minutes after Oldenburg's departure, before Krylov's rage had cooled. "Viktor, my God,' he cried in his excited boy voice, "I had no idea what I'd let you in for. No idea at all. Are you all right?"

"Go away."

"But I *must* hear your story," said Churches, taking the spare chair, leaning earnestly forward.

"You would be 'mystified.'"

"Oh, I see, you've already heard from Klaus. I didn't want to give anything away. Not before I talked to you."

"What? You didn't want to tell him you arranged to have me kidnapped?"

"Kidnapped….much too strong a term, Viktor."

"Abducted."

"No, no, delayed en route. An hour or two out of your life. I had no idea about the cave, none at all."

"Bullshit. The Americans asked you for a Russian inspector. You gave them me."

"I wanted to go, but they wouldn't take me. British, staunch Coalition partner, all that. They needed someone more, um, unengaged."

"So, ask them for the story. Or watch it on television, like everybody in the world."

"I did watch it. Amazing. You, and those Americans. You may not have meant to, but you may have fixed their problem about invading Iraq. Ours too. I mean the UK's. You gave them a lovely dirty bomb. I bet you're a hero back in the States. Ticker tape, Freedom Medal."

"Not funny."

"Not fond of our cousins?"

"*Your* cousins. Mine are quite different."

"Mongol hordes. Genghis, all that."

Krylov leaned forward. "Listen to me, Churches. If you were a grownup, I would already have dragged you into Imler's office and squeezed an explanation out of you. Not just why you set me up, but why you're in the pocket of people like Emerson. Imler hates spies."

"You would know," said Churches, withdrawn now, angry in the way of guilty boys.

"My glamour days are over. Cross me like this again and yours will be too. You can grow roses in Surrey."

"Devon."

"Whatever."

"Now I've been scared out of my wits, Viktor, and threatened with physical harm….may I help? I mean, you've been in that hot cave, you must've taken bags of samples. I'll pass them to one of our weapons guys at Aldermaston. Analyze them on the quiet. Off the books. Find out what, when, where, maybe who and why. Least I can do. Anything for my Cossack pal. Yes?"

"The Americans took the swipes."

"Oh."

"Didn't they?"

"How would I know?"

"If they didn't have them they would call you. They would say, Churches my lad, we want you to chat up your Sov, find out what he's done with the stuff from the cave, get your little paws on those swipes and send them over. Have they called?"

Churches shook his head, lying, of course.

"Well, then, they must have the samples."

"Yes, I see that."

"Good-bye, Churches."

On the way out, Churches turned to give the Russian an angry frown and stamped his foot on the old linoleum. Krylov laughed and went back to his desk.

Imler was next, a taller man than Krylov, dressed like a village undertaker, thin as a heron, black hair going grey and thin, mad-scientist glasses, eyes so pale they seemed to have no irises. Some people feared him, but Krylov had discovered that inside this rather distant Argentine lived a wise and gentle man. They were about the same age and equally unreconciled to history.

Imler's German father had fled to Argentina after the war, for reasons that were never discussed, and found work at the Mercedes plant outside Buenos Aires, where Imler was born. As a boy, he told Krylov on one of their Heuriger evenings out in Grinzing, he'd lived in the suburb of Olivos and played football with Nikolaus, the son of a Mercedes foreman named Ricardo Klement, who, as Adolf Eichmann, had ended up at the end of an Israeli rope.

"I never understood all that hatred of the Jews," Imler said. "It intruded so upon fighting the war. Ah, how I dreamed about the war as a boy. About victory slipping through our fingers."

"There was a moment when everybody thought you'd won," said Krylov, being kind. He had never forgiven Germany anything, but had decided to cut his friend some slack.

"Hitler was crazy to invade Russia."

"We thought so."

Imler laughed. "Maybe just crazy?"

"Maybe. A lot of that around, then."

Despite the steady shrinkage of the tobacco universe, Imler still smoked when he could. His sharp-boned cheeks were as red as a clown's, and he had the translucence and cough of someone dying; but he had been that way for years. Now, slipping into the extra chair, he held up a pack of Marlboros. "May I?"

"Will they fire me for harboring a smoker?"

"Not for that."

"Then I don't mind." Krylov passed him a cut-glass ash tray looted years earlier from a London hotel.

Once wreathed in a grey veil of exhaust, Imler said, "Oldenburg's in a state."

"Good."

"One day you will wind him up so tight he explodes."

"I look forward."

"Churches also."

"Yes, he was so angry he stamped his foot."

Imler chuckled and leaned back in the chair and smoked quietly for a moment, watching Krylov. Then, "Very well, we go to work. What happened to you down there?"

"Are you talking to an underling or a friend?"

"What can an 'underling' tell me?"

"Almost nothing."

"And a friend?"

"Everything. Well, almost everything. But it stays with you."

"Fair enough."

"In Bonab we were offered a helicopter ride to Tehran. It sounded better than the commercial flight from Tabriz so I took it. Churches wanted to stay on. I don't know why, we accomplished nothing there. But he stayed and I went off with the multichannel analyzer on an Mi-8 with Bulgarian crew. They took me to Tehran, all right. But first they took me to Iraq."

"How did you hear about this ride?"

"One of the Bulgarians offered it to Churches."

"And he passed it to you?"

"Ask him."

"He never tells the truth."

"No, he never does."

"But if I must have one of the American's flies on my wall, I prefer our little Englishman. If he goes too far, I send him back to grow roses in Sussex."

"Devon."

"Whatever."

"We landed in the northeast, not very far from the frontier. An American named Emerson was there. Ralph Emerson."

"Truly?"

Krylov nodded. "He had some contractor muscle with him. Also a female commander in the Navy. They'd found a powerful radiation field in a cavern. They asked me to go in with her. Take some measurements."

"And you could not say no?"

"A long walk back to Tehran."

"You would walk before helping the Americans."

"All right, it became one of those moments when you have to choose between doing something stupid and sounding like a coward."

"Ah." Another Marlboro flared to life, visibility in the little room declined.

"Inside the cavern we found a strong cesium 137 signal, radiation you could feel through the suit, on your skin. Signs of a very hot fire, everything molten or turned to ash. Human remains. When we came out Emerson had reporters waiting. So I said whatever I said and they let me go on my way. End of story."

"And your samples?"

And now, thought Krylov, you have to tell your friend a tiny lie. "The Americans took them."

"How?"

"I had the stuff in the instrument case. But when I opened it in the helicopter, everything was gone."

"You know what I think?"

Krylov shook his head.

"I think you anticipated the theft and made a clever substitution."

"I'm glad you think I'm so smart."

"Oh, Viktor, I *know* how smart you are." Imler waited a couple of beats, then, "Years ago, when you went off to Bolivia, you were not merely being helpful." Seeing Krylov begin a protest, he held up a hand. "Let me finish. You also smelled American involvement and wanted to have a little war with your old enemy."

Krylov shrugged.

"So my question is: are we now seeing another front in that war?"

"This isn't just a faint odor. Americans are everywhere. You saw the television."

"Didn't you?"

"Of course. Over and over. Why did they want me? To have a Russian ratify their discovery. Why? So they could crow about finding a dirty-bomb factory in Iraq. Why? To clean up their disgraced president." This time he held up a restraining hand. "No, let me finish. The answer to your question, is no, I am not going to war with the Americans. I am finished with them. Absolutely."

Imler smiled his undertaker's smile and shook his head. "You know, Viktor, I think you actually believe that. But I think you are into something fairly complicated and dangerous. So, speaking first as a friend, let me warn you not to go too far out on this limb. We, meaning the Agency and I, cannot protect you."

"And speaking as my boss of bosses?"

"We shall not lift a finger to protect you."

"You would throw me overboard to quiet the sea?"

"If the sea needed quieting."

To Krylov's relief, the telephone intruded with its soft double ring. "They can leave a message."

"No, take it."

Krylov picked up the receiver, listened for a moment, then put his hand over the mouthpiece, grinning. "The girl of my dreams."

Imler ground out his cigarette in the ash tray and stood up. "I was just leaving."

ILSE HEILIG REALLY HAD BEEN THE GIRL OF KRYLOV'S DREAMS, ONCE upon a time. In a way she still was, for he remembered her as one did one's dreams, and his heart lifted at the mere sound of her, especially on a day when it offered an escape from Oldenburg and Churches and, yes, even old Juan Carlos Imler, the friend who would not lift a finger to protect him. Now, free of UNO City's steel and glass towers, booming southward on the A4 in the Benz, windows open, hair flying, Krylov felt free as a crow.

It always surprised and pleased him that the city gave way so quickly to the manicured farmlands of Austria. With the Danube a narrow grey ribbon off to the left, on the right the old gas works that developers were turning into retro-condos, the tangled plumbing of the Schwechat refinery, and then, just beyond the airport, a turn southwest toward Enzersdorf—and suddenly, there you were, traversing a rumpled quilt of fields decorated with trim walls of poplar and willow. Krylov smiled and hunkered down into the crazed leather seat of the Benz, which, he now remembered, had been with him almost as long as his sweet dreams of Ilse.

They'd met at a going-away party for a Russian at the Safeguards lab at Seibersdorf, where she worked as an analyst. It had snowed heavily all afternoon, huge flakes gliding earthward in their trillions, an invasion of snow from the grey winter sky. Russians being Russians, it had required much of the night to launch the departure, with toasts longer than a big man's arm, one tiny glass of cold vodka after another. Then everyone had gone slithering out into the frozen night, gingerly picking a path down the slow lane to Vienna.

Until the party, Krylov had only seen Ilse at a distance, and had known only that she worked at Seibersdorf and was not, once seen, easily forgotten. Even in passing, he had taken note of her sharp but finely drawn features, hooded green eyes, and a broad mouth that told the world she found it droll, although not necessarily funny. She was, Krylov thought, like a slender bowsprit figure, breasting the sea of life, auburn hair streaming, head held high. He could not remember why he'd attended the party; it was during his Lada Period, when he had mainly stayed away from such gatherings. But for some forgotten reason he had pedaled the Lada to Seibersdorf that night, and there she had been.

Below Enzersdorf, Krylov turned the Benz down the Leitha Bundesstrasse, a long diagonal road through a world that had changed little in centuries. He liked to come this way, which was not quite as direct as a straight southward drive from the city, because this portion of the road reminded him of Russia, or, rather, Russia with a nice haircut, all of her teeth, and a little money.

As always, the low oblongs of the laboratory complex appeared as if suddenly and he braked to make the turn into the driveway. The guard, an extremely tall Sikh in the livery of UN security, studied his badges, then studied him, and then gave an almost imperceptible salute to pass him through the gate. He pulled into a guest space near the Safeguards wing of the facility, parked, and shut down the Benz. For a moment, he rested there, still trapped in reverie.

Ilse had been the first person Krylov had noticed upon entering the conference room where a crowd had assembled to say goodbye to their colleague. He had spotted her among the eddying figures, the amused expression, the luminous face, the confident stride; he had watched her furtively as he worked his way through the chilled vodka and Swedish meatballs. Whenever he looked up, there she was, across a crowded room, as they say. Finally, it had dawned on Krylov that she was also watching him. When their eyes met for a moment, they both looked quickly away, startled by the unexpected intimacy of the exchange. They had fled in opposite directions, escaping into the knots of people, until, finally, they found themselves standing side by side.

"Are you following me?" The faint, not unfriendly curl of the lip, green eyes laughing.

"I thought *you* were following *me*."

"I don't follow men."

"What, you lead them?"

She laughed. "I do what I can."

"You remind me of a Russian girl."

"I knew I was a little overweight…"

"Don't be nasty. Russian girls are strong and beautiful."

"Well, I am fairly strong. Beautiful, never."

"You would be the last to know."

"It's just the party. Tonight everybody reminds everybody of Russia. Everybody is beautiful."

"Well, if you're not a Russian girl, what sort of girl are you?"

"An Austrian girl."

"You're fooling me."

"Austrian through and through."

"Do you live out here?" He'd waved his arms, trying to evoke the middle of nowhere. "On a farm?"

"You make a face when you say 'farm.' But, no, I live in Wien."

"Where?"

"Behind Karlsplatz, in the Fourth." She smiled. "And you would be up in the Eighteenth, with all the Russians."

"Yes, we have a crowded barracks up there. Earthen floor. Goats and chickens. Barbed wire. You know how we are. Serfs at heart."

"You really do remind me of Russia."

"Through and through. Where in the Fourth?"

"I'd rather not say."

"Why not?"

"You might follow me home."

"What if I did?"

She shrugged and sipped her vial of chilled vodka. "I would have to entertain you."

"Feed me."

"Give you something to drink."

"Listen to my life story."

"You could tell me about your wife and children."

Krylov shook his head. "I haven't been married for a long time and my children are…" He'd started to say lost. "Grown. What about you?"

"My husband is away."

"On business?"

"You could say that."

"Snowbound somewhere."

"It would not surprise me."

"Would he mind if I followed you home?"

Ilse had gazed into Krylov's eyes for what seemed a long, serious time. Then, "No."

"Then that's what I shall do."

"You're in no condition to follow anybody. Here, I'll tell my ride I've had a better offer." With a laugh she wandered away, and for a time Krylov thought he'd lost her. But no sooner had he grabbed another vodka than there she was, eyes sparkling, pulling on a dark fur coat. "Follow me," she said.

"No, no," protested Krylov, "follow *me.*"

"Don't forget your coat."

"Russian men don't wear coats."

"Sorry, I forgot."

"This way. Have you driven much in a Lada?"

She shook her head, frowning. "Never."

"Well, then, you're in for a lovely surprise."

They had charged off into the blizzard in what she would later name The Little Red Monster, the cabin cold as Siberia in winter, the defroster icing the windscreen, the little engine complaining at being left outside in such weather. But it had got them to her street behind Karlsplatz and almost to her building before expiring like a Disney auto, panting and heaving against the curb.

"Follow me," she said and led Krylov into the foyer, the white and black tile slick with snowmelt, and to a tiny cage of an elevator, and up four stories to her door as the hall-light timer clicked down to nothing and the place went dark. Her flat was a set of three high-ceilinged rooms with tall, lace-curtained windows peering out into the Vienna night. But, in a rush of postwar improvisation, this pretty old place had been given a strange new superstructure: a bathtub in the kitchen, a WC off the living room, pipes everywhere for central heat.

"I think we should skip the life story," she told him. "I think we should just go to bed."

ILSE WAITED FOR HIM JUST OUTSIDE THE ENTRANCE, NURSING A PAPER cup of coffee and smoking her tenth morning cigarette. She wore a long white lab coat and carried a notebook held against her breasts, like a school girl. When she saw Krylov she lifted her chin and tried to give him her amused, green-eyed look.

A week earlier he had materialized in her office with a shy "Hello, Ilse." Then, into her silence, he added, "You're looking fine." Then he'd seen how thin she was and the dark crescents of fatigue beneath the clever eyes, emeralds in a pallid mask. "No, better than fine."

"Better than fine. And you look very sleek. Very KGB. Have you put on weight?"

"A little. How is Walter?"

"We are always the same."

"I came to ask a favor."

The green eyes had watched him, opaque as a cat's.

Krylov held out a plastic bag. "Can you look at this for me?"

"What is it?"

"Swipe samples."

"I'll put them in the queue. Come back in a year."

"I need you to look at them now."

"Whose are they?"

"Mine."

"I'll look at them when I can and send over the usual report."

"I'd rather we just talked about it. Kept it between us."

"Us? Is there an us?"

"There used to be."

"How long has it been, Viktor?"

"A lifetime?"

"A lifetime. Well, not quite. And here you are wanting me to give you something I would not give anyone." Like my bed, like my body, like my heart; Krylov heard the unspoken refrain. For a moment she'd studied him. Then, with a resigned shake of her head, she'd taken the baggie and turned back to the dune of paper on her desk. "Goodbye, Viktor. I'll call."

The problematic us had lasted barely a month. The business that had kept her husband, Walter, out of Vienna had turned out to be ten years in Hirtenburg for selling marijuana, a high crime in Austria. Good conduct and poor health had got him out in three, and soon he and his seriously compromised immune system were back in Ilse's life. She had been unable, on her own, to tell her dying man to leave; she may have hoped Krylov would lure her away, talk her off the ledge. But he had felt too unreliable, too disconnected from the world, to help. So she had sailed away, the bowsprit breasting the angry sea of life, head high, auburn hair streaming, to serve what remained of Walter.

Although the sight or sound of Ilse could still lift Krylov's heart, as chance encounters with him might still lift hers, there had been no road back to their happy, ardent moment. It had been just further evidence, as if any were needed, that life was a bad joke. Krylov believed the love they'd made still existed in what a laboratory would call detectable traces. Parts per billion.

The trouble was, thought Krylov, watching her across the parking area, we had not made enough love to see us through.

"Hello, Ilse," he called.

She nodded toward the Mercedes. "Au revoir, Little Red Monster?"

"It died, years ago."

"Like everything."

"Yes, exactly." Everything, he thought, but Walter.

"Let's talk out here."

"Beautiful autumn day."

"Beautiful."

They were close enough that Krylov could have swept her into his big arms and carried her off. They exchanged glancing looks, then looked away. Finally she said, "I've run your samples."

"So you said on the telephone."

"Let's walk."

"Is that like follow me?"

She ignored him. Lighting a fresh cigarette, she wandered toward a line of poplars. Her grip on the notebook tightened and she turned to Krylov. "The analyses are in here with your MCA readouts. I burned a CD for you and kept a copy. The swipes are properly stored so they won't kill anybody."

"So, tell me."

"No, you tell me. Where did you get them?"

"I can't say."

"Then I can't either."

"But it's the rule. You're never told where samples come from because that might skew the result."

"A secret analysis done off the record isn't already skewed?"

"What if I just take the notebook?"

The old smile flickered and for a moment some color crept into her face. "You would have to knock me down. Rip it out of my arms, like a baby. Would you do that, Viktor?"

Krylov's heart gave a sad lurch. He shook his head.

"So, tell me," she said.

"Tell me what you found. Then, maybe, maybe not."

Ilse was quiet, but one could see her spirits had risen a little. For the first time in a long while she wasn't thinking about the dying man at home. "Okay," she said at last. "Cesium 137 has a thirty-year half life, decays to metastable barium 137, half life a couple of minutes, and then stable barium 137. If the cesium is fresh, you would see less barium. If old, you would see more."

"And you found very little."

"You think the cesium is fresh."

Krylov nodded.

"In fact, I found quite a lot of barium."

"That doesn't make sense."

"We don't know if it does or not. If we look at the proportions of cesium 137 to barium 137m and stable barium 137, we can conclude that the cesium has been decaying for ten, maybe twenty, years." She smiled for him. "Since before we were lovers."

"You're wonderful."

"I'm more wonderful than you think. I rummaged around and found readouts from cesium-137 released at Chernobyl in 1986. They're older than your stuff by five to ten years." She waited a couple of beats, letting him think things over, then, "I have more, but first you tell me where you took the swipes."

"Ilse, some people are going to be very pissed off about all that barium."

"Look at me. Do you see a girl who worries about pissing people off?"

"I don't want them to kill the messenger."

"You are the messenger, Viktor. I am just an instrument. Besides, Walter killed me years ago."

"I took the swipes in that cave."

"What cave?"

"The one in Iraq that everybody saw on television."

"I don't watch television."

"The Americans got me to go there, never mind how or why. Very hot, radiologically. The Americans immediately concluded it was a dirty-bomb factory. Proof that Iraq was working on unconventional weapons right up until the 2003 invasion."

"If any of your samples had been fresh, we would have seen less barium. So either the work was done ten or twenty years ago, or the cesium is old. Why would they use such old material?"

"Because that's all they had?"

"If you were making a dirty bomb in your bathtub, you might use old cesium, you know, discarded radiotherapy sources near the end of one half life. But a wealthy nation would have access to fresher material. I think your cave is like a pharaoh's tomb. Your cesium is a relic of a time when Iraq really *was* working on WMD."

"So the Americans got it right about intent, but wrong about time."

Ilse shrugged. "No, they got what they deserve."

"Meaning?"

"Meaning they got intent wrong as well. I found traces of some relatively high melters. Steel, tungsten, glass. Everything melted. But here we have cesium 137 and its daughters surviving more or less intact. What do you think of that, Mr. Bond?"

"The radioactive material was deposited after the fire."

"And not a lot of it. Remember Goiânia? Disperse a tablespoon of cesium chloride salts from a radiotherapy machine and a whole Brazilian village sickens. The radiation you measured in the cave would have required more tablespoons, maybe a Coke bottle filled with cesium chloride. So, yes, there was enough bad stuff in there to build a dirty bomb or two. But why would it have been sprinkled around the place after a fire?"

"Because dogs follow the strongest scent."

"The radiation is what you notice."

"You erase whatever you're doing with fire. Then you mask the remains with a powerful radiation field. And off the dogs go."

"Clever Arabs."

"Stupid dogs." Krylov turned to Ilse, she of the profound fatigue. "I was worse than stupid to involve you."

"I'm not involved, Viktor. Neither are you. I gave the package an invented number: 55555. Remember it. Five fives."

"Why?"

"To separate it from the system."

"But my name is on it."

"Not any more. I changed it."

"To what?"

"Churches." She held up a hand to silence him. "Don't worry, he'll never know. He hasn't been out here in years."

"But why do it at all?"

"Because I also thought someone would be pissed off about all that barium. Because I care about you. A little. Always, a little."

"Does anyone else know about the swipes?"

Ilse shook her head. "Just me. Just us."

"Ah, there *is* an us."

"There will always be an us, Viktor. Long after we are gone, there will be an us."

Krylov put out a big arm and drew her toward him, kissed the crown of her auburn hair. "Sometimes I wish…"

She put an index finger against his lips and, very gently, eyes gleaming, pushed him away. "Shh. Sometimes I wish also."

"We should have an evening."

"I cannot."

"I'm extremely harmless these days."

"You, harmless?" She laughed.

"Seriously. These days my idea of a big evening is dinner with the daughter of an old friend. She calls me Uncle Viktor."

"Uncle Viktor. Well, goodbye, Uncle Viktor. This has been rather nice. It will last me a long time."

Ilse walked with him to the Benz and watched as he strapped in and cranked the engine. "Where do you go from here?"

"I wish I knew."

"Be careful."

"You be careful too."

Then she leaned toward him, frowning. "You know, in the lab we use cold to preserve life and heat to end it. That fire in the cave wasn't just destroying evidence. It was killing something."

VI

Peter Gayle liked Brighton best as it was tonight, wrapped in fog, its lights faded to glowing nebulae, its human clamor muffled. Driving in from Folkestone, he could just discern the low relief of the coastal hills, like a sleeping silhouette against the lighter sky, resting on a bed of mist and diffused illumination beneath the low moaning of the foghorn at Shoreham-by-Sea.

"Cerberus," Mother had liked to say, "would have a voice like that."

"That makes Brighton Hell, doesn't it?" young Peter would reply.

Neither thought much of the Hell idea. They had both loved the old city by the sea, its rows of terraced homes coiling up the heights, even the seaward rank of fun fairs, as vibrant with false promises of happiness as a phalanx of brassy prostitutes, of which there were more than a few, along with buskers and souvenir vendors and criminals and the subterranean species that feed on the noise and strobing light of a carnival. Ordinarily, the sight of Brighton in its cloak of stratus would have lifted Gayle's heart, like the unexpected glimpse of a lost love. But tonight, although he had never felt more relieved to be home, or to hear old Cerberus guarding the gates, his heart didn't budge.

When they went well, writing assignments left Gayle high and wired; but this time he was returning like a castaway crawling through shoals onto the beach, exhausted and edgy. A dispiriting malaise had overtaken him in Bern, which he at first attributed to the extreme dullness of that city, and then to a mild flu; he thought he might have a low fever. And his attitude had been just wrong. When the Swiss said they would have to think a bit longer about letting him into a Hornet cave, he'd felt more relief than disappointment and hadn't bothered to protest.

Instead he had slouched back to the Saab and headed for Coquelles to catch the Chunnel train. Even that routine crossing had seemed nightmarish, the illegals scurrying like huge rats along the tracks, clinging to the fencing in the stark mercury-vapor light, then all those kilometers under the seabed, all that water pressing overhead....He had driven out of Folkestone harbor like a man fleeing ghosts.

Gayle thought he might have more than a touch of flu. The business with the girl had left him with an emotional hangover that persisted like a minor form of grief; people were supposed to walk away from *each other*, not just walk away. It annoyed him that he missed her. Add to that the brushing contact with Al-Rabiah, reminding Gayle that he'd once lived frightened in his own shit, and his complaint lost some of its mystery.

He grinned bravely and shook his head. "All we need," he told the rushing night, "is a bit of whisky and lots of sleep in our own sweet bed. Alone."

Then he took the Saab down into the cloud, threaded through the shrouded seaward streets, now almost empty of traffic, and turned uphill, back into the clear night. A few streets up he turned again and slid the Viggen into the narrow entrance of the garage where he leased two spaces, and parked it next to the older Saab. He gathered his bag and overcoat and hurried toward the exit.

"Good evening, Mr. Gayle."

"You're up late, Ali," said Gayle without looking.

"Oh, very sorry, Mr. Gayle, I am Abdel."

Gayle looked more closely at the man as he stepped out of the shadows. Tall, whiskered, cratered skin, sweet dark eyes that darted like a bird's, a soft mouth. "Then good evening, Abdel."

"I hope you are fine, Mr. Gayle?"

"Fine enough, thanks."

"You had a pleasant journey?"

"Oh, yes, very."

The dark eyes danced around, now and then settling upon him interrogatively, like the eyes of a doctor, thought Gayle, willing you to tell all.

"But I'm in rather a hurry to be home."

"Of course, excuse me, Mr. Gayle."

Then, pausing, "How do you know my name?"

"From the car. Ali told me."

Gayle thought of the vanished man, small, dark, often funny, once a lawyer, now the keeper of a small parking garage. Well, now gone, now nothing at all. "What happened to Ali?"

The big rounded shoulders shrugged. "He found another position. In London."

"Where do you come from?"

"London, Mr. Gayle."

"Before that."

"Mosul, Mr. Gayle."

Another bloody Iraqi. "Well, keep the vandals off my Saabs."

"I shall, Mr. Gayle."

LIKE THEIR VISITS TO THE HOTEL VICTORIA, THE PLACE IN BRIGHTON had cost Mother more than she really had, but offered things she could not quite live without. "If you spend your life on an island," she would tell Peter, "you should by God have a view of the sea."

The leasehold occupied the entire third storey of an old Regency townhouse, tarted up in turquoise and white trim, like a Wedgewood vase; two beds, tiny kitchen, bath, w.c., floors fitted with a cheap beige carpet to match the walls, except in the sitting room, which had fine old parquet that still took a shine.

She had chosen the flat for the sitting room's view. Its seaward wall was a broad window that looked across the Channel toward Brittany, whose coast she claimed could be seen when The Visibilities were right. Ferries, tankers, container ships and liners, bright sailboats and grey men of war sailed back and forth across this grand tableau, towing their white wakes. Seabirds glided past the window, watching the world below as though they understood and owned it.

She had brought in what remained of her family furniture, carved chairs standing on cats' paws and chests with snarling snouts for drawer pulls, worn upholstered pieces, lamps made from eastern balustrades and ginger jars, faded rugs from Afghanistan and China, a mahogany dining table and chairs sized to the smaller males of an earlier century, a sideboard with more snouts, a single bed for her, another for Peter, a stuffed colobus monkey named Avery who had hung by its frazzled tail in a cage since her childhood, staring at nothing through glass eyes.

"Graham Greene would love it," said Peter.

"Perhaps. It is designed for solitary creatures."

"Perfick for us, then."

"Yes, perfick."

And it was. After his mother's death, Gayle had left the flat pretty much as it had always been, adding a color television and setting up his computer as a visitor might on a cheap wooden table near the window, where he could do his work in view of the sea. He felt no ghostly presence of his mother, whose remains he had launched into the atmosphere above Montreux; but she persisted as a faint, rather pleasant scent of ladies' powder, about as much company as a solitary creature wanted.

"Perfick," Gayle said as he entered the familiar room. "Perfick."

He dropped his bag inside the entrance door, next to the monkey, threw his trench coat on the flowered settee, and sank into a comfortable old chair with carved lion claws on the arms and feet. His heart thumped from his hurried climb up four flights of stairs, he felt shivery and worn out. A definite touch of flu. He closed his eyes and leaned back against the familiar hibiscus pattern of the chair, relieved that this odd lassitude, this flatness, appeared to have a physical cause.

The knocking made so little sound that Gayle at first thought it must be something overhead, a mouse in the ceiling, wind across the shingles. But when it came again, he got up and padded down the hall to open the door, expecting old Gurney, the little Yorkshireman who kept the common spaces picked up and more or less secure.

"Hello, Mr. Gayle. Do I disturb you?" Voice like a song, another new boy from the east, a big fellow, color of creamed coffee, mustache, the worried eyes of a stalked doe.

"Do you know what time it is?"

"Yes, I am so sorry to be knocking so late."

"Where's Gurney?"

"Mr. Gurney is gone."

"What do you mean, gone?"

"He stopped coming to his work."

"Did he say why?"

"I did not speak with Mr. Gurney."

"Was he sacked?"

A shrug. "How would I know?"

"I'll find out. Who are you, then?"

"Yusuf."

"From Mosul?"

"Mosul?"

"Abdel, the new man in the garage, is from Mosul."

"Ah. But, no. I am from Samara, Mr. Gayle."

"How do you know my name?"

A beat of hesitation. "Why, Mr. Gurney told me all about you."

"You said you didn't speak to him."

"I did not speak to him about why he stopped coming to work. But I did speak to him about you." Then, conspicuously shifting gears, "Was your journey a success?"

"Did you come up all those stairs to ask me that?"

"I was thinking you were perhaps tired. I can see you are not feeling very well."

"Long drive. People knocking on my door at all hours."

"Shall I call a doctor?"

"Just a cold, it'll be gone by morning." Then, feeling a grand sneeze expanding within, he brought up a handkerchief to contain it.

Yusuf stumbled backwards and nearly fell.

Gayle grinned, dabbing his nose with a handkerchief. "Don't hurt yourself. It's only a cold."

The young man kept his distance.

"Well, I don't blame you. You don't want what I've got. I'll say good night."

"Good night," said Yusuf, backing away toward the stairs.

Gayle closed the door and, because the night had been crawling with strange Iraqis, turned the deadbolt and put up the chain. On the way back to his chair he poured a tumbler of whisky and thought how he would miss Gurney, whom he'd liked.

Tom Gurney had been a Bolton-Paul Defiant gunner in the War, so now and then they'd nattered over a whisky about wars past and present. Then Gurney would take his bike, which he proudly described as one of the last of the British-built Raleighs, and thread his way through the Brighton traffic to Hove, where he and a grown son shared a cottage purchased years before the neighborhood went rich.

Gayle thought it a sad business that the wonderful old British boys were going extinct, driven out by the tide of labor flowing from the east. He didn't see himself asking Yusuf or Abdel in for drinks, or even a mug of tea. He might have to give Gurney a call.

With the single malt percolating within, Gayle began to feel more himself. He poured another whisky and stuck a frozen shepherd's pie into the microwave. Then he switched on the television to catch the ten o'clock news on BBC1, read by a pretty red-haired girl who looked about thirteen.

It was the usual stuff. Conflict in the Horn of Africa, rape and dying babies in Darfur, Taliban resurgence in Afghanistan, fighting in Sri Lanka. In Iraq, suicide bombers and roadside bombs, more dead and wounded, rent garments, coffins cresting a sea of mourners, shrill lamentations rising to the skies. Britain pulling out sooner rather than later, Americans staying till the job was done, or not. The president this, the prime minister that. Airbus warns of further delays on the A380....

"Ah, the MUMBO Jumbo." Will Anna remember that, and will it make her smile?

The reader turned over more of the day's Tarot. Euro and British pound up, dollar down. Bourses torpid, as if the world had lost interest in making money.

When the microwave buzzer sounded, Gayle took out the shepherd's pie, found a chunk of bread in the fridge and buttered it, and brought the lot back to his chair. It took him a moment to recognize the blonde woman on the screen. "Anna," he said, leaning toward the set, his heart giving an involuntary leap of pleasure. "Is it you?"

Of course it was not. This one was wrapped in black like a Muslim widow and the name floating below her image on the screen was Sophie Nieman. Christ, she looked almost exactly like his Anna. Gayle grinned. My Anna. Indeed.

"Coalition sources," said the reader, "say the car in which Ms. Nieman was riding approached an American checkpoint at speed.

The soldiers fired warning shots, then fired at the vehicle." The screen showed the bullet-riddled, burnt-out remains of a rusty Toyota sedan, guarded by the tattered body of what looked like an Iraqi boy. A few meters away another supine figure was surrounded by young men in desert camouflage.

"Sophie Nieman was kidnapped several weeks ago while on assignment for Deutsche Welle television. Sources say she had evidently been released and was on her way to safety. Ironically, her ride to freedom ended in a hail of American bullets. Her Iraqi driver, also killed, has not been identified."

A small, wiry man with wild graying hair and a mad gleam in his pale eyes appeared. "Lou Bell, the *Times* Baghdad bureau chief, knew Sophie Nieman. Lou," said the pretty reader, trying to sound like Bell's oldest chum, "thanks for joining us at what must be a very bad time for all of you."

"We all liked Sophie, and we shall all miss her," Bell told the camera, visibly discomfited by the prospect of unwanted fame. "She was one of the rising stars among journalists here. Very good at her work. Quite incapable of fear. She will be missed." His voice cracked slightly, his crazy eyes misted, possibly for the first time ever, and he waved the camera away.

Like a referee, the reader stepped back in. "Thank you, Lou Bell in Baghdad." A short pause, then a shot of the low Vienna skyline, followed by the Austrian chancellor as the reader continued, voiceover. "The Austrian government has denounced the incident and demanded an explanation." The British prime minister appeared. "Great Britain has called Ms. Nieman's death a tragic accident." Then the American president on-screen: "We are investigating the circumstances of the incident and send our prayers to Ms. Nieman's family."

"The victim's sister," said the reader, now back on screen, "declined to comment."

And suddenly there was Anna herself, precisely the girl Gayle remembered, dressed in sky-blue hospital scrubs, glaring at the camera, shielding her face from the lights, pushing away down the gleaming hall of what looked like a ward. Anna Nieman. Anna the nurse. Anna the one who got away.

Gayle leaned back in his chair, his heart thumping like a pile-driver in his chest. Was it Anna or the flu? Anna Nonperes. Why Nonperes? Why the fibs about Paris? Why the Air France credential? Why the fake *everything?* A tint of rage colored the unexpected pleasure of her company. *"Why bloody me?"*

He picked at the shepherd's pie, now going cold and clotted on its plate, and took a couple of bites before putting the meal aside and fetching another whisky. His legs felt rubbery, his skeleton ached, he was sweating beneath passing waves of chill. A cold. Gone by morning. Now he was not so sure. His temple throbbed. Avian flu? Perfick.

Back in his chair, Gayle sipped his whisky and watched the screen, hoping Anna would return, but the program had moved on to Crimewatch. "Shit," he muttered, using the remote to move to BBC2, where Newsnight would almost certainly reprise the kidnapping, the checkpoint incident, the angry Anna, fleeing cameras in her hospital scrubs. When it did not, he switched off the set.

Nonperes, he thought.

No father? Fatherless?

Non-person?

No one?

Anna No one?

Wasn't Nieman nobody in German?

No, niemand.

Anna Niemand?

Anna Nieman.

But why all the bother?

Why bloody me?

Gayle shut his eyes. The pretty girl at the press conference in Toulouse had not been there by chance. She had credentials in a fake name. So, in the worst case, she had not been irresistibly attracted by his famous charm; she had come to Toulouse for him to find. *She* had picked *him* up! But to what purpose?

They had lain more than comfortably in each other's arms, they had shared some heat and laughter. Was that all just nurses' training? Did you need such training to tolerate an afternoon with Peter Gayle? He hoped not. "Once in my clutches," he told the empty room, "she fell a little bit in love with me. I know she did. And, all right, I fell a little bit in love with her." File under unintended consequences, he thought. Like everything. Put something on your ego's swollen black eye and move on.

All right, all right, thought Gayle, there I was with this pretty Austrian nurse in the Hotel Victoria and suddenly here came Dr. Al-Rabiah, my old Iraqi benefactor. Another wild coincidence? Well, hadn't Anna fled before dawn in the good doctor's car?

Ah, but if they had some secret agenda, something must have gone wrong. I wasn't supposed to find her again. She was supposed to vanish. Our little moment was over, over, over. Except it wasn't, now that the Beeb had brought her back on news of her dead twin.

Iraq was seeping back into his life. Gayle thought of the two new Iraqi boys who'd stayed up late to greet him. And then what? Had they called Al-Rabiah to report Mr. Gayle's safe return, touch of flu, rudeness? Why would Al-Rabiah care? Why would anyone?

Besides, Iraq was history. Gayle's experience there had ended when he and the rest of the April Ten arrived in Landstuhl after the ordeal of captivity. A brief encounter with Al-Rabiah at a Swiss hotel umpteen years later did not a conspiracy make. These dots were just dots, few and very far apart in time; only astronomers and lunatics would try to connect them. Seen in a certain way, Gayle told himself, all our lives contain enough grassy knolls to make us crazy. Except you needed a plan, a motive, something that made more than paranoiac sense.

Anna at the press conference with fake credentials, fake name, fake everything, up to something— but nothing to do with me. I was a happy accident. Hell, maybe I helped her escape. Maybe I drove the getaway car. All I suffered was the great pleasure of her company. Definitely no harm there.

Al-Rabiah appears. A separate occurrence. But it has to be coincidence. No known connection with Anna, and only that ancient one with me.

Al-Rabiah and Anna leave together before dawn. But what had Theodore said? The doctor saw her waiting for a taxi and offered a ride. Again, thought Gayle, nothing to do with me.

For him, then, all this botheration was just some parts flu and some parts bruised ego.

What if I wish to kidnap you again?

Then you come to my quiet corner of town.

And there you will be?

There I will be.

"I'll come to your quiet corner," he told his vanished girl, "and there you will be." He smiled, thinking of Anna's surprise when he strode into her hospital. Then, more or less contented, Peter Gayle dropped into exhausted sleep, and, dreaming, was restored to his Captivity.

WHEN HE OPENED HIS EYES TO THE GREY, AQUARIUM LIGHT OF EARLY morning, Gayle thought the other members of the April Ten were still with him, as they had been all through the night, actors in dreams already slipping out of memory. Indeed, he could almost see them adrift in the cold air of his sitting room, dissolving as the day took hold.

Whatever they had been up to in dreamland, it hadn't done much for his flu. He felt rotten, his skeleton hurt, his head throbbed. The congealed remains of the uneaten meal lay on its plate nearby, along with a crystal tumbler holding an amber smear of whisky. He shuddered at the sight. Old Doc Gayle's magic remedy: a night in a chair, too much to drink, nothing to eat. Works like a charm.

For a time Gayle lay curled among the faded hibisci of his chair, wrapped in a blanket he supposed he'd fetched from one of the bedrooms during the night. He still felt the residual presence of his spectral visitors, a faint cold touch upon his psyche. He could not remember ever feeling so close to his comrades, if one could really call them that. And yet, here they'd come, crowding in around him.

There was Boots Anderson, a lieutenant in the American Navy, an F-14 backseater still mourning the loss of his pilot, with whom he had spent a thousand hours in type. He had the pale, flushed face of a Minnesota suicide; it had always relieved Gayle to see Anderson survive another long, grieving night of captivity. Mickey Williams, as a backseater himself, understood such things, and had tried to console the pale, young American, without much success. If Anderson was alive, thought Gayle, he'd still be mourning his lost pilot.

Char and Maby had been SAS sergeants, whose chevrons carried about the same weight as generals' stars almost everywhere except in Iraqi prisons. Both were Irish dark, small and strong; you could see how they would have romped through the desert night, carrying their weight in kit and weaponry. Their squad had been on what they called "a challenging op" far behind enemy lines. When, inevitably, it collapsed, a Republican Guard regiment had tracked them into the mountain snows and, when they had exhausted their food, ammo, luck, and hope, scooped up the two survivors.

Like mad twins, the SAS boys communicated mainly with each other, although now and then they made amiable sounds toward Gayle and Williams, their compatriots, more or less. The Iraqi officers were always pissed off at Char and Maby, though, and let them know it. By the time the April Ten went off to hospital, the pair hadn't much left, although they survived and, for all Gayle knew, had returned to fight again.

There'd been four Yanks, Gayle thought they were a Blackhawk crew, a couple of warrant officers, a couple of ranks. He couldn't remember their names or much about them. Mouse would know.

Hell, Mouse would know the color of their grandmothers' hair. He'd made a point of learning such stuff. "Situational awareness, Boss," he'd explained.

And there was poor Koenig, from Malmö, tall and thin and frail as a flamingo, with a thin shock of strawberry hair. He'd walked across the Syrian desert into Iraq seeking fame and fortune as a freelance journalist. Instead he'd found himself chained to a petroleum storage tank, sharing human-shield duty with a group of American evangelicals.

The Americans were sent home, but Koenig went to prison, where he was somehow shuffled in among the April Ten. The Iraqi officers did what they could to teach him how bad life could be with neither credentials nor friends at court.

"Like poor Lawrence," Williams had murmured, rolling his eyes, "and the ruthless Turkish bey." As Anderson's had become the iconic face of grief, Koenig's evoked a terrified despair.

The Ten had barely known one another in prison, their paths crossing mainly as they were herded between their cells and some new humiliation. After the American medics had let them out of Landstuhl, they'd gone their separate ways, exchanging Christmas cards that first year, then a call or two the next, then nothing at all.

Gayle thought their dispersion was probably a good thing, for they could only remind one another of those bad times. So the Ten had moved on, or had until last night, when, summoned by God knew what, they had converged on his little flat in Brighton.

And what about Anna? Had he really seen her on television? Or had she arrived with the others, another spectral child come to play? No, Anna had been real. There'd really been a dead twin. He remembered everything, so it could not have been a dream.

Moving like a man interred in gravel, Gayle pushed his way out of the chair, and stood for awhile watching the grey Channel become a blue sea. Still using the mental lash, he drove himself to clean his teeth and shave and stand under a hot shower until the water began to cool. Drying off with one of the Hotel Victoria towels he'd liberated years before, he noted a faint pink stipple along his forearms and thighs. Prickly heat. "Perfick!" He took a couple of Codis and put on fresh jeans and a gun-colored cashmere turtleneck.

He put three eggs on to boil and poured out a glass of orange juice only a day older than its sell-by date, a half liter of milk still good enough for tea, and cut up a baguette that, toasted, could probably be chewed. While the electric kettle roared and the eggs bumped around in boiling water, he scraped the gummy ruin of the shepherd's pie into the disposer, stuck the plate in the dishwasher, and washed and dried the tumbler, as the machine had an appetite for crystal.

Gayle ate at his computer table, beyond which a quilt of Brighton rooftops marched down to meet the water, now bathed in sunlight. The only clouds were a few stratospheric fingers of cirrus stealing in from the southwest. A stiff breeze raised whitecaps and sent a trio of early windsurfers flying like one-winged birds from swell to swell. He watched the gulls play with the moving air and thought, not for the first time, that, cuisine aside, he might like to return as one of those big grey and white chaps.

After making himself another mug of milky tea and wiping up the last bit of egg with the last bit of toast, Gayle decided it was time to rejoin society. He emptied his Hartmann garment bag and dumped the week's accumulated laundry into the washer-dryer.

Then he took the computer off standby and waited while the screen composed itself into a Norman Hoad painting of a Tornado on a night raid. The beloved machine hurtled through the desert sky like a startled grey ghost, illuminated by an Iraqi airfield going up in flames in its wake. Gayle had chosen the painting because it seemed to halt time seconds before he and Mouse were hit. In a way, the image was a ticket back to the days when he still flew and had never sat down with an officer in the Republican Guard. The days before the end of life as he had known it.

Ah, there the pretty airplane came, swift and spirit-pale, hurrying away from harm, oblivion-bound. The icons popped onto the night sky and Gayle headed for his e-mail.

His editor wanted to know how Toulouse had gone. One of the public relations people in Bern said he was sorry the cave deal had foundered and that he would keep trying. An Airbus flack thought Mr. Gayle would be interested in a symposium, "Production Delay as Economic Strategy—the Case of the A380." His editor again: "Swiss Hornet hangars?" Booksellers were after him with special sales, which he put aside. The rest of the messages offered cures for erectile dysfunction, cheap pharmaceuticals, Nigerian legacies, low-rate mortgages, hot stocks, intimate apparel, Russian girls. Gayle sent them to spam heaven.

A small queue had gathered in his telephone voice mail, stepping up to the speakerphone one by one, like actors at an audition. A lady reminded him it was time to give the annual bit to Lifeboats. The Saab garage said his Viggen was due for service. There was, "Hi, Peter, it's Stephanie," a young woman with whom he'd once spent a week end at the Hotel Victoria. She was in Brighton, she'd love to see him, here's the number, been a long time. "Ah," said Gayle, "but not nearly long enough." Stephanie hadn't worked out, he could not remember why.

A week-old message from Mouse: "Hey, Boss, give me a shout, won't you?" It was the usual brave rasp, but Gayle thought he detected a faint signal of something else, a quavering note that only he or a dolphin might hear. In anyone but Williams, it would denote fear, but Mouse had never been afraid of anything. Indeed, without brave old Mickey Williams, Gayle knew, he would have died in Iraq, lying broken in his own shit.

Then another week-old message from someone who sounded like Sam Small: "Ahm Toby, Tom Gurney's boy. Please call," and there followed a number in Hove. Gayle dialed it and waited through ten double rings before the connection clicked.

"Aye?"

"Toby?"

"Aye."

"Peter Gayle."

A silence, then, "Ah called Sunday a week."

"I was away."

"Ah see."

"I only learned last night that Tom doesn't work here anymore."

"Dah don't work at all, Mr. Gayle. Dah's dead. Ah were calling to ask thee to t'funeral."

"God. I'm very sorry."

"So are us all."

"What happened?"

"It weren't his health, he were fit as a fiddle. It were t'damn bike. Coming home in darkness. A motorcar knocked him clean out of t'road and kept right on going, t'bastard. Right on going. Dah died in hospital."

"That's terrible."

"Worse than terrible, Ah think. Des-picable, maybe."

"I only heard he'd stopped coming to work."

"Well, so he did. Happen that were t'general idea."

"What, you think it was deliberate?"

"Ah don't know what to think, Mr. Gayle. But Dah told me there was Arabs looking to take his job. And, well, here it come, suddenly vacant. And who got t'job, may Ah ask? An Arab. So there tha be."

"With respect, your dad's job wasn't one you'd kill for."

"It were everything to Dah. He couldna live without it." Toby was quiet for a moment, then, "Well, or with it, either, as things turned out."

"I wish I'd known."

"Ah do too, Mr. Gayle. But Dah would've understood. It were a nice little service we had. There's more Defiant men alive than Ah thought."

"I liked your dad. I'm very sorry he's gone."

"He liked thee too. Which is why Ah called."

"Can I do anything?"

"Nay, it's all been done. But thanks. Good day, sir."

For a time, Gayle sat still, his spirits descending. The news had left him tired, frangible, haunted. His old ghosts jostled him again, restoring him for a moment to his cell and what he had bravely called his aches and pains. Anna drifted past, but only briefly; his mind, tuned to Death, saw instead the pretty twin cut to rags by a hail of bullets, and then cut to rags again.

He imagined poor Gurney on his old Raleigh three-speed with its basket and leather saddle, weaving through the crowded streets of Brighton. One of those black-windowed Chelsea Tractors rounds a corner at speed and strikes the cyclist a glancing blow without even noticing the contact; and Gurney, inoculated with all the kinetic energy of the juggernaut, goes flying through the air with his twisted wreck of a bike to crash on the pavement, where he lies until someone notices and the summoned help arrives.

"Christ, poor Gurney," Gayle whispered. He goes through a war in a dangerous kite like the Defiant and then gets killed on a bloody bicycle. Mortality, his, Gurney's, everyone's, hung in the room like an acrid vapor. If that had been waiting for Gurney, what must await him? A fatal slip in the shower, a fall off a ladder? "Christ." And Mouse, what sort of mundane, useless accident had Cosmo in store for him?

The telephone, still in his hand, began to howl and he shut it off. Then, worried that the day's visitation by Death might not be over, he rang Williams' number in Lyme Regis.

"Morning, Boss."

"How'd you know?"

"Situational awareness."

"Okay."

"Actually, caller i.d."

"I got your message."

"High time."

"I just came in last night."

"From?"

"Bern."

"A dirty weekend in a posh hotel?"

Gayle decided to lie. "Just Bern."

"You're slipping, Boss. As who isn't, right?" A pause, then, in a voice suddenly sad, "Well, maybe slipping doesn't quite describe it."

"Tell me."

"Kind of embarrassing."

"You're among friends."

"I picked up a dose of something."

Gayle laughed, relieved. "Just stop seeing her."

"Very funny," although Williams' voice said there was nothing funny anywhere in his universe.

"Go on. I promise to behave."

"A couple months back I felt a bit fluish, you know, low fever, dragging around like a fly in winter. Then it left me alone for a time, I felt grand, and then, maybe a fortnight later, the dying fly again, with a bit of skin rot. It comes and goes quickly, like it's racing through an entire illness in a day or two. For all I know it's an old syphilis—a bloody miracle of latency given the time between girls—or AIDS or maybe some affliction known only to God. It doesn't hurt, but it preys on my mind. That's what destroys me, that preying on my mind."

"What's the doc say?"

"No doctors yet. I know, I know, that's not the way. But I can't bring myself to go in and be told I've picked up Ebola from a lavatory seat and best hurry into quarantine for a bloody awful death."

Gayle was quiet for a moment, thinking of his own flu, the pink cloud of rash on his limbs. Ebola from a lav seat. "Mouse, everybody's got the bug. I picked up something in Bern…"

"Just stop seeing her."

"Ho ho. But the difference is that if mine gets serious I'll take it to a doctor. You should do the same."

"I know, I shall," but Gayle could tell he'd moved on, for his voice trailed off, as if into reverie. Then, "Do you ever wonder about the others?"

"The others?"

"The Ten."

Only in my dreams, Mouse. "No, and they don't ever think about me, either, or about you."

"I wondered how they were doing. I checked them out."

"Wonderful, we can resume sending Christmas cards."

"They're all dead, Boss."

Ah, another visit from Sir Death. "It's dangerous in the military, as we know."

"These were all accidents."

Accidents. Gayle saw Gurney hurtled against the pavement, his spare little body crumpled like a dying child's. "But you're thinking something else."

"I'm thinking we all started from the same square one, down in Iraq, and now there's just the two of us left."

"We'll wrap you in wet sheets."

But Williams wasn't listening. "When I go out now, I see Arabs everywhere, I hear that snaky English, I feel their eyes upon me, like it wasn't over."

"Britain's full of Arabs." He thought of telling Williams about the two new ones wanting to know how he was doing, or about running into Dr. Al-Rabiah, or Toby's views on how his Dah died— and decided not to. He didn't want Mouse going off a cliff. "Look, I know the feeling you describe, but it's just the heebie-jeebies. A hangover."

"It's more than any hangover. It's a web that we were all stuck upon, and I'm just the first to figure it out."

"Listen to how this sounds. Because every couple of years one of our number dies in an accident, you think there's some colossal conspiracy. Further proof is that you see Arabs everywhere, looking at you. Right?"

Williams didn't answer.

"This isn't a conspiracy, Mouse, it's a bunch of unconnected dots in time and space that you think ought to be linked up. I have dots too. Everybody has. But I know it's just a bloody fruit basket. Apples, oranges, kiwis, you name it. But don't try to add them up in the same column."

"We shouldn't do this on the phone."

"Why, because They are listening?"

"Because we shouldn't."

"Because I've hurt your feelings."

"I'll send you an e-mail."

"Do that."

Williams was silent for so long that Gayle wondered if they were still connected. Then, "Peter?" When had Williams last called him by his Christian name? "Can you come down?"

The thought of the long gallop to Lyme Regis along the coast, hours on the highway, and a day or two devoted to Williams and his conspiracy theories was more than one should have to bear. Gayle shut his eyes, rubbed his temple. "I'm just back, I'm on deadline, I've got a cold...."

"Boss....I'm scared."

Mickey Williams, who'd kept everyone alive during their captivity, who'd never been afraid of anything, was scared. "If I come, will you see a doctor?"

"Yes."

"Promise, hope to die?"

"Yes."

"I'll be down in the morning."

Gayle put the telephone back in its nest and pondered what he could do to ease Williams away from whatever was scaring him.

Mainly, he thought, Mouse needed protection and a sign that he'd been taken seriously. Gayle grinned. He had just the thing. All he had to do now was remember where he'd hidden it.

It had been a gift from Trout and the boys in his squadron. After The Powers had thrown Gayle out, Jamey Trout had come by for a drink and a natter, really to deliver the gift and say goodbye forever. Predictably, Gayle's captivity had severed the comradely umbilicus linking a squadron leader to his squadron.

Trout was not very tall, or very friendly, or neat. His freshly pressed blue RAF uniform was rumpled before he finished doing up the buttons and his neck tie seemed to have been knotted by a maladroit child. No matter what fixative he applied, his unruly black hair rose like a sudden burst of smoke above the pale circle of his face. The matching black mustache above thin, unsmiling lips usually contained an embedded crumb or two. His eyes were like currants, but sharp, as though they were always aimed at something. He was not a man who inspired friendship everlasting, but he'd been very good indeed at flying Gayle's wing.

On this visit, perhaps because he knew it was probably the last time he'd see Gayle, perhaps because he was on his way to a new assignment and a Tornado squadron of his own, Trout had been as nervous as a boy. The two had chatted rather obliquely for half an hour and downed a couple of whiskies before Trout got down to his real mission. Rummaging around in his chart case, he'd brought out the gift, wrapped in a chamois cloth. "Something from the boys," he said. "And me."

Gayle hefted it, then, knowing what he would find, unwound the swaddling to reveal an Iraqi Tariq nine-millimeter pistol with mother-of-pearl panels on the grip. "Ugly little thing, isn't it?" was all he could think of to say. He ejected the magazine and saw it was full. "Ugly and dangerous."

"Boys asked me to bring it by. It belonged to the head guy where they kept you. Unable to send you his balls, they settled on this as the next best thing."

"Well, he was never without it." A cold sheen of perspiration had condensed upon Gayle's forehead and upper lip. His temple remembered the cold snout of the thing he held in his hand, he saw the hairy, olive finger tightening on the trigger; then, tensed for the sudden explosion of his brain, he'd heard only the click of a hammer on an empty chamber, followed by delighted laughter all round.

"Ah, I'm sorry, Boss. We weren't thinking. This is like giving a man his old waterboard. Shall I take it back?"

Gayle shook his head. "It's the thought that counts, Fish. Thank the boys for me."

"I shall."

"It's illegal as hell, you know."

"Not to worry. Our SAS chaps brought home bags of AK47s. This is pretty small potatoes. But try not to hurt yourself with it. And keep it in a safe place."

Now Gayle wondered where that safe place might be. He'd concealed the relic of his captivity more than a decade ago, somewhere out of sight and mind. He cast about the flat, trying to jog his memory, and finally came eye to eye with the dead colobus. "Avery, you devil," said Gayle, "*you've* got the bloody thing." He walked over to the cage and reached under the papered floor until his fingers touched chamois. "Thanks for keeping it safe," he told the monkey. "But old Mouse needs it more than you do."

MICKEY WILLIAMS SMILED AND LEANED BACK IN HIS WORK CHAIR, a sternly ergonomic design in stainless steel and black leather. He wore only a faded yellow terry cloth dressing gown, shorts, and slippers, as if he'd narrowly escaped a house fire, and kept one hand curled lightly around a tumbler of tepid gin.

He'd spent part of the day writing and rewriting a long e-message to Peter Gayle, and had stripped down to his underwear to add a digital image of himself, "warts and bloody all," which he attached to the letter. Another read-over, a bit of trimming and shaping, some kind of droll conclusion, and off it would go. Gayle would have it tonight, so that what he saw on his arrival tomorrow would not be quite such a shock. Christ, running sores, he thought, feeling panic stir within. He gulped a mouthful of gin and tried not to care.

Beyond the computer screen the ocean had begun to lose its color, preparing for the night, and the sun yielded up its furnace golds and crimsons as it dropped into the sea. Long-shadowed and still, the rounded hills above Lyme Regis glowed in the lingering afterlight. Dawns and dusks were Williams' favorite times of day, but this evening seemed especially favorable, now he'd had a chance to chat with Peter Gayle.

Of course, he thought now, Gayle could be splendidly opaque, as with that: *Promise, hope to die?* As a matter of fact, one hoped *not* to die, but saw that hope losing wattage day by day. Still, Williams believed in his pilot's ability to make things better, and, at the moment, belief was everything.

Six-foot-two and lean as an oak, Williams had the look and stride, the presence, of a man who feared nothing and was ready for anything, ruddy of face, auburn of hair, freckled and green-eyed. Looking him over after his captivity, The Powers had seen the RAF poster boy looking back at them, so they'd kept him on as a Tornado navigator, while Gayle went off to brief misery at a desk, thence to the sweet hereafter of retirement.

Although he said nothing, Williams had known it was a bad idea to keep him on as backseater. He'd come home from Iraq with flickering distractions that made it difficult to keep his mind on his work. Often he found himself back in the dark halls of the prison, an Iraqi hand under each armpit dragging him somewhere, when he should have been minding the radarscope. On a night intercept in dirty weather, or on nocturnal grass-cutting runs southward out of Scotland, such inattention in a navigator could scare a pilot half to death. The real trouble was not so much the distractions as Williams' being as stuck to Gayle as poor Anderson had been to his lost pilot; he had little interest in flying with young strangers.

Hearing of the odd close shave, The Powers had decided Williams should be invalided out after all. He'd taken what his parents left him and the bit he'd saved and bought a tiny stone cottage a mile outside Lyme Regis, where he could just survive on what the government gave him, but with a fine view of the sea.

The place was wreathed in red and yellow roses that fattened on the ocean mists, and he put in a small truck garden, with a sign marked *Peter Rabbit's,* behind the house. For transport he revived a tapped out Deux Cheveaux. When he felt like working he drove down to the Cobb to help at a boatbuilding school run by a former Sea Harrier pilot. But Williams rarely ventured beyond his crazed, unpainted wooden gate, and had not spent a single night outside the cottage in years.

The large single room was sparsely furnished, although, to a man who'd spent years in the rear cockpit of a Tornado, it was quite comfortable, with a small galley kitchen off to one side, a bedroom and bath off to the other. One wall had been given to shelves on which hundreds of books were stacked in no particular order. The center of action was a computer with a large flat screen and vast memory. Capable and lightning quick, it sat on a sturdy oak kitchen table bleached almost white by years in sunlight, in a rat's nest of coiling wires—Williams believed wireless systems were too audible to others.

With the computer and an outsized self-built sound system, and everything interconnected, his home resembled his weapons-navigation station: an impossible clutter whose true order was known only to him. The computer and the ergonomic chair were his main luxuries, and he spent much of his time there, peering into cyberspace. When he looked up, there was the blue sea.

Rather to his surprise, this simpler life had rendered him a satisfied and happy man. The occasional natter down at the boat school, followed by a pint or two and fish and chips at the Cobb Arms, and the odd call from Whitey Gayle—these were all that any man needed if he had the roses and Peter Rabbit's and a view of the sea. Now and then a woman would pass through his life; some stayed until they saw just how immutably Williams was what he was, and that knowledge drove them away.

Fear had been an unexpected guest. As he had little experience of it, he'd failed to see it coming. For a time, fear had been no more than a distant presence, a small and nameless stranger traversing a familiar landscape. But then, on a nostalgic whim, Williams had begun tracking down the other members of the April Ten and discovered, one by one, the whole lot dead, killed in fiery accidents.

Nothing to do with me, he thought. But then his mind began tugging at the accidents and gradually kneaded them into murders. The murderers could only be conspiring Iraqis from the first Gulf war. They had killed eight. It followed that they would go on and kill nine, then ten. God knew why.

Having established to his satisfaction that he would also be murdered, Williams had brooded over the indignity of the event, which seemed to be the proverbial fate worse than death. It was then that fear had stepped into the room, planning to stay. Once afraid of nothing, Williams was, as though suddenly, afraid of almost everything.

Fear rendered his first flulike symptoms sinister. He felt, and feared, a kind of turbulence within, as if a jungle weed had taken root and now grew rapidly inside him. He was afraid to go out, fearing he might be contagious, and he was ashamed to be seen with his face bright with what at first had seemed a bad acne. He feared Muslims, who were everywhere, all careful not to meet his gaze, but studying him whenever he turned away.

His only human visitor was the delivery boy from his grocer's, instructed to leave the food and his weekly liter of Bombay gin—his other luxury—outside the front door. The boat school called a few times to see if he was coming down, but he let the telephone ring to silence and erased the messages. Soon the calls stopped altogether.

Now Williams looked at the computer screen, where the last paragraphs of his long note suspended on a white field. Setting his thoughts down on virtual paper had calmed him. For the first time in weeks he felt his inner jitters subside. Fear seemed to retreat to a far corner of the room and Williams sensed he was once again alone. Gayle was coming. They'd find a doctor. They'd find out what this thing was. He smiled, seeing himself and his good friend turning toward the fight like chums on a cinema poster.

I believe I know what to expect, Boss, he wrote across the flat screen. *In some ways it would have been better to forget the others. Well, it is always better not to know the future. But now it's too late. I've brought upon myself a crippling fear of being dragged out and humiliated further by those snake-voiced buggers...*

He stopped typing and listened. There was the steady buffet of the wind, a hum from the fridge, the gentle whir of the computer fan—and something else. An automobile engine, cracking the silence of an empty land. Peering past the screen into the descending night he saw a dark estate creep into view, no lights, and no more velocity than a parade float. It crept past his window and down the narrow road until it vanished over the crest of a hill. The silence mended itself. The threat, if threat it was, had passed.

Death doesn't frighten me, Williams continued, *but I hate to think of my simple, reasonably happy existence just ceasing to be and my poor old place going up in smoke with Peter Rabbit's and the roses charred to ash. Well, how I careen. I shall be very glad to see you. Mouse*

Ah, here came the estate again, now just a silhouette against the western sky, crawling back along the same track past his cottage. As he knew it would, the car stopped outside his gate, doors snapped open, snapped shut, he sensed movement in the darkness. He saw the future.

Williams typed: *visitors boss in ford or vhall estate knock on door enter three men dressed as bugs look me up and down*

The men wore goggles, clear plastic rain capes with hoods pulled up around their heads, held in place by the straps of painters' respirator masks; plastic bags covered their boots. Like kids playing Star Trek, except, thought Williams, they're not kids and they're not playing. They've come for me. The shortest of the three pulled down his respirator and raised his goggles to his forehead. Williams typed: *shit heres rdoc im9 watchoutwatchoutwatchout* as the man brought out a long-barreled pistol and aimed it at Williams' chest.

The first silenced shot caught him just left of his heart, which leapt about like a small, round fish inside him. But look there, thought Williams, the bullet passed through as neatly as a ray of light. When they were finished with him, why, he would be a regular crepusculation of beams shining through his perforated body. He didn't care about the light beams, though, or the humid hiss of a perforated lung. He needed to regain control of his mouse hand, which felt as if someone else had got hold of its strings. The cursor arrow flew around the screen like a frightened sprite, clap if you believe in cursors, until, at last, he forced it to settle on SEND, and clicked.

The second bullet found his heart just then, and again passed through him neatly as a ray of light, although it also seemed to take all his inner light with it, for his mind diminished until, to the surprise of Mickey Williams, it disappeared. He did not live to see one of the goggled intruders vent a gas cylinder into the room, creating a sea of vapor along the floor, nor did he see the final explosion of light in which his simple, reasonably happy existence just ceased to be, the old place going up in smoke, and Peter Rabbit's and the roses charred to ash.

VII

Krylov had been serious when he said his idea of a big evening was dinner with the daughter of an old friend. He cherished such evenings, but carefully conserved them, not wanting Svetlana Trulova to get the wrong idea and stop calling him Uncle Viktor.

He'd first seen her in Moscow when she was not yet ten and the old city was still grey and rather serious, and the only people having much fun were high officials and spies. Because Maxim Trulov and he had good English, they often found themselves in the same meetings and, sometimes, working the same streets in the same foreign city.

Maxim had been a decade older and a major, Viktor a young lieutenant, and those differences might have kept them apart had they not been so congruent in other ways. They were about the same size and had about the same degree of belief that what they did served a higher purpose, although neither man was ideologically blind. They were perfectly comfortable trading jokes about the Soviet Union conquering the Sahara, then running out of sand—the kind of jokes Czechs and Hungarians liked to tell.

But at heart they were loyal Soviet boys who believed equity lay more on their side than on the other; neither had the slightest doubt that America was the enemy. When they worked in the field they were adroit and could be deadly, although, said Maxim, laughing over drinks, "don't ask us to part the Red Sea."

When Maxim Trulov was happy, there was no one warmer or funnier in the world; he entered a room like the returning sun. But his temper, once loosed, could melt snow for miles around. It could cause a man to go off on his own—the eighth sin, they'd called it, back when they still believed it couldn't happen to them.

They liked to think of themselves as two bears with a little money, Canadian passports, good suits, and a job that now and then produced a sensation Trulov said was better than sex. "Have gun, will travel," he would announce, raising his glass and laughing. They were always laughing.

They had tried to bring their families into this friendly embrace. The Trulovs and the Krylovs had endured a few miserable hours together on country picnics in the broiling Russian summer, a ski weekend, an exchange of dinners in their modest flats on the northwest edge of Moscow. It hadn't worked. The wives could not ignore the differences in age and rank; the children barely spoke. Still, something familial and permanent had passed between Svetlana and Krylov, and she took to calling him Uncle Viktor.

The Moscow interlude had lasted only a couple of years. Then they had gone their separate ways, Maxim to a contrived position at the Centre for Analytic Studies, near Vienna, where he could tap into the American computer networks and make American scientists his friends. Viktor went to Afghanistan with Spetsgruppe A, the KGB's so-called Alfa Group, after the Soviet invasion.

One always heard eventually of murders when the murderers were not colleagues, and word of Trulov's death had finally trickled into

Kabul. Krylov was left with his imagined re-creation of his friend's final moment in the Hauptallee: the single round fired from one of the idled Riesenrad cars, the big, cheerful Russian face suddenly a crumpled mask in a slurry of brain and snow. When he thought of Maxim afterward, Krylov's memories of the good times always tapered to that mask in the snow.

From Afghanistan, he wrote amusing letters to Svetlana to give her something besides her father's death to think about. He told her stories of the two bears in Moscow and here and there across the world, bringing Maxim back to life, in a way, but without the mess and mayhem. He sent her happy postcards when he went on mission to Angola, or Vietnam, or Cuba.

When Svetlana wrote him that she and her mother were being sent home, Krylov had called in a marker to let the girl finish at the International School and go on to Universität Wien. When he was assigned to the Agency in Vienna, he'd called Svetlana and found her genuinely delighted to receive Uncle Viktor back into her life.

Vera Trulova and Svetlana and Krylov had formed an occasional threesome, out for a concert or a Heuriger evening, or a Schnitzel in the old city. He taught Sveta to drive, and helped her with her French; he went with her to the Feuerhalle after Vera died. When Svetlana finished at the university Krylov had reminded the Centre for Analytic Studies that, in a way, they owed her something for the loss of her father; they took her in reluctantly, only to discover they could not get along without her.

That had been the beginning of the cherished evenings, the still-young spy and the tall, luminous twenty-year-old Russian girl, and they continued now she was a wise woman with a life of her own. Without making a great fuss over it, they had become a family of two.

Krylov rationed their time together. Usually he waited for some external impetus, some reminder that he was Russian and could use a few innocent hours in the company of a nice Russian girl. His motive today, however, was less clear. Something to do with seeing

Ilse, no doubt, or the lingering business of the famous cave, which had settled on his spirit like a layer of ash.

A woman answered when he called, an unfamiliar, somewhat slurred voice he couldn't recognize. "No more calls please," she said in German. "Leave us alone."

"Sveta?"

"Viktor?"

"Yes."

"This is Anna."

"Hello, Anna. I called…"

"I know, how sorry you are."

"I don't understand."

"About Sophie?"

Krylov's neck hairs bristled. Like almost everyone on earth, he knew Sophie had been kidnapped in Iraq. Now he heard her death in Anna's dulled, hopeless tone. "What about Sophie?"

"They killed her."

"Christ."

"The Americans. The kidnappers said they would give her to the Americans. Well, they did. And how!"

"Terrible."

"Diabolical."

"What about you, Anna?"

"No one shot me to pieces. I am perfect." She sounded far from perfect, though. "Are you coming over?"

"Maybe this is not such a good time."

"I would like it."

"May I bring something?"

"Somebody drank all the vodka."

"I have some."

"Then you can definitely come over. Here, I'll fetch Sveta."

"Uncle Viktor?"

Ah, there she was.

Svetlana had helped him find his flat, which occupied the upper floor of an old stone house in Oberdöbling. It was not much larger than his place in Moscow, but he loved it. When he sat on the narrow balcony he overlooked a deep garden shadowed by ancient trees and shrubbery gone wild; he could have been at his little dacha north of Leningrad, as he still called the old city.

There were two bedrooms, his and another kept ready for visiting children who never came. Aside from a few books and his clothing, all he had brought to the flat was a genuine icon depicting Gabriel and a heavenly host announcing the end of everything. Krylov called it nuclear proliferation.

The furniture, which was dark, solid, and from a much earlier time, belonged to Frau Steiner, a pale, tiny, nearly bald woman in her eighties, who silently shared the ground floor with Stella, a shorthaired dachshund of equivalent age. Krylov saw so little of them that he sometimes feared they'd fallen to dust. But then one or both of them would suddenly appear and greet him before vanishing again into their tranquil oblivion.

"Grüss Gott, Herr Krylov," she called now, materializing in her doorway, Stella staring silently from between her slippers.

"Grüss Gott, Frau Steiner."

Krylov opened the rusted iron gate and strode into the fading light, the Stolichnaya bottles in his UN commissary bag clinking like a milkman's. Indeed, he looked like a man delivering something, for he'd left his business costume hanging in the wardrobe and put on khakis, walking shoes, and a leather jacket that was still faintly radioactive with microscopic debris from the cave.

It was less than a kilometer from his place to Anna and Svetlana's flat on Sternwartestrasse, following a circuitous route that took him through the looping paths of Türkenschanzpark. This had been the high-water mark of the Muslim tide that had flowed into Europe four centuries earlier, the battlefield from which it then slowly ebbed, draining into the desert. Now Islam was back, Muslim émigrés were everywhere one looked. Krylov thought this time they were here to stay.

Autumn filled the park with big Ukrainian crows, just now arriving for the milder Viennese winter. When there was snow on the ground, Krylov often sat on one of the wooden benches with a bag of corn and the birds, who seemed almost a civilization unto themselves, strutted up to him, leapt onto the bench beside him. One half expected them to speak, although what they would say, and whether they would speak some avian dialect of Russian, was unclear.

On the far side of the park lay the astronomical observatory, half hidden among black evergreens and old trees whose autumn leaves had begun to fly away on the wind. It had been laid out in the shape of a giant horizontal cross, with the main dome where the arms met the stem, and smaller domes at the ends of both arms. Krylov had read somewhere that when the observatory opened, its 62-centimeter refractor had been the most powerful telescope in the world. But then Vienna's night sky, never exactly awash with stars, had vanished in the glare of the growing city's lights.

Krylov had no idea what was done there now, if anything. It looked to him like a haunted castle, its rusty brick walls dark and brooding. He had never seen anyone inside the fence. Perhaps it had been abandoned after all. But he didn't care about the work. He was charmed by the existence of such a place in the heart of Vienna, and by the German term: Sternwarte; star watch.

The press had almost given up on Anna Nieman. Several determined paparazzi huddled outside her gate, smoking, idling like dogs, and a television camera and a business-suited reporter—what the Americans called talent—waited for that shot of Anna in tears. Across the street, a pair of Cobra Unit guards protecting an Israeli residence cradled their Steyr AUGs and watched this weird, unwelcome swirl of activity for signs of imbedded terror.

When the idlers saw Krylov, they surged tentatively in his direction. "Don't think of it," he growled in English, holding up his hand like a traffic cop. He looked toward the nearest Cobra, who gave him what might have been a smile before turning away. No help there.

A strobe flashed, and then another. The night leapt back from the video camera's light. The reporter stepped forward, microphone presented like a popsicle he wanted to share. "Are you a friend of the Nieman family?"

The others joined in.

"What's in the bag?"

"Did you know Sophie?"

"Are you a family member?"

"What's your name?"

"When did you hear of Sophie's death?"

The bored strangers converged on him, cameras popping.

"I know him," someone yelled in German. "He's with the Agency. I saw him on TV."

Krylov placed his bag gently against the metal gate, then faced the little crowd. When another strobe went off nearby, he shot out a hand and ripped the camera away from its owner, who began to shout and dance in circles.

"Nice," said Krylov, hefting the camera, giving the enraged young man a hard smile. "Nikon D-80. Fifteen hundred euros, easily." He ejected the card and put it in his pocket.

The others moved away a meter or two, getting themselves clear of what they hoped might be a fight.

"Put your cards on the ground," Krylov told them, "or this boy loses his Nikon."

The photographer threw himself at the big Russian, hopelessly, like throwing oneself against a wall. Krylov batted him away, then stepped into the street, holding the camera like a flat rock, ready to skip it all the way down to the Gürtel.

"You can't do this," called one of the photographers.

"We're a free press," cried another.

"On three," said Krylov. "One…"

"Bitte, bitte." The boy who was about to lose his Nikon put out his hands, as though trying to calm a violent sea, and rattled off his plea in German. "Do what he says, we didn't get anything anyway, I can't lose my camera, Christ, I wouldn't let you lose yours, do what he says, please…"

"Two," said Krylov.

Grumbling about the Russian bastard and what he had done with his mother, the other paparazzi shuffled about, fiddling with their equipment.

"I want the video also."

"Fuck you," said the cameraman.

"Your camera's next. Two point five."

"Please do what he says," said the boy. "Please."

The TV cameraman looked at his reporter, who nodded. "We got nothing much," he said in German. "Go ahead."

"I can't afford to throw away my cassette, Russky," the cameraman said. He held his camera out where Krylov could watch him erase the tape. "There. Now give the boy his Nikon."

"Good man," said Krylov. "But you two, two point six is the count."

Like a clutch of birds readying themselves for takeoff, they eddied for a moment or two, muttering and wanting to be tougher. "We'll be back," said one.

"Two point seven," said Krylov.

One of the CF cards hit the pavement, then another.

"Okay, we're leaving. Give him his camera."

They edged downhill, pissed off boys kicking stones, throwing angry looks back at Krylov. When it seemed certain they were on their way, he handed the Nikon back to its owner. "If I see you again, I send it flying."

He watched them vanish down the dimly lighted street, listened as their complaints were subsumed in the traffic noise rising from the

Gürtel. Then he picked up the cards and his jingling bag and stepped
through the gate.

Svetlana met him on the other side. "Papa would have thrown
the camera," she said in Russian before giving him a double kiss.
"After breaking it in half."

Krylov laughed. Max would have sent them away with their
cameras stuck up their arses.

"You were a long time getting here. Were you feeding the crows?"
She was changing the subject, fleeing another evocation of her lost
father. Even after all these years, grief was never more than a memory,
a sentence, away. "We began to worry."

Krylov shook the bag, causing the bottles to clink, hoping to
make her smile. "But here we are. Safe and sound."

"Anna has already drunk more than enough."

"How is she doing?"

"She isn't grieving, exactly. She's angry. Something happened
with her, she went off for a weekend but she won't talk about it. And
now this thing with Sophie."

"I won't stay long."

"We can both escape after you've had a little visit. I've taken so
much time off because of Sophie. I need to go by the office for an
hour. But then we can go find a Heuriger or something. Okay?"

Taking his hand, she led him into their building, which had been
a fine home until after the war, when someone had cut it into four flats
with high ceilings, crystal chandeliers, and imaginative plumbing.
Krylov liked the place for its light, which poured in through tall
windows filled with the melancholy Vienna sky and the writhing
arms of old trees.

The women had kept things simple, furnishing the flat mostly
from IKEA. But there was a samovar Krylov recognized as Maxim's
and, from him, an Afghan rug, green-leaved golden boughs on a
blood-red field. He thought the shelves of books must be mainly
Anna's, as was the small upright piano, whose mahogany case was

covered with silver-framed photographs of their families. Their ghosts. People had been busy sending flowers and cards saying how sorry they were about Sophie and the room dripped with floral scent.

Anna sat cross-legged on a leather poof, a glass tumbler balanced precariously between her thighs. She was still in her blue scrubs, her hair was straggly, her pale, red-rimmed eyes ringed with olive crescents of fatigue. She'd had enough to drink that it took her a moment to recognize Krylov, and then she smiled. "Hello, Viktor."

"Anna." He bent down to give her a double kiss.

"Make yourself a drink." She emptied the tumbler and held it out toward him. "Make me one too." Her exhausted eyes, he saw, were now dry as porcelain; one could not imagine their producing tears. Svetlana had seen anger in them. He wasn't sure what he saw.

Krylov poured vodka over a tumbler of ice, then made a smaller one for Anna. "The next hour of life," he said, passing her the glass.

She nodded. "Prost."

He sat down on the floor next to her. "Tell me what happened."

"To Sophie?"

"Yes."

"They let her go."

"Because some demand was met?"

"Yes."

"By?"

"By me," she whispered.

"Will you tell me what it was?"

"Not yet."

"But you did something for them."

"Yes."

"And they said they would free Sophie in return."

"They said they would give Sophie to the Americans."

"Ah."

Anna squeezed her eyes shut. "They fed her to them."

"So they kept their bargain, but set her up for the Americans to kill. Is that what you think?"

"Yes."

"To silence her?"

"Yes."

"Except that her death doesn't guarantee her silence."

"Why not?"

"You're still alive."

She gave him the saddest smile he had ever seen, and he realized that what he had detected in her eyes was not anger, but fear. "For the moment."

"Tell me what you did for them."

"I cannot."

"If they have decided to kill you, they will do it anyway."

"Not if I keep silent."

"Is that what they said?"

"They said they would have my silence, one way or another."

"You were actually in contact with the kidnappers?"

"No. With their….agent." She would not look at Krylov.

"So all of this stuff about what 'they' said is really what he said?" Anna nodded.

"Iraqi?"

"Yes."

"He met you here in Vienna?"

"He came to the hospital."

"So he knew you were a nurse."

She held up a palm to stop him. "Please, Viktor, no more."

Krylov wasn't finished, but Svetlana gave him a glare that said Anna had endured enough for one day. For a time the three of them sat in silence, as if alone. Krylov was turning over what Anna had told him for the twentieth time when someone knocked on the entrance door.

"Oh, Christ," Sveta exclaimed, "I left the bloody gate open."

Krylov got to his feet, rocking a bit to get the circulation going in his legs. He no longer felt like fighting paparazzi.

"Sorry to pop in this way," came a man's voice. "I didn't have a phone number and I'm only in Vienna for a day. But I thought you'd want this…"

Svetlana came into the room, followed by a man Krylov didn't recognize at first, dragging a wheeled carry-on bag. "Anna, Viktor, this is Mr. Bell from the *Times*."

Bell still looked mad, but less so in a jacket and tie; everybody looked crazy in the wilderness. Bell gave Anna an almost imperceptible bow, then noticing Krylov, his shaggy eyebrows shot up and his burned-out blue eyes brightened. "Viktor, by God. Small world!"

"Sometimes too small."

The two men shook hands, then stepped back, giving each other space. Bell said to Anna, "We were all devastated by Sophie's death. I'm so sorry."

"Thanks," said Anna.

Bell nodded at the bag. "As I was coming to town I thought to bring Sophie's things. I fear she traveled very light."

"She never cared about stuff," said Anna.

"No, she never did."

Taking the proffered handle, Anna wheeled the bag into a far corner of the room, then stood as if listening to it. She touched the leather flank gently, gingerly, and drew away, like a child touching live mussels on a rock.

"Will there be a service?" asked Bell.

Anna shook her head. "We will think of somewhere nice to spread her ashes." She studied the reporter for a moment, then, "Will you have a drink?"

"Thanks, but I can't linger. I just wanted to tell you how sorry I am, everyone is. How we shall miss Sophie."

"What lured you out of the desert?" asked Krylov.

"Big thing tomorrow at the Agency. Iran. Nukes and spooks. What's your view?"

"Don't make me famous again."

"As far as I'm concerned, your fifteen minutes are up."

"Those who can afford it will build real bombs. The poor boy next door will improvise on a nuclear theme."

"Whew. I may have a glass of that purple Kool-Aid after all."

Krylov laughed. "Well, it is not so bad as that already."

"Tell me about the cave."

"You were there."

"What did the samples show you?"

"The Americans have the samples."

"I don't think so."

"Ask Emerson."

"I did."

"And?"

"Angry shrug."

"Is he still bragging about his dirty bomb factory?"

"He's gone rather quiet, actually. We, by which I mean the paper and I, did very little with the dirty-bomb idea. Once burned, et cetera. My hunch is Emerson and company went a bridge too far in the first round of claims, and now they're under some pressure to make things right." He grinned at Krylov. "Christ, you've already figured it out, haven't you?"

"I figured out what it was not."

"Are you sharing?"

"When I know what it was, I will tell you."

"Promise?"

"Hope to die."

THE MERCEDES ALMOST UTTERED A CRY OF JOY when they reached the Sudautobahn and Krylov took it up to one hundred fifty, where it loafed along happily. Bell had declined their offer of a ride south and a Heuriger meal and had gone off into the autumn night, promising to keep in touch, to stop by again time permitting, to give any help he could.

Anna, after some persuading by Svetlana, had numbly agreed to go with them, uncomfortable, Krylov thought, about staying home alone. By the time he'd fetched his Mercedes, she had showered and put on black jeans and the sweat shirt from Greece, pulled back her hair into a bright ponytail, and done something to her face, which seemed less haggard.

Now, glancing over at Anna in the passenger seat, Krylov saw she had begun to relax a bit, lulled by the gentle roll of the Mercedes, the sense of being among friends and on her way somewhere. She'd evidently thrown off the effects of the day's vodka, for her voice was clear and steady, and her eyes no longer looked ceramic. He could see Svetlana's face in the rear-view mirror, the usual bright oval dimmed now by the fatigue of empathy. When their eyes met, she offered a melancholy smile, then turned to watch her reflection fly across the dark fields outside.

South of Mödling, Krylov turned onto the B11, crossing empty farmlands, "Blacker," he told his passengers, "than Bulgaria at midnight." Another turn onto Wienerstrasse brought them into the village, which soon opened into a broad plaza flanked by a great cake of a palace done up in Habsburg yellow and trimmed in white, the Schlöss where the Centre for Analytic Studies did whatever it did.

"Here we are at the fun farm," Krylov announced.

"You mean the Centre," chided Sveta.

"Sorry."

Anna looked around the square. "I haven't been here in years, but it's just the same."

"More Mercs, fewer Ladas," said Krylov.

"I used to come out with Svetlana. We played tennis, we did some riding. We went out to Heurigen with visiting scientists from America, from Russia, everywhere. Those were the days, right, Sveta?"

"The days when you took time to have a little fun?"

"My mother hen. But it's true, now I get home too late and too tired to play."

Krylov parked near the castle entrance. "I'll wait here, you and Anna go ahead."

"No," said Anna, "you go. I'll stay here."

"Anna and I will wait," said Krylov. "My final offer."

"I could be an hour," Svetlana said, getting out. "I could be all night."

"We don't care," said Anna, already scrunching down in her seat, getting comfortable.

"You're both impossible." Shuddering with mock impatience, Svetlana stepped out of the car and marched into the hemisphere of light around the broad entrance door, then passed into the castle.

"There she goes, into the eighteenth century," said Krylov. "I had hoped to come while Maxim was still here. I wanted him to show off the fancy nest he had built for himself."

"But you never did?"

Krylov shook his head. "Max was long gone by the time I came to Vienna. But I know the place a little. Some Russian friends from the old days are still around. And I've come here with Svetlana."

"I'm trying to think when I was last here. I think it was before the Wall came down. They were still talking about East and West."

"A note from Max would reach me in Afghanistan, always something funny." Krylov smiled at the recollection. "Joke science, he called it. But I think it was more interesting in those days. Well, so was the world. Now it's not East-West, it's Occidental-Oriental, or North-South. As for this," and he waved a hand at the yellow castle, "It's like the Sternwarte—who knows what it does now? Ah, well, scientists will always want places far from home with tennis, horses to ride, and pretty girls."

"People used to say it was a nest of spies."

"Maybe not a nest, but, yes, plenty of spies. Max told me that in the beginning we got more out of the arrangement than we put into it. Now and then the Americans or British would send over a young scientist who was political, or an old fellow from the intelligence services. But they took home very little. Well," and Krylov gave an elaborate shrug, "the painful truth is we needed more than they did. We needed everything."

"But it must have been deadly serious. Maxim was killed, after all."

"It *became* deadly serious. It turned out that beneath the little scrums everybody was running on the surface were secret roots going down to the center of the earth." He smiled at her. "People like Max and me, we do whatever our business cards say we do, but we also have this other thing, like a second head. It sees the world the way a cop does, or maybe a criminal. A spy. Things leap out of the background unexpectedly. Something leapt out at Max. He inferred the existence of that deep root system. But by the time he'd figured it out it was too late."

Krylov was quiet for a time, musing over the vanished pleasures of being a bear until his memory produced the human mask crumpled and bloody in the snow. He uttered a long sigh. Then, "But I have to say, it was no bad thing when we and everybody else thought we were going to win. In those times, we really earned our living."

"You miss the old days?"

"I miss old Maxim."

"But not the, what, the epoch?"

"Sometimes. Now and then, yes, Heaven help me, I miss Russia when she was great."

"Everyone says she's coming back."

"She is, but in a new form. I am too old for a new form." Krylov laughed. "But, here comes the new Russia anyway."

"Sophie was made for the new Russia."

"Yes, I think that's true."

"You knew her, a little."

"I met her once or twice at your place." Krylov tried to remember the lost twin, but could only conjure Anna. Sophie had been prettier, but harder too; her constant calculation was almost audible.

"They say that twins never quite separate, even if they become totally different people. So, for me, losing Sophie is not like losing a loved one; it's like losing an arm or leg. I feel deformed but I also feel the limb still in place. I haven't a clue what to feel about *her.*"

"I was a little afraid of her."

Anna nodded. "Everybody was. But she feared nothing, just as she cared for nobody. I think our mother was like that."

"But not you."

She shook her head. "Or my father. He was good-hearted. A good-hearted failure. A dreamer."

"There are worse things than dreamers."

"Not to Sophie. She hated dreamers, although she was quite the dreamer herself. I imagine her standing in a rain of bullets thinking how famous she was going to be. But she hated Papa's always drifting. She would lecture him about getting back to reality, as though she were behind him. He adored her, even when he lay dying and she never came. I always found her difficult…no, impossible…to love. Still, being twins, there is that psychic joining at the hip. That phantom limb."

"Sveta said you would walk into the Underworld for Sophie. Even knowing she would not lift a finger for you."

"It sounds foolish when you put it that way."

"No, just loyal. May I tell you what I think?"

"About what?"

"About what's happened to her, to you. Then I promise to shut up. Okay?"

"But if I say stop?"

"I will stop."

"Okay."

"I've been looking at this puzzle all evening, using that extra head I mentioned."

"The cop?"

Krylov nodded. "We've got this backwards. It wasn't: We have Sophie the famous journalist, now let's ask her sister the nurse for some favor. It was: Anna Nieman is a nurse, how do we get her to do this thing we want? Whom would she do anything to save? So we kidnap Sophie."

"The world is full of nurses. Why would they want me?"

"I don't know."

"And when the thing was done, why not just give her back? Why have her killed?"

"It wasn't to keep her quiet. She didn't know anything. No, they just wanted a diversion. They wanted the nurse business to be lost in the glare of Sophie's death." It was, thought Krylov, like sowing a fire scene with a radioactive isotope, to decoy one's attention. "Magic."

"Magic," Anna echoed.

"And they don't care about your silence either, because you don't really know what you did for them. That's true, isn't it?"

"I know what I did."

"Tell me."

"Not yet."

The entrance door opened and Svetlana stepped into view, followed by a compact man in a rumpled dark pinstripe suit and no tie. They talked briefly in the light, then turned toward the Mercedes as Krylov cranked the engine and switched on his headlamps. The sudden light glistened on the man's sleek, olive skin, glittered on his amber aviator glasses. His small, soft mouth formed an O of surprise in the dark triangle of beard, and he spun away, holding up a hand against the glare.

"Good night, Dr. Muckeltee," called Svetlana as she climbed into the car. "See you tomorrow."

But the man was already hurrying across the Schlössplatz to a Paris-green Ford Focus parked in the shadows.

Krylov put the Mercedes into reverse. But as he looked back, his eyes caught Anna's, and he saw the ghost that she had seen. She watched the stranger as a staked goat would a stalking tiger, hypnotized by the appearance of Death where it was least expected.

"You were quick," Krylov said, catching Svetlana's eye in the mirror.

"I am quick. Now feed me."

"In a minute. Who was that fellow?"

"Dr. Muckeltee."

"He's out late tonight."

"He just drove in from England."

"Ah." His eyes met Anna's, and she looked quickly away.

THEY FOUND A HEURIGER a kilometer up the Vienna road, a low place with beige stuccoed walls and the hanging bundle of pine twigs that said the place was open. Krylov steered them to a table in a quiet corner of the large room, empty except for one other couple. A plain woman in a Dirndl came over, showing a good deal of breast, and took their wine order. When it arrived, they went to the counter to assemble breads, meats, and cheeses to go with it. They said very little, but sat like three strangers, sampling the food, remarking on its quality, sipping at the Viertels of red. They might have been sharing a table on a train.

Finally, Krylov leaned back on his bench. "Sveta, tell me about this Muckeltee. What does he do?"

"He's a visiting scientist. Something to do with public health."

"From?"

"Bangladesh."

"How long has he been here?"

"Not long. Less than a year."

"You work together?"

"We are both in Environment."

"So you meet, you talk, you have lunch?"

Svetlana laughed. "Don't worry, we are just good friends. Are you going to interrogate me, Uncle Viktor?"

Krylov was not inclined to play. "You talk about your life."

"I suppose."

"So he would know about Anna?"

"Sure."

"Would he know she is a nurse?"

"Maybe. I'm proud of her after all. She's a wonderful nurse."

"Another mystery revealed."

"What mystery?"

"The mystery of how they knew Anna was a nurse."

"They?"

"Sophie's kidnappers."

"Sveta, this Muckeltee was the one who contacted me," Anna explained. "He called himself Al-Rabiah."

"Dear God."

"It is time to tell me, Anna," said Krylov.

"Svetlana will hear."

"Why shouldn't I hear?"

"I've been so stupid. I'm ashamed."

"Of trying to rescue your sister? Don't be silly."

Anna looked from one friend to the other, and then, in a small voice, she began. "He came to me at the hospital. He said he was just an intermediary. But later he boasted that the others were cogs and he was the wheel."

"What did he want?"

"He said the kidnappers wanted me to inoculate a British stranger without his knowing it. A nasty and horrible thing to do, but easy for a nurse. Almost a prank, in a way. I would have done much worse to save Sophie." She spoke into the dim light of the room, as though alone, and, indeed, Krylov sensed that she was no longer quite with them.

"They sent me to Toulouse with false identity. I was called Anna Nonperes."

"Nonperes?"

"An anagram of *personne*. 'Magic!' he said."

"A lot of magic going on," said Krylov.

"I went to an Airbus press conference, and, as they knew he would, this British journalist picked me up and took me to his favorite hotel in Switzerland."

"As they knew he would?"

"I guess I was not the only girl he took there."

"What was he like?" asked Svetlana.

"Far too nice."

"You got to the hotel," said Krylov.

"In the afternoon." She paused and her companions could almost hear her remembering a sweet moment or two. "When we went down to dinner we were happy and laughing. Then *he* …"

"Muckeltee?"

"Yes, he was at the hotel with his family. He came over to our table. He had known my Englishman in Iraq."

"When?"

"After the first Gulf War. He was an RAF pilot. He was one of ten prisoners this Muckeltee helped when the war ended."

"So your man was glad to see him."

"No, he hated seeing him. He drank a lot and I gave him something to put him to sleep. Then I gave the inoculation."

"What was in it?"

"I don't know. A small amount of clear fluid. I watched to see if I had killed him. He didn't die. I did, a little, but he did not. I tried to get away early in the morning, but Al-Rabiah, Muckeltee, whoever, was waiting and brought me back to Vienna in that little green car."

"How did you part?"

"He reminded me that I had committed a crime. He said they would have my silence one way or another. He said I would never see him again." She managed a wan smile. "He was wrong about that."

"He was wrong about a lot of things. Sveta, did he know they were twins?"

"I might have mentioned Sophie as Anna's famous sister working in Iraq. But I never spoke of her as Anna's twin. I never thought of her that way, Anna is so different inside."

Anna said, "He didn't know. On the way back to Vienna he asked if we were much alike, was there a family resemblance, that kind of thing. I almost told him we were twins, but something made me stop."

"Had they known, they might have gone elsewhere," said Krylov. "They knew that Sophie's death would be widely reported, her face on television, in newspapers. But they didn't know her face was also your face, Anna. So now you are not just Anna Nonperes. You are Anna Nieman. Your Englishman can find you, if he wants."

"Why would he want to?"

"A good question I cannot answer. Anyway, they make mistakes. Sveta, did you tell him Anna was with you tonight?"

"No."

"Good, another mistake. He doesn't know we've seen him. He thinks he can still hide in plain sight. That gives us time."

"Time for what?" Anna wanted to know.

"First, to find out more about our little doctor. Second, to see where he goes and what he does there. And third, to make sure he has no way of reaching you."

Svetlana laughed. "One, two, three. You sound like a Russian."

"You said I am in no danger," said Anna. "You were right, I don't know what was in the syringe. I don't really know anything."

"I said they didn't care about your silence. But you see how readily they kill. Sophie was thrown to the Americans just for effect. As a magic trick. When this Muckeltee realizes his mistake about twins, he will see his plot is a house of cards. Your Englishman will find you. You will have to tell him what you know. He will see that it was medical, and that it was linked to his time as a prisoner of war. From there, he can bring in the authorities and Muckeltee's plot, no matter what it is, is finished."

"But only if my Englishman finds me."

"Our little Bangladeshi, or whatever he is, is not going to wait for that, Anna."

VIII

Churches spent a good deal of time engaged in imaginary conversations, hoping to sand away the poor fit between what he wanted from others and what he got. Long after his parents died, he continued his efforts to persuade them that, never mind his size, he was twenty, he was thirty, he was forty—he was grown. He talked things over (and over) with the several women who had stepped briefly into his life, then left him trying to repair a heart that cracked as readily and deliciously as an adolescent's. On that front he had made little headway; everything still hurt.

Tonight, as he pushed his Mazda Miata southward on the A3, top down, chill wind like the vortex of a tornado, his imagined conversation was with Viktor Krylov, with whom some grievances were long standing. Like the business with the car. When Churches had driven up in his new Miata, the Russian had nearly spoiled his pleasure by noting that his toothbrush was the same color. Churches had turned away in angry silence, his head ringing like a cage of finches.

It's metallic aquamarine, what they call Aquapulco, you stupid Russian bastard, and I suppose you people want something metallic to brush all those steel fillings with, fillings that are, now I think about it, the color of an aged Mercedes. Yes, and I had a red toothbrush once, the color of a certain clapped-out Lada.

But the conversation currently in progress had nothing to do with cars. It was about their encounter in Krylov's office; it had inflicted wounds that would not close.

You don't tell a man what you would do if he were a grownup. You don't threaten a colleague. I am the sort of man who forgives everything, Viktor. But I forget nothing, ever. You'd best watch out for me now. I no longer have your interests or friendship at heart. Nor am I your oh-so-transparent Mr. Cellophane.

The transparency issue had to do with Krylov's sensing immediately that he, Churches, was reconnoitering for the Americans.

You just caught that odor wafting off Emerson. Anyone in our line of work would smell it. No big deal. Yes, I do the odd thingy for the Americans. We have a special relationship. Brits and the U.S. onward together. But I don't do anything bad to anybody. And I'm not a whore. I am not a minion.

He was not so sure about the minion part. Emerson had called the night before, complaining that Krylov had done a switch and left blank swipes and an empty disk. They had nothing, nada, rien, sweet Fanny Adams from the cave. "You have to find those samples for us, Churchy."

Don't call me Churchy.

"And not sometime next year. Now, tonight."

"Rafe, I'm not sure I can."

"You saying our special-relationship eggs are in the wrong basket?"

Special relationship eggs, for God's sake. Well, I'm not your bloody Churchy minion chap. But that notwithstanding I bloody well tried. I offered Viktor a way to get his stuff analyzed on the quiet, no waves, at Aldermaston, and he just swatted me away.

"Christ," Churches complained above the roar of the slipstream. "Christ."

Had you shown an iota of collegial respect, Viktor, I would have gone back to Emerson with a shrug and a sad shake of the head. Not possible. Sorry. And that would have been that. Emerson wouldn't change our relationship. He wants a certain fly on a certain wall. Buzz, buzz. Very well, it ain't big money, but it's reliable money, if you follow.

Churches had stomped back to his office thinking duels, thinking bombs, thinking slashed tires on a certain old Mercedes. His little body had vibrated with frustrated anger. Seated in his swivel chair, his feet barely skimming the carpet, he rotated this way and that, unable to be still, asking himself how he might repay Krylov's cruelties.

Then, as his temper steadied and cooled, he saw the way ahead. He would find where the samples had gone, retrieve them, and hand them to Emerson. He was an irresistible force. He would bring down the temple. Make them think twice.

You needn't be Sherlock Holmes to solve this one, Viktor. You're not the type to share such stuff. No sending the samples back to Dubna for analysis at the Flerov Lab. Where would you turn? Seibersdorf? Have you a chum there? I think not. Ah, but hold on a moment. Don't I remember some chatter about you and a bit of pussy at the lab? Before my time, no idea who she was or if she's still there. Oldenburg will know, and he has no time for you, Viktor. I just walk up and say, Klaus old chap, was there any truth to those tales of Viktor and that Seibersdorf technician, whatsername?

"Ilse Heilig?" asked Oldenburg, not bothering to look up.

"That's the one."

CHURCHES TOOK THE EBREICHSDORF EXIT AND DOUBLED BACK TO the northeast across the black fields until he made out the low cluster of lights marking the laboratory. He pulled up at the gate with a big smile for the Sikh guard, who towered over the Miata. "Good evening, Anthony."

"Mr. Churches. You're working late."

"No rest for the weary, I'm afraid."

"I haven't seen you out here for a long time."

"Too long. Been working. Donkey in a mine, if you know what I mean." Churches gave a helpless shrug. "But, here I am."

Anthony pondered the proffered credentials. "You're visiting someone?"

"Miss Heilig."

"But she's not here. No one is. It's late."

Feeling the first light touch of panic, Churches leaned toward the giant as if wanting to whisper something to his knees. "Actually, Anthony, I don't need to see her. My colleague, Viktor Krylov was here a few days ago…"

The guard nodded. "I recall."

"He asked her to leave something for me to pick up. On her desk."

"But her office will be locked."

"No problem, Krylov gave me her key." By way of proof, Churches brushed the keys hanging from the ignition. "But, you know, it *has* been a while. Which wing is she in now?"

The Sikh gestured toward the Safeguards door.

"Thanks. I'll not be long."

"Very good," said Anthony in a voice like distant thunder, and waved him in.

Churches parked outside the ring of light at the entrance and marched confidently into the place. People left you alone if you looked like you belonged. The reception desk inside the door was unoccupied, and the only sound of human habitation was the distant drone of a floor buffer, touching up the pea-green lino. He padded down the hall, checking names, and soon came to I. Heilig. A swipe of a Visa card and the lock popped open. Churches entered and, in the light from the hall, found a desk lamp, which he switched on, then closed the door.

There were files everywhere, on the grey metal desk, in bookshelves to the ceiling, even stacked on the floor, creating revetments of bulging manila folders. On a small table across the room files poised like a cliff of old snow getting ready for an avalanche.

Ah, Ilse, Ilse, Ilse, what a messy place you've got here. Spontaneous combustion any moment. A child did the decorating for you? I thought so. Now, how did that child organize this stuff? Because I know it's organized. Technicians always organize, even when the result is apparent chaos.

He grinned and rubbed his hands. Where to begin?

At the beginning, of course.

The folders stuffed into bookshelves and stacked along the walls looked as if they'd been there forever; some of the higher strata were gauzed with spider webs. Churches pulled over Ilse's swivel chair and sat down, studying the desk for a time.

What I'm looking for, Ilse, is something pretty fresh. Viktor's stuff. Only a fortnight old. Time to run your analysis. Time to talk it over. Time to give him the stuff. But you're a technical gel, you aren't going to just hand everything back to him. You're keeping a copy.

He began sorting through the folders on the desk, one by one, each labeled with a five-digit number beginning with three, the name of the client, and the date of arrival at the lab. Three four zero five six, Imler. Three four zero five seven, Imler. Three four zero five eight. Oldenburg.

You don't know where these things come from, Ilse. But I do. For me it's like looking into people's souls. Imler's stuff from Atucha-1, Oldenburg's from Loviisa-2. Ah, here's a vintage Krylov, last year's refueling at Leningrad-I. The secret lives of all my fellow Safeguardsmen, piled up on your desk.

Quickly, he ran through the folders, ranging outward from the desk to the precarious column of files on the table, then to the bookshelves, then to the stacks along the baseboard. It was all just the normal stuff…

And this?

He held up a yellowed folder. It looked centuries old.

55555, Churches, no date.

Years since I sent anything out here.

He swept away the rubber band holding the folder closed, then spread the contents on the desk.

Readouts, a CD, some notes from you, Ilse. Brand new material in that antique folder. Hidden in plain sight, as they say. Not my stuff, either. No, it's bloody Viktor's. From the bloody cave. No cotton swipes. You must have put them in safe storage.

Churches turned to Ilse's notes, composed in her clear, calligraphic hand: cesium-137 .6 half-life (.2 younger than Chernobyl Ce-137). MCA readouts show abundant barium daughters, meaning…

Meaning it's gone through more than twenty years of radioactive decay. Emerson, old bean, your dirty-bomb factory's old enough to drink. Churches uttered a delighted yodel of laughter. "Old enough to drink!"

EMERSON WAS NOWHERE IN VIEW when Churches pulled up at the Augarten, where they had agreed to meet. The American favored these lonely venues, "where," as he put it, "you don't find a lot of people speaking English."

Or German either, Churches secretly replied.

Vienna used to be so safe, Krylov had told him in one of their more companionable moments, that you could send your little girl out at two in the morning, covered with hundred-dollar bills, and no one would touch her. Now, it seemed to Churches, that same little girl's green feathers would be plucked before she reached the next street; she would be raped and murdered.

The old city had always had its share of displaced, desperate people, yet it had somehow remained safe. Not now. Vienna was a modern city, to which the displaced and desperate came from south and east with a mad shine in their eyes, abundant guns, and traditions of exquisite cruelty. Churches shivered, although the night was far from cold, feeling what it would be like, to be a girl cloaked in hundred-dollar bills in this lonely place.

He would have much preferred the Blue Bar at the Sacher or even one of the Bürgerhof's corner tables. But, no, Emerson had wanted the usual haunted house, so here he was, down among rows of stunted black trees near this weird anti-memorial to an era many Austrians wanted to forget.

Two of Vienna's three pairs of Flaktürme, the antiaircraft platforms arrayed in a large isosceles triangle around the city's center, loomed in the dimly lighted park, one a twelve-storey petaled cylinder of thick concrete and steel—the Gefechtsturm, carrying the heavy guns—the other a matching oblong with emplacements for smaller guns and searchlights jutting like jug ears from each corner.

"Don't you love these things?" It was Emerson, coalescing out of the darkness, wreathed in pale smoke from his cigarette. He was dressed in his usual costume of navy blazer, blood-red bow tie, white shirt, pale blue jeans, beige desert boots.

Emerson of the bloody desert.

A huge shadow followed Emerson, some American muscle, Churches supposed. Yes, he could see the man more clearly now. The one with all the tattoos. Lamont.

"You two know each other?"

"Evening, Mr. Churches," Lamont said in his tiny Louisiana voice.

"Hello, Lamont," said Churches, giving a wave to avoid taking the man's curiously small, gloved hand.

"Frederic Tanna's indestructible brain children, or maybe Albert Speers's," Emerson went on, waving his cigarette at the near tower. "Built to last a thousand years, like the Third Reich. After the Nazis won the war, they were going to plate these things with black marble inscribed with the names of German dead." He took a long draw on his cigarette, then let the smoke drift like a thought out into the night.

"Regime didn't make the thousand-year mark, but these babies will. Sovs tried to raze them, but that's ten feet of concrete and steel. Artillery and bombs just bounced off. Put in enough explosive to destroy them, you take out the whole neighborhood. Empty now, stained the color of dog shit by the elements, defiled by graffiti. Austrians of a certain age hate them. The young think they're for wall climbing. Too bad. Anything men make that will stand through all eternity deserves some respect."

He shook his head and laughed. "Little history for you, Churchy."

Don't call me Churchy.

Emerson guided him to a bench where twin rows of linden trees marched toward the southwest tower's entrance door. Lamont moved off into the shadows, covering the flank.

"Now, Churchy me boy," said Emerson, "what've you got for me?"

Churches passed him an unmarked folder secured by several large rubber bands. "I found what you wanted."

"Never doubted you could do it."

"At Seibersdorf. Folder had my name on it, quite clever, stashed with a pile of ancient stuff. No swipes, probably in radioactive storage. I burned a copy of the compact disk and photocopied her notes…"

"Her?"

"The technician who analyzed the swipes."

"Friend o'Vik's?"

"I suppose."

"Okay, and….?"

Churches launched his punch line. "Your dirty-bomb factory's old enough to drink."

"Ho, ho, and ho. Just tell me."

"The cesium-137 in the cave has been decaying for decades. It's almost as old as Chernobyl cesium."

"So what?"

"Whatever the Iraqis were doing in the cave that produced cesium-137, they stopped doing it a long time ago."

"Before Gulf One?"

"Maybe."

"So it's what we thought, only earlier." Emerson cracked a broad smile. "Shit, Churchy, we were more than half right." Then he looked skyward, seeming to sample the air. He frowned at what he discovered there and gave Churches a penetrating look. "Weren't we?"

"I don't see how you get from the isotope to the fire and end up with so much isotope."

"Easy." Emerson relaxed. "It's called nuclear fission. Sometimes known as: *Oops!*"

Churches shrugged. If Emerson wanted there to have been a fission accident in the cave, let him. Krylov had said not, and, whatever his faults, the Russian knew what he was talking about. Well, it was academic. Churches thought he'd done enough for these boys tonight. Let the Americans work out how all that isotope had survived a fire hot enough to melt glass and steel *without* a fission event. Let old Lamont apply his keen intellect to the problem.

"There, there, don't brood," said Emerson, giving the Englishman's shoulder a manly squeeze. "It's a good job done, Churchy, right out of the top drawer. You'll get your reward in Zurich." He stood up, fading into the shadows. "Good night."

"Night." Churches peered into the darkness, where the bodyguard's bulk was still just visible. "Good night, Lamont."

The reed of a voice came back, "Night."

Churches waited where he stood, diminished, as always, by contact with Emerson. It was like certain kinds of sex: one always felt such a naughty boy afterward.

In the distance a big engine cranked and revved noisily; he thought it must be one of the black embassy Suburbans favored by Emerson's crowd. When he heard it pull away, its metallic growl echoing through the narrow streets, he turned back toward his car, thinking he might just pop into the Blue Bar for that Martini after all.

"Mr. Churches."

Christ, don't sneak up that way!

"Just leaving, Lamont."

Now several shadowy figures moved in between him and the Mazda, men not much taller than he was, but feline in their motions, as if they drifted weightlessly through the gloom. But he could sense their latent velocity; if he ran they would be after him like cheetahs. They wore jeans and black sweatshirts with hoods and as they approached he could discern their dark faces, their beards, the bright brown eyes of the desert. Christ, how one began to hate the bloody desert.

"Just a minute, Mr. Churches." The new voice again, right behind him now, and definitely not Lamont. This one was deeper, with a foreign hiss in it.

Churches stopped without looking around. His life had brought him into tight corners before, and he'd been pleasantly surprised to discover that, while he could be plenty scared, he was not a coward. "What do you want?" Good, the voice was steady, no tremor in the hands.

"We wish to speak with you."

"Who are you?"

"Men in a patriotic cause."

"If you're collecting, perhaps you could send me something through the post?"

"We are not collecting money."

"Then what?"

"Information."

"You've come to the wrong man. I have none."

"Sometimes we have more of everything than we think. For now, please walk along with us."

The men—he saw there were four of them in all—formed a kind of star around him, and impelled him along the gravel walkway between lines of silhouetted trees that writhed against the lighter sky above the city. The great curve of the monolith's concrete flank, invisibly black at night, glimmered like the walls of a prehistoric cave with generations of graffiti, of swastikas, the Che Guevara glyph, the stylized Christian names of adolescent artists who had by now vanished into their maturity. There were admonitions in all the languages of the old city: peace; solidarity; death to Bush, Jews, and Crusaders; no blood for oil; no nukes; save the whales.

One of the Arabs pushed open the heavy metal entrance door, which moved enough on its corroded hinges for a man to squeeze through, which they did, Indian file, with Churches in the middle. Inside, Churches found the darkness palpable and fetid, as if he were wrapped in soiled black velvet. The ammonia stink of urine brought tears to his eyes and as he walked his feet scattered God knew what kind of filthy detritus across the concrete floor. An electric torch beam jabbed through the blackness for just a moment and Churches saw they were headed for a steep flight of metal steps. Then, restored to the heavy darkness, they made their clanging ascent to a higher, less cluttered level.

The room occupied half the storey, its thick curved outer wall pierced with a tall slit window that admitted cooler, sweeter air. Churches wanted to gulp it down, but did not. A shaft of pale light pooled upon the rough wooden floor. The place had been swept up, a little, and furnished with a few large kilim cushions, their deep colors greyed in the dimness. A wooden café chair sat in the middle of the room, and the sight of it, the implications of there being such a chair, in such a place, in such company, made Churches' knees wobble briefly, his stomach roll with nausea. Then he steadied himself. They had no reason to hurt him. They would let him go. He would wake up and find this had all been a terrible dream…

"Sit down."

Churches eased himself into the chair. His heart, he thought, must be audible in the distant suburbs, and no doubt he emitted some odor, some detectable element of fear, that these boys could smell. One of the figures came up behind him, he felt him kneel, then plastic loops cuffed his wrists behind one leg of the chair, his ankles behind another.

"Now we work on that exchange of information," said the man who'd first accosted him. He was dressed like a Russian detective in a shiny black leather jacket and black trousers, and he was older than the others. The faint light bounced off the tiny circles of his glasses and his face was all facets, partly masked by a shallow black beard. His dark hair was lush, spumed with white, and parted in the middle, like black waves breaking on a tan beach. He half-reclined on his cushion, as if at any moment boredom might drop him into sleep. "Are you aboard, Mr. Churches?"

"Who are you?"

The man laughed. "Call me Ishmael. Or whatever. It does not matter who I am. What matters is what you know and whether you are willing to share it."

Churches' tongue seemed to have swollen, it flopped around his mouth like a captive toad. "I can't imagine....what I...."

"Let me place my cards face upwards, so we know precisely where we stand. First, the cave."

"What cave?"

"Please, don't make things worse. Of course I mean Mr. Emerson's cave. The cave of your Russian colleague."

"*That* cave."

"Good for you. We know what the Americans said they found there. Now I want to know what they did not say."

"I know awfully little." It was not much of a protest, for Churches had already decided not to fight the problem. The cave was Emerson's business, not his. He would allow these fellows to extract every little thing he knew. They would hear the ring of truth and let him go. He waited a couple of beats, taking a breath, trying to shake the tremor from his voice.

"We were in Bonab, Krylov and I...," He spoke to the man in the leather coat, confidentially, as if they were alone. He gave him the Bulgarian pilots, the idea of borrowing Krylov, the Emerson connection, the cave; he poured out everything he could think of. "Because there was a very hot fire and large amounts of cesium isotope, the Americans decided there had been some kind of fission accident in the cave."

"They took samples?"

"Krylov did. But he didn't share with the Americans. He had them analyzed here."

"Here?"

"Our lab in Seibersdorf."

"And what did this show?"

"A lot of barium…"

"Not too much chemistry, please."

"Cesium-137 that had been decaying for twenty or thirty years."

"As you say, old enough to buy a drink."

Churches flinched, spooked by the sound of his poor little joke, then pressed on. "I think the cesium went in after the fire."

"Why would anyone do that?"

"I have no idea."

"Nonsense."

"To mask something else?"

"That's better. But what?"

"I don't know. Nobody knows."

"I think you are mistaken. No, let me be up in front with you. I think you are lying."

"I'm not." Churches heard a shrill note in his protest, and tried to take it back. "Really, I've told you everything I know."

"Lend me your ears, Mr. Churches. My comrades and I have been thinking this over for many years. Because of our history, rumors of a secret project in a secret cave wonderfully concentrate our attention."

"Kurds."

Churches saw the man's shoulders move in a shrug. "We are what we are. In the desert, in the wilderness, information flies around like leaves in a whirlwind. We reach out and catch them, one by one, hoping we shall eventually be able to see the tree in full. So. One leaf speaks of Saddam's secret cave in the northern hills. Another tells us Saddam has hidden a nuclear-weapons program. But then another says, no, worse than nuclear, the mother of all weapons. Other questions arise. What happened to this man from this village and that man from that village? We try to fathom this, but all we have, really, is a handful of dead leaves. We do not even know if they fell from the same tree."

"I have no leaves to add."

The speaker ignored him. "So we ask: Was Saddam's mother of all weapons the project in the secret cave? Is that where the Disappeared have gone? We think we are making progress when, suddenly, the cave is abandoned. The whirlwind dies. No more leaves. A few of our people go into the cave. They find what you have described. Signs of a terrible fire, human ash. Not much later, they begin to die. You see, we are no wiser about radiation than cats are about motorcars."

He was silent for a moment, as though trapped in angry reverie. Then, "People invent frightening stories about the cave, ghost stories, punishment from God. They shun the place. The leaves that might tell us the reason for its existence turn to powder in our hands. The years walk by. Our awareness of the cave fades to nothing. But then," and here the man paused, his face creasing with a broad smile full of huge, crooked teeth, "here comes the American named Emerson, drawn to the cave by the same rumors and, we surmise, something more. Our interest stirs."

"You know rather more than I do," said Churches, "More than Emerson."

"The Americans claimed to have found a factory for dirty bombs. But we believe the entity in the cave was something worse. Now I rely upon you, Mr. Churches, to tell us what that was."

"But I've no idea." Churches felt his nerve begin to ravel. "We didn't even know there was a cave until the other day."

"This is what I believe, Mr. Churches. I believe you—you, Emerson, perhaps your Russian—learned about the cave as we did. But, unlike us, you discovered what was in the cave. You thought it was too terrible to waste, so you went in and found it."

"That's not true. We found nothing. We know almost nothing now."

"People talk. The air is full of their talk, if one only listens. Listening, we hear names associated with the cave. Names we have never heard before."

"I'm very confused," murmured Churches, beginning to realize that his captors pursued information he did not possess. He saw his severed head held up for the cameras on a jihadist website.

"How could we know so much and you, so little?"

A brief whirring sound came from the darkness, then silence, then another whir, and another, as if someone gunned an electric motor. The hand torch switched on, the beam aimed away from the window.

"What's that?"

"Mister Black & Mister Decker."

I must not shit.

"Talk to somebody else, talk to Krylov, talk to, God, I don't know, but anybody. You know I'm empty, why go on with me?"

"Because you are here."

Churches felt his will collapse. *Think of courage.* He shut his eyes and saw, as on a screen, Ann Boleyn parting her hair to expose the pale nape to the axe. Sidney Carton in the shadow of the guillotine doing a far, far better thing than he had done. Saddam trading jibes with a noose around his neck… They were all images of brave behavior, but also of how one must accept the inevitable, how one can be numbed by knowledge of the future.

Now, from a childhood memory, Churches found himself in the Devon countryside, watching cattle march up the abattoir ramp. An almost visible veil of fear descended upon their bewildered minds like night coming down and he could see them take in the stink of oblivion in the air ahead of them and hear the awful cries of their comrades. Shitting with fright, their hooves slipping on a slurry of excrement, they went terrified to their deaths.

I must not shit.

In a voice devoid of hope, Churches said, "I can't help you. Sorry."

"Yes you can. Tell us about Mohammad Al-Rabiah. Tell us about Peter Gayle."

THE LOW AUTUMNAL SUN HAD JUST STRUCK THE PALE UPPER RIM OF the Allgemeines Krankenhaus when Krylov arrived. Traffic on the Gürtel was just waking up, he could sense its clamor gathering, like a vast nineteenth-century factory starting its lathes and belts and presses. He locked the Mercedes and strode toward the entrance, still dressed as a Moscow delivery man, head down, moving like a rugby forward, as if he expected heavy resistance along the way. Of course, there was none. The place was almost deserted, for the night's gang of sick and injured, dying and dead, was usually dispersed by sunrise.

Krylov had spent a good many days in hospitals, seeing after his people, visiting old friends run down by a violent event, having his own wounds repaired. The experience had given him a peculiar aversion to medical venues of any kind, and especially to immense, faceless places like Vienna's general hospital. Sveta said this only meant he was too keenly aware of the human suffering around him; she always erred on the side of kindness. Krylov thought it was more like the fear animals had of veterinarians, an apprehension that if one entered such a place, one might never leave.

The night before, as they drove back into the city, Anna had announced she was going to stand her midnight shift after all. "Sober up first," Krylov told her, only half in jest.

"You think I'm drunk?"

"I think you were."

"I was blind until I saw the light." She gave him a tired smile. "Until I saw Sveta's Dr. Muckeltee."

"Take a taxi," said Krylov.

"It's such a nice walk."

Christ, the woman was like a dog who won't come out of traffic. He was glad to see them to their gate, where Sveta paused, locking it behind them, and waved him a kiss. Krylov grinned, wondering what men did without a Svetlana of their own.

Then he'd driven home, poured himself a vodka nightcap, and sat down among the faded flowers printed on Frau Steiner's old divan. Almost immediately, he was asleep, the dreamer dropped back into the cave with the not quite beautiful American Navy commander. The gamma fell around them as a gentle, golden rain. She took off her hood and mask, shook out her strawberry hair….The multichannel analyzer suddenly announced a dire, mysterious threat, and Krylov grabbed for it….

But it was the telephone, Anna at work, begging him to hurry.

A sleepy clerk at the information desk gave him a map with the Abteilug Intensiv highlighted in chartreuse, and Krylov forced himself into the maze of corridors, long, empty, shiny-clean halls that ran off to a vanishing point, as in a Dali painting, or an anxiety dream.

Anna waited for him outside the ICU, looking tiny and exhausted in her blue scrubs.

"Where is he?" Krylov asked.

"This way."

She led them into the ward where intensive-care units were arrayed like spokes around a central nurse's station. Across the open floor, a grey curtain shielded one of the beds. "Over here," said Anna, parting the curtain for Krylov.

Churches had always looked like a boy. The shock of pale blonde hair, the face almost unmarked, the small white teeth, the sapphire eyes had imparted an aura of innocence that had given some protection from the real, adult world. Now he lay in a tangle of tubes, reduced as if by magic from ageless youth to little old man, the bright face shrunken and ash-grey beneath a plastic oxygen mask. On the readout his pulse accelerated and faded, the heart line jumping like a seismograph needle between too much and too little. His life seemed to be slipping away faster than the tubes could replenish it.

"What happened?"

"He ran off the road down by Seibersdorf. His car caught fire, but it didn't burn. The police say he fell asleep. They're testing for alcohol."

"How did you know to call me?"

"He asked for you. When he came in he said, Viktor Krylov. So I called."

"It must have been quite a crash."

Anna shook her head. "The crash was just a final touch. He was tortured beforehand."

"Tortured?"

She suppressed a gag reflex. "With a power drill."

"Christ."

"Viktor? Is that you, Viktor?" The ruined creature in the bed had opened its one good eye, which darted from Krylov to Anna and back again, sending frantic, incoherent signals to the brain.

"It's me, Churches. Be quiet. Anna's a friend. She'll make you good as new."

A moist chuckle from behind the oxygen mask, a brief light in the good eye. "I look forward."

"Who did this?"

"Kurds."

"Try to rest now," said Anna, glancing nervously at Krylov. "Really, he has to rest."

"Thought I was a goner." A hideous Jack o'lantern smile appeared beneath the mask. "Iraqi dentist." Another gargle of laughter. "Not the best."

"What did they want?"

Churches took a long, scratchy breath. "The cave."

"But you weren't there."

The Jack o'lantern grinned once more. "They didn't care. Not detail men."

"What did you tell them?"

"Every fucking thing I could think of." The phrase took all his breath. For a moment the little old man seemed to die, to suffocate, but then revived, gulping oxygen. "Nothing was enough," Churches whispered.

"Please," said Anna, "please."

"Okay," said Krylov. "Churches, you rest now. I'll be around. Later we can talk some more."

"Thought I was a goner."

Krylov looked at Anna, who closed her eyes and turned away. "Anna will make you good as new."

"Viktor?" The good eye had ceased its darting around, and peered at him, half closed, its light subsiding.

"Yes?"

"I gave your cesium stuff to Emerson. Sorry."

"Don't worry about it," said Krylov, thinking he would like to give Churches a good shaking. Emerson meant more trouble, endless woe, on and on. "Now rest."

"And Viktor?"

"What?"

"Do you know a Peter Gayle?"

IX

Beyond Lyme Regis, Gayle steered the elder Saab onto the Ware road, then turned down a narrow country lane that, he hoped, was the way to Mickey Williams' place. In the ten years that Williams had been in the stone cottage, Gayle had visited him just twice, and even out in these meadows that seemed immune to change, navigation points came and went; once out of sight of the sea, it was easy to lose one's way. But this morning Gayle was in a fine mood and didn't mind having to reconnoiter awhile. He would come upon Mouse eventually, and had begun to look forward to the visit.

After a night of the usual febrile dreaming Gayle had awakened to find himself lathered like a blown horse, but otherwise much improved. His skeleton felt less like tallow and more like bone, his head had ceased pounding, and the naked man in the bathroom mirror bore no rosy whorls of prickly heat.

He'd dressed quickly, thrown on an old bomber jacket, and started for the garage, then remembered to collect the pistol, still wrapped in its chamois cloth. By the time the sun boiled up out of the sea, he was hurrying down the A35 into a dazzling bright autumn day, the farmlands smooth as moss, the ocean like a field of diamonds off to his left.

Gayle and Williams had made a point of seeing each other about once a year, but hardly ever where they lived. Instead, they'd gone up to London for dinner at Wheeler's and a West-End play, or driven into the countryside to spend the day in Oxford or some charming Cotswold village. Because they had shared, as Gayle put it to himself, every bloody thing but a woman, they needed to meet. But they also needed to meet on neutral ground, so as not to come too close for comfort. They were like a couple who, after a long marriage, had decided on an amicable divorce, then got together now and then to chat about their grown children and people they'd known. This amiable tradition kept the friendship alive by making no demands on either party, although each believed he might ask anything at all of the other. Today's visit was the only favor Mickey Williams had ever requested of his pilot.

A woman constable in a dark Macintosh and a yellow reflective vest was stepping into the lane ahead of him, her hand raised to signal a stop. "Sorry, sir," she said, coming up to his window, "road's closed." She was a pretty, stocky girl with a blonde pony tail poking out behind her checkered cap and tiny square hands that looked strong as a baker's. Her eyes were a wonderful blue.

"Is there another way?"

"Depends where you're going."

"I'm visiting a friend. He lives just a mile up this road."

"May I have his name, sir?"

"Michael Williams." But Gayle had seen the pink-cheeked country face unconsciously avert itself, the blue eyes cloud. A chill drifted through him. "What's wrong?"

"One minute, sir." She put her back to him and called someone on her handheld radio. He couldn't hear what she said, but after a short exchange, she came back to him, still holding the radio. "What is your name, sir?"

"Peter Gayle."

"It's Peter Gayle, sir," she told the radio. "Yes, sir, thank you, sir." She shut it off. "My guv'ner says you can go up. Do be careful, though, it's a bit crowded up there now."

Gayle had found his first visit to the stone cottage awkward. Williams had just moved in and the little house, beneath its wild coils of red and yellow roses, still wore an aura of penury, failure, and decay. He hadn't known what to say, except what a fine view it had. He thought he might send a little money, although Williams never asked and he never did.

Three years on, when he paid his other visit, the cottage had felt more like his friend's true home, with the roses tamed and happy and Peter Rabbit's garden neat and fertile, and the inside livable, clean, and cluttered with piles of books, electronics, and what looked like miles of wire. "You're one lucky mouse, Mickey," said Gayle. He'd meant it, too.

Now the place looked like one of those crash sites in which the aircraft and its passengers have been deconstructed utterly. Behind a gaily strobing cordon of police cars, an ambulance, and what looked like a crime scene van, the remains of the grey stone walls stood like ruined molars in a bed of ash still exhaling thin wreaths of smoke. A bunting of black and yellow police tape trembled in the breeze. The Deux Cheveaux lay inverted far down the slope, as if kicked there by a pouting giant child. No roses, no roof, no Peter Rabbit's sign, no garden. Yes, thought Gayle, and there would be no Mickey Williams, either. He didn't like the idea of a world in which there was no Mickey Williams.

You're one lucky mouse, Mickey.

Christ.

Gayle parked the Saab off to one side of the lane, well clear of the police vehicles, then waited as a sudden inky swirl of grief spun itself out and his eyes ceased gleaming. "I wish I could help you, Mouse," he told the brilliant morning, the ruin, and the sea, "I wish

I could bring you back, I wish I had come sooner, I wish, I wish, I wish." When he thought he had his emotions capped, he got out and walked toward what had once been the true home of Mickey Williams.

The ground had warmed enough that a cold breeze poured inland off the sea, and he zipped his bomber jacket against the chill. As he approached the ruin, a tall man who had been standing with a group of uniformed police approached him.

"Mr. Gayle?"

"Yes."

"Detective Inspector Wickers." The man put out a huge farmer's hand and gave Gayle's a good, hard shake. Wickers looked about sixty, a good deal of fine etching around the mouth and grey-green eyes. His teeth, which glistened when he spoke, seemed cut from a single block of antique marble, and a wisp of collie-colored hair crept out from under a grey tweed cap. He wore a white shirt and striped blue and yellow tie under a Navy blue pea coat, which Gayle thought would be too hot by noon. "I fear you'll not have much of a visit, Mr. Gayle."

"What happened?"

Wicker shook his head. "Our techies are still piecing it together," and he nodded toward what had been the cottage's main room, where men and women in white coveralls were taking samples. "As you can see, there was one hell of an explosion. Just look at that poor little French motorcar. About nine last night, everybody saw it. From Lyme Regis it looked like the end of the world. We thought we had a volcano. By the time the fire brigade found the place, it looked much as you see it now, although much hotter."

"Was it a bomb?"

"Oh, I don't think so." Wickers uttered a soft chuckle at the idea of a bomb in his corner of the countryside. "Mr. Williams cooked and heated the cottage with propane. We haven't yet found the tank, no doubt vaporized in the explosion. So propane looks the prime suspect here. Doesn't take very high concentrations, less than ten percent in air I think, to brew a very explosive cocktail. Hotter than a crematorium when it goes, hence…" and he nodded toward the bed of ash.

"Where's Mickey?"

"I fear he's gone. Our chaps found human remains, enough to work up an identification, but nothing to tell us exactly how he died. In these explosions, things happen rather quickly. I doubt he knew what hit him."

"He knew. He always knew everything. Situational awareness, he called it."

Boss…I'm scared.

"Good friends, you and he?"

"He was my navigator."

"Navy, then."

"RAF. Tornadoes."

"In our Gulf war?"

"The first one."

"Ah. Long time ago, that."

"Yes, a long time ago." But, thought Gayle, not nearly long enough ago, or far enough away.

"Can you think of anyone who would wish Mr. Williams dead?"

Gayle hadn't listened. "Sorry?"

"Do you know if Mr. Williams had any, um, serious enemies?"

"Mickey was always short of enemies."

"Do you know any reason he might do this?" He darted a look at the ruin. "To himself?"

"We were prisoners of war together. If you don't do it then, you're not good suicide material."

"Oh, I see, sorry. But I take your meaning. Then one might imagine his being asleep, the propane pooling along the floor. Perhaps he lost consciousness as well. Then some spark—a telephone, a pilot light, something—and Bob's your uncle."

"An accident?"

"Yes, I believe we can say that, preliminarily of course. Naturally there will be an inquest." When Gayle did not respond, Wickers harrumphed and said, "I'd like to have your particulars, Mr. Gayle, in case we need to talk further."

Gayle got out his wallet and gave the detective one of his business cards.

"Hmm," murmured Wickers. "A journalist. I trust we won't see our conversation in the press?"

"I write about aviation."

"Jolly good."

"You'll let me know how this turns out?"

"I'll make a point of calling." The big policeman shifted uncomfortably, watching his colleagues. Then, "I guess that's all, Mr. Gayle. I'd best rejoin my chaps up there. Stay here if you like, but please keep this side of the yellow tape. As you see, we've begun drawing a crowd."

Between the smoldering remains of the cottage and the sea, several cars had drawn up and a few people stood where they could watch the police dig around in the ruin. Among the little band of spectators was a tall fellow Gayle thought he recognized. The man was bigger than Gayle remembered, powerful through the shoulders, and close enough that one could see the cratered skin, the whiskers, the dark eyes....

It was Abdel from the garage, watching him.

Gayle quickly looked away, pretending not to have seen the Iraqi, pulled open the door, and dropped into the driver's seat. To his surprise, his heart was thrumming as it had in a desert sky full of arcing tracers, as it had when he'd heard the approaching footfall of his captors, coming to molest him. He waited for a moment, willing the excitement to subside. Then, with the threat mentally contained, he cranked the Saab and crept back down toward the road to Lyme Regis.

When he stopped at the bottom of the lane, the policewoman came over. "Very sorry about your friend, sir," she said.

"I thought the road was closed."

"So it is, sir."

"Then how'd we get a crowd of spectators up there?"

The cheery, open face closed like a fern. "I've no idea. Maybe they were up there all night."

Maybe, thought Gayle, pushing the old Saab toward Lyme Regis, toward the A35, toward home, maybe they were up there when Mouse was burned to ashes. Maybe Abdel had taken part.

Boss….I'm scared.

Me too, Mouse. Me too.

ABDEL WAS NOWHERE TO BE SEEN WHEN GAYLE PARKED THE SAAB in its narrow slot next to his Viggen, nor did that other eastern lad, Yusuf, come knocking at his door. Gayle put the wrapped pistol on his computer table and tossed the bomber jacket on the sofa, then poured himself a tumbler of whisky. Feeling leaden as a dead man, he sank into the faded bouquet of his chair and watched the ocean yield its color to the descending night.

When Gayle tried to conjure the Mickey Williams who had been, nothing came except the smoking ruin outside Lyme Regis, the unspeakable stuff the detective called human remains, the improbability of Williams dying in a propane accident.

But if not an accident, what?

Suicide?

Not a chance.

Murder?

By whom, and why?

And, if murder, what did one do? Take it to Detective Inspector Wickers, who thought the idea of a bomb too droll for words? Put the Tariq's muzzle into Abdel's mouth and torture out the motive, the names and locations of the guilty?

It was, Gayle realized, the Hamlet problem: action required certainty, and he was certain of nothing. He wasn't even sure he could remember enough of their last conversation to reconstruct the strands that Williams had braided into a conspiracy.

I'm thinking we all started from the same square one, down in Iraq, and now there's just the two of us left.

Started what, Mouse?

Ebola off a lavatory seat. An old syphilis.

Gayle pushed up his sleeves and studied his forearms. Nothing. No aches, no pains, no pimples. Heartbroken about old Mouse, everything else okay.

Ah, but what about Abdel?

When I go out now I see Arabs everywhere. I feel their eyes upon me. It's a web that we were all stuck upon, and I'm just the first to figure it out.

Figure *what* out, Mouse?

I'll send you an e-mail.

Gayle moved to his table and took the computer off standby, waited while the spectral Tornado coalesced with its constellation of icons, and went to his mail box. There was another missive from his editor wondering when he could read about Swiss Air Force caves. Several fresh slices of spam promising to increase size and endurance, reduce mortgage payments, and introduce Hot Russian Girls. And there was the promised note from Mickey Williams.

Boss, sorry to burden you, but time is short and you will need to know what I think I know. Like in our old kite, always good to have that second pair of eyes.

First, about the others of The Ten. We were repatriated the end of April 1991. For years, nothing. Then we began to die.

Boots Anderson. *Continued as active backseater. Miramar Naval Air Station, near San Diego. Late on the night of 9 July 1996 he went off the cliff at Torrey Pines in his little Zed Four. Girlfriend at his side.*

Rainy night but the car burned like a magnesium flare. Identified by DNA.

*   **Bill Elliott, Stan Lieb, Tommy Wilson, Geraldo Fuentes.** Our four American comrades in captivity. Stayed in army, all warrant officers flying Blackhawks from Stuttgart. On 12 November 2000 with ski party down to Austria's Kitzsteinhorn Mountain. Their funicular train started up one side of Kaprun tunnel, 3300 meters long. About 600 meters in, carriage caught fire. Electrical heater and hydraulic leakage blamed. Tunnel acted as chimney, nozzling fire which reached 2000 F or better. Twelve escaped by running downhill away from the smoke, 155 trapped and killed, eight Yanks, including our four. Identified by DNA.*

*   **Char & Maby.** Our SAS sergeants. Didn't know they had Christian names, but they did, Cecil and Crispin, respectively. They shook off captivity, no problem. On 12 October 2002 they were patrolling in the Kush with small contingent of Royal Marines and Afghan trainees. Things relatively quiet, Taliban licking wounds in Pakistan, Americans talking glorious victory, etc. But our boys were caught in a green on blue by their Afghan chums. Bodies burned to ash. Big stink in press at the time about this. Char and Maby id'ed by DNA.*

*   **Koenig.** Never knew his Christian name either. Dag, it was. Iraq broke him utterly. Wound up living alone on the Swedish coast up Göteburg way, selling travel blurbs a penny a pound. Nobody knows what happened exactly. His shack went up in flames. They said you could see it from Copenhagen (which I doubt). Human remains assumed to be Koenig's. Poor lad. Probably glad to have it over.*

*   So, Boss, that leaves just you and me to ask the questions. Like are these just random events or are they pieces in a mosaic? Is there a design?*

*   Eight of us dead, eight of us also reduced to ashes. We come home and all is good. Then, four years on, poof, there goes Anderson. Four years further, the tunnel fire kills four more. Two years later, Char and Maby. Then Koenig. So, are we waiting our turns? Or am I just infected with the heebie jeebies?*

*   I admit to being puzzled. The four Yanks, for example. They were flying Blackhawks. Nobody easier to kill than helicopter crew, fluttering*

around in those flammable shells. And why, if you only want the four, kill a hundred fifty others? Doesn't make sense.

And Char and Maby. How would anyone find them, much less murder them, in the vastness of Afghanistan? Special ops aren't in the social columns.

And poor old Boots. State trooper who was first on the scene said Boots was hot-dogging it along the top of the cliff. Dangerous play, it sounds like. But can you imagine Anderson playing, ever? I don't think he did even as a child.

None of this quite parses. And yet in my gut I just damned well know that these weren't accidents. Somebody is picking us off, God knows why.

So we go back to those few weeks in our shitty little spa. The ten of us are nicely softened up by Republican Guardsmen. Then, suddenly, the war is over and done, all the other prisoners of war go home, but we do not. Instead, this kindly doctor "rescues" us, puts us in a nice clean hospital, and supposedly gets us strong enough to go back to our so-called lives.

I remember almost nothing but good treatment, gentle nurses, white sheets, the doctor always sweet. But I also remember we had no natural light, nor ever heard a sound from the outside. We could have been in a sunken ship at the bottom of the sea. And I remember waking moments as the exception, where the rule was sleep. We slept like the dead.

I think we were drugged and kept in a secret place so they could do something to us. Use us as lab rats. Brainwash us. God knows. But I wager that, were we to return to Iraq, we would find no trace of that hospital, or those nurses, or the good doctor.

The good doctor, thought Gayle. I should have told Mouse about seeing Al-Rabiah. I wish, I wish, I wish.

Something was done to us, Boss. I keep thinking of those Tuskegee syphilis experiments in America in the thirties, infecting black men to chart the course of the disease. Maybe the Iraqis used us as guinea pigs to study Mesopotamiosis (is there such a thing?) or some other disorder close to their black hearts. Maybe there were more than ten of us to begin with and we're the surviving half of a nerve gas L:D 50 experiment. Or maybe we were rewired in some way, made into Manchurian candidates, had our memories fucked with. God knows. Then off we went back to the world, none the wiser.

Except, over time, we began to come apart, wires rusting, synapses reviving, immune system working the problem, post-traumatic stress, whatever. And as the Iraqi creation came apart, the Iraqi hand became more and more visible.

Maybe this crud of mine is what happens when the thing unravels. Maybe Anderson and the four Yanks and the SAS boys and our Swede also caught the crud and had to be eradicated. If so, the people who did the others will want to do something about me.

I bloody well know I have a monitor. There's this young chap from somewhere out east, a powerful-looking bloke with a thin beard and scars from an old pox. He has been everywhere, unable to take those soft, heartless Arab eyes off me. If my surmise is right, and he sees my middle-aged acne, the terrible thing will happen.

I believe I know what to expect, Boss. In some ways it would have been better to forget the others. Well, it is always better not to know the future. But now it's too late. I've brought upon myself a crippling fear of being dragged out and humiliated further by those snake-voiced beggars.

Death doesn't frighten me, but I hate to think of my simple, reasonably happy existence just ceasing to be and my poor old place going up in smoke with Peter Rabbit's and the roses charred to ash. Well, how I careen. I shall be very glad to see you. Mouse.

Then: *visitors boss in ford or vhall estate knock on door enter three men dressed as bugs look me up and down shit heres rdoc im 9 watchoutwatchoutwatchout*

"Well Mouse," Gayle murmured, "the terrible thing has happened." He shut his eyes for a moment, envisioning the ruined cottage, then the Iraqi man, Abdel, watching him. Now, thought Gayle, the minders, if minders is what they are, can concentrate on me.

At the foot of Williams' message Gayle read:

Attachment 1: softporn.jpg(image/jpeg)

Opening the file was like resurrecting the dead. As Gayle watched, the person who now existed only as human remains was reconstituted on the screen, bit by bit, until, at last, there was Mickey Williams sitting in nothing but sky blue boxer shorts, a broad grin on the thin red lips, green eyes twinkling, ruddy cheeks clear. Very soft porn indeed, thought Gayle.

But something had gone wrong with the pale, freckled skin. A russet stipple of what looked like tiny, red rivets crossed Williams' chest and ran along his limbs, here and there marked with a sheen of clear serum pinked with blood. Looking at it, Gayle sensed that what he saw was just a faint suggestion of a more intricately tangled web beneath the surface.

Gayle closed the snapshot, restoring Mouse to the aether, and returned to the letter.

visitors boss in ford or vhall estate

He thought of the cottage in early evening, night just draping the coastal hills, a Ford or Vauxhall estate gliding silently up to Williams' gate.

enter three men dressed as bugs

Dressed as bugs. Masks? Goggles? Antennae? Gossamer wings? Enter three men wearing some sort of costume. Why? To hide their identities? To avoid contamination? To keep from catching what Williams had?

shit heres rdoc

Gayle wrote the message out on a foolscap sheet:

HERES RDOC

Here's our doc.

Gayle imagined the tableau inside the cottage, Williams near his computer table, seated, as in the photo, the intruders a few meters away. Guns come out. One of the three men drops his mask. Deliberately? Of course. Al-Rabiah wants Williams to recognize him. Surprise, the Angel of Mercy is really the Angel of Death.

Surprise, Mouse, it isn't just a bunch of unconnected dots. I told you wrong. When I mix in the circumstances of your death those dots snap together like Lego blocks.

Encountering Al-Rabiah at the Victoria could no longer be seen as a coincidence, nor could the fact that Anna, lovely, loving Anna of the false everything, was a nurse. They'd wanted to give their English squadron-leader chum a secret medical once-over, check him for leaks, for neutrons, for a brain in need of further washing. "Anna," Gayle muttered, "you should be on the bloody stage."

Hoping to generate rage, Gayle found he could summon only regret and a kind of general grief, for himself, for that lying girl, for poor lost Mouse and the other eight. His first impulse was not to fight, but to slip into mourning and despair.

Gayle peered past the computer screen at the fading glow upon the sea, the necklaces of light winking on along the ocean front; a low, surf-like murmur rose from the congested streets where workers crept toward home. He pressed closer to the glass, where he could look down into his own road, knowing that, if he looked hard enough, he would see his Iraqi minder. Ah, there he was, and not at all difficult to find, either.

Abdel stood just outside a cone of light from a streetlamp, his eyes on Gayle's lighted window as he sucked on a cigarette, the veil of smoke drifting off into the gathering darkness. Now the other lad, Yusuf, came over, the two men chatted, shared another cigarette. Yusuf would have been the third guy in a bug suit. Cocky bastards, strutting about like dangerous men. Well, and maybe they *were* dangerous enough for Peter Gayle. Almost certainly they'd wiped away old Gurney to put Yusuf in his place. They'd fixed poor Mickey Williams. If Al-Rabiah said the word, they'd come after him.

And now, at last, the sight of these self-important boys from the east, recently returned from murdering one's old friend, caused rage to flicker within. Gayle felt the angry leap of the heart one needed going into battle, the low flame that let a man dogfight an enemy into the slow, tightening spirals of the merge, or raze a neighborhood with bombs, no questions asked. He looked at Williams' letter on the screen.

im 9

"Nine you may be, old Mouse. But I'll not be bloody ten."

MUCH OF THE EVENING WAS SPENT FIGURING OUT HOW TO REASSEMBLE the Tariq pistol, which Gayle had separated into small parts arranged like metal chessmen across his computer table. Its years spent with a stuffed monkey had not been kind to the weapon, which had begun to rust; the slide caught and cobwebs clouded the bore.

Because pistols of the same epoch are much alike, Gayle found, once his memory engaged, that the Tariq broke down more or less like the Browning nine-millimeter in his RAF survival kit. Looking at the pieces arrayed before him, he thought it would be just the time for Abdel and Yusuf to burst through his door in bug suits, guns drawn. "Perfick." He'd have to ask them to wait a minute, while he tried to put the damned ugly thing back together.

But as he cleaned and oiled each piece, as he ejected and wiped down each round in the magazine, and finally got the device back together, Gayle thought it was not such a bad looking bit of machinery after all. The bore was a gleaming whorl of rifling and the slide now seemed frictionless. He pulled the trigger on an empty chamber—the hollow click made him start—and slid the cartridges back into their magazine, which he pushed into the grip with his palm. Now all he needed was a target—that and time, distance, and money.

He bought some time with an e-mail to his editor: *Swiss Hornet caves are back on, maybe a ride in their F-18, off to Bern in a.m. EADS also active. Will return via Toulouse for more on JUMBO and the new American tanker mess. I'll check messages. Home in a fortnight.*

Distance was more difficult, and Gayle wished, not for the first time, that Britain were not an island and that Europe were a bigger place. In North America you could swing a two-thousand-mile radius encompassing vast, empty spaces. Had he wished to flee, he would have headed for Montana or British Columbia, places as remote from Brighton as the moon.

But fleeing was never an option. If one fled, Gayle understood, one's enemies simply followed at a leisurely pace until they overhauled you at the end of your tether. Europe's empty spaces were a bit closer together than America's; swing a five-hundred mile radius from Zurich and you got the whole thing. This meant that any pursuers would never be more than a day's drive away. Gayle thought he could still cut himself some geographic slack.

Once across the Channel, the Viggen would take him a thousand miles in a day, to Vienna tomorrow evening, where he could shake some truth out of perfidious Anna the Nurse. By the time Al-Rabiah and company found him, he would have wrung enough from her to take the matter to the Ministry of Defense. From there, Her Majesty's government would work the problem.

As for money, Gayle's RAF war pension already went automatically to the account at the UBS branch in Montreux, where his mother had once cached what they'd called the Victoria Fund. Money from Jane's went into a current account at the Royal Bank of Scotland branch down the road. He would leave that as it was; in time, his editor would realize his correspondent had gone missing and cut it off.

The local bank also held his mother's secret cache, a savings account into which she had quietly siphoned some ten thousand pounds, a pound or two at a time, like a magician pulling coins out of the air. Gayle had left that money where it lay, gathering interest, growing like a tumor for more than twenty-five years.

Gayle composed a letter asking Henry Munro, the erstwhile Harrier pilot who managed the branch, to transfer all but a thousand pounds to the USB account in Montreux. He said he was looking at a Swiss condo, time was of the essence, signed hard copy to follow by post, many thanks, happy landings, bye-bye. He faxed the letter to

Munro, then put the original in an envelope, sealed it, and pressed on a file of green Elizabeth II profiles from a roll of stamps.

Dinner was another pair of four-minute eggs and a Cornish pastie thawed in the microwave, washed down by a couple of tumblers of whisky. While he ate, Gayle watched the eight o'clock news, hoping for another glimpse of Anna or her twin, but there was none.

"Mystery explosion near Lyme Regis" made the news, however, with a woman reporter named Trilla Something on the scene, banks of lights illuminating the rubble that had been Williams' cottage, festively wrapped in yellow police tape, men and women in white coveralls haunting the place. Wickers suddenly filled the frame, rolling his eyes at the reporter's calling it a mystery explosion. "We are about ninety-nine percent certain it was propane," said the detective. "Ninety-nine percent."

Bored with such practicality, Trilla moved on to a young witness she called Ali. Gayle leaned forward. It was Abdel, posturing on national television.

"You actually saw it happen?"

"Yes," said Abdel, cool as could be, although those soft eyes moved around like a bad dog's. "I thought it was a car bomb, like at home."

"Home being…?"

"Baghdad."

"Was anyone near the cottage that you could see?"

"I was too far down the hill. I saw nobody. Just this big flash." He gave his broad shoulders a shrug. "Very scary," he added, showing off.

Gayle thrust his chin toward the screen. "Walk her through the murder, you lying bag of shit."

But Abdel was gone, replaced by Wickers. "We know very little about Michael Williams, the man who we believe died in the fire. Quiet chap, kept to himself. We understand he flew Tornadoes in the first Gulf War. He did occasional work at a boat-building school down in Lyme Regis."

The BBC father figure returned. "Thanks, Trilla." When he said, "Elsewhere…" Gayle switched the television off. He didn't give a damn about elsewhere. Then he and the pistol went off to bed.

At five Gayle got up in darkness, showered and dressed in a black cotton turtleneck and khakis, stout socks and walking shoes. He packed what he thought he'd need in the weathered olive-drab garment bag, adding a couple of fresh shirts in plastic sleeves and a spare tie. He drank what remained of the orange juice in the fridge, put some cherry jam on the last fragment of baguette, and brewed a mug of milky tea.

Eating at his computer table, Gayle peered at the street below, still empty at this hour, and no sign of his minders. He washed up and put everything away, in case his flat had visitors. Finally, he went to the computer and copied Mouse's last message onto a compact disk, deleting it from his mail box and emptying the e-trash.

He pulled on his bomber jacket, stowed the disk in one deep zippered pocket and the pistol in the other. Picking up his bag and khaki raincoat, he stood for a moment in the sitting room of the flat that had been home for so many years, sad as a sailor abandoning a beloved ship to the sea. Closing the door would be a bit like dying. "Not to worry, Avery," he told the colobus. "I'll be back." Gayle thought it sounded like a lie.

Dawn was just a molten suggestion in the eastern sky when Gayle left his building, the city almost silent, its morning clamor still an hour away. He crossed to a red pillar box to post the Munro letter, then turned back toward the garage.

Gayle was sentimental about his machines, and the first sight of his Saabs roosting side by side always lifted his heart. He gave the elder car a pat, then opened the Viggen's boot and dropped in his raincoat and bag.

As he closed the boot, Gayle caught something on the air, an odor he could not immediately place, then recognized. It was the familiar interrogation-room recipe: old blood, human waste, and perspiration spread on musty stones; add a dash of cold fear. He gripped the pistol in his pocket. "Abdel?"

A voice he'd never heard before replied. "Good morning, Mr. Gayle. And, please, no guns. This is not the All Right Corral." The speaker stepped out of the shadows, and Gayle turned to look at him. Another visitor from the east, leather jacket, khakis, mad-scientist glasses glinting against a finely cut olive face with a short, untended beard just going grey. Several other figures moved silently in the shadows beyond.

"Who are you?"

"Call me Charlie. Or Bill. Harry. Whatever."

"What do you want with me?"

"I was hoping you might help us." He fiddled with a pipe as he spoke, then lighted it, sending a plume of fragrant smoke into the dank air of the garage. "Come."

Gayle paused, weighing his options. Flight was not among them, as two of the enshadowed figures had drifted toward the entry. He could see their silenced pistols, long as short swords, against the rising light outside, waiting for him to yank the Tariq out of his coat pocket.

He followed the visitor into the darkness.

Yusuf knelt against the far wall, hands cuffed in plastic rings behind him, eyes fixed on the cement floor, his body trembling and fouled with fear, his face a child's finger painting done in blood.

Several meters away, Abdel sprawled, hands cuffed behind him, but all resistance gone. A shining stream from what remained of his skull meandered across the cracked cement floor.

"As you see, we are a serious lot." The stranger leaned close enough that Gayle could smell his breakfast, "Serious, but not infallible. For example," he went on, moving away slowly, motioning for Gayle to follow, "we wasted a good deal of time talking to your friend, Mr. Churches."

"Who?"

The man chuckled. "He had not heard of you either. And yet, everything suggested that you and he must be linked."

"Never heard of him."

"I fear we put him through quite an ordeal before we realized he was not being strong; he was empty. We will try to spare you that, Mr. Gayle."

"Good, I like being spared things."

"Then tell me about Mr. Emerson."

"Emerson?"

"American agent of all work, it seems. We keep hearing his name, always murmured, always in the distance."

"I don't know this Emerson."

"Well what do you know, Mr. Gayle?"

Gayle glanced at Abdel, at poor Yusuf, and thought he would have to begin turning over some of his cards if he wanted to walk out of the garage. "Very little. My friend Mickey Williams died night before last. Yusuf and Abdel may have played a part."

"Yusuf said as much."

"Did he say why?"

"Even under some duress, he did not."

"Maybe he doesn't know."

"And you, do you know?"

Gayle shook his head.

"But you know enough to pack a bag and get an early start. Where are you going?"

"I have business in Switzerland."

"Nonsense, you were taking it on the lam."

"I hate trouble."

"You were a prisoner of war in Iraq."

"Yes."

"There were ten of you. The April Ten, so-called. I remember. Tell me about your captivity."

"Rather brutal, wore us down to nothing. Some took it more to heart than others. Then this Iraqi doctor…"

"The one calling himself Al-Rabiah."

Gayle nodded, taking a moment's silence to palm the Hotel Victoria card, and also Anna, his duplicitous queen of hearts. "Al-Rabiah moved us to a proper hospital."

"Where was this proper hospital?"

"God knows."

"In a mountain cave?"

"I've no idea. We were somehow moved from prison to a hospital. We woke in a ward. Beds, nurses, doctors. I never saw a cave." Never mind the cave of my bad dreams.

"We have a special interest in a certain cave in the north of Iraq, Mr. Gayle. Churches knew about it. Emerson has sent people into it. The same people who whisper about this cave also whisper your name. How do you explain that?"

Gayle shook his head.

The man studied him, eyes hidden behind the shiny disks of his glasses, the face quite closed. "Very well," he said at last, "we turn the page. What do you think they did to you in this hospital? Feed you up for repatriation?"

"I don't think anything," he said, deciding this Charlie-Bill-Harry-whatever fellow didn't need to know about Williams' skin problems. "Mickey believed they'd done something to us. He couldn't say what, but he was sure they'd fiddled with us in some way. Used us as lab rats, played with our minds. Mickey began checking up on the others of the Ten. All eight died in accidents. He saw a conspiracy, and thought that he'd be ninth. He was right about being ninth."

"With any luck, you will not be number ten, Mr. Gayle."

"I'd like that. Which side are you on?"

"Side?" The man shrugged. "I wish it were so simple. We are just looking out for ourselves. We are on the way to having our own homeland after centuries spent wandering the lands of others. Milk and honey, prosperity, stability, autonomy." He smiled. "Oil. Chicken in every pot. Good times just around the corner."

"If things are so good, why bother with this?" Gayle nodded toward the captives.

"Because the voices we hear, the fragments of information we gather by this means and that, say Saddam developed a terrible new weapon."

"Saddam is history."

"But his successors gather in the wings." The man was silent for a moment. "The new dictator in Baghdad will want our homeland, our milk and honey, our autonomy, our oil, perhaps our lives. We have been what you call lab rats too. Our history tells us to expect the worst. So when we hear of a terrible new weapon our ears prick."

"If you find it, what then?"

"We take it out of play."

"But it could give you an advantage."

"What we need, we have. But what we have we intend to keep, at any price."

"Did these boys tell you anything at all?

"Yusuf said he was ordered to look after you. Indeed, we first heard your name in intercepted wireless calls between Yusuf and his mentor. 'I am transferring you to Peter Gayle,' he told Yusuf. 'Keep a close eye on Peter Gayle. Apprise me of the condition of Peter Gayle.' That is what led us to you."

"Why were they minding me?"

"We asked these poor dogs that very question, over and over. They displayed a convincing ignorance."

"What happens now?"

"We detain you for a time."

"I have other fish to fry."

"So have we all. But we must finish this business. The thing we seek, whatever it is, has been concealed behind a very complicated lock. You are the first thing that looks at all like a key. So we must hang on to you for a little while."

"Stake me out for the tiger to find?"

"No, no, no. We are both in the same ship. While you are our guest, we shall let slip a few hints as to where you are and with whom. When the people who sent out poor Abdel and Yusuf come a-knock-knock-knocking at our door, we shall ask them what they've been up to. When they reply to our satisfaction, you will be free to carry on frying those other fish. But I must have your weapon, lest it lead you into temptation."

Gayle handed over the Tariq. "It has sentimental value. I'd like it back."

"Of course. All in good time."

They had circled the garage floor as they talked, and were now back near Gayle's Saabs. Yusuf still knelt, but seemed calmer, lulled by his growing knowledge of the inevitable. A young man in a hooded sweat shirt and jeans stood just behind him, a silenced pistol in one hand, watching for a signal. When the leader nodded the boy shot Yusuf in the back of the head. The dead man flopped forward, his skull leaking everything he'd known; he lay like someone dropped from a passing airplane.

"Too bad, but we need his silence. One of the sad things about our situation, Abdel's, Yusuf's, mine, is that we are so expendable. Nobody outside the immediate family notices when an Iraqi disappears. No one will miss these two boys." He gave another of his shrugs and regarded the two cars. "As we have fair weather, Mr. Gayle, let's take the soft top. You drive. It isn't far."

X

Painted kelp green and smelling of mould, lime, cement, and human waste, the concrete enclosure could have been centuries old. The brushed-out scratches on its walls spoke of vast fetches of time, of days ticked off one by one until the timekeepers lost the temporal thread. Entering the room, one felt the river of seconds and minutes and hours, of days and years and decades, begin to freeze.

A narrow plastic cot was anchored to the wall in one corner, next to an American-style toilet and sink, both made of a tough, grey polymer. The only decorative touch was an olive drab blanket spread on the scuffed surface of the floor, bearing a small table and two lawn chairs, all in flamingo-colored plastic. There was no window. Light came from a fluorescent tube in a ceiling fixture covered with wire-reinforced glass, well out of reach of the man who lived there.

Dressed in tangerine prison coveralls, he lay supine on the unyielding cot. His round, melancholy face retained some of the shrewd sleekness of the westernized scientist; beneath the Arab mask one could still discern a British subject. The dark eyes gleamed with longing, as if in constant expectation of looking beyond the walls into the open distance, which they had not done in years. The outside world was just a fading visual memory.

His teeth, once rendered perfect by a Minneapolis clinic, were no longer quite the gleaming white fangs the world had seen on television, where he had expounded on the futility of the American search for Iraqi weapons of mass destruction. His scalp gleamed through a thin thatch of hair, now almost entirely grey. His beard was starkly black or white, like the pelt of a skunk, its growth regulated by a large tattooed Nubian who never spoke, but arrived once a month with his scissors.

Like all men who live alone and in silence, the resident longed to speak, to hear a human voice; the slightest kindness made him want to weep, although he had never shown his captors anything like a tear. The approach of familiar footsteps made his heart leap like a dog's; he thanked God he had no tail. Now he kept his gaze fixed on his visitor's face, trying not to look at or think about what might be in the Lord & Taylor shopping bag.

"Hello, Salam," said Emerson, taking one of the pink chairs.

"Ah, another visit from Satan." Salam Nasser sat up, put on a droll smile. "Welcome to Hell."

"I would say Purgatory, my friend. Hell is forever. Purgatory, well, you never know."

"I know. I am here for the rest of my life."

"Maybe not," said Emerson, aware that both of them heard the lie. "Lot of people out there working for your release."

"I once thought they might succeed, as I did nothing to warrant this." He waved a hand at his shrunken universe. "Politics, of course, is interested only in itself."

"You sneered at the Coalition."

"I only told them the truth."

"With a sneer. With contempt."

"You lot *were* contemptible. I called a spade a spade."

"You called a big, strong Negro a Spade, my friend."

"I did not."

"Metaphorically. You wrapped the truth in an insult. Proof you're English-educated maybe, but it hasn't helped your case."

"It's true, I don't suffer fools gladly."

"We fools are still outside, Salam. While you suffer."

Such banter had become the overture to their occasional meetings, to a day or week of interrogation, some further erosion of the prisoner's knowledge of who, what, and where he was, and why. The first round had been conducted years earlier in the detention center at Baghdad International, after Salam Nasser, believing himself innocent of any crime, had walked into an American checkpoint, hands raised, hopes high.

Then, festooned with chains and blindfolded, he had taken the long flight to this tiny room. The interrogations had resumed with added vigor, the usual humiliating stuff: days of wandering naked among his captors, exposure to menstrual blood and human excrement, female interrogators coyly revealing a nipple or a shadowy crotch; now and then a visit to the water board, or a mock execution. But he never feared the Americans would kill him. Their belief that he knew something was too strong. "This old goose has no golden eggs inside," he told them, but they had pretended not to hear.

Except for those sessions, Nasser spent his life alone and left his cell only for an hour's mild exercise each day. He never saw the sky, or other prisoners, he never felt the kiss of the living atmosphere, never knew whether it was night or day. He would have killed to see a bird in flight. His seventieth birthday had come and gone without his knowing it.

"I retired from the army in 1993," he told his tormentors. "Since then I have given some scientific advice to the government. But I directed nothing, I arranged nothing. My wife Esme is a British subject. I have spent as much time in England as in Iraq. I have invariably told you the truth."

Because such straight talk took him nowhere, Nasser tried fiction. He allowed them to extract details of his work on mobile biolabs, where anthrax powder was grown and loaded into bombs, which were strapped to small radio-controlled aircraft capable of reaching Israel. He confessed to secret shopping trips to Niger's uranium mines, of plutonium stashes now lost in the Iraqi desert, of using contacts in Pakistan and Germany to acquire aluminum tubes for centrifuges. You want mushroom clouds, here you are. Robot submarines no larger than a dolphin? Why not? Suicide dogs? Links to Al Quaeda? Here they are. It was never enough.

"What about nine-eleven?" they wanted to know.

And there Nasser would stop, beam a smile at them, and begin laughing like a madman. "Everthing I've told you is shit," he would cry, tears running down his cheeks, "all just shit. It's what you asked for, and what you so richly deserve."

Emerson didn't mind the fiction or the mad laughter. "You want to crack his nerve without his quite realizing it," he cautioned his colleagues. "We *want* these excursions from reality. We *want* him to wonder who he is. But we also want him to look at me as his one and only."

They had reached that point more than a year ago, when both Emerson and Nasser privately acknowledged that nothing much would ever change, that they were yoked. They remained adversaries, captor and captive, but the fight had gone out of them. Now they leaned upon each other like exhausted boxers, lifting leaden fists in soft jabs that had become almost caresses.

"So, what brings you to Hell, Sahib? Did you miss me?"

"I did."

"Enough to come all this way?"

Emerson feigned surprise. "All what way?"

"To this place. We flew for hours, I remember. Thousands of miles."

"Maybe we did. Or maybe we just went out and circled and came back to Baghdad. Maybe all I had to do today was helicopter out from the Green Zone."

"This can't be Baghdad."

"Sure it can."

"I would know it. My heart would tell me."

"Your heart hasn't a clue."

"But I hear things."

"Of course you do."

"I hear people speaking."

"What do they say?"

"I can't understand them."

"Italian?"

"No, I would recognize Italian."

"Not Japanese?"

"Definitely not."

"Rumanian?"

"I haven't heard those slippery vowel sounds."

"So you're not in Bucharest?"

The prisoner chuckled dismissively. "The game's over, Emerson. I know where I am. I figured it out."

"Tell me."

"You will just deny it."

"I won't."

"Well, then….Bulgaria!"

Emerson shook his head in mock admiration. "By Allah, Salam, you old fox."

Nasser beamed. "You see? You see?"

"What tipped you off?"

"Voices. Speaking something very rough, but like Russian."

"I thought maybe you'd had your windshield wipers stolen."

"What?"

"That's how I know I'm in Bulgaria. My wiper blades disappear."

"But I have no car."

"Then how do you know you're in Bulgaria?"

Nasser was silent for a time, and sad. Then, "I am not in Bulgaria, am I?"

Emerson shook his head. "Afraid not."

"Then where?"

"It doesn't matter."

"It does to me."

"What time is it?"

"I don't know."

"Day or night, morning or afternoon?"

Silence.

"Spring or fall, summer or winter?"

Nothing.

"A man who doesn't know when he is doesn't really need to know where."

"Am I really at the Baghdad airport?"

Emerson shrugged. "Your whereabouts are a closely guarded secret, which I cannot divulge to anyone." Then he waved a hand, acting impatient. "Enough foreplay already. Look what I brought you."

With canine interest, the prisoner got off the cot and approached the Lord & Taylor bag. He licked his lips, and wiped at them with his sleeve as his mouth filled with saliva.

"For the chess machine Esme gave you," said Emerson, holding up a four-pack of batteries.

"The original batteries died a year ago."

"Rome wasn't built in a day." Emerson's hand went back into the sack and came out with an ivory-colored envelope. "From Esme, with love and squalor. Uncensored, unread. The real stuff."

Nasser grabbed the envelope and retreated to the cot, where he put the letter under his pillow, then went back to watch Emerson with the bag.

"Something special," said Emerson, pulling out a pair of tangerine and white running shoes that had Velcro tabs instead of laces. "Color coordinated. Extremely comfortable."

"I can wear them when I make a run for it."

"Sure you can. But, wait, there's more." He fished out a crisply folded copy of the *International New York Times.*

Nasser snatched it away, controlling himself only with difficulty. He had not seen a newspaper since 2003. Then, wary of such kindness, he asked, "Is it real?"

"Printed in Paris."

"October thirty-second?"

"Made up. I was for just handing it over to you, but The Powers thought you could be dangerous if you got your calendar going again."

"So the stories are all so much shit."

"I don't know."

"This one. Saddam finds asylum in the Netherlands."

Emerson shrugged.

"You never caught him?"

"Slippery as an eel."

"And he surfaces in Amsterdam?"

"Whatever it says."

"I like this one. Vice-president shoots friend while hunting doves in Texas."

"Comedians had a field day."

Nasser flipped through the paper. "Henman takes Wimbledon?"

"Now *that* strains credulity."

"The Dow at twenty thousand?"

"Happy days are here again."

"So this paper is like the BBC's April Fool's broadcast. The Italian spaghetti harvest. That sort of thing."

"Don't worry about reality. Just lie back and enjoy having a newspaper."

"Is Saddam really in Amsterdam?"

"Like a gorilla in the mist."

"I don't believe you."

Emerson was busy studying his watch and made no reply.

"You got him, didn't you?"

"What do you think?"

"How could you not get him?"

"Good question. But let's move on. Let's dance."

Nasser sat down across the plastic table. "You want to know about our secret moon base."

"No, and I don't want a lot of invented shit from you either."

"How about the nuke we buried under the White House?"

"Come on."

"Our dirty little secret: we have no oil?"

"Then we've gone to a ton of trouble for nothing. Can we get serious now?"

"All right."

"Good. Forget Iraqi Freedom."

"I forgot it long ago, when you lot made it disappear."

"Be serious. We're back in the early nineties. You're, what, a brigadier general?" Emerson took out a pen and reporter's pad and pretended to take notes.

"Lieutenant general."

Emerson grinned. "Whatever." It always surprised him that men in Nasser's situation could still strut when it came to rank and position. "You're their weapons honcho."

"That's one way of putting it."

"You know about every sparrow that falls, weaponry-wise. Nuclear. Conventional. Germ. Gas. Everything."

"I had a broad portfolio, yes."

"We know about most of the stuff."

"Then you know everything I've told you was true. After the first conflict, we couldn't even find a coffee tin for hiding secrets. Besides, we had no secrets worth keeping. Dead in the water. Well, in the sand."

"But before that, there was a facility in the hills north of Erbil."

"Why not? We had facilities everywhere."

"This wasn't an arms cache. From what we could tell, it was a laboratory. In a cave."

"I'm thinking."

Yep, thought Emerson, you're thinking like a guy looking at his cards. "We went into the cave."

"You did?" Genuine surprise.

"Not me, my people. There'd been a hell of a fire, hot enough to melt rock and glass. Lots of gamma radiation, cesium 137 everywhere. And human remains, ash and some bone."

Nasser smiled. "And what did you make of all that, Emerson?"

"I'll tell you the honest truth…"

"Shall I alert the media?"

Emerson ignored him. "At first we thought it was a dirty-bomb factory where something had gone seriously wrong. A fission accident, maybe. What can you tell me?"

"I can tell you there has never been a nuclear fission detonation in Iraq."

"Okay, that fits. Turned out the cesium in the cave was more than twenty years old. So we think it must have gone in about the time of the first Gulf war. You would've heard about it."

"You weren't in Iraq in those days, Emerson. It was like Carthage at the end, we were eaten alive by rumors. Nobody thought you would stop where you did. We expected your victorious troops to march into Baghdad. So our orders were to rip out all the wires, the nuclear ones, the germ ones. To become like Caesar's wife." He shook his head sadly. "Nothing turned out as we expected. We overestimated your appetite for conquest in that first war. Then we underestimated your president's attachment to stunts and special effects. To Shock, to Awe. So, yes, I heard all sorts of stuff, hardly any of it true."

"What did you hear about the cave?"

"I'm trying to remember."

"Try harder."

"You know, Emerson, my memory would perform ever so much better if I knew where I was."

"Bulgaria."

"Where they pinch windscreen wipers."

"That's the place."

"I wish I could believe you."

"Unless I got it wrong."

"You prick."

"Maybe it's Ohio."

"Bastard."

"Tell me what you heard about the cave."

"I can't remember."

"Shall I ask my associates to help?"

Nasser paled, but did not flinch. "Do what you will." He left the chair and retired to the cot, where he sat cross-legged, his back against the corner of the wall. "I think our interview is over."

"Not until the lieutenant general sings."

For a time they sat in silence, Nasser pouting in the corner, Emerson studying the doodles in his notebook, knowing that no man who lives in silence can resist the opportunity to speak.

"We had so many facilities in those day," Nasser said at last. "Lots of arms caches, lots of buried rockets and tunnels. We had nuclear sites. Biological ones, chemical ones." A calculated pause. "But no caves in the north."

"I don't believe you."

"Too bad."

"Salam, here is what I will do. If you crank up your memory, I will tell you where you are."

"And tell Esme?"

"I can only tell you."

"Then tell me."

"What did you hear about the cave?"

Nasser hugged his knees, rocking slowly on the cot, until silence again became unbearable. "We did hear of one cave facility. It was never in my portfolio."

"But you know what they did there."

"Not really. It was very secret. After the first war, we heard that they had dismantled it. Well, more than dismantled. Made it as if it had never been. But nobody told us what they did there."

"You must have suspected something."

"It wasn't nuclear, I knew where all the nuclear work was, and there wasn't enough electricity up there. So we assumed chemical, biological…"

"And the human remains?"

"Probably Kurds, used like rhesus monkeys and beagles in nerve-gas experiments. You know, L:D 50s, stake them out and see what it takes to kill fifty percent of them." He smiled. "It's considered bad form to use humans."

"Hence the urgency to make the place disappear."

"I suppose so. They wouldn't have wanted that coming to light."

Emerson waited for more, but nothing came. Again, silence congealed in the room. "That's it?"

Nasser nodded.

"And for that you expect me to divulge state secrets?"

"I expect you to keep your word."

"Have I ever?"

"It's never too late to start, Emerson."

"You didn't get me where I needed to go, Salam. You fucking let me down." The American got up, stowed his notebook and pen, and rolled up the Lord & Taylor bag. "Enjoy your chess game. Enjoy the *Times*. I'll see you in a year or two."

"There *was* one other thing."

"Tell me."

"Where am I?"

"Bulgaria."

"I was right."

"Cunning dog. So tell me."

"Am I really in Bulgaria?"

"Cross my heart and hope to die. Tell me."

"Not all the subjects were Kurds. We heard that some prisoners of war were there as well. At the end of the conflict, in early March of 1991, we repatriated a group of ten prisoners, then another group of thirty-five. But there were rumors of a third group of ten, kept in prison until the end of February, but not repatriated until late April."

"The April Ten. I remember."

"We heard they spent those missing weeks in the cave."

"Doing what?"

"God knows. As I say, Baghdad was like Carthage at the end. Most of us didn't think the prisoners story was true."

"It's true. Enjoy Bulgaria."

"Next time, bring me some hemlock." The voice had already begun to die, silence filling the room like the fall of night. "When do you come back?"

"I never know." Emerson hammered on the door, which was opened immediately by an American guard in a polo shirt and denims. Emerson looked back at Nasser, crouched on the cot, broken without quite knowing it. "Bye bye," he said. Then, with the door shut behind him, he marched in step with the faux civilian toward a faint light at the end of the corridor.

A female Army captain in desert camouflage with IVY stenciled on her nametag sat behind a grey metal desk near the entrance. "How'd it go?"

"Pretty well. He's decided he's in Bulgaria. Change some of the ambient sounds. Give him someplace else. Texas, Taiwan. You pick the place. Surprise me."

Crossing the parking area, Emerson experienced the chilly reptilian tremor that was, for him, a leap of the heart. His old Iraqi chum had produced like one of Al Capp's shmoos, tons of milk and eggs. Now the boys back home could begin running down that April Ten, names, ranks, serial numbers, whereabouts, fates. What had been an impossibly cold trail suddenly bloomed with scent.

He would head back to the hotel, have a couple of vodkas in the room, from which he could see the whorls of the old city spread across the broad bowl between the mountains, the dying light on minarets and golden domes. He would take dinner in the Losenets Restaurant, where a slender, translucently pale blonde tirelessly stroked her piano keys with red-nailed porcelain fingers. Then a good night's sleep and out to Vrazdebna to catch the Gulfstream back to planet Earth.

Emerson unlocked the black embassy Audi and started to climb behind the wheel, then stopped. The wiper blades were gone. He uttered a great haw of a laugh and shook his head in amused admiration. "Welcome to Bulgaria. Son of a bitch."

XI

Alexey Ivanovich Palev appeared on the green horizon of Kolomenskij Park, moving down the tree-lined path with an old man's deliberate slow motion, as if the ground might at any moment part beneath him, as if each step would be his last. He kept his eyes fixed upon the sandy track, now and then shuffling to a stop to look up and check his surroundings.

Krylov watched him approach, the legs swinging forward carefully, like limbs of glass, one-two, one-two, with the contrapuntal pecking of a birch cane. He had expected the Palev he remembered from the old days, the assured academician who had bent like a giant tree over his band of KGB cadets, seconded to Biopreparat to learn about germ warfare, as the world called it then, and leaving months later with a fount of new knowledge and Palev's dictum engraved upon their minds: "Life is the bridge between birth and death; biology is the study of bridges." Now here came this poor fellow, vanishing almost before one's eyes, like a figure carved from wax.

His brown tweed jacket, worn smooth as velvet, was sizes too big, his grey corduroy trousers gathered like a draw-string purse around his narrow waist; his shirt was the color of ancient bones, with a vivid green tie looping his thin neck like a noose. As always, he wore a lapel pin that told the world he had fought in the Great Patriotic War—that he had accompanied his motherland through her grand, heart-breaking climb to the twenty-first century. The pin said he had seen it all and was old Russia right down to his toes.

"Alexey Ivanovich," Krylov called, "I'm over here."

The older man looked up with the immediate sharp interest of a sparrow, then, recognizing an old friend, he smiled and accelerated ever so slightly. Krylov met him halfway, offered an arm to lean on, and steered them to a wooden bench overlooking the steep descent to the pinched blue curl of the Moscow River.

Palev sank gratefully upon the bench, and for a time seemed to have forgotten about Krylov. His blue eyes strained toward the water and beyond, over the old industrial ghettos of southeast Moscow, where he had spent much of his career. "I shall be with you in a moment, Viktor Viktorivich," he said in Russian, breathing with some difficulty. "When my heart beats more like a man's and less like a hummingbird's, then we talk." He gave Krylov a pat on the arm to apologize for the delay.

Krylov didn't mind waiting. He was happy to be home. The old city had never looked more beautiful than in this woman's summer. The trees resisted autumn's impulse toward sleep, the sky glowed like a blue ceramic bowl, the southbound sun touched drab buildings with gold and transformed golden domes into globes of molten light.

Not very long ago, in the interval when Mother Russia seemed to have died and gone to Hell, the city had stunk of poverty, abyssal hopelessness, an oxygen of fear. Now Mother Russia was back, although no longer the robust peasant girl from the old Soviet posters, pink-cheeked and large of bosom in her coveralls. This incarnation was young and beautiful and a bit hard, cold as a film star in a fawning crowd of strangers, hard-hearted toward the old folks buzzing like moribund flies around the edges of the new prosperity. But Krylov didn't care what form she took, or how well she was doing, or whether her heart was hard or soft. He was just glad to have her back.

Now he breathed in the sharp scent of abundant food and money drifting on the air. He didn't recall Moscow girls being so pretty, the boys so assured, everyone so brisk. All the young people seemed to be headed somewhere, to have a future. Even his own grown children might be lifted on this tide. The roads were full of black BMWs and Mercs with opaque windows and blue flashing lights. Such Ladas as remained looked like Toyotas, although he suspected they hadn't lost their ability to surprise.

Mainly, it was wonderful to uncork his native Russian. He rarely noticed the strain of being always in a second or third language; but when he returned to Russian, it was like removing a steel helmet after a long march, you thought your head would float away.

"I was so glad to hear from you, Viktor." Palev had regained his breath, and now sounded more like the man Krylov remembered. "It's a great compliment to an old teacher, having a star pupil keep in touch. I suppose you've come all this way to tell me you want to be a biologist after all?"

That career choice had been their recurring joke, repeated in rare letters and in the New Year's greetings they still exchanged. "I fear not. Too old for new tricks."

"You know absolutely nothing about 'too old,' my friend. *This,*" and Palev opened his arms so that his jacket parted, revealing his wasted torso, "is too old." When Krylov said nothing, he went on, "You are too polite to ask where the rest of me has gone, but I will tell you anyway. God decided to play one of his fine little pranks on me. After watching me spend four decades as a virologist, he sent one of the little fuckers to kill me."

"Which little fucker?"

"Cancer of nearly everything you can think of." He uttered a hard laugh. "My love affair with the virus is coming to an end."

"But you're still working…."

"Oh, yes, I go over to 15 Dubrovskaya every morning. I watch the buildings crumble, the iron gates rust, the trees try to grow. I do a little thinking, a little writing. For this every month they pay me the equivalent of three hundred euros—now we see everything in euros or dollars. We are still an institute for viral preparation, but the truly interesting work has moved to Vektor, in Novosibirsk. They have our live variola, they have our ebola and Marburg, our anthrax and VEE. Well, and people whisper that they have a good deal more. So, Viktor, you should have called someone at Vektor." He chuckled. "Vektor? Here is Viktor Viktorivich. Viktor, Vektor."

"I needed an evil genius."

"Ah, then you came to the right place."

Krylov had called Palev from Vienna early that morning, after Churches had asked about a man called Peter Gayle. Hearing the name, Anna had uttered a muted cry. Krylov saw her ashen face and knew immediately: "Your Englishman!" Then, as Anna had told him everything she knew, Krylov saw his cave and her Englishman and a cohort of still unresolved figures converging, like images in a viewfinder.

Once away from the hospital, he had called Ivan Silmov, a former colleague at the Russian embassy in Vienna. Krylov had dragged Silmov's inert body from the burning remains of a crashed Mi-8 north of Kabul and more or less cajoled him back to life, establishing a debt the survivor was happy to repay. Silmov promised to get back to him about the April Ten and Peter Gayle. Then Krylov had booked a seat on an early Air Austria flight to Moscow, and called Palev to ask for this afternoon meeting.

"I have two isolated sets of events that have unexpectedly connected," Krylov told him now.

"That means you have a circle where you thought you had two lines. But why come to me? I'm a biologist. Why not call a chum at the FSB?"

"Because this involves that famous bridge of yours."

Palev smiled. "Now you have my undivided attention. Tell me everything. Really, every damned thing. Then we see if I can help."

Krylov began with the Bulgarians and the helicopter, and, as the low sun drifted westward, he described what he had seen, and heard, and suspected. Palev listened like a man hypnotized, head cocked, eyes half closed, as his former pupil took him into the puzzle of the cave, the nurse, the dead twin, the Englishman, the April Ten, poor Churches.

Palev was quiet for a long moment after Krylov finished, his head nodding as if a tiny man inside were sorting what he'd heard. At last he straightened up. "First, on the matter of the secret injection. I believe we can rule out vitamin supplements and performance-boosting drugs." He chuckled at his little joke. "So we ask, was this Al-Rabiah-Muckeltee fellow hoping to immunize the Englishman or infect him, or both? Or was he masking a chemical sign of abuses during the man's captivity? You tell me that Anna herself doesn't know. Because of the secrecy, I would vote for infection."

"I rather liked the masking idea," said Krylov. "Destruction of lingering evidence. Those Serbian boys in The Hague would like some old evidence destroyed."

"But it's a long time for this 'evidence' to drift around in the blood, fooling the liver, the kidneys, the immune system. Even if the substance could survive there eternally, we have to wonder: why now, why not then, why not later?" Palev shook his head. "All these possibilities. I begin to hear the clamor of too many moving parts, like in an old helicopter. Nothing makes sense except having a skilled nurse do the injection. But then why kill her twin after the job is done? It makes my head hurt."

"Let's try the cave."

"I can see the molten rock, the dust, and I can feel the radiation. Your Americans…"

"Not *my* Americans, please."

"This American, this Emerson, hopes it is a WMD laboratory. There are what appear to have been flasks and test tubes, office furniture, beds, partitions, that sort of thing. But," and he leaned toward Krylov and poked his chest with an index finger, as he once had in the classroom, "no mention of expensive stuff. No one asks: where are the melted computers? Where are the charred remains of monitors, containments, air filtration systems, power generators, fermentation tubs?"

"There was nothing like that."

"I tell you why. Iraqi science may have been fairly well endowed in those days, but never what we would call flush. Word comes from the regime: rub this cave facility out of history. So the scientists spin the illusion of something like a nuclear accident. But they also tell us, without intending to, it is an illusion. They remove the expensive stuff before the 'accident.' Clean it up. Sell it. Move it to another laboratory. They could not resist being thrifty."

Palev gazed out across his corner of Moscow, perhaps thinking of what extreme thrift had done to his institute. "And since when," he continued, "is anybody so fastidious as to scrub history so clean? People are messy when they do things they shouldn't. Nobody burns all his clothing because of lipstick on one collar, so the partner always finds the remnant stray blonde hair, the scent. We let stuff lie around to be discovered. Think of the Nixon tapes. Think of the Nazis and their meticulous record of the Holocaust. Think of the top-secret but universally known camps of the Gulag.

"In my line of work we have our share of messy relics. In the village of Aralsk, there were open-air tests of what we now call the Aralsk strain of chiornaya ospa, black smallpox. They lit an epidemiological fuze that was only extinguished by the grace of God. Ten cases, three deaths, forty-some thousand vaccinations, strict quarantine. All top secret, but also known to everyone everywhere. Not that such things are entirely bad. No one on earth is more immune from variola than the people of Aralsk.

"Rebirth Island still sits like a pellet of poison in the Aral Sea after years of 'secret' tests of every kind of biological weapon. You can visit the empty cages and pens, which evoke hundreds of monkeys and sheep waiting for death in a toxic fog." He shuddered involuntarily. "One doesn't dream about the human dead, but about the murdered animals."

Krylov made a sad smile. "It was the animals that caused me to leave Biopreparat. All those little primate hands reaching out from the cages, beseeching, like the hands of the very poor."

"Good Lord, is this the same Viktor Krylov who drops miscreants out of windows for a living?"

"Not for a living. Strictly recreational. Anyway, humans at least know more or less what to expect."

"Nonsense. We have no idea what the future holds, only that it exists. Besides, our minds are clouded with hope. As in, I hope this brute doesn't drop me out the window."

"Speaking of dropping things, let's drop this windows business. It is funny but also untrue."

"Completely untrue?"

"It never happened."

"How could I get that wrong?"

"People say anything."

"I shall miss it. It always made me think of getting big dogs into a tub for bathing. All those arms and legs."

"Big dogs are easier," said Krylov. "Now, okay, we move away from the windowsill and go back to work. My colleague's interrogators linked the Englishman to the cave."

"So you are thinking that he and his comrades were taken there for some nefarious experiments, which the regime then wanted disappeared. I wonder. The Iraqis were so untidy when it came to covering up even the worst atrocities. They didn't bother to pick up the dead Kurds killed with sarin gas at Halabja. Instead, they left the bodies for the world to see. And yet they took the trouble to eradicate whatever was in your cave."

"Leaving us an abandoned stage and no playbill to tell us who performed there."

"We must use our imaginations."

"Ah, now at last our own secret weapon comes into play. To tell the truth, it was the hope of tapping your imagination that brought me to Moscow. Given what we know, given the resources we know about, if the cave had been *your* playpen, what would you have been up to?"

Palev displayed an exaggerated evil genius smile and rubbed his liverish, translucent hands together. "It is not easy to imagine myself an Iraqi, but I shall try. It is January 1991. My country is losing a short war with the rest of the world. Soon it will be under various embargoes. Its secret weapons programs will be rolled up by UN and other inspections. A humiliating denouement for us, so we think of taking some kind of revenge. Is this the sort of thing you want?"

Krylov nodded.

"I direct a modest project in a secret laboratory in northern Iraq. Because I am I, the project must be biological. Virological. By the grace of God, my research has reached an interesting point. The basic work is over, I think I am onto something big. Maybe big solutions to old problems. And maybe some payback for our legion of enemies.

"What problems? Well, biological agents are easy to manufacture—once you start them they more or less manufacture themselves. But of course in our little cave, there is nothing like the Level Four isolation cells found on Atlanta's Clifton Road or at Vektor. So as we do our work, it seems to me, we contaminate our facility. We turn it into a kind of subterranean plague ship. Some of our players drop by the wayside."

"What are we making?"

"It doesn't matter. All of the bad things are dangerous in about the same way. Ebola, variola, Marburg. Remember poor Ustinov, a cut in his suit and he becomes, for a short time, the world's leading expert on Marburg. We are working with less protection than he had."

"Like the people who go into the Chernobyl sarcophagus."

"Yes, about that well protected. So that is what we are doing in our imaginary cave. But if we want to apply our work to taking revenge on the rest of the world, without the rest of the world coming after us again, we must find a way to deliver our product to the enemy. For people in the bioweapons trade, this has always been a big hemorrhoid.

"If you are the Soviet Union—sorry, Russia—or the United States, you can launch a squadron of jets to lay down a fog of anthrax or Venezuelan equine encephalitis over a battlefield, over a town, hoping to God the meteorologists got it right about the wind. With this stuff, you are always praying that you won't kill your own soldiers.

"On a much grander scale, if you are a past or present superpower, you can load powdered variola into multiple ICBM warheads and drop them on cities an ocean away. They explode at altitude, dispersing a fine, invisible cloud of particles that find their way into the lungs, where they come to life. No worries about infecting one's own forces. Having launched the attack, you have to wait, and wait, and wait, until people begin to sicken and die. A week, two weeks. But as soon as that happens, everyone gets quarantined and vaccinated. The illness confers immunity on its survivors. So your target eventually vanishes. Your weapon of mass destruction goes poof."

"Then what's the point?"

"Terror. The evil genius wants to terrify. So he infects his enemy with a disease that is not just deadly, but hideous and messy. It turns loved ones and neighbors into blackened, repugnant strangers bleeding from every orifice, every pore, and mad with misery and fear." Palev paused for breath and shut his eyes for a moment, as if what had been conjured might become real.

Then, his feelings once more under his control, he continued. "Between the time of dispersal and when your WMD goes poof, the evil genius kills people in their tens of thousands. For the afflicted, it is as bad as Armageddon. It is the end of the world."

Krylov shuddered, for the old man had littered his mind with imaginary dead. "Let's go back to our fantasy. You are not Russian or American. You are a poor Iraqi scientist."

"In a defeated, ruined nation. I have no aircraft and no long-range missiles. Even if I did, I would still have the problem of randomizing my attacks in space and time to make them more difficult to contain. I am in my tuxedo, but I have no driver to take me to the ball."

"So the work in the cave bangs into a dead end."

"Maybe not. Perhaps, I think, we could organize a brigade of infected hosts and send them into the world. Like a gang of suicide bombers."

"You advertise for masochists."

"Don't laugh. It's true that most diseases worth sending aren't contagious until the carrier himself is incapacitated and visibly infected. Nobody lets a young Arab board an airliner with blood leaking from his eyes. The soldiers in this imaginary brigade must somehow propagate the agent without catching the disease. Symptomless carriers. And they must be innocents, with no knowledge of what they carry."

"And here imagination veers toward science fiction."

"On the contrary, I have two historical models for just such a delivery system. One is Mary Mallon."

"Mary Mallon?"

"Typhoid Mary. An American cook in New York a century ago. She carried *Salmonella typhi* without knowing it, and without catching typhoid fever herself. But food from her kitchen could kill you. Especially the cold desserts. In fact, only a few people died because of her, but she entered the language anyway as the perfect delivery system."

"And the other?"

"The long-haul truck drivers of East Africa. Hundreds of miles of a route lined with prostitutes, through a continent in which

AIDS has reached epidemic proportions. But they screw with wild abandon, believing themselves immune. Of course, they are not, hence the epidemic. Yet here and there, one comes upon a driver, or a prostitute, who seems naturally resistant to the AIDS virus, although they can transmit it like everybody else. So we know the symptomless carrier is possible. I don't know how you would go about creating one. But perhaps there is a way."

Palev smiled, enjoying himself. "So we can imagine me in my secret cave. We can imagine that I have somehow solved the symptoms problem. Let us also imagine I have solved the time-delay problem as well, and figured out how to activate the agent, so that the outbreaks come when and where I want them to, not while my soldier is off fishing on a deserted lake. The on-switch could be a secret injection, Viktor. You see the possibilities."

"What a busy little cave you have."

"All imaginary. And some problems remain. The war has taken me to the end of my tether, research-wise. I am stuck with what results I have, for we are out of money. Worse, I am out of human specimens, for, in making my unholy omelet, I have used up all my eggs. Those human remains in your cave, Viktor, are pioneers. I have no way to test my terrible weapon. I rend my garments and moan that all my work has been in vain."

"But it has not."

"No, because just at that dramatic moment, praise be to Allah, word comes of ten badly abused prisoners of war who are available if I want them. I take them in, fix them up, and send them home. Then, on the regime's orders, I destroy every trace of their presence. I wipe the biological adventure, the plague ship, out of history. As far as the world is concerned, it's over."

"But is it over?"

"Viktor, my boy, it has just begun!"

"Job tvoju matj!"

"But," and Palev held up a hand like a sorcerer calming the sea, "keep in mind that this may be just wishful thinking by a thwarted evil genius. To be frank, I don't think anyone could survive working with the really virulent stuff in the facility you describe. I have no idea how to solve the symptoms problem. And then there is the matter of control. You need that on-off switch, and it isn't clear to me what you would be turning on or off. It's beyond my experience.

"The main trouble is that, having sent out ten Typhoid Marys, you must then send out ten more people to monitor them. Because the one thing I find inconceivable, Viktor, is a biological weapon that sits for years without springing a leak. Outside their host, viruses are just dirt, matter. But once they come to life, they have a mind of their own. So, once in a host, why would they wait?"

"Do you think Al-Rabiah fielded this brigade?"

The old man shrugged. "God knows. You will know too, I think, when you find out what happened to the other prisoners. I think that is all I can invent for you now."

"Just as well you're not an Iraqi scientist."

Palev grinned like a bad boy. "Being an evil genius is a marvelous sensation. I am completely exhausted, but the ordeal by imagination has added hours to my life. Thank you for those hours, my friend. I wish I could be with you to the end."

By now the day had dwindled to a pale line of fiery light beyond the low relief of the Sparrow Hills. Guards were moving through the park, jabbing vagrants asleep on benches, herding stragglers toward the gate. When they approached, Krylov stood up. "We're going," he told them. "But don't try to hurry us." Then he got an arm under Palev's and began the slow dance toward the exit.

"Here is the agenda," the old man said as they traversed the dark estate. "First we go by the institute. You can see how the mighty have fallen. I will give you a cocktail."

"Why don't we just find a bar?"

"No one else makes this particular cocktail."

"What is it called?"

"Immunity from everything but God."

Krylov laughed. "I've been immune from God since my Pioneer days. But this cocktail sounds like a lethal injection."

"No, no, no. A suit of armor. The deeper you go into this labyrinth, the more protection you will need. Trust me."

"And after the cocktail?"

Palev paused, unable to walk and take such large decisions at the same time. Then, "I propose that you buy me a fine dinner. Where are you staying?"

"The Metropol."

"I love the place." He shut his eyes, the better to remember it. "A time machine. Welcome to 1910, am I right?"

Krylov nodded. "The dining room is fantastic."

"Yes, all that glass. And a pretty woman with a harp."

"Then we go there."

"But not much of a bar."

"So where shall we go?"

The old man suspended once more, thinking. "I wouldn't mind going somewhere new. Broaden my experience."

"What do you have in mind?"

"I was thinking restaurant O'Mar."

"I don't know it."

"After your time. It's right by the Metropol, outside the Kremlin walls. It evokes a ship under sail. In Moscow today it is as easy to find good seafood as it is in Chicago, Illinois."

"You've been to this place?"

"No, it's too expensive for me. But I reconnoitered. The menu made my mouth water. Good smells. Comfortable interior. Lots of young people. Fewer tourists than you'd think. A cheerful piano. I was waiting for some oligarch on a white horse to take me."

"I'm your oligarch."

"Tomorrow, my assistant will ask where I ate, expecting me to say, Oh, I went to Il Patio for a pizza. Instead I say I ate sole meunière at the restaurant O'Mar. She will think I have hit the lottery."

"Maybe you *should* hit the lottery. I have some money lying around. Let me do more than buy you a meal."

The old man gave Krylov a long, admonitory look. Then, having quietly chastened his former pupil, he grinned. "A taxi would be nice. And on the way we will get you that cocktail."

LAMONT COULD HARDLY BELIEVE HIS EYES. While waiting for Emerson in Schwechat's general-aviation terminal, his attention was drawn by a peripheral movement on the inner surface of his right bicep. There, as she had for nearly twenty years, Leda trembled beneath a huge, white swan. But now, Lamont saw for the first time, the swan moved its wings and body, it thrusted, when he flexed the inflated muscle. The big bodyguard grinned like a dog. All these years and he hadn't noticed what the artist—he thought it must have been the old hippie in San Diego—had actually created on him.

Leda and the swan had been inscribed when Lamont was a year and a half out of high school and a bit over a year in the Marines, the first bit of color on his pale white skin. Since then, a multihued forest of tendrils, branches, and leaves had grown around the mythic figures, interspersed with things both celestial and material: a supernova detonated farther down the right arm, and on the opposite forearm, a sketch that looked something like the young Lamont fired an M-16 that, when he made a fist, recoiled. Along his spine the dark-haired lady from one of his Klimt coasters stood in a golden rain, against a landscape borrowed from the Hindu Kush. At the moment, however, Lamont was hypnotized by what his bicep did to the swan, and he was still watching the rape when, above the hemisphere of the muscle, he saw Emerson's airplane taxi in.

The long-legged Gulfstream IV seemed to stalk the yellow FOLLOW ME jeep to the general-aviation apron, where a man in blue coveralls waved paddles to move the aircraft into its final position. Lamont loved flying on this particular Gulfstream, even when they had a guy or two in an orange suit, shackles, and a bag over his head. He liked its call sign, Nine Four Juliet. "Nine Four Juliet, with you at forty thousand" was music to Lamont. "Nine Four Juliet, twenty northwest with Lima." It just flat rolled off the tongue!

His natural inclination was to trot out as the door lifted open and the steps deployed, but he noted a large Cobra guard watching him, his automatic rifle cradled in one arm. Lamont raised his eyebrows interrogatively and nodded with his chin toward the Gulfstream. The Cobra replied with an almost imperceptible shake of his head. So Lamont remained behind the glass wall as Emerson emerged from the Gulfstream, looking pissed off about something, as always, and Lamont knew what it was. Emerson liked to be met *at* the airplane. Now there would follow some genuflecting and eating of shit, after which, Lamont knew from experience, things would settle down.

Wearing the usual blazer, blue jeans, bow tie, and desert boots, Emerson stormed across the tarmac with his small leather bag, expending energy like a man beset by invisible bees, and into the general-aviation terminal. For a long moment he peered at Lamont, who looked away.

"I like to be met," said Emerson.

"Security," said Lamont, nodding toward the Cobra guard.

"I thought *you* were security, Lamont."

"Sorry, Ralph."

"You're telling me."

Emerson looked Lamont up and down, the Heat tank top, the khaki cargo shorts, the child-sized red, white, and blue cross trainers. Erase the tattoos and he looked like an Ohio tourist. Emerson thought it might be time to get himself another breed of dog, something more up-market than this big mutt. He stared into Lamont's eyes, into what he regarded as the empty rooms beyond, until the younger man grew nervous and his gaze began to dart.

"How was your trip?" The child's voice was half an octave higher than normal.

"Successful. Actually," and Emerson, deciding the big mutt wasn't so bad after all, put a hand on the illustrated shoulder, "better than successful." He felt Lamont relax under his paternal touch. Good, good. Easy, boy. One didn't want these fellows too excited or too sad—well, too anything. Running an entourage like his, Emerson had once confided to a senior colleague, was like driving a nitro truck. "You know, like the movie." The colleague hadn't a clue what he was talking about.

Lamont picked up the bag. "I saw your Sov in the terminal."

"My Sov?"

"You know, that Viktor."

"Oh, Viktor. I remember Viktor, he tried to screw us."

"He looked like shit."

"Was he coming or going?"

"Coming, I think."

"Ah," mused Emerson. "Think he's still there?"

"We could look."

They got into the black Suburban Lamont had left outside the general-aviation area and circled back toward the main terminal, then pulled up to wait. At first, Emerson didn't recognize Krylov. He just saw a big man stumble past the automatic doors and grab a metal railing, on which he leaned heavily, his eyes closed, his face pallid and shiny with perspiration.

Emerson leaned out his window. "Yo, Viktor. Need a ride?"

Krylov opened his eyes to a narrow slit and made a face. "My car is here."

"Arriving, then?" When Krylov did not respond, Emerson asked, "From where?"

The Russian grinned and tried to stand a bit straighter. "Beijing. I've gone over."

"Sure you have."

"And you? Coming or going?"

"Just back."

"Renditioning?"

"Naturally."

"Anyone I know?"

"Nope."

"Good. Wonderful seeing you again. Now I pick up my car." Krylov started to move off, slowly and with effort, as if struggling against gravity.

Lamont let the Suburban idle along beside him. "Must have been a hell of a night," called Emerson.

"Those crazy Chinese."

"Viktor."

"Yes?"

"I heard about Churches."

"Me too."

"He gave me the cesium stuff."

Krylov nodded. "He told me. Now you have to find a new whore."

"Interested?"

Krylov turned back toward the Americans, and now he was looking them over, like a tormented bull with enough *pics* in its shoulders to throw its life away. "What else did you hear?"

"The April Ten?"

"I love their new CD. Especially the accordions."

"My people at home gave them to me on the radio. Nine dead guys. They also gave me Peter Gayle."

"Peter Gayle, Peter Gayle. I am weak on English opera. Hum a few bars, maybe it will come back to me."

"He's the sole survivor."

"Who?"

"Peter Gayle."

"Of what?"

"The April Ten."

"Why would I care?"

"I've been wondering the same thing. But I know you do."

"Then you know more than I do."

"Should you see Mr. Gayle, tell him I'd like a natter."

"I'll tell him to run for his life."

"His life doesn't interest me. I'm after his body. Hell, I'll settle for a gallon of his blood. Nothing we can't handle post-mortem. Entirely his call."

"As the wife said in the film, Try the cock."

"Fuck you." His cheeks scarlet with anger, Emerson turned toward Lamont, prepared to launch the big man, who was fiddling with his seat belt, waiting for the command to pounce.

"Don't start anything, Lamont," said Krylov, nodding toward a pair of Cobras watching from the far side of the glass wall. "They see you as a pretty lampshade."

"Another venue, another time," said Emerson. "Remember to tell Gayle what I said."

"I'll remember that lampshade shit," added Lamont.

Krylov made no reply, but rested against the wall, watching the black monster roar off toward the exit. This must be what Churches would call the cherry on top, he thought, running into Emerson after a night out in Moscow with Palev, a bottle of good vodka and that special cocktail. He supposed Palev's cocktail had infected him with a mild case of every viral ailment known to man. His head pounded, he could barely make a fist; he felt as if he carried an invisible refrigerator on his back. Immunity from everything but God. Now he wasn't so sure.

Saddled with this hydra of a hangover, Krylov had hoped to avoid all human contact until he found his bed. That was about as far ahead as his mind would take him today. But then, the Americans had demonstrated their uncanny knack for materializing at just the inconvenient moment. When I die and go to Hell, there will be Emerson and that tattooed gorilla, waiting with Cerberus. Krylov considered offering up a little prayer of thanks that Lamont hadn't jumped him.

Even through the haze of his discomfort, however, Krylov could feel time draining away. The April Ten. Peter Gayle. Emerson, who had known nothing, now knew quite a lot; the American was overtaking him. But he still had a step or two on Emerson, who had not yet made the connection with Anna and her lost twin, or with the Iraqi scientist who called himself Al-Rabiah and Muckeltee. There was still time. He took out his mobile phone and dialed Svetlana's work number.

"Environment, here is Svetlana."

"Sveta…"

"Uncle Viktor. Where have you been?"

"To Moscow."

"Without me? How could you?"

"Next time, I promise. Now, quickly, where is Muckeltee?"

"Who knows? We haven't seen him in days."

"And Anna?"

"At work."

"Christ." Krylov forgot the hangover and sprinted for his car. The hospital was half an hour away, and he could almost hear the steps of the Iraqi, stalking Anna through its vast, echoing halls. "Give me her number."

XII

Anna came and went through the broad automatic doors separating the Intensiv's manifest of the desperate and the dying from the unthreatened and alive. She seemed not to have a care in the world beyond the care of patients, and moved briskly in clean blue scrubs, head high, eyes clear. Nothing apprehensive, no obvious preoccupations, which, Al-Rabiah decided, meant she was not yet aware of her new status as prey. And yet, he noted, she was never alone, and never very long in the same place. She moved with the herd, and kept to its center.

Al-Rabiah moved along the fringes, wearing purloined scrubs over his street clothes, dark glasses, a cap over his hair and a surgical mask loose beneath his chin; a clipboard conferred an aura of medical urgency, as if he were on his way somewhere. Sometimes he and Anna almost brushed in passing, but always in an eddy of staff and patients and visitors. He had lunched not ten meters from her in the cafeteria. But she avoided those quiet corners of the hospital where he might silence her and get away undetected.

Still, Al-Rabiah was confident the opportunity would finally come. Meanwhile, he hovered in disguise, one hand wrapped around the grip of the silenced semiautomatic pistol in a deep trouser pocket. The weapon, which he now used with an abandon that surprised him, seemed too refractory and massive to escape the notice of others, like an unbidden erection at a middle-school dance. People would see it and roll their eyes; they would laugh at him behind their hands.

The possibility of such laughter and the elusiveness of his prey had tempted Al-Rabiah to give it up. Let Anna live, he told himself. We have done what we have done. Leave this irrelevant girl alone. But he could not. She had shown her hand, and it was the hand of an enemy.

"Are you and your sister very much alike?"

"Well, you know, we're sisters."

Sisters. Not twins, just sisters. Why had Anna not told him Sophie was her twin? Because she had decided to deny him that crucial particle of information. If she had the will for that, she had the will to contact Peter Gayle, the will to go with him to the authorities, the will to expose Al-Rabiah's enterprise, to destroy it with light.

He had thought about little else since the night he saw Anna and Sophie on television. He had just completed the marathon drive from England. Not twelve hours earlier, he had killed Michael Williams, because, like the others, Williams had begun to rot. Returning to Vienna to find the Nieman twins on world television had tipped him over the edge. Silfer and the little angels had taken cover, frightened by the magnitude of his rage. Al-Rabiah had wanted to tear out his hair. His reason left him; he imagined it drifting away like a soul departing the body.

When the idiot in Baghdad said, on a scrambled mobile telephone, "I thought you knew," Al-Rabiah had imploded. The man was an imbecile, a turd, a dwarf, a sodomist, the incestuous son of a mongrel dog. But all he said was, "When did you learn she was a twin?"

"Just before she left."

"And still you let her go?"

"I thought of stopping her. But as you know all things worth knowing, I decided you must know this as well."

"I did not."

"Perhaps you should have."

Al-Rabiah heard the hiss of fealty leaking away. "Excuse my rudeness, brother," he said quickly. "I am exhausted. My brain is like a tolling bell. Forgive me."

But he knew the damage had been done. The man in Baghdad was finished with him and would now go on to other horrific acts closer to his heart and home. One could not help but envy him that option. He had a homeland, as Al-Rabiah did not. Baghdad was as irretrievably lost to him as the hanging gardens of Babylon.

"Stuff happens," he muttered.

The matter of the twins was just another mishap in a long string of them. And killing Anna? Almost certainly another mistake. Think what the world would make of twins shot dead within a fortnight of each other, a thousand miles apart.

Still, the idea of Anna's death, of guaranteeing her silence, would not leave him alone. The morning after his return, and the morning after that, and now, today, Al-Rabiah had resisted briefly, feebly, then marched helplessly toward murder. He lived for the morning visit to the Allgemeines Krankenhaus, hoping to isolate and kill the pretty young woman who came and went through the automatic doors between the world and the flickering lives of the Intensiv.

Now, juggling a paper cup of coffee and his clipboard, Al-Rabiah saw Anna appear suddenly on his side of the doors. She held a mobile telephone to one ear, listening, eyes wide, distracted, nodding or shaking her head as she searched among the faces that passed her in the hall. For a moment their eyes met, then hers veered away with no sign of recognition. She closed the telephone and dropped it into a pocket of her scrubs, and set off almost at a run. Something had spooked her; she was bolting from the herd.

Al-Rabiah tossed away his coffee and pulled up his surgical mask, then started after her, careful to keep his eyes mainly on the empty clipboard. His heart drummed like a young lover's, his grip tightened on the pistol that bumped against his leg.

Where was she going?

Around one turn into a broad hall stretching out to the vanishing point, a few figures in the distance, floating in the hard fluorescent light like mirages in the desert. Al-Rabiah quickened his pace to overtake her.

Now Anna turned sharply into a narrow corridor, dimly lighted, with a red AUSGANG sign glowing above a glass door, through which poured a rectangular slice of the brilliant autumn morning. Al-Rabiah slid the pistol out of his pocket, holding it flat against his leg.

Barely three meters behind her, he reckoned, able in a few more steps to reach out and touch her shoulder, startle her into spinning around. He would drop his mask, as he had for Williams, watch fear and recognition saturate that pretty face, and then the double cough of the pistol, perhaps a cry of pain, or maybe nothing...

Al-Rabiah stopped. A large shadow eclipsed the light streaming through the door, which she opened, admitting a ferocious-looking man with hair like a black lion's. He seemed almost to fly into the corridor, quick and light as a huge raptor, then paused for a second, getting his bearings.

"Viktor," Anna cried. "What's wrong?"

The newcomer ignored her, his full attention fixed upon the small man in scrubs with a clipboard and a gun. He pushed Anna out the exit door, then, as it hissed shut behind her, he sprang for Al-Rabiah, who brought up the pistol and quickly squeezed off two rounds, *pok! pok!* that went wild, ricocheting crazily between the walls and ceiling. The man seemed not to notice. Feeling the bile of panic rise in his throat, Al-Rabiah pocketed the gun, pivoted, and sprinted down the corridor, the pistol banging painfully against his thigh. Now his heart drummed more like a rabbit's, hearing the beat of large wings behind him.

He turned down another hall, and then another, the footfalls of the stranger echoing after him. When he encountered a swarm of visitors and patients creeping down the hall, he quickly threaded through them with a litany of Sorrys and Pardons. Jittery as a disturbed school of herring, they moved in agitated circles, trying to coalesce behind him, only to be penetrated by his pursuer, who scattered ailing Wieners in every direction. The collision added a few seconds to Al-Rabiah's lead, letting him fly out of sight around another corner.

Seeing an exit door ahead of him, Al-Rabiah ran to it and wrenched it open, then doubled back and darted into a door branded with a large yellow and black radiation symbol. The nurse inside looked up and smiled. He nodded, trying not to breathe too audibly, consulted his clipboard, and marched past the changing stalls into a room where an idle X-ray machine suspended like a waiting python.

Pretending to examine it, pretending to write on his clipboard, Al-Rabiah listened. Footsteps went past, then nothing. He imagined the big stranger standing in the open exit, looking for his quarry in the torrent of traffic on the Gürtel, breathing hard, scratching his wild head.

Minutes later, having shed his disguise, Al-Rabiah was just another Arab in blue jeans, hooded grey sweatshirt, and white trainers, strolling along the Gürtel to the Michelbeuern-AKC stop for the number six U-bahn, which ran on the old elevated Schnellbahn tracks. Waiting for the southbound train, he looked back toward the hospital, and there they were, Anna and her mystery man, crossing the parking area together. The man scanned the ground ahead of them, and even looked up the road to the station platform where Al-Rabiah stood. Had their eyes met? The Iraqi almost hoped they had.

The train arrived and Al-Rabiah took a seat on the hospital side, hoping to catch another glimpse of them. But they were nowhere to be seen. He held up his hands, palms outward, willing them to be still; he thought his heart rate had begun to slow. He shut his eyes and leaned his head against the window, wondering who this "Viktor" was, besides someone else he would eventually have to kill.

As a visiting scholar at the Centre for Analytic Studies, Dr. Simon Muckeltee could afford to lease a five-room flat a few streets from the Schloss Schönbrunn, on a broad tree-lined avenue where the ground rose toward the hills and the city opened to the sky. It was a neighborhood of UN officials, technical people, and diplomats, where Dr. Muckeltee was always running into colleagues. Everyone knew and liked him there, and Silfer and the two angels were able to quench their awful addiction to show.

But Al-Rabiah spent much of his time some distance away, in a flat not much bigger than a closet off the Margaretengürtel, where he was just another member of an Arab multitude trying to make a living in a foreign land. The place had an ageing WC and shower, a wooden bar for hanging clothes, sagging parquet floors, a tiny refrigerator and electric kettle; a small crystal chandelier sparkled hopefully in the center of the room.

A narrow window shrouded in stained white chintz overlooked the crowded lane three floors below, always teeming with pilgrims from the east, always noisy with traffic and the jack hammers of Vienna's constant reconstruction. In the summer the stifling room might have been in Fallujah, and in winter the oil heater could not even dent the cold. But it was his lair, his secret place. Silfer didn't know of its existence; no one did. The man whose name was on the lease had died years earlier in an unfortunate laboratory accident.

On a small table under the window Al-Rabiah had a five-year-old computer with a large flat screen, on which he did his writing, some research, and, in moments of loneliness or depression, watched the odd adult film. It was also where he did his serious smoking and drinking.

Now, having debarked at Längenfeldgasse and walked the several blocks along the Margaretengürtel warily on the watch for shadows, he had gone to ground in his hideaway. He sat facing the computer screen, his feet elevated on the table, a pack of Turkish Specials and an ashtray by his left hand, a crystal tumbler and liter of Johnnie Walker Red by his right.

He sipped from the tumbler and lighted a cigarette, then held up his hands to verify that they had steadied. His heart no longer felt ready to explode with fear, although he was still afraid; his body tingled with the electricity of being chased by a dangerous stranger.

But not entirely a stranger. Al-Rabiah thought he'd seen the fellow before. And the name, Viktor, that rang a bell. The sight of the black screen revived a memory: the Russian Safeguards man. Al-Rabiah had seen him on Austrian television, but where? Silfer always watched a drama when the news was on. And then another memory popped to the surface. He and the other Environment people at the Centre, working late, had gone to dinner at a Gasthaus where a small color television glittered above the bar. Svetlana watched it for a moment, then gave a delighted start, grinned broadly, and exclaimed: *Look, there's my Uncle Viktor!* As they watched the Austrian version of the CNN story, Al-Rabiah had become aware that this Uncle Viktor person had just been inside *his* cave.

That explained why this same man had been with Anna Nieman. He knew her through Svetlana. Al-Rabiah frowned. The other night, the old Mercedes waiting for Svetlana. Had there been a big Russian at the wheel? He wasn't sure. The windscreen had been as opaque as a mirror in the dim light of the village square. But if the Russian had been there, would he have recognized Al-Rabiah at the hospital?

He picked up his mobile and scrolled through the phone book to *s+angels*. Silfer picked up after two rings, as though she'd been waiting. "Where are you?"

"I'm at work, darling."

"I tried your office."

"I must have stepped out."

"Someone called."

The hairs on Al-Rabiah's nape stood up. "Who was it?"

"Someone asking for you."

"For Muckeltee?"

"No, for you."

"Man or woman?"

"A man. Are you in trouble?"

He waited several jarring heart-beats before replying. "Why would I be in trouble?"

"Well, you know, these deceptions."

"Please, sweetheart, not on this telephone."

"I'm sorry. I just worry, you know."

"Listen, darling, I've been working on a little trip. We could all use a change of scene."

"That would be nice, but the angels are in school."

"It wouldn't be so bad if they missed a week or two."

"What are you thinking of?"

"The Third World Academy has asked me to deliver a paper in Trieste. The conference lasts a week. Then perhaps a drive south along the sea, perhaps some time in Switzerland. You know, the Hotel Victoria."

"We could take their lessons with us."

"We could home-school, like Americans."

"When would we leave?"

"Tonight."

"Drive in darkness?"

"In moonlight, my precious."

She uttered a voluptuous sigh.

"Yes, I was thinking the same. Get some things packed. I will finish up here."

"Hurry home," she said.

"I shall, dearest."

Al-Rabiah rang off and set the phone down on the table. Such calls exhausted him. But the adroitly improvised trip was just the thing; it would buy him time. He could work out where they went from here in the relative peace of the road. And he could pick the right moment to tell Silfer and the angels that their Vienna days were over, that they would be....what? Moving to North Korea? The Sudan? Iran? He would have to be damned careful to reveal this without actuating their hair-trigger hysteria; sometimes it took weeks to settle them down. Al-Rabiah shook his head in melancholy resignation, acknowledging that his sweethearts were now and then a cross to bear. He took a long pull at the tumbler and lighted a new cigarette. Then he clicked the mouse, starting the video disk labeled *HANGEDMAN* for the hundredth time.

AT FIRST, THE SCREEN was a vortex of motion as the photographer, evidently using a mobile telephone as his camera, got his bearings. A figure in a black overcoat slowly climbed clanging metal stairs, moving in the awkward way of bound men, to a railed landing, where he stood, gazing into the surrounding darkness. His long, handsome face had settled into an expression of sad equanimity, he seemed bemused by his surroundings, but also interested in them, as if eager to help, and not at all afraid.

Al-Rabiah's vision blurred with tears. He froze the frame. Here was the man he had come to love, to the degree (he hastily appended) it was proper for one man to love another, the man for whom he had done the wonderful, terrible thing, but also the man who'd rather let him down.

A click and the video advanced.

The man stood very straight by the metal railing as a rising chorus of rough voices and laughter flew out of the surrounding darkness, the cries of jeering spirits flapping around the gates of Hell. Now two masked companions appeared on the landing. One wound a black scarf around the man's neck. The other came forward with the thick hemp noose and its heavy coiled slipknot, and lowered it like a garland of flowers around the man's neck.

Al-Rabiah froze the frame.

"Thanks to you, I spend my life like a fox in the English countryside. But, I have thus far foiled the hounds. I wish you had done the same."

The young chemist from Samarra who worked in pharmaceuticals at the Salman Pac complex south of Baghdad had never thought about packs of hounds. Life had been simple, satisfying, and sweet until the man on the screen had appeared and the world had changed.

"Remember your first visit? You asked what we were doing. I said something like, 'We are encasing tiny doses of medication in a chemically inert shell.' You laughed, and asked why we should do such a thing, and I told you that, as the shells drifted in the blood, they slowly decayed, releasing the medication over various intervals of time."

Al-Rabiah laughed softly, recalling the moment. "Of course my hands shook like a girl's, I was a cataract of perspiration. We were all afraid of you." But there had also been the sense of a powerful and not unfriendly gravitation, drawing him in.

The visitor had watched the demonstration as a dozen pellets no larger than grains of sand were produced from metal nozzles, dried, and separated. "How many of these can you make?"

"Each concentric pair of nozzles gives us twenty to thirty per minute, sir."

"Twenty to thirty per minute. Why, in an hour you could have, well….many of them." His eyes turned cold, warning Al-Rabiah not to do his arithmetic for him. "Twelve to fifteen hundred." The smile returned.

Al-Rabiah had been just thirty then, a freshly minted PhD chemist trained in the United States and Germany, and the young architect of this first micro-encapsulation facility at Salman Pak, its catchments and containments and drying bins and gleaming nozzles brand new, enveloped in a forest of copper and steel piping.

The important guest strode around, sharp as a British general in his olive-drab uniform, web belt, holstered pistol, boots shined to a metallic finish. His small, black eyes darted this way and that, and now and then he made some comment to one or another of his uniformed entourage, or smiled and nodded to one of the white-clad lab technicians.

When he returned to Al-Rabiah, he said, offhandedly, as though he spoke of weather, "this medication business is all very well. May God bless you for doing it. But what else can you en-cap-su-late?"

"Anything."

"Aphrodisiacs?"

Al-Rabiah stammered. "I, I suppose so, sir."

"Ground tiger penis? Rhino horn?"

"I know very little about such things."

"But you've just told me you could mi-cro-en-cap-su-late," and he rolled the word around, tasting it, "anything."

"Yes, sir."

"Well, Mohammad....you don't mind my calling you Mohammad instead of Doctor Al-Rabiah?"

"No, sir."

"And you don't mind my little joke about aphrodisiacs?"

"No, sir.

"Anyway, they are a waste of time. They are just psychology." He gave a savage grin. "I don't need help in that department. I need weapons that will cut down those waves of children sent against my army. I need something that brings the flat hand of God down upon the Persians, crushing them like flies. Perhaps you can think of a way to use your mi-cro-en-cap-su-la-tion against those cowards and dwarfs."

Al-Rabiah had replied in a whisper: "How shall I do that?" He felt faint; he heard the doors to his future slam shut.

"You will find a way." Then, putting an arm around the younger man's shoulders, enveloping him in a mist of masculine odor and cologne, the visitor said, "Don't be afraid of me, Mohammad. I liked you immediately I saw you. We both come from the north. We may be cousins. Tell me what you need, and I shall provide it. And if, at the end, you tell me you have tried honestly and failed, I shall even forgive you." His eyes had danced, the hard line of a mouth below the black mustache had softened in a smile. "We shall talk again."

Al-Rabiah was enthralled less by the man's awful power than by a strange charm, a kind of incompletely formed, adolescent magnetism that he found irresistible. Being in its presence had been like sipping a rare and wonderful wine, like nodding in an opium den, like sleeping among wolves in the wild desert, sweet and dangerous and dreamlike and, although one would never articulate it, sexual.

The video advanced.

Off-screen voices chanted, "Muqtada al-Sadr, Muqtada al-Sadr," a Satanic chorus of derision.

The man half-smiled. "Muqtada al-Sadr," he mimicked, speaking the name as he would speak of shit.

Al-Rabiah stopped it there. It made his hair stand on end to watch his leader and friend, a noose around his neck, still capable of spitting at the men who shouted from the darkness, like a tangle of vipers hissing in a desert cave. The man was very tough, tough as the Prophet, tough as Macbeth, without the Scot's crippling belief in ghosts.

"In time, Mohammad, you will find it as easy to kill a man while looking him in the eye as it is to infect a litter of puppies to test a mi-cro-en-cap-su-la-ted poison. But killing is just a beginning. You must drag your enemy's remains through the streets. You cut him into pieces, urinate upon them and cast them into the desert for jackals and vultures to eat. You reduce him to carrion." He had grinned and clapped Al-Rabiah on the shoulder. "I see I've made you green around the gills again. But you're coming along. And there's no hurry. We shall never want for enemies."

Al-Rabiah rubbed his eyes, lit a new cigarette, took a mouthful of warm whisky. "Truth be told, I would have thrown Silfer to the wolves for you, even with all your warts and crazy moments. God help me, I might even have sacrificed the angels." In the event, he hadn't sacrificed his family, but he had put them to one side as his humanity flaked away like rotted garments and a monster stirred within.

"You were never a coward. You kept your word."

The man in the computer screen gazed calmly back at Al-Rabiah, seeming to listen, seeming almost to smile while he tried on his heavy hemp cravat.

"I was unable to give you the weapon you wanted in time for the Persian war, and you forgave me."

But Al-Rabiah had been telling the truth when he said he could encapsulate anything. He had successfully encased any number of reactive substances in inert microscopic shells, and set the pellets adrift in the bloodstreams of dogs and monkeys, and taken notes as the material was slowly, incrementally released. Nothing went perfectly, of course. Now he chuckled. "We used to say the place was so contaminated we would be safer working as American spies."

By then, as his friend had known would happen, Al-Rabiah was able to look into the eyes of a primate as it died in pain that he inflicted, and feel nothing. Just nothing. He had taught himself to kill his subjects with less feeling than a butcher has for a beef. He had ossified into a hard man, if not a very brave one.

In 1989, the year after the war with Iran had ended, the year before the invasion of Kuwait, a woman calling herself Dr. Daura had contacted Al-Rabiah. Effective immediately, she said, his micro-encapsulation research was in Directorate Eight of the Mukhabarat. He and his staff would be transferred from the complex at Salman Pac to a new, secret facility in the north. "You shall have whatever you need. Biological agent. Computers. The best Germany can provide." She laughed like a girl of seven and grinned around small, yellowed teeth, tangled like a shark's. "And primates. You will not lack for subjects." More girlish laughter.

The video advanced.

The man in the screen still watched Al-Rabiah with interest as the noose was tightened, the knot laid at right angles to the left side of his neck.

The picture froze.

"Dr. Daura was as good as her word," Al-Rabiah told the suspended image. "The cave. Every possible resource. And, finally, the ten prisoners. My chalices of death. By the time Satan had destroyed your army in the south, I was ready to set their fuzes and send them into the world. But you said, 'No, Mohammad, wait until we get Satan off our shoulders. Their inspectors and patrols will go away. They will not care about us forever.' And so we waited, and waited again.

"Meanwhile," and here Al-Rabiah's voice rose, suddenly shrill, "your delusions brought the Americans back to Iraq, this time to defeat and occupy my country. You did not ride out to meet the Jews and Crusaders, as Saladin did. You hid like a rodent until they found you and dragged you back into the light. You went to prison, showed your open mouth on television, appeared on the front pages of newspapers in your underwear. You suffered their trial. You went to the gallows where I see you now. So you are finished. But I am not. God left me a tenth chalice."

A click and the video moved on.

The clamor in the darkness grew louder. The man on the platform remained calm, watching the crowd who had come to see him cower, to see him unable to speak for the fear in his mouth. Well, they would be disappointed. He had told the world he was not afraid to die, and he was not. Al-Rabiah's anger melted away, his eyes misted over.

When the end came, it came at the speed of thought. One instant the man stood on the screen, looking sadly, pityingly, upon his tormentors. The next he was gone, dropped from the frame; the rope snapped taut with a sound like a shot.

"Ah, my God," murmured Al-Rabiah. "My God, my God."

He closed the video file, then leaned back for a time, reflecting, sipping his whisky, drawing on another Turkish Special. Finally he reached forward and ejected the disk, replacing it with another labeled *ARALSK-I.*

THE SCREEN FILLED WITH A DARK OBLONG the shape and texture of an old brick, its ends rounded as if by the elements, its surface covered with a dark, tubular moss. It looked like something dredged from a deep ocean trench, where its cylindrical hairs would have waved like the serpentine locks of the Medusa as it made its way through the abyss. It was mysterious and immediately recognizable as evil; one could imagine it turning men to stone.

Framed on a black screen, it seemed huge, reminding Al-Rabiah of the Juggernaut, or the Death Star, for its sides were not smooth, but seamed, like an irregular mosaic of armored plates riveted together. The creature, if one could call it that, was among the largest and most complicated of its kind, and yet it was only several ten-millionths of a meter long; millions could dance on the head of a pin.

Al-Rabiah knew it was inert and only potentially alive, but that did nothing to dispel a sense that somewhere in that hidden interior was a synapse, a bare wire, a rudimentary natural transistor, something that did the work of a brain—some apparatus of evil intelligence.

In its way it was as sensitive to the presence of a human host—its only host in nature—as a shark was to blood in the water, and as determined. It possessed a curious mobility for something not yet quite alive; it performed tricks and gambits. The dark, Medusan figure on the screen was the most amazing creation Al-Rabiah had ever encountered. And he had made it his, more or less.

"If you can encapsulate anything," the hanged man had challenged him, "encapsulate this."

A sealed, refrigerated box containing what amounted to frozen dust was duly handed over. The hanged man had grinned. The woman, Dr. Daura, said, "Aralsk-I. What they call chiornaya ospa. It means from Russia with love." She giggled and showed her yellow shark teeth.

The frozen dust had immediately rendered the laboratory in the northern cave a very dangerous place. In the lower level, beds of sedated human subjects drifted in and out of tormented slumber, their bodies incubating billions of the creatures, as they invaded, exploited, and ultimately destroyed their host cells, whose ruptured remains lay across the interior bioscape like cities bombed to rubble.

The technicians who inadvertently inhaled a grain of Aralsk-I became new incubators en route to a sedated death, thence into a bunkered dune of ash, where they joined the dogs and monkeys, Kurds and Jews, Al-Rabiah and company had sacrificed to science.

He clicked ahead one frame.

The new image was illuminated by a kind of cosmic radiance, like a galactic nucleus glowing in its envelope of stars. Al-Rabiah closed his eyes and let his mind animate the static micrograph. Dark oblongs cascaded slowly through a structure so complex that he had to remind himself that here, as before, the scale was not galactic, but microscopic, and what he envisioned was not the drift of vessels through infinite space but the invasion and conquest of a single human cell.

The dark bodies were Aralsk-I particles pouring through the outer membrane of the cell and releasing a dumbbell-shaped core. Now there came a quickening as the long genetic coil in the core stirred like a charmed courtier awakening from centuries of sleep, and, harnessing the resources of the host, began furiously to replicate itself.

Soon a horde of progeny drifted off, maturing, growing. Some grew tails and wriggled out into the cellular membrane, hiding in tubes they pushed into the walls of adjacent cells, which they then invaded. Others marched off to trick the cell's Gogli apparatus into giving them a coat of camouflage—a safe conduct through the host's immune system. Then the cloaked marauders burst through the cell wall and began their terrible campaign against the body that sustained them.

Al-Rabiah opened his eyes. These reconstructions of the life and replication of Aralsk-I left him excited, but also exhausted, his nerves on end. He ignited another Turkish Special and poured out two more fingers of whisky, then clicked the mouse.

A grey figure shaped like an elongated American football appeared on the screen, its sides smooth and seamless as glass. It was an artist's rendering of what Al-Rabiah had believed would be his masterpiece. As before, the scale was deceptive. The object on the screen seemed as large as an airliner, but was barely a thousandth of a millimeter long. The exterior, an inert polymer of Al-Rabiah's invention, encased several million Aralsk-I particles, isolating them from the external world, theoretically, forever.

Once put into a human body, they would circulate undetected until the inert shells were breached by the addition of a chemical solvent. Then those with the thinnest casings would rupture, and pour out their legions of dark bricks. A few weeks later, the thicker casings would dissolve, beginning another attack, and finally the thickest would fail, and a final siege would begin. Theoretically.

Theoretically, the human host could be immunized against the invaders mobilizing within. When a vessel released its evil little captives, the host might experience a mild flu, a head cold, a transient skin rash. But each release would both strengthen his immunity and diminish his symptoms. While the hosts were at their most contagious, the invaders would be expelled in droplets of saliva, mists of phlegm. Then the contagion would cease—until the next viral release. Finally, when the host's load of vessels was expended, he would disappear back into society, knowing nothing and forever unknown.

"Theoretically," Al-Rabish murmured now, aware that he was a little drunk. "The-o-re-ti-cal-ly."

He clicked to the next image. Five of the actual pellets produced by his laboratory stood like suspects in a police line-up. He had turned them out like a potter at his wheel, one by one by one; no two were alike, and none bore much resemblance to the idealized football shape in the illustration.

One pellet was almost spherical, the next almost a cylinder, like a grain of rice. The next preserved the football shape, but seemed uninflated. The next seemed about to burst. The last might have been a wadded sheet of paper. Al-Rabiah could not have said within a factor of ten thousand how many particles each contained. He could not have said when which pellet would rupture and begin the process of infection, or how long that process would last.

Nor was the grey polymer coating anything like the smooth, blimpish casing he had envisioned. The encapsulating shells looked more like the cratered surfaces of asteroids, and, again, Al-Rabiah had no accurate measure of their wall-thickness.

"Look at you," he muttered irritably, "a bunch of sports and freaks from a fucking cave."

Encapsulate this.

In time, Al-Rabiah had told himself repeatedly, he might have solved the problems of quality and reliability, and brought theory and reality closer together. But that first batch proved to be his last. The rest of the world was marching on Baghdad, Saddam was finished, the inspectors would spread across Iraq like a plague of vermin, getting into everything. He had just enough time to immunize his ten prisoners against Aralsk-I, then introduce the coated pellets into their bloodstreams. "Desperate science for desperate times." Then off they had gone, his ten chalices, back into the world, and he had been ordered to obliterate the laboratory and its work.

But the Americans and their collaborators had decided not to come to Baghdad that time. Al-Rabiah was left with his ten chalices out in the world, none of them fuzed. The order to arm them with an injection of chemical solvent never came.

By then, the country was crawling with UN inspectors, its ceramic blue sky latticed with the contrails of foreign jets enforcing no-fly zones, the desert air humidified by constant rumors of imminent invasion. Al-Rabiah and the small cadre who had survived and still believed in the enterprise chose not to wait. He and his men had set out like the whalers of an earlier century, knowing it would be years before they returned to Iraq, if they returned at all. They gave their lives to following the chalices.

There was no money for this, and, really, no credit in doing it. Al-Rabiah had kept back the expensive gear, the computers and air conditioners and containments, to be sold on the black market. He sustained himself as a visiting scholar at institutions like the Centre for Analytic Studies and the Third World Academy of Sciences. The others joined the Middle Eastern diaspora, working illegally in foreign hospitals and garages and takeaways, as janitors, concierges, nurses, night managers, cooks, news-sellers, rubbish collectors, whatever came to hand. Al-Rabiah took his family with him on this long voyage. The others left their wives and children at home.

Home. The word had once brought comfort. Now it conjured a ruined land defeated and occupied by the Americans, then cut apart by civil strife, a hopeless place.

Over time, the chalices began to fail. The immunity of the hosts diminished; when a pellet released its cargo of particles, more serious symptoms ensued. In some the pellets ruptured all at once, so that the person threatened to go off like a bomb. The failures were destroyed, reduced to ashes.

Now, Al-Rabiah thought, only the one remained. But this one, thanks be to God, he had managed to arm.

He closed his eyes for a moment, thinking of how things should progress. The first wave of contagion from the tenth chalice would infect ten or twenty victims, and each of them would infect ten or twenty more, and so on into the millions. Then the infection would stop until the next pellet detonated within, and the sequence would begin all over again, in another place.

Public health agencies would hurry rapid-response teams and materiel to each new ripple of contagion, hoping to arrest its spread. But on the electronic screens at the World Health Organization center in Geneva, the outbreaks would continue to bloom like digital explosions, now in England, now in America, now in Indonesia, now in Japan, now in Argentina. There would be no pattern in time or space, no predictability, no way of conferring immunity on every one of the billions of people at risk, no means of identifying the symptomless carrier. God knew how long the process would continue. Perhaps it went on forever.

Al-Rabiah raised his glass to the screen. "Here's looking at *you,* Squadron Leader."

THE BUZZING SEEMED TO COME from a great distance, during a dream of viral brigades dropping through host cells like German paratroopers filling the Dutch sky. Al-Rabiah finally recognized the sound of his mobile, but had no idea how long it had been ringing. He must have drifted off to sleep.

Shaking himself alert, he groped for the telephone, annoyed that Silfer would call again. And then it came to him that in all probability it was not his wife, but Abdel and Yusuf calling from Brighton. Al-Rabiah smiled with relief. Abdel and Yusuf, as close and reliable as two loyal sons. Peter Gayle, they would tell him, was intact and on the move. Thanks to a once-obscure chemist from Samarra, they would tell him, smallpox was back in the world. God is great!

XIII

On that first day, driving out of Brighton, Gayle had pondered ways of escaping his new captivity, which could only end in his execution, kneeling, like those poor Iraqi lads back in the garage, surrendering to death. Out of the corner of his eye, he'd seen the Tariq pistol held loosely in the passenger's lap. If he made a move, there would be the sharp crack of a shot and the world would slowly fade away.

Road signs pointing to Winchester, to Aldershot, to Newbury and Swindon, told him they headed north and west, across the Downs south of the M-4. He had pleasant memories of this countryside. He and his mother had made just this journey many times in the hated old Vauxhall estate in which, as they were not on the Continent, Peter was allowed the front passenger seat.

"Time for a Drive," his mother would say, somehow imparting to the term a capital D. Then off they had gone, away from the sea and into this lovely, undulating patchwork of trapezoidal green and golden fields bound together by narrow lanes and hedgerows, ragged strips of ash and beech, with the odd bone-like outcropping of chalk, as if a white giant had been buried there. Above them curved the maritime sky beloved of English painters.

"I think we might quite enjoy life on the Downs, Peter," his mother had declared on one of these outings. "A lovely part of England, a venerable part, an honest part." She had something good to say about every corner of England and some praise for parts of Scotland; she was silent on the merits of Ireland and Wales. "We could find one of those little cottages of pale stone. We could have animals. A dog for you, a cat for me. A pig. A pony, if you like. A cow."

"We could live in a shoe."

"Not possible."

"Why not?"

"Because I am not yet an old lady, and I know precisely what to do."

"That's because you don't have so many children."

"One is more than enough."

They'd laughed, knowing they would only abandon the seaside for their fortnight at the Victoria, and, after all, Lake Léman was rather like a sea, wasn't it? Gayle grinned, remembering, moving for a moment leagues and decades away from the hurtling Saab and his quiet, dangerous companion.

"Something funny?"

Gayle shook his head. "Reverie." He kept his eye on the thin line of cracked macadam not quite two vehicles wide, widened at intervals for passing. At any moment a lorry might come screaming around a bend and sweep them away. Well, better that than dying on your knees.

"Do you know the Downs?"

"Not really. We were city mice."

The man barked a hard laugh. "I shall try to keep the country cats away." He had lapsed into silence, then, except for occasional steering commands that kept them to the minor roads.

Half an hour out of Brighton, a beige Volkswagen bus had crept up behind them. "Ah, here come my young men."

"Having cleaned up their mess?"

"Having disposed of two unfortunate Arab boys nobody will miss."

Gayle said nothing. He could launch the Saab off one of these rising turns and hope he wouldn't get his neck broken in the roll-overs. Harder to work out, now a Volkswagen full of killer boys was tailing them.

"You know, Mr. Gayle," the passenger said at last, "I can almost hear the gears meshing in your head. Because I've let you see where we are going, you think we must leave you out here to amuse the foxes and crows. You think of desperate alternatives. But I meant what I said. When we have confronted our enemy, off you go." He held up the Tariq. "I will even return this object of sentimental value."

Another half-hour's driving and he told Gayle to take the next right turn, and then another, and, a few miles on, another. Finally they had come to a faded FOR SALE sign dangling from a length of rusted chain stretched across a driveway. The sign bore the name of an estate agent in Swindon. The passenger got out to drop the barrier, and signaled Gayle to drive in and stop. The Volkswagen followed close behind.

Back in the Viggen with the chain in place, the man nodded up the drive, and Gayle drove on. "Thank you for not running me over."

"Never occurred to me," said Gayle, although it had.

The rough, one-lane track arced uphill through an abandoned orchard of ancient apple trees, their old limbs bending with autumn fruit, then up a treeless slope rising beneath a blanket of wild grasses and stubble, seared brown. At the top of the hill was a stone cottage that seemed to have erupted spontaneously from the terrain.

Gayle pulled the Viggen up beside a ruined gate, bleached grey as driftwood and supported by a single hinge. The Volkswagen swung in behind him, blocking the drive. A plume of dust settled across the path.

He got out and walked around the low garden fence, which was missing a good many slats. Everything about the place, even its stone walls, radiated decrepitude and decay, as if no one had lived there for ages, if ever.

It was a nicely elevated spot they'd found, offering what an infantryman would call excellent fields of fire over the empty, scorched fields. He thought they must be Set Asides, for they lay fallow, barren of the stubble of recent crops. Behind the cottage stood a pair of grey outbuildings, turned by time and weather into driftwood, like the fence. An open cistern rose between them, a three-meter cube made from the same beige stone as the cottage; where it was not streaked with green algae, the water mirrored the blue sky.

There was not another structure as far as Gayle's eye could see; this England seemed an unpopulated relic of the distant past. "Very nice," said Gayle. "How much are they asking?"

"We are not buyers, Mr. Gayle. A compatriot put us onto this place. It has been on the market since the owner died two years ago. Unless the estate agent gets lucky, we have it for as long as we need it."

"This is where we wait to see who comes a-knock, knock, knocking?"

"Yes."

"And when will that be?"

"Word is percolating out. Two dead Arab boys. Peter Gayle abducted. A trusted friend in London tells a trusted friend in Baghdad the whole thing, including where to find us. The trusted friend tells his trusted friend. Finally, at the end of a daisy chain of friendships, the last trusted friend sells us to our enemies. And *voila!* They come a-knocking. But this all takes time. A day or two here, a day or two there, and so on and so on. We are in no hurry." He nodded toward the cottage. "Come, I'll show you your room."

Gayle followed his host through the front door into a small mud room that opened into a dining area with a sink, the remains of an ancient cooker, and a fridge of antique manufacture beneath a tier of windows looking out across the fields. The grey stone floor still bore the stains of old spills, but someone had swept and mopped it and cleaned the windows.

"Not the Ritz, Mr. Gayle. No gas, no electricity. The fridge is just a sealed container to keep the flies away. The cooker is useless. But we have a good spring that keeps the cistern filled with water. We have candles, torches. Provisions. Pretend you're off at camp."

Camp! Gayle heard his mother nearly gag on the term. "*We English do not do Camp!*

"I missed that," he said.

"Then this will flesh out your experience."

"I thought it might."

His room lay beyond the kitchen, through another door and down half a flight of steps to a kind of sitting room. A small alcove offered a sleeping bag and a towel and a feeble light through a narrow clerestory window. Someone had swept the place, so at least one wouldn't be sleeping in shit.

"I'll have my men bring your luggage in."

"Leave it in the car. I'll get what I need as we go along."

"As you wish."

They went back outside, where the man sat down cross-legged by the fence and lit a pipe, relaxed as a farmer in his fields. Gayle sat down nearby, his arms around his knees. It was a strangely amiable gathering, not much like the old captivity at all, although captivity it certainly was. When night came, the door to that alcove would be locked, the steps guarded by the three boys taking turns. If Gayle bolted, they'd shoot him with no more feeling than frogs spearing insects. He looked up at them now, where they unloaded the Volkswagen.

"Do they have names?"

"Tom, Dick, and Harry."

"I thought you were Harry."

"One nom de guerre is as good as another."

The three were almost identical, all within an inch or two of the same height, all dark, all just sprouting a thin black beard. They wore huge white cross-trainers, jeans with hooded navy sweatshirts over soiled tees bearing the name of some famous team. The new army of the night. Their soft brown eyes were as opaque and illegible as those of reptiles. The lads looked quick and strong, trained up as guerilla muscle for this Harry chap. "I'll call them Huey, Dewey, and Louie."

"That will be fine." The man grinned, but behind the rimless lenses his eyes were cold. "Ducky."

"You can be Uncle Donald."

The smile disappeared. "Harry will do."

"What do they call you?"

"What I tell them to."

Now the boy Gayle decided was Huey came out of the VW leading a lamb by a length of colored cloth.

"Pet?" asked Gayle.

"Dinner."

The lamb gave the two men a tranquil glance, then it followed Huey at a cheerful trot around the side of the cottage toward the outbuildings. "Poor little bugger."

"Are you a vegetarian?"

Gayle shook his head. "Your boys seem to enjoy fleshing things out."

"Young soldiers don't brood about what they have to do. They try to stay alive and kill their enemies. Well, you know how that goes, don't you?"

"Touché."

"As for your poor little bugger, had we not liberated him, he would have gone to God at an abattoir with legions of his fellows. All those bewildered, frightened cries. The stink of singed wool from the electric stunners. The odors of death floating like poison gas upon the air. He would have seen his future. Whether you're a lamb or a man, you don't want to see your future so clearly."

"I trust mine will be full of surprises."

"I guarantee it. So is the lamb's. It has gone with, um, Dewey?"

"Huey."

"Whomever. It grazes a bit, thinks lovingly of its mother, perhaps. At some point Huey, whom the lamb now trusts, will put an arm around its little shoulders and, with a razor-sharp blade, sever its jugular. The world goes grey before the wound begins to sting. He dies in Huey's arms." Harry released a plume of fragrant pipe smoke. "Fade to black."

THE BOYS KILLED THE POOR LITTLE BUGGER early that afternoon, hoisted it head downward on a hooked chain in one of the sheds, removed its entrails, and cut away its wool until it hung washed, naked, and pink as a Baptist missionary among the cannibals. The body spent the rest of the day on an improvised metal spit over a fire dug into the earth behind the cottage, with such delicacies as the head and edible organs wrapped in wet rags and put among the embers to bake. The three boys took some pains to keep the smoke down, although, given the remoteness of the place, a mushroom cloud would not have summoned the fire brigade.

Gayle had dozed off, lulled by his own helplessness, the whir of bees, and the sweet touch of the autumn afternoon. He slept until the sun grazed the rolling horizon to the southwest and the long shadow of the cottage covered him with a blanket of cold. Then he started awake, fleeing a horrific but unremembered dream. Iraqi boys dying on their knees, he thought, or lambs to the slaughter.

He stood up slowly, clinging to the fence for support until he got his balance. He looked around for Harry, but the man was nowhere to be seen. The boys were in back with the lamb. It looked like opportunity.

He started down the driveway, past the Saab, past the Volkswagen, trying to hurry, but moving like a man underwater; his feet weighed tons, his lungs sucked at the atmosphere as if he were about to drown. Huey, Dewey, and Louie would come after him like three greyhounds, and they would not bring him back alive.

"May I join you?" Harry came up behind him, wreathed in sweet smoke.

"I don't mind."

"Are you all right?"

"A bit stiff, lying on the ground." Gayle coughed, then turned and spat into the grasses.

"I thought you might be eloping."

"So did I."

"Better you relax and enjoy camp. It will be over before you know it."

"That's what they tell lambs."

Harry uttered a clanging laugh, releasing a cloud of smoke like a talk balloon. "Lambs, yes. And suicide bombers. Pregnant women. Dental patients. Boys at camp."

"One size fits all."

"My lads sent me to fetch you to the great feast they've prepared." He pulled on his pipe. "Come."

The five of them sat on cushions arranged around large dishes on the kitchen's freshly swept stone floor, dipping up chunks of roast lamb and its juices with cupped shards of flat bread, which they wielded like oven gloves. The boys had added a plate of apples from the abandoned orchard, tomatoes and cucumbers and onions and a lentil paste. China mugs held sweet tea.

The preparations and the food had been like a ticket home for the chefs. The blank-faced young killers now looked more like happy young men. Like aircrew back on the ground after a difficult raid, thought Gayle, infantry back from the front. They spoke like excited hornets, words pouring out in staccato streams, arms and hands waving. But they spoke only to one another, as if Gayle were not there. None of the four, it was clear, had ever met an Englishman he liked.

But Gayle found his invisibility agreeable. He wanted to be left alone. The tea felt good in his throat, and he stabbed with his bread at the meat and tomatoes, although his heart wasn't in it. The bug he'd brought home from Bern had revived. His temples were hot to the touch, his head pounded. He felt as if he'd been in a fight. It had been so bloody stupid to lie out in the wind, reviving his cold.

The buzz of conversation suddenly died, as though a switch had thrown. "You worry me, Mr. Gayle," said Harry, one hand suspended with a fold of flatbread sandwiching a chunk of lamb in a nest of cucumbers and tomatoes. "Here our lamb has given his all for us, and you merely pick at it. It will never be this succulent again." He chuckled, although his eyes remained empty of mirth. "Indeed, before we leave this place, the meat may be moving on the plate."

Gayle coughed behind his hand and shook his head. "Not up to a big meal. Apologies to the chefs."

"I fear we've worn you out."

"You may have done." He stood up unsteadily. "I'm going to make it an early night. Get rid of this bug."

An interrogative buzz ensued among the four.

"A bug?"

"A head cold. Nothing to worry about."

Wrapped in his sleeping bag and sealed in the alcove, Gayle spent a febrile night, soaking his clothes with perspiration, then shivering with chill. Sleep dropped him back into his Iraqi cell, which he now shared with the charred remains of Mickey Williams. The dreamer believed that Anna the Nurse secretly looked in on them, whether to help or hurt he couldn't say.

Dewey brought him warm tea during the night, and water to drink, and some aspirin. In the morning, Louie arrived with some flatbread and marmalade and another mug of tea. No one spoke and there was no warmth in these contacts. Gayle dozed fitfully through the day, waking long enough to note the return of prickly heat to his limbs and neck.

"How are you doing, Mr. Gayle?" asked Harry, arriving from nowhere.

"I feel like shit."

"You may not be camp material."

"Does that mean you're sending me home?"

"Not yet."

"Don't let the bait spoil."

"I'll pop by later."

"I'll be here."

Then back to dreamland. Mickey Williams was on the intercom now, telling Gayle he'd caught the real honest to Christ crud, which meant a bunch of snake-voiced boys coming around in their bug suits, setting fires.

We're fucked, Mouse. Out we go.

But the ejection handle actuated nothing. The Tornado was rolling crazily across the desert sky, among that smoke of stars, and Gayle couldn't get the fucking canopy to blow. He felt Mouse's arm encircle his shoulder and wondered how the navigator could do that in their cramped, tandem cockpit, but then he realized he wasn't in the kite after all, but on a bloody patch of stubbled ground, and the arm around his shoulder wasn't Mouse but Huey, whose razor-sharp blade was icy cold against the jugular…

Gayle sat up, suddenly awake, disoriented, wondering where he could be, and why, and what had happened to poor Mouse. Then, remembering the dream, he fingered his throat to make sure the jugular was intact. He remembered the drive from Brighton and the abandoned cottage on the Downs.

He rolled out of the sleeping bag, and stood up to peer out the clerestory window. A spreading crack of furnace light along the horizon looked like dawn; his watch said it was six. His clothing hung like Spanish moss upon his limbs, damp and musty with cold sweat. But his headache had diminished to mere background discomfort, his forehead was cool to his touch. When he pulled back his sleeves, he saw the prickly heat had faded to faint pink freeforms that floated like submerged flowers beneath the skin.

It didn't much resemble Mickey Williams' crud. Perhaps one needn't dream of Arab boys moving up the slope dressed as insects. Gayle sat down with his ankles crossed, his back pressed against the cool stone wall, and pulled the sleeping bag around him, waiting in his locked alcove for the others to wake up.

LIFE AT THE COTTAGE SETTLED into a quotidian routine. Recovered from what he thought of as the Bern Bug, Gayle began his mornings with a long walk around the edges of the cleared area; soon the walk became a trot, the trot a pounding run, as if he fled the certainty that they would finally kill him.

One of the boys, silenced pistol in hand, always ran with him, staying just behind and to his left, a blind spot from which he could be easily picked off. Up by the cottage, the other two boys watched the morning runs, Kalashnikovs cradled in their arms. Harry watched and nursed his pipe.

Then there was a bit of flatbread and tea and an apple for breakfast. Gayle got the first freezing shower most mornings, which, Harry said, was his right as an honored guest. One of the lads waited outside the bath, just in case. Standing under the trickle of cold water, Gayle thought of other things. He thought he was losing fat, which was all to the good. He thought he might let the blonde stubble on his face grow into a beard.

At mid-day, another apple and bit of honeyed bread with another mug of tea. In the evening, the boys would devise some novel use of the poor little bugger's remains, although no amount of spices and onions could disguise its increasing age.

"In a year or two, it will be right for haggis," said Gayle.

"Haggis?"

"Scottish cuisine. Road kill."

"The meat is still stationary."

"I know my old food, Harry. Any pub can give you a pickled egg from Roman times. Meat pies from Victoria's reign."

Even the boys, who knew a bit of English after all, smiled at the ancient pickled eggs and pies. Be a clown, thought Gayle, all the world loves a clown.

Most afternoons they would take turns around the chess board, with Harry teaching the boys, then showing them how little their British guest knew about the game. Harry avoided ambuscades, he rarely sent his knights galloping in to hem in and assassinate the foreign king. Instead, he deftly kept things going, like a master playing with a smart child. And they would talk.

"Who are they, really?" asked Gayle one night, nodding toward the three boys.

"Really?" Harry hesitated, studying Gayle, as if weighing whether this Englishman should ever be told the truth about anything. Finally he said, "They are my sons. Some of my sons."

"How many do you have?"

"A goodly number. All of them warriors." Harry's eyes gleamed and he fiddled with his pipe, thinking of other times and places, his armor temporarily pierced. "All loyal, all brave. Immune from dishonor."

"And cold blooded," Gayle added, thinking of the Brighton garage.

"The enemy is the enemy. It doesn't matter if he is young or good-looking or from a fine family or has eyes like a doe. To me, to my sons, he is just the enemy. In the desert, you live like scorpions or you do not live at all."

Gayle thought they lived more like dogs, the days drifting by as they ate and shat and slept, occupying space without occupying time. He was ready for a change. "Maybe the boys could go pick up some fresh provisions," he told Harry during the daily chess lesson. "Run up to Swindon, bring home something tasty."

Harry shook his head. "I need everyone here when they come."

"The other scorpions?"

He nodded.

"When will that be?"

"Who knows? They are already overdue. But they will come. And when it is over we will free you."

As you freed the Arab boys, thought Gayle. As you freed the lamb.

Next morning the chummy atmosphere had chilled. A different Harry met Gayle at the gate, where he waited for a running mate to appear. The man's face was grey and drawn, the mouth a hard, bitter line, and he held the Tariq pistol in one hand. "Huey and Dewey took sick during the night," he said. "Louie is caring for them."

"Rotten meat."

"No, a flu."

"Think I'm a carrier?"

"I don't know what to think, Mr. Gayle. My sons have not been sick a day in their lives, yet here they are, like flies in winter. And here you are, the picture of health. I find it very suspicious. So now we give up the little jokes about camp, the funny duck names, the niceties. What Americans call the bullshit." He waved the pistol toward the cottage entrance. "You will stay in your room until my men have recovered."

"That could be a long time."

"It could be a very long time. Come."

THAT WAS THE END OF THE MORNING RUNS and cold showers, the communal meals and chess lessons. In the early morning, Harry arrived to replace the plastic pail that served as a toilet and delivered a liter of bottled water and an apple and scrap of bread. Gayle had forsworn the mottled remains of the lamb. The Tariq pistol always in one hand, Harry executed his detail without speaking and without taking his tired, furious eyes off Gayle. As he'd said, no more niceties. No more bullshit

The smaller increments of time, the minutes and hours, punted slowly by, as they do in captivity. But the days burned swiftly away like a temporal fuze sputtering toward his invisible future, toward the sound of someone knocking, to the moment when Gayle would be made to kneel, then shot through the back of his skull.

He had endured worse. The filth was nothing a hot bath wouldn't fix. There were no interrogations, no sportive humiliations by grinning Iraqi officers. He could do this kind of time, as American gangsters used to say in films, standing on his head. Nor was Gayle inclined to scratch marks on the stone wall to mark the passage of days. It would be over when it was over. Like everything.

The idle mind being what it is, Gayle spent hours roaming his memory, favorite cars, the names of lost and deceased pets, the Drives with Mother, the lovely afternoon with Anna the Evil Nurse at the Hotel Victoria, the girl who'd tried to reach him in Brighton, what'shername, Stephanie, and the other fine times overlooking Lake Léman, although such recollections were mere portraiture. Not for the first time, Gayle recalled the poor doomed bloke in *Paths of Glory*, who said he hadn't had a sexual thought in a fortnight. Sex had gone the way of Empire.

He spent some time flying, sometimes an imaginary Tornado, not in combat, but just flying, its wings his wings. Sometimes he was out in a Chipmunk, sometimes he balanced precariously, like a man on a huge beach ball, hovering in a Harrier. Often he traversed the indigo calm of the stratosphere. Now and then he rolled the Tornado into a low-level pass, the planet a slurry of blue and green rolling past him fifty feet below.

He was always alone on these flights, not wanting to have the remains of Mickey Williams strapped into the back seat. When memory steered him toward the Iraqi lads shot in the garage, or the sad fates of the other eight members of the April Ten, he veered away. He tried not to dwell upon his own plight, the inexorable advance of his own death, although, of course, now and then there was nowhere else to dwell.

Like all prisoners, he thought about escaping. He supposed he could kick his way through the locked wooden door, but then what to do about his guards? Harry or one of his boys would be sitting on the stairs, laughing his head off.

Gayle probed the clerestory window for a soft spot, a crack, a finger-hold in the long wooden frame, but the trellis of panes had been set into the stone wall to admit light, not air; heavy mortar nails held the frame rigidly in place. Gayle believed he could knock out enough glass to squeeze through the narrow aperture, although not without a clawing by the remaining shards. He saw himself stand up on the far side of the wall, streaming blood like a flagellant pilgrim, Harry fiddling with a pipe and one or all of the boys ready to give Gayle's experience a bit more fleshing out.

The idea of escape slowly evaporated, as it does in captivity. Running in place and doing press-ups and sit-ups to keep limber lasted only a few days. His forays into memory became less frequent, as the shapes and colors of the past blurred and faded. He settled into a torpor he recognized, passing the time like an impounded dog.

It would be over when it was over.

The first morning Harry failed to appear barely registered on Gayle. Not until late afternoon did he notice that the fetid pail had not been replaced, no new apples or bit of bread or water had arrived. "I must write an angry letter," he told the room, thinking inanely of what he might say to Harry about the service in this place.

By the next dawn, however, hunger and thirst had begun to burn away the torpor. Gayle waited for Harry, and when the man did not come, he tried to apply some of Mouse's cherished situational awareness. Maybe Harry and the boys had left him here to die. Had he heard the Viggen drive away? The Volkswagen?

He cocked his head to listen, but the cottage was quiet. Were they off shopping? Were they waiting on the other side of that door, bets laid on whether Gayle would pop out and who would be the one to shoot him? Working out the possibilities was like cutting a path through jungle: one saw little evidence of progress.

As the light faded, however, and Gayle found himself out of water and almost hungry enough to try the remains of the lamb, maggots and all, he decided it didn't matter who or what awaited him. It was over.

His second kick shattered the oak door, weakened by wood rot, around the metal lock. Then, standing in the open threshold, Gayle waited to hear a voice, an alarum, the sound of someone moving. A shot. But there was nothing. No one waited in the adjoining room, nor on the steps. The kitchen was devoid of life, save for a squadron of moribund flies spending their final hours with a bit of old lamb on platters among the cushions where he and his captors had taken their meals. The room seemed to have been suddenly abandoned, its stone floor littered with rubbish, nothing put away. The Tariq lay in a stratum of debris along the countertop. Why had Harry left it there? A piece of cheese in a trap? Was he returning an object of sentimental value? Gayle scooped up the pistol and stuffed it into a pocket.

Then he stepped into the sweet open air, the furnace light of a fine sunset. The two vehicles were parked where he'd last seen them. Had Harry and sons simply walked away? Had the boys in bug costumes arrived and quietly destroyed them? Did he care? God no. Gayle headed for the Saab.

"Not even a goodbye, Mr. Gayle?"

Harry stood in the doorway behind him, leaning on the frame for support, one of the AK-47s pointed at Gayle's torso. The older man's face was drawn with pain, his black hair wild and flumed with fresh patches of grey. A cascade of rivet-like pustules flowed downward across his face and into the neck of his shirt, as if a raspberry sauce had been emptied over his head. He exuded an odor Gayle could not identify, a stink not of death so much as death impending, a miasma of the scents that men emit toward the end of their lives.

"What happened?"

"What do you care?" Harry gestured feebly with his free hand and added in an exhausted voice, "Well, you see. I have caught the thing too."

"What about the boys?"

"My three sweet ducks? They are dying, Mr. Gayle."

"I'm sorry."

"Of course you are." Harry laughed, coughed, and spat something into the shadows, then gestured with the rifle. "Come, I will show you my sons."

The small bedroom buzzed with sleepy flies, intoxicated by this trove of human wreckage. The three lads lay like fallen soldiers waiting to be collected by a graves detail, supine, side by side, one two three.

Louie wore only a Manchester United tee shirt and blue briefs, his body like a map of dark continents where blood pooled beneath the pallid olive skin. He seemed to be dissolving into a caviar of tiny pustules, dark and porous, leaking blood and webs of serum. He was still alive, for the dark eyes tracked Gayle as he entered the room. Their irises were the rust color of dried blood, and the boy frowned, distracted and worried. Louie emitted an infrasonic moan; his fever was palpable in the close atmosphere of the bedroom.

Huey and Dewey were still alive, just. They were past caring about their pain and their fever seemed to have passed, leaving them suspended in shock as life dwindled toward its vanishing point. Their blood-dark eyes were open, staring with disconcerting interest at something Gayle did not much want to see. But they were no longer quite recognizable as men. It was as if their affliction had charred them, inside and out, then basted them with blood and sera. They saw what was coming and had given up.

"Jesus," whispered Gayle.

"Do you know what it is?"

Gayle shook his head.

"I am old enough to recognize the Devil when I see him. As a young civil servant I visited a village in the north, where this plague had swept everyone away. It was like the hot breath of God himself. It was like the radiation in the cave. No one knew it was there until too late, and few survived it." He leaned toward Gayle. "Smallpox,

Mr. Gayle. A disease wiped off the earth fifty years ago and here it is, killing us. Killing us, not you. Don't you find that odd?"

"You think this is mine?"

Harry nodded. "I know it is. This is why no one has come a-knocking. They know you will kill us."

"You're fucking crazy." But, Gayle thought frantically, what about Mickey's crud? All those little red rivets? He shook his head furiously. "I had the sniffles, and they're gone. This is yours, Harry."

"Call it ours. I haven't time to argue the point. I am burning up with fever. These little bumps are streaming down my body like a rain of blood. The pain is constant. I dream like a mad man. I feel myself losing the will to die." He studied Gayle for a moment, then, "I have not lost it yet, nor am I so weak as to let you run away. We have work to do."

"What work?"

"The dirtiest you can imagine." Harry leaned heavily against the wall, his eyes fluttered; for a moment the Kalashnikov drooped. But when Gayle took a step toward the door, the man revived and aimed the muzzle at Gayle's face. "We must stop this thing here," he said. "We must not let them have their epidemic."

"Them?"

"The men who made you what you are. And the others, who would like to have you in their arsenals." Seeing Gayle about to protest, Harry waved the gun. "No, no, we don't have time to argue." He gestured toward his lads. "Here is my dilemma. If I shoot you now, which I am powerfully inclined to do, I destroy their terrible new weapon…"

"You're crazy."

"But then someone comes upon our infected remains. They carry the virus away with them. Perhaps they restore us to our families, to our new land of milk and honey, and the enemy gets a very satisfactory epidemic after all, if not the global one he desired." He paused, drawing deep breaths with difficulty. "So here is what we do. We take the jerry cans from the bus and soak the boys, me, the cottage, everything in petrol. We light it off. We slay the dragon."

"And I go my merry way?"

"You are welcome to join us in the fire. You can go live in isolation until the thing they have grown in you dies. You can run until the mother of all scorpions overtakes you and stores you in formaldehyde, like John Dillinger's cock." Trying to laugh, Harry coughed into a hand and spat something at the floor. "My choices are very simple compared to yours, don't you think?

"I think you're full of shit."

"Worse than shit, I assure you."

"I'm not throwing myself on your fire."

"No, you would rather leave a wake of death." Harry nodded toward the boys. "Of this."

"I didn't do this."

"Then we blame God." Harry gave an exhausted shrug and waved the rifle at Gayle. "Now we go to work." He propped himself just outside the door, where he could cover both the bedroom and the kitchen with the Kalashnikov. "Bring my sons in here," he said. "Arrange them on their cushions."

Gayle shuddered. "Arrange them yourself."

"The only reason you are alive, Mr. Gayle, is that I need your help. Helping me is your only chance of surviving the day. Take it or leave it."

The trick, Gayle thought, was to make an engineering problem of it, so that the boys were not great bleeding sides of rotting beef but mere sacks of shit to be lifted and dragged from one room to the other. It was not an easy illusion to sustain.

Kneeling behind Louie, whom he had coaxed to a sitting position, Gayle embraced the slick smear that enveloped the body, placed his cheek against the sheen of excretions, as he lifted Louie under the arms. He half expected the boy's flesh to slide off the skeleton, like cooked beef from its bone. But the ravaged surface remained strangely taut, with a soft, velvety feel that evoked a beautiful black woman from Dakar Gayle had met in Paris years before. Theodore and the others at the Hotel Victoria had almost genuflected. Protectively wrapped in tactile memory, Gayle wrestled Louie's dead weight out of the bedroom and laid him among the cushions.

"Excellent," said Harry, "but, please, more of a sitting position. We are not stacking firewood."

Gayle rearranged the boy's limbs, conscious that Louie's frightened eyes never left him.

Huey was surprisingly light. Gayle lifted him in his arms, bore him like a bride into the kitchen, and lowered him onto his cushion with his back against the wall. The boy watched him attentively, but made no sound. Neither did Dewey when he was transported. Gayle studied the grim tableau for a time, then stood back, feeling like a man dipped in blood, no longer able to conjure the lady from Dakar.

Harry came into the kitchen, eyes gleaming, the red-stippled skin of his cheeks shining with tears. He approached his sons, reciting something in the excited, indecipherable language they had used at meals. In one hand he held the assault rifle, keeping it pointed in Gayle's general direction. In the other, he gripped one of the silenced pistols the boys had used in Brighton. He stepped toward Louie, who watched his father with frantic eyes, and shot the boy through the forehead. Huey was next, and showed some interest in what must follow, but no fear. Another silenced shot through the forehead. Dewey did not even look up when his turn came.

"Now," Harry said, his voice heavy and sad, "we bring the petrol."

The Volkswagen held ten jerry cans, which Gayle hauled into the cottage, two at a time, always under Harry's gun, and, as darkness fell, the blinding beam of his electric torch. Fifty gallons would make a grand fire, but not as grand as the one at Mickey Williams' place. Poor Detective Inspector Wickers, should he get the case, would be mystified by the absence of a propane tank.

When the containers were in the cottage, Harry said, "Pour out two of them in the bedroom and the hall." When that was done, he said, "Put seven on my sons." Then, as Gayle dribbled fuel across the bodies, Harry picked up the last of the jerry cans, cracked the seal, and upended it over his own head.

Still carrying the Kalashnikov, and refreshed by the cold evaporation of the petrol, Harry strode to his own cushion and sat down in the gory bosom of his little family, in a room that had become a firebomb of vapor. "Thank you, Mr. Gayle." He held Gayle in the beam of light for a time, as though studying him. "Poor thing," he said. Then Harry gave an odd, lunatic smile, and aimed the rifle at Gayle's heart. "Now we stop this thing."

Gayle was in motion before Harry fired, two long strides and a dive through the open entry door into darkness, followed by a barrage of automatic fire, the rounds whining off the stones. A fireball of ignited petrol fumes detonated behind him. Gayle rolled and kept rolling, then regained his feet and leapt the low fence, the fire like a monstrous breath behind him.

By the time he stopped and turned to look, the cottage was all burning beams held in a cauldron of charred stone. Now and then, ammunition went off like a string of firecrackers, as the flames took the silenced pistols, the Kalashnikovs, and, in a sudden and unexpected drum roll, a clutch of rocket-propelled grenades.

For a time Gayle watched the flames play over the ruin. Then, his mind and body numb with fatigue and melancholy, he slowly undressed, tossing everything but his shoes and the Tariq into the fire. When the clothing had burned to ash, Gayle walked slowly around the remains of the cottage, hoisted himself up the side of the overflowing cistern, and slid into the cold, black water like a merman returning to the sea.

FROM THE FRINGES OF THE OLD APPLE ORCHARD, three men had watched the cottage since early afternoon. They were armed with silenced pistols and dressed in plastic raincoats with hoods and respirator masks, clean-room booties, and goggles loose around their necks, like an off-duty Panzer tank crew.

Indeed, Mohammad Al-Rabiah may have felt a bit like Erwin Rommel as he lowered Silfer's tiny mother-of-pearl opera glasses. The burning cottage was as clear an emblem of victory as a desert full of ruined Allied armor.

From the moment in Vienna when he had learned that Abdel and Yusuf were dead, that Peter Gayle had been taken, that the carefully nurtured epidemic had been effectively put on hold, Al-Rabiah had seen the matter conclude in just this way. The captors would use Peter Gayle as bait, unaware that his presence would destroy them. They would have done better, Al-Rabiah mused at the time, had they stolen a ton of radioactive waste.

Sure enough, the betrayals had begun trickling in. A man and three of his sons from somewhere in the north of Iraq had executed Abdel and Yusuf, whose tortured bodies had been discovered in a Kentish ditch. They had taken Peter Gayle hostage. They were in England. Finally, the last piece of the puzzle had arrived: they were in an abandoned cottage southeast of Swindon with such and such GPS coordinates.

But Al-Rabiah had a rat's intuition when it came to traps. He would not be lured by this easily acquired information. Instead he went with Silfer and the angels to Trieste, attended the workshop, delivered a paper, then drove down through the Italian boot. He'd taken his time, letting the viral clock tick down to the enemy's extinction.

On this day, the virus seats itself in their lungs. Today it spreads through the lymphatic system. Today the early symptoms appear: headache and fever and mental anguish. Today pustules pour down their bodies. Thus cued, he had left his family in Glion and set out in the green Ford Focus for the South Downs.

In a sense, Al-Rabiah thought now, the abductors had inadvertently arranged a verifying experiment. They were dead, the

Englishman lived on. No pustules on his body. He seemed none the worse for wear, barring a fatigue one could detect even at this distance. Well, and perhaps some depression, as he began to realize what he had become.

Ah, here he was, back from the cistern. "There is not enough water in great Neptune's ocean to clean you up," Al-Rabiah murmured, watching Gayle through the glasses.

The Englishman stood as naked as first man, primitive and alone upon the earth save for a crowd of dancing lights and shadows cast by the burning cottage. For a time Gayle scanned the illuminated slope, the black trees and fields beyond, the starry night. Then he went to his convertible, opened the boot, and took out a shirt, which he used to towel himself dry. He dressed in jeans and a black pullover, fresh socks, and pulled on his leather jacket against the chill. He walked to the wall where he'd left his shoes and the Tariq. He wiped off the shoes and slipped them on, and stuffed the pistol into a jacket pocket. Then he walked to the smoldering ruins and tossed the damp shirt into the flames.

"There, you think it's over." Al-Rabiah smiled. "But it is just beginning."

Gayle got into the Saab and maneuvered it clear of the Volkswagen, took a final look at the ruin, and headed down the drive. The three men pulled back into the night. When they heard the Viggen turn onto the tarmac lane, Al-Rabiah and his two minions started up the slope. As they reached the cottage, they pulled on their hoods and adjusted their goggles.

Inside, the four bodies were badly charred but still vaguely recognizable. One could discern patches of stippled skin, the glaze of baked discharge. Three had been shot through the skull by the fourth, who had collapsed into the fire. He had almost certainly intended that their captive die with them. But Gayle had slipped away. "Clever English."

One didn't want one's epidemic to begin in such a lonely spot. The place would need a more all-consuming fire that would reduce the bodies to ash. The cistern would have to be drained and scorched with petrol. The Volkswagen would have to be driven into the ruins and ignited. The police, if police there were in this remote corner of England, could treat it as a traffic accident. Al-Rabiah chuckled into his mask, pleased with his little joke. He would have to share it with the others.

Or not.

There were no more chalices to monitor, no more chalices to destroy. Wherever Peter Gayle went, an outbreak would follow in a week or two. His potency might last another fortnight. It might endure forever.

Either way, it was time to move on. Al-Rabiah thought he would offer his skills in the global bazaar of horrific weaponry. Somewhere there was a man, a movement, a government willing to support him, someone to give him money, staff, a modern laboratory with pressurized suits and level-four containments like those in Atlanta and Novosibirsk. A facility worthy of his achievement.

But these two minions, the last of his cadre of watchers and waiters, knew far too much about his secret creation. He would have to leave them here as well, once the hard labor had been done. He would give them God's blessings for their long and loyal service, but he would see that their ashes stayed on the Downs. Then he would put his raincoat and respirator and goggles and booties into the flames and drive away.

It was still early. They would finish their work by morning. Then, with a bit of determined driving, he could join Silfer and the two angels for supper. He loved dining at the Hotel Victoria.

XIV

Anna had never believed Churches had a chance. She'd watched him lying in the Intensiv, his body mending as his soul corroded with despair. He seemed never to close his eyes, never to move; he spoke less and less as he became more aware of what his captors had done to him. Like a trapped animal, he suspended in the moment when the steel jaws had clamped about his life; there was nothing before the event, there would be nothing after.

She recognized the will to die when she saw it. She also sensed his shame at being the person upon whom such humiliating horrors could be inflicted. For, to be that person, one would have to be despised by all the world, despised by God.

Anna understood shame. She still dreamed of injecting Peter Gayle, of looming over the poor man, wicked and uncaring as a black widow spider while she dripped her venom….dripped whatever had been in the syringe. Had it brought Sophie home, safe and sound, Anna might have put the sin away. But as it was, the magnitude of the transgression grew day by day; she was the betrayer, the evil one, the cheater in the game of life, the loser in the game of twins. She was the object of a hatred that, in her dreams, burned like the desert sun.

Thus, when Churches began caching his opiate tablets instead of suppressing his considerable pain, she looked the other way. The days drifted by until one morning she found him wound in the stillness she had seen so often in the Intensiv, a small man rendered smaller by death, like a fallen sparrow. Of course, being Anna, she had shed a few tears for Churches. Then, dry-eyed and efficient, she had cleaned him up for the official visits she knew would follow.

An Austrian detective had dropped by for a chat with Anna. Where was the crash? How long was he in the Krankenhaus? Anna had answered each question calmly, telling the truth about everything but the opiates and the Black & Decker.

When a doctor from the coroner's office came to ratify the Englishman's death, Anna told him the injuries were from a car crash; she omitted the wish to die. The doctor poked at the cast shell of the man, noting abrasions and perforations but inclined to waive the autopsy normally mandated for road deaths. He was careful not to look too closely at what remained of Churches, or too long into Anna's eyes.

The coroner's report led to preparation of the necessary Todesbescheinigung, which was forwarded to the registrar, from whom, almost a week after Churches' final night, an Austrian Certificate of Death emerged.

A stately young woman from Senegal came over from the Agency's human resources office to view the former employee, make some notes on survivor benefits, and to explain that because he was British his remains would be handled by his consulate.

Next day, a pink-cheeked, rather well-tailored and crew-cut young man named Smythe-Weymouth looked in. "Embassy sent me over to help with all the, you know, nitty-gritty." The consulate would get an Austrian mortician into the picture, see to the paperwork, and get Mr. Churches home to Kent.

"Devon," said Anna.

THE SUICIDE HAD SURPRISED Viktor Krylov. He hadn't spent enough
time in an Intensiv to have inhaled the bouquet of hopelessness that
floated in the ward. In such an atmosphere, suicide was often the first
solution that came to mind. He had always thought it went the other
way, and that self-slaughter was a last choice requiring uncommon
bravery. He'd never thought Churches very brave. "But I am often
wrong," he'd told Svetlana.

"You get over the physical damage," she said, being the wise
Russian girl. "It's the psychic stuff that kills you."

Anna, by then exhausted, eyes as darkly rimmed as Cleopatra's, had
almost wrung her hands over the slowness of Churches' disposition,
although she had been over this same ground countless times before.
"They want his passport. I don't have his fucking passport!"

Not wanting a lot of crap from Oldenburg or questions from
Imler, Krylov went looking for the document in Churches' office
after hours. A bunch of passports were in the middle desk drawer,
held together by a stout elastic band. There were several of the grand
old British blues, all expired, and a valid EU passport in red. Like
animation cels, the successive photographs showed the blonde boy
grow into a boyish little man.

There were also two official United Nations passports, both valid,
which Krylov took a moment to look through. Evidently, Oldenburg
had intended great things for Churches; the passports held half a
dozen open visas. Krylov pocketed the red EU document and the
two blue UN-issued ones. You never knew what the authorities
would want.

But the passport business was just another distraction. Krylov
was having trouble focusing on anything, so busy was he with all the
other moving parts that had, as though suddenly, accreted around
his existence. He tried to keep close to Anna, hoping to grab the
Bangladeshi, or whatever he was, should he try for her again.

The day of the first attack, Krylov got Muckeltee's number from Svetlana and called the flat, asking for Mohammad Al-Rabiah. The woman at the other end, the wife, Krylov supposed, said there was no one there by that name, he must have the wrong number. But her voice shook with apprehension.

That night he'd driven over to the flat in Heitzing and found it dark; no one answered his knock on the door. A day later, Svetlana reported that Muckeltee had been called away by a death in the family. His landlords were complaining about his broken lease, a default the Centre would have to cover. Vienna International School wondered what had become of the two girls. "Your birds have flown," said Sveta. "Whereabouts unknown." But she would keep looking.

"Find him, Sveta." Krylov, nervous at having the enemy running submerged, had stepped up his Anna patrols.

Meanwhile, Oldenburg pelted him with sarcasms. Good of you to grace us with your presence, Viktor. Is the doctor in? Can you spare us a minute of your time? That kind of thing. Worse, the terrible Dane had begun waving distant assignments at Krylov. The Argentines were about to refuel the Embalse reactor, the South Koreans, Yonggwang Unit-1. Leningrad-II was due for a snap inspection. So was South Africa's Koeberg-2.

"I can slow it down, Viktor," Imler told him, responding to his appeal. "But I cannot stop it. At some point, the argument will be made that you either work for Safeguards or you work somewhere else. You know how these things go."

AND THEN THERE WAS THE MATTER of Ivan Silmov and the April Ten. Silmov had asked to see him "regarding his recent query." They'd met on a warm day at Konzert Café Schwartzenberg on the Ringstrasse.

Silmov had greeted him in Russian. "Viktor Viktorivich! Good to see you!"

"And you, Ivan Borisovich."

A manly handshake.

They took a table out in the amber autumn sunlight, the air filled with the metallic songs of the red and white trams and streaming traffic. They could just hear a violin and piano speaking to each other inside the café. Krylov laughed. "In the old days we would have done this behind Stephansdom at midnight."

"Or on the Prater wheel, like in the movies."

Krylov studied his old comrade in arms. Silmov had once resembled the kind of spy one saw in films, trading secrets and flinty dialogue in a Riesenrad car. He had been lean and graceful then, cunning as a fox, unafraid, a true believer, something of a ladies' man. Now, while greyer and thicker, he was still a good looking fellow, and successful, judging from the quality of his charcoal silk-wool suit and ostrich attaché case. But his movie-star days were over. His eyes held no more light than a shark's, and one could sense nervous tremors going off like seismic detonations far below the skin.

Perhaps, Krylov thought, something vital had been lost in the wrecked helicopter north of Kabul. But, no, Silmov had emerged intact, more or less, and his eyes had shone with gratitude when Krylov revived him. Evidently something else had overtaken him in the intervening years. There was always something else. That was their big occupational hazard.

Over coffee and a Linzertorte, Silmov had walked Krylov through the April Ten: prisoners of war transferred to a hospital unit at a northern location still to be determined, not repatriated until late April 1991. Eight accidental deaths over the years, remains consumed by fire.

"The ninth died just recently. Do you know England?"

"Are you kidding?"

"I forgot. Of course you do. Near Lyme Regis. Another very hot fire. Michael Williams. Interestingly, he was the navigator for the last surviving member of the Ten."

"Who is?"

"Squadron Leader Peter Gayle." Silmov opened his attaché case and took out a manila envelope, from which he produced a stapled sheaf of papers. With an impresario's flourish, he passed them to Krylov. "The Ten."

One page was a poor black-and-white copy of the newly repatriated prisoners, photographed outside the Hercules that had flown them back to Germany. Someone had scrawled *Anderson, Fuentes, Koenig, Elliott, Lieb, Wilson, Maby, Char, Williams, Gayle* under the images.

Krylov took in the group, then studied the one labeled *Gayle*. A calm-looking fellow, fair-haired, a bit shorter than his navigator, but not as short as the SAS boys, which put his height just under two meters. Gayle looked very young. Well, everyone had looked young in 1991. Krylov felt a spasm of pity for Gayle. What did they do to you down there?

He flipped through the other pages, each devoted to one of the Ten, then returned to the group photograph. They all looked normal, happy to be out of Iraq, to be alive. They looked like all prisoners on their way back to freedom. "Were they badly treated?"

Silmov nodded. "There was maybe a microsecond during which the Iraqis believed they could get away with anything." Then, almost inaudibly, "A microsecond can be a long time for a prisoner of war."

Ah, there it was. Ivan had been through one of those microseconds himself. That's what had doused the light in his eyes. "Chechnya?"

Silmov wouldn't look at him, but kept his head down. "Let's stay with the Ten."

"Sorry. Where can I find Peter Gayle?"

Silmov looked up and shook his head. "We...I wish I knew. Gayle has gone missing."

We? Krylov's interior alarms went off. "You wish you knew?"

"I'd hoped to give you something more definite. Sorry." Faux smile, faux regret.

"No problem."

The two were silent for a time. Then Silmov asked, "How was Moscow?"

"How would I know?"

"You said you were going to Moscow."

"Did I?"

"So, how was Moscow?"

Krylov shrugged. "I don't know. The trip was a family thing. You know, grown children needing money?" He saw that Silmov heard the lie.

"Too bad you didn't drop in on old Palev. He always liked you."

"Why do you think that?"

"I was in the Biopreparat class after yours. He spoke highly of you. Wistfully."

"I'll see him next time."

"I doubt it."

"What do you mean?" Krylov felt a hand close around his heart.

"Palev's gone. I suppose that's why he came to mind."

Silmov's eyes were all over the place as he spoke. He should get out of this business, thought Krylov. He was completely useless now. "He can't be. We spoke on the phone just the other day."

"He had cancer everywhere."

Yes, everywhere, often traveling in pairs and wearing leather overcoats and pistols. "How did you hear of it?"

"Moscow let us know."

"Why would they care?"

"Oh, you know. Their eye is on the sparrow."

"I know all about their eye."

The trouble with these broken comrades, thought Krylov, was that when they broke, their heads cracked open and you could read their minds. Krylov already knew how it had gone. His call to Silmov had stirred the bored spies in the embassy to see whom else he'd called, and that had taken them to Palev. Nobody talked to Palev about old times. You talked about virology. So here was Krylov, flying Austrian Air to see the old man in Moscow. How did virology connect to the query about the April Ten and Peter Gayle? They'd put the question to Palev, giving a squeeze. Of course, the old man had told them to kiss his ass. They'd squeezed harder.

"May I ask you something, Viktor?"

"What?"

"The April Ten, that was a long time ago. Why are you interested?"

Krylov fiddled with his coffee spoon, eyes down, a bit of manufactured diffidence on display. "You won't like it."

"Tell me."

"They were a crossword puzzle clue." Krylov held Silmov's wandering eye. "Do you want to know the answer?"

"What?"

"*LATE REPATES.*"

"Okay." Silmov held up a palm. "I get it. Very funny. Ha ha."

"When I finish this crossword, Ivan, I may go to work on what happened to Palev."

"I told you."

"I know, but you lied."

"Viktor, I couldn't get your information without giving them something in return."

"So you gave them Palev."

"He was dying anyway."

"And then you gave them me."

"All I said was there was interest in Peter Gayle and the April Ten. I didn't bring you into it."

"But you brought *them* into it and they soon teased me out." Silmov started to protest, but Krylov held up a silencing hand. "My query to you had nothing to do with Russia. It is none of their business." He leaned across the table. "Listen to me with all your ears, Ivan Borisovich. Years ago I made you a gift of your life. If I detect the slightest threat from those people, I promise you here, on this fine autumn day, that I will take it back."

Silmov's spirit had been cracked, but not his nerve. The man had never been a coward. "You know how these things go, Viktor. You have your information, but it came at a price. There's always a price." He stood up with his oligarch's leather case. "As for your coming after me, a look into my eyes will tell you I don't worry about such stuff. My fear gland was removed years ago. Anyway, you're the one who needs to be careful." He nodded politely and clicked his polished heels. "Finished?"

"Finished."

No manly handshake this time. Silmov walked away without looking back, without a wave, and vanished into the sidewalk crowd.

Feeling haunted, Krylov had gathered up the pages on the April Ten and stuffed them back into their envelope. But out of sight, they were by no means out of mind. He shivered in the warm sunlight. Footsteps on his grave, wherever that might be.

XV

It was raining when Churches, ratified and stamped and paid for, finally went off to the Feuerhalle at Vienna's Zentralfriedhof, the vast city of the dead on the low, damp ground of Simmering. Juan Carlos Imler had expressed a wish to attend, then Oldenburg had come in, making nice for a change, to say he and a couple of the other inspectors also wanted to be involved.

Krylov thought Churches would have liked a few kind words to launch him into the afterlife. "We should have something," he'd told Anna and Svetlana one evening. "After all, Vienna is the funeral capital of the world."

But Anna had warned against it. "If anyone takes a serious look at the body, the questions will never stop."

Sveta had concurred; she held the Russian view that authorities were to be avoided at all costs. "Once we get stuck on *that* web…." and she'd given an elaborately hopeless shrug. "Besides, I have to work."

"What you have to do is find Muckeltee."

So Krylov told Imler and Oldenburg, "There's no funeral. We're just making a delivery."

"No memorial service?"

"Nothing."

"But someone will say a few words?"

"One word: goodbye."

Krylov thought Anna would ride with him, but at the last minute she rushed up to say she would come over in the hearse. She wore scrubs spattered with a brown spray of old blood and looked like a woman about to pull out her hair; her voice shook as she spoke. But, seeing Krylov's eyebrows rise in consternation, she'd grinned like her old self and patted him on the shoulder. "Not to worry, I'm just busy and tired and filthy. I'll see you there."

So Krylov headed for the crematorium in his old Mercedes, Smythe-Weymouth following in his black Golf. The grey Mercedes hearse from Hockstein's funeral home was somewhere behind them in the crawling traffic. They crept southward along the Simmeringer Hauptstrasse, the pavement shiny and slick beneath the sheets of rain, neon-red with reflected brake lights. Krylov could just discern the steel ribbon of the Danube off to his left, and the green cross hatch of farmlands—Vienna planted her vegetables as well as her dead in Simmering.

A few kilometers farther south the cylindrical brick towers of the old gasworks rose into the weather, with the Schwechat refinery lighted up like a cruise ship a kilometer on. In the distance, the airport beacon flashed its contrapuntal green, white, green, white, against a slab of pewter clouds.

They drove into the crematorium grounds, past the cluster of visitors' cars and into the park that led to Clemens Holzmeister's 1922 creation. Watched by the crumbling towers of the Schloss Neugebäude a few roads away, the Feuerhalle seemed to hover in the rain, exotic and impenetrable. The architect had been guided by his vision of an Asian fortress from some imaginary past. "The temple of doom," was what Svetlana had called it when, years earlier, they'd brought her mother's body to the furnace. Krylov thought the pale, stuccoed building looked more like an anchored freighter riding out a storm, a grey smear of smoke rising from its superstructure.

Krylov took a turn around the inner parking area, which was nearly empty, looking for intruders. The Russian embassy Mercedes with black windows was parked on the far side, partly hidden by a line of trees. The Americans had stashed their Suburban behind another screen of trees. Some things never changed.

Parking as near as he could to the entrance, Krylov got out and popped his umbrella. Smythe-Weymouth pulled in beside him and walked over under a small blue umbrella with a circle of yellow stars. "Europe forever," he said, giving Krylov his ready smile. But he'd taken note of the Suburban. "Friends of the deceased?"

"Sentimental Americans, come to pay their respects."

The dimly lighted entry hall preserved the nautical severity of line, the Expressionist touch evoking hatches, ladders, and companionways, without suggesting the presence of a human crew. A ghost ship, then, thought Krylov.

A weak sepia light fell from the translucent amber pyramid that formed the ceiling, turning everyone a little older. Some metal-legged tables with chairs were arranged around the room for mourners seeing to the departed's paperwork. A faint, sweet lavatory odor hung in the air, although it could have been Krylov's imagination. Crematoria in German-speaking countries had always given him the willies.

People eddied in small squads, as separate from one another as planets orbiting different stars, each group held together by the gravitation of shared grief. Some had priests with them, some stood bravely alone, like grieving anarchists. Now and then one of the chapels would disgorge the living and another group would shuffle in to say goodbye to their lost person. Krylov told himself, not for the first time, that he did not want to grow old in Vienna.

He waited while Smythe-Weymouth trotted over to the reception desk to handle the nitty gritty. After chatting for a moment in good German, he turned back to Krylov. "Passport?"

Krylov reached into his coat pocket and pulled out the three passports he'd taken from Churches' desk. He passed the red EU document to Smythe-Weymouth and put the other two back in his pocket.

The Americans stood in the shadows on the far side of the room. Emerson wore his usual desert boots, jeans, and blazer with a large scarlet bow tie. Lamont stood next to him, natty today in an ivory sports jacket that hid all but a few loose tendrils of his tattoos. And, a surprise: the Navy commander from the cave, almost invisible in a black pants suit and shiny black blouse except that her pale freckled face seemed to glow, her red hair to flare like a port light. Liz, thought Krylov. Her name is Liz.

Emerson raised his eyebrows and mouthed: *A word?*

Krylov crossed the floor.

"Viktor, good to see you." Emerson crowed. "You remember Commander Mabrey? Of course you do. And Lamont? Ever seen Lamont looking so good?"

Krylov ignored the two men. His impulse was to lift this small, not exactly beautiful woman, with whom he'd shared an eternity in a strong gamma field, into a bear hug she would not soon forget. But he settled for a firm, friendly handshake and a hello.

"We meet in the oddest places," she said.

"Don't we? Did you crack the mystery of the cave?"

"A funny thing happened to the samples. All blanks."

"Bizarre." Krylov watched her carefully, wondering whether it was possible that she didn't know Churches had passed everything to Emerson.

"I knew you'd be amazed."

"Emerson has a talent for finding lost things. It will turn up."

Liz shrugged. "Not my problem."

"Out of the cave business?

"And how. Thank God."

Krylov looked around the lobby. "Is this Ralph's idea of a date?"

"He's just giving me a ride. I'm meeting someone at the airport."

"*Mister* Mabrey?"

She grinned, animating the fine scrimshaw of her face. "That would be my dear, late dad. This is my cousin from the States."

"You meet him…"

"Her."

"Her. Show her old Vienna, then back to Iraq?"

She shook her head. "I'm here now. They seconded me to the Agency."

Krylov was quiet for a long moment, reflecting on the news. He didn't want this admirable woman to be the Americans' new whore, but he couldn't imagine what else she might be. "Of course, Emerson's sudden vacancy."

"Seconded. Not indentured." Her face closed.

"And on the way to the airport he brought you here, to watch poor Churches go up in smoke?"

"He wanted to pay his respects."

"He has a heart like Siberia. Vast and cold. Well, maybe not all that vast."

"Okay, I guess that'll do for now. Nice seeing you, Viktor." She turned to Emerson. "I'll wait in the truck. My plane comes in at 1700." Then she was gone.

"I'm surprised you bothered, Emerson."

"No man left behind."

"Lamont going to whistle *Taps*?"

"We're giving Churches the Medal of Freedom." A hard chuckle that nobody shared. "But seriously, I thought you and I might have a chat." Emerson took him by the elbow, but Krylov shrugged away the guiding hand. "Viktor, we need to start turning up our cards." The American spoke almost in a hiss; some of the old grievers who still had their hearing turned toward the unfamiliar sound, puzzled. "We have a situation we've got to get under control. People are beginning to figure it out. My people, your people."

"Do I have people?"

Emerson gestured with his chin at two stocky men in Navy blue suits. "Why not just tattoo *Russian* on their foreheads?"

"Good idea. I'll pass it up the line."

"In the meantime, let's find Peter Gayle, the Brit you've never heard of. Let's find the Iraqi pharmacist who fiddled with the April Ten. They've lit a very short, very dangerous fuze. We've got to stomp it out."

"So, stomp."

"You're thinking you can work this one by yourself, like some guy building a ship in the back of his Lada. But this isn't something one man can handle. This is big, it needs a government. The cavalry. To tell the truth, I'm surprised you haven't brought in the authorities already." When Krylov did not respond, red patches bloomed on Emerson's cheeks, he sucked in breath like a dying halibut. "Say something, goddamn it."

"Have you taken your lithium?"

"Fuck you, fuck you." Emerson almost stamped his foot.

"If you're looking for these people, just go find them. You have Predator drones, satellites, what you call HUMINT. You go through everybody's mail. You're game to invade anything. When you catch your men, drop them into a cauldron of boiling zinc, like Jimmy Hoffa. Make them into bumpers. You don't need me for that. Bye bye."

Lamont stepped forward, light on his feet, sneering. "Where've you been, Viktor? They don't make bumpers outa chrome anymore." His pig eyes darted at Emerson, silently asking: *Now* can I have this guy?

Krylov nodded toward the two Russians across the room. "Like you, Lamont, they're as dumb as they look. But they'd rather rip off your bumpers than rape and pillage. And they *love* rape and pillage."

"Fuck you," piped Lamont.

Krylov walked back to where Smythe-Weymouth waited. "Looks like trouble is food and drink to you," the Englishman said.

"Only drink." Krylov laughed. "Those boys talk about nothing but sex."

Smythe-Weymouth cocked his head toward a door opening in the far wall. "Hullo, I think we have some news, at last." He put up a hand so the arriving Feuerhalle official would see him and darted away. "Back in a jiff."

But Krylov's mind was busy with Emerson. The American wanted to share everything, which meant he didn't yet have it all. What pieces was he missing?

Krylov believed he understood Emerson rather well. He was like the optimistic child who digs through a room full of horseshit looking for the pony. Emerson was looking for the weapon. He wanted to be the one who laid this new horror before the generals of the war on terror. And he wanted to control it. That was why he hadn't handed the matter to his government. That was why the streets weren't full of people wearing level-four protective gear.

The disease is not just deadly, but hideous and messy, poor old Pavel had told Krylov in Moscow. *It turns loved ones and neighbors into blackened, repugnant strangers bleeding from every orifice, every pore, and mad with misery and fear. For the afflicted, it is as bad as Armageddon. It is the end of the world.*

Emerson didn't care about the end of the world. He didn't care if the epidemic swept across a village or a continent, or whether it took ten lives or a million. No, Emerson just wanted to have the option of wielding Al-Rabiah's terrible new sword. He wanted Peter Gayle supine on a morgue table and disassembled like an unexploded bomb. He wanted the Iraqi chemist to explain how he'd solved those tough bioweaponry problems. Hell, if the Iraqi could do variola, why not Marburg, ebola and those hybrid viruses for which the only palliatives were prayer and the healing hand of Jesus?

But Emerson couldn't be interested in new ways to wreck civilizations. There were plenty of those around. No, he hoped to add another dimension to the game of terror. If a mad Arab blew up the London Underground, Emerson would see to it that his surviving comrades took home the seeds of, say, Spanish flu, extinguishing their tribe by sunrise. No visible national hand involved, just the invisible one of Allah. The price of deploying young men and women in explosive vests would become more than most villages were willing to pay. The light in the extremists' eyes would dim.

In Emerson's fantasy, all that was needed to work such magic was a certain anonymous Iraqi scientist and a British squadron leader who'd gone missing. *Those* were the absent pieces Emerson was digging for.

And Krylov had them, more or less.

Krylov thought the odds of his stopping what Al-Rabiah had started were close to nil. All Peter Gayle need do was board a flight from Heathrow or sit down at a crowded dinner table, and the pestilential wave would begin to build. After it broke, governments would intercede; eventually the epidemic would be brought under control, the dead buried, the psychic scars wiped away in a generation or two. But in the end, there this new capability would be. The world would have another weapon too terrible to use and the human condition would stagger onward to the next square.

But Krylov didn't think Gayle was flying anywhere. He would want to drive to Vienna and shake some truth out of Anna. Sveta meanwhile was trying to find Muckeltee/Al-Rabiah. So there was a chance that Krylov could take Gayle and Al-Rabiah off the table and send smallpox back to oblivion, where it belonged.

Odd, thought Krylov. This was what he'd once hoped to do with The Bomb. Cosmo must be giving him a second chance.

Smythe-Weymouth interrupted his train of thought. "Everything's set, but no point in our staying. A good many dead chaps queued up ahead of us, each needing a couple of hours to render. I'll pick up Mr.

Churches tomorrow and send him off to Devon, his mum's to spread beneath the roses." He scanned the room, then gave Krylov a smile. "Excuse me, there's our driver." Smythe-Weymouth darted over to talk to a slender man dressed like a Ukrainian crow in mortician's livery.

"Where's Anna?" muttered Krylov. He called over to the driver, "Where is Anna Nieman?"

The man looked up, startled to see a big Russian about to charge. He tensed to flee, but the polite young man from the British embassy restrained him with a surprisingly powerful grip on his upper arm. "He wants to know where is the nurse."

"What nurse?"

"She was going to ride with you from the hospital."

"Ah. She never come."

Krylov advanced on the man. "She said she was riding with you."

"I drive hearse, not tourist coach. I carry dead people. If living wish riding with me, then come on time."

"*Job tvojo matj!*" Krylov lashed out at a nearby pew with his right fist, taking away a shard of polished mahogany. Then he was hurrying toward the exit, patting his pockets for his mobile phone.

Emerson watched, amused. "Anna Nieman. Rings a bell." He turned to his illustrated man. "Lamont, get me everything there is on a nurse named Anna Nieman."

Krylov ran to the Mercedes and hopped in, his umbrella still furled, his good grey suit spattered with rain. He fished out his mobile and began fiddling with the buttons. The young could write sonnets with their thumbs. Krylov had to do everything like a blind man, one digit at a time with an index finger. But finally he had the hospital, then the Intensiv.

"Anna?"

"No," said a musical German voice, "Here is Renate. May I help you?"

"Is Anna Nieman there?"

"She's gone to a funeral."

Krylov dialed Anna's flat, letting it ring until a recording came on to tell him in German that no one was there. He called Svetlana's office number. When she answered, he said, "Sveta, Anna's gone."

"You think Muckeltee?"

"Who else?"

"Are you sure? He'd be mad to come here."

"Mad perfectly describes him."

"But she wouldn't just walk away with him."

"I'm afraid she would," said Krylov, beginning to think more clearly. "She would walk to her death to protect anyone in her care."

"Or a fledgling fallen from its nest. You're right. But wait, I have another call." Svetlana was silent long enough that Krylov thought the connection had been lost. But then she came back on the line. "That was the Academy in Trieste. There was a radiologist calling himself Al-Habira traveling with a big Scandinavian wife and two daughters. He attended a week-long conference on third-world oncology. Then he told the registrar he and his family were going on holiday."

"But he must have come back to Vienna, lured Anna...."

"Let me make a call. Wait where you are."

Krylov rang off and simmered in the Mercedes behind its steamed windows. A moment later, his telephone buzzed. "Sveta?"

"I found them."

"Where?"

"Where Anna saw them. In Glion, the Hotel Victoria."

XVI

Although Anna spent her life among the dying, she was not inclined to spend more time than she had to with the dead. When her lost patients left the Intensiv they left her world, and good luck to them in the dark silence of the afterlife.

Even so, she had been uneasy about letting Churches vanish into the flames completely unattended. He was one of those heartbreakers you now and then got in the unit, a man who looked like a boy, a boy who seemed to have no friends unless one counted Sveta's Uncle Viktor. Anna always found the heartbreakers irresistible, and, besides, she admired the little Englishman's calm march toward death, head high, no apparent fear of the blackness waiting on the other side. But, mainly, she felt she owed him some special treatment for bringing her a favorable omen.

Do you know a Peter Gayle?

When Anna heard the name, her heart had lifted briefly, a lark rising against a falling net of dread. After Sophie's death, Anna had waited for Peter to arrive, certain that he was on his way to Vienna.

He would have seen the Sophie story on television, Anna Nonperes would have been revealed as Anna Nieman, captured in blue hospital scrubs, and Peter would come, angry, no doubt, hating her, no doubt, but unable to keep away. His heart would bring him to her.

He would surprise her, take her firmly (but gently) by an arm, steer her toward his steel-colored Saab. It would be raining. It would be a glorious autumn afternoon. It would be three in the morning. He would say, *Don't be afraid, I'm not going to hurt you.* He would say, *I should beat you to death.* He would ask, *Why?*

She would say, *I'm not afraid. I won't try to get away.* She would say, *Peter, I'm sorry, so very very sorry.*

And then?

Anna had no idea. Sometimes she thought the encounter would last five minutes, sometimes an hour, sometimes for eternity. She could not propel the imagined meeting much further than *Don't be afraid.*

But as the weeks crept by with no sign of him, she had given up. Her heart knew exactly what had happened. Peter had heard about Sophie and seen Anna on television. And he had said, *So what? Who cares?* and other dismissive things. *Plenty of pretty fish in the sea. I shan't come looking for you in your quiet corner of….was it Paris?*

Such musings had chilled Anna's quadrant of the universe, from where Peter had become a point of light fading into darkness, like a distant galaxy receding from her at some unimaginable velocity. He was gone, forever.

Do you know a Peter Gayle?

By asking the question, Churches had brought Peter back within range of her signal. She neither wanted nor expected anything from him, no residue of affection, not even forgiveness. All she wanted was to make one final contact, confess her sin, apologize, grovel— whatever would quench his hatred of her. For hatred there would certainly be.

In her dreams of dripping venom into Peter Gayle, the atmosphere crackled with his scorn, a flickering radiation, hot upon her skin, dessicating to her spirit. Of course he would despise her, this girl with all the false names and colors, who'd made a fool of him; this girl who'd abandoned him to men like the ones who'd driven Churches to the brink of death.

But now Anna knew that her enemies and Peter's were the same, that they were serious, dangerous men, and that they did not all fight on the same side. By his example, Churches had illuminated a continuum of threat that touched everyone, not just her. Al-Rabiah was linked to Peter Gayle and to her, but now Viktor Krylov was linked to them both through the cave in Iraq and the torturing of Churches. And somewhere out there was yet another perimeter of Americans she'd never seen, this "Emerson," stalking the true purpose of the cave, stalking Peter Gayle. The players were all conjoined; their destinies formed a circle. Ah, but if a circle, where did it close?

On the day Churches left the hospital a car crash north of the city had saturated the Intensiv. By noon Anna was spattered with brown free-forms and ugly with fatigue. She'd seen fatally overdosed young women who looked healthier than the girl in her mirror.

It had been all she could do to trot out to Viktor, who waited in his Mercedes, to tell him she would be along later, in the hearse. Then she had run back to the nurses' changing room, tossed the soiled scrubs into a bin, and stepped into the shower, where she would have stayed until Christmas, except for needing to see Churches off.

Not wanting to go to the Feuerhalle in the jeans and Greek sweat shirt she'd worn to work that morning, Anna had also packed her mauve woolen knit dress, last worn to dinner at the Hotel Victoria. She unrolled it and gently ran her hands across it, deep in reverie. Then she gave her head a fierce shake and slipped the dress over her head, letting it drape her slender body. There, she felt almost pretty again. She put on hose and heels and grabbed the down-market shearling coat she called The Bratislava, picked up her pack and hurried to the loading dock. But Hockstein's Mercedes hearse was nowhere to be seen. She ran back to the hospital entrance, waving at every cab that slid past in the rain, already hired.

"May a colleague offer you a ride?"

Anna turned toward the voice, heart pounding. Almost in a whisper she replied, "But you don't know where I'm going."

"Oh yes I do," said Peter Gayle.

THE SAAB BORED THROUGH the darkening Vienna afternoon, fingers of rain playing on the soft top, the metronomic thump of wipers, now and then a sidewise gust of wind. It was, thought Anna, as if they were just leaving Toulouse, with the Hotel Victoria waiting for them somewhere in the future. But, no, that was over. All over.

Nothing had gone as she had imagined. There had been no *Don't be afraid,* no *I'm not going to hurt you,* no *Why?* Gayle had nodded toward the parked Viggen and she had followed him to the car through the rain. No gentle hand under her arm. No further conversation. She had offered no resistance, and he seemed to expect none. He held the passenger door for her and she got in. Then, as they had before, they drove away together in silence, like a worn-out couple, like two people holding hands as they sank into the sea.

Anna stole looks at him. He seemed years older than the Peter Gayle she'd met in Toulouse, his face drawn by some new extreme of experience. His shock of blonde hair needed cutting and he'd grown a scruffy beard. She thought he'd lost weight, five kilos or more. His hands, formerly fine-boned and well kept, a gentleman's hands, were dark around the fingernails, rough, the hands of a man who earned his living with a rake or broom.

Mainly, she noticed his odor. She supposed coal miners smelled like that when they returned to the light. So did patients brought to the Intensiv. Hard labor and animal vitality mixed with a few parts of despair. It was, she realized, the smell of a prisoner. Had he been kept prisoner? Is that why he had taken so long to find her?

Gayle seemed unaware of his passenger, but concentrated on pushing the Saab through the clotted traffic on the Gürtel, his eye darting at street names, trying to navigate. Finally, as they waited at a traffic signal, he leaned his head on the steering wheel with a deep sigh and said, "I lied. I don't know where we're going. I don't know where I am."

"Where do you want to go?"

"Somewhere I can stop the bloody car."

He faced her then and she saw his profound fatigue, and something febrile and unstable in his pale eyes. Had her betrayal made him mad? Anna shuddered. She would rather murder people than make them crazy; she preferred the dead to the insane.

"Somewhere in your quiet corner of town," said Gayle, giving her a terrible grin.

Ah, she thought, the first hint of bitterness. That wasn't the same as being crazy. She could handle bitterness. "Turn left when you can."

Anna took them northwest, out of the dense metal herd of vehicles circling the city center and up past the snake of tourist coaches creeping past the villas and Heurigen of Grinzing and beyond, until, as if suddenly, Vienna was behind them and they ran through woodlands, emptied of people by the cold rain.

Gayle followed a narrow lane that wound among the dark sentinels of beech and oak, and larch like giant druids draped in sable rags. Then, as if both man and machine had exhausted their fuel, he let the Saab coast to a stop and switched everything off. He leaned back in his seat, as tired, thought Anna, as a man cut from a cross. The only sounds were the rain whispering around them through the branches, the engine ticking as it cooled.

"I've been driving twelve hours," he said without looking at her. "Dragging dead boys around before that. A pretty rum day."

"I'm sorry."

"For what?" He closed his eyes. "For the long drive? For the dead boys?" When she started to speak, he held up a palm to silence her, and she, seeing its tremor, said no more.

"Sorry was what I felt when I saw Anna Nieman on television. Sorry for myself, being such a predictable bounder and so easily deceived. Sorry for you, being a deceiver. I wondered why bloody me, otherwise no problem. Except from the day I met you, my life has been one surprise after another." He extended the palm again. "Keep still. I'm trying to tell you where we stand. My first impulse was to shake you to pieces, find out what this shitty little panto was all about. Put you away."

"Why didn't you?" Her heart felt like a stone. Where was the *Don't be afraid, I'm not going to hurt you?*

"I was unavoidably detained."

A prisoner, again, thought Anna.

"So now I must know exactly what happened. Exactly what and exactly why."

Anna took a deep breath. "I gave you an injection."

"Of what?"

"I don't know."

"But you did it anyway."

"They had my sister. They said if I did this one bad thing Sophie would go free. I would have done anything to save her." She paused, catching her breath. "I stayed with you afterward, to make sure…"

"What, that it wasn't cyanide?"

"To make sure you were alive."

"Next time, use cyanide."

"There won't be a next time."

"We don't know what there'll be. You gave the shot. What then?"

"I was supposed to stay with you to Bern and come home Sunday. But I left."

"With Al-Rabiah."

"I didn't mean to. He was in the lobby. I went with them back to Vienna. He told me I had done a criminal thing. If I spoke of it he would have me silenced. And that was that."

"Was it?"

"No. After Sophie died, he tried to kill me in the hospital."

"Yet here you are."

"A friend chased him away. He's left Vienna."

"He may have been in England last night. A cottage out on the Downs. Several blokes in among the trees, dressed like bugs, as old Mouse would say."

Anna remembered Peter asleep: *We're fucked, Mouse. Out we go!* "Who is Mouse?"

"Mickey Williams. *Was* Mickey Williams. My former navigator. Men in bug suits killed him, reduced his cottage to ash. Same thing last night, only they let me leave, I don't know why. Do you?"

Anna shook her head and watched the rain streaming down her window. She had no idea what to do, where to go, how to end this unhappy encounter. She wanted to wring her hands and scream.

Gayle was studying her. "You're quite worn out," he said. Then, "I remember the dress."

"I was going to a funeral."

"Perfect day for it."

"Not a real funeral. One of my patients went to the Feuerhalle. I thought I should be there." She smiled, thinking, I owed him something for bringing you back to life, ha ha.

"Sorry."

"His name was Churches. He asked if we knew you."

"I've heard of Churches."

"Of course you have," and she detected a bitter note in her voice now. "That's because we are all connected, like a bunch of sausages."

"The same lot who took him also took me. They said they'd put my friend Churches through the grinder. I didn't know what they were talking about."

"But they didn't torture you."

"They just wanted me for bait. No head-screws or water-boarding."

"Or Black and Decker."

"Is that what Churches got?"

She nodded.

"I didn't know they were handy. Lucky me." He leaned against the headrest as though he weighed a ton. "Anyway, those lads are off to Valhalla, Paradise, wherever they go when they die."

"Maybe it's over." She thought: We can find proper treatment for you, we can bring back the charming fellow who takes pretty women to his favorite hotel, we can fall in love.

"It's never bloody over."

"Do you still want to put me away?"

Gayle shook his head. "I'm the last living member of the so-called April Ten. Ten unfortunate prisoners of an ancient war, sent home via Al-Rabiah's laboratory. Somehow modified. All murdered, every one but me. Now death follows me around like a black dog. In the class photograph I'm the chap standing on that pile of bodies."

Anna heard the accelerations in his speech, the signals of a man letting go of the buoyant shard that had borne him across the sea. He wasn't mad; he was just at the end of his endurance, and had relaxed, believing himself to be with a friend. Her heart cracked. "Let me take you home. You need a hot bath. A good meal. Sveta will make you dumplings. We have vodka. We can wash your clothes. You can rest, Christ, you are so tired, please come home with me."

"I can't, Anna."

"But why?"

"I need to disappear for awhile."

"And after that?"

"I don't know. Rather soon, every time I hit a cash point or use a telephone, a blip will pop up on a map somewhere. They know about us. They'll be listening to your telephone, watching your house. They'll follow you everywhere. They…"

She put a hand on his arm. "You sound like you need a nurse."

"And how."

"Why can't you just give them what they want?"

"They want *me*. They want to study Al-Rabiah's creation."

"And what is that?"

Gayle leaned back into the headrest, eyes tight shut, jaw working, arms crossed upon his chest as if he held himself together. Almost inaudibly, he said, "I think it may be a monster."

BACK IN THE CISTERN, ANXIOUSLY SCRAPING at the bloody slag that had glued itself to his body, Gayle surfaced, gasping for air. A few meters away the cottage still dissolved in fire. And there were Huey, Dewey, and Louie, watching from the flames, eyes fixed upon the man floating in the cistern. But where's Harry? wondered the dreamer, realizing in that instant that Harry, or what remained of him, was also in the water, the charred skull wearing a horrific grin, the bare arms reaching out for an embrace....

Gayle gave a strangled cry and sat upright, not yet quite awake, uncertain where he was, or why, or with whom. One thing at a time, he told himself. One thing at a time.

He was in the Viggen, but in the passenger seat. He looked across at the driver. It was the pretty girl from Toulouse, Anna Something, driving like an angel, which must mean he still lay in the coils of a dream, although this was a definite improvement. He watched that smart, serious face, the tinge of ivory upon the English skin, the long neck, all remembered from some previous dream, or had that been reality? Gayle bit his lip. One thing at a time.

"I didn't know you could drive," he said at last, testing the apparition. If it answered it might not be a dream.

"I am a very decent driver."

"I just gave you the wheel?"

"You put yourself in my capable hands."

Anna had not responded to his monster comment beyond a faint suggestion of movement, a reflex of apprehension, behind the blue eyes. She hadn't asked what sort of monster, how many tentacles, how many heads, how much venom. She had just reached out her capable hands and he had collapsed into them.

"This isn't a dream, is it?"

She shook her head. "We changed places. I drove us out of Vienna. You went immediately to sleep. I stopped once, at the Oldtimer in Guntramsdorf. We needed petrol."

Gayle thought he remembered their stopping, or, rather, his surfacing in the parking area, partly awakened by the silence and garish lights, to find himself alone in the Saab, God knew where. A moment's terror, then back to the abyss of sleep. Was it memory or another compartment of the dream?

"I got money from the machine. Some water and sandwiches. Orange juice. Coffee. When did you last eat?"

"I don't remember."

"Want a sandwich?"

"Not just yet. What else have you been up to?"

"I used the public telephone to call Svetlana …"

"Svetlana?"

"My flat mate. I told her I was all right and not to worry. Please tell the hospital my grandmother is dying in Klagenfurt and I am rushing to her side. And now," and she raised her head defiantly, "we disappear."

"Into thin air?"

"More or less."

"This really is you, isn't it?"

"Unless *I* am the one dreaming."

Gayle looked out the window, the day fading behind a raspberry-colored sun, which suspended between the rainclouds and the hills. He held up a hand between the sun and rough horizon. About an hour of daylight remained. "Where are we?"

"On the Sudautobahn, Wiener Neustadt passing on the left."

"And where are we going?"

"Into thin air." She laughed for him. "But now try to sleep some more. Usually when I meet someone as tired as you were, he's already dead."

"I'd rather watch you drive."

"*That* will make you sleep, for sure."

"Do you own a car?"

"I live a kilometer from the hospital. I walk everywhere."

"Then how is it you're a decent driver?"

"My father taught me and also Sophie. He drove for a living."

"What did he drive?"

"He could drive anything, but his job was driving the ÖAMTC van. He would find somebody in difficulty and help them get going again."

"That sounds a nice sort of job."

"It gave him time to think, is what he used to say. Actually, it gave him time to daydream. He was quite the dreamer."

A sign for Edlitz and Aspang Markt drifted into focus and she dropped the Viggen down to fourth gear, slowing for the exit. Then they were hurrying along two-lane roads bounded by dark forests, the land becoming rougher as it rose toward the falling night.

For a time they were quiet, Gayle trying to get his bearings, but unable to see anything but black trees and a charcoal-colored stratus spewing rain.

"Are you all right?" she asked.

"A bit disoriented, otherwise fine."

"Let me ask you something."

"Sure."

"At the hotel, you said we might go to Sion and watch the Swiss do touchings and goings. What does that mean?

Gayle laughed softly. "You mean touch-and-goes. You fly an approach, touch your wheels to the runway, then put on power, clean up the plane, and take off again. You touch, then you go."

"Ah."

"Like the human condition."

"It sounded mysterious."

"When you're in love, everything sounds mysterious."

Anna blushed and concentrated on her driving.

She slowed as they entered what seemed an empty forest beyond Molzegg. "Years ago," she said, "my father bought a piece of land up here, that's how I know where I am. He lost it, of course, but the memory lingers."

"Sounds thin air indeed."

"There are small vacation homes scattered through the forest. People from Vienna come here for the summer and come back for Nordic skiing after it snows. But in the interval the places are closed up. So we are looking for one with no lights showing. No dogs barking. No cars, no one about. Something remote enough that the nosy neighbors won't come knocking on the door."

"A-knock, knock, knocking."

"Yes, exactly."

As they climbed the terrain roughened and the rain began to mix with graupel. Now and then Anna would stop where a narrow drive angled away into the trees, kill the engine, and listen quietly as a stalking cat. Gayle heard nothing, saw no human sign, but Anna evidently sensed something and kept moving on, farther into the mountains.

Finally, she stopped the Saab where a rutted path about one vehicle wide veered into a tumble of boulders and black trees. Gayle could just discern the A-shaped silhouette of a small chalet behind a wall of spruce. Anna listened in silence for a time, then cranked the engine and drove slowly uphill for some fifty meters, to stop in front of the silent structure.

The place was more hut than chalet, Gayle decided, built on the cheap and rough-finished, with a coat of crimson paint and windows trimmed sky blue, the colors leached by the gathering darkness and fall of sleet. It poised on the rim of a rocky cliff, overlooking what seemed an empty valley. Off to one side Gayle made out a small utilities shack where fresh firewood had been stacked and covered with a tarpaulin. On the other side he saw a sheltered area for a car. He nodded toward it, but Anna was already turning the Saab around to back into the space. If they had to, they could make a dash for the main road.

Again they waited in silence, listening for footsteps, voices, dogs. But all was quiet. "Thin air," said Anna.

She brought her backpack and the food from the Oldtimer stop, Gayle his one bag and bomber jacket, which sagged with the weight of the pistol. The owner had secured the front door with the usual Austrian deadbolt lock, but, this being thin air, he'd hung the key on a nail under the low wooden stoop. Anna found it and let them into a single room, with a sofa and chairs on one side, a painted white dinette near the kitchen area, and a low IKEA pine bed against the other wall. The floor was a concrete slab covered with a coarse beige polyester carpet. The walls were rough cedar planks on which a column of tiny red-deer skulls, with antlers no longer than coat hooks, climbed to the ceiling.

"Ugh," said Anna. "We feed them through the winter just to kill them later."

She roamed the house, trying everything. "We have water and gas," she reported. "No electricity until we find the main switch in the morning. But here are some candles. We can eat by candlelight." Then, "There is some mail here. The name Franz Trauber, at a postal box in Wiener Neustadt. That's good. No mail delivery, no postman."

Gayle watched her move through the darkness, watched the flare of a match illuminate her features as she lit another candle. So pretty, he thought. So very pretty. On that first day, they had melted into one another's arms like loving dancers. Now, he realized, they were careful not to touch. "Not the Hotel Victoria, is it?"

"That was then."

"You're right. I need to clean up. I'm covered in filth."

"I'll put out the food," she said.

The demand water heater in the bathroom ignited with a small detonation. Gayle filled the basin and gingerly sheared away a fortnight's beard. "That's more like it," he told the optically distorted image in the aluminum mirror. He examined himself minutely, looking for a fresh spray of rash or some other sign of Al-Rabiah's monster. But there was none. His skin was clear, he had no fever, no flu. Perhaps this monster was like most of that species, a myth. Perhaps whatever they had grown in him had died.

Somewhat reassured, Gayle stepped into the coffin-sized shower stall and stood under the comforting stream for several minutes before adding soap and shampoo. But it seemed that no amount of scrubbing could quite rid him of those dead Iraqi boys. His body refused to forget portaging the viscous Huey, Dewey, and Louie to their pyre.

He picked up one of the small, stained towels, not much more absorbent than a sheet of newsprint, and began drying off. The door opened behind him. He shut his eyes as he felt Anna begin to pat his back with another little towel.

"Anna…"

"Shh, be still." Her sure hand gently dabbed away the drops gathered along his spine, down the buttocks and legs, the towel rising and falling in a rhythm, Gayle realized, with which she might soothe a dying patient. It stroked away the three Iraqi boys, and Harry, and all the other dead. The pleasure of this human contact left Gayle weak; he dared not move, fearing she might stop.

At last, into the atmosphere of relief and desire rising around them, Anna said, "In my imaginary conversations with you, I have told you over and over how sorry I am for deceiving you, how dirty I feel about it, but also how sad I was that you were gone forever. I could not quite turn loose of our mysterious touching and going, you see."

"Touch-and-goes."

"Whatever. Finally I believed that if we met again your hatred would hit me like a flame. I would ask your forgiveness. Maybe you would give it, maybe not. And then you would walk away. And that would be that. But now you're here, I must ask for more than your forgiveness, Peter. I must ask you to love me. I must ask you not to walk away, for that would break my heart."

Gayle turned and found that she was naked too. "Christ," he whispered, his heart full to breaking. Then they melted into one another's arms like loving dancers.

XVII

The stone cottage on the Downs had taken nourishment from their efforts to destroy it, or so it seemed to Mohammad Al-Rabiah. Ramming the Volkswagen into the structure at speed had caused little further damage, although the minion driving the bus had been badly scraped when he leapt from the cab.

Once they'd seated the Volkswagen in the wreckage, the second minion had scampered down the hill to bring up the Ford Focus, hidden behind trees off the lane, and the propane tank in its boot. But the sun had risen before the ruin had cooled enough that they could disperse a low stratus of the gas, seed it with petrol, and set the place burning like a Hindu bier.

The other delay had come from trying to get the two minions into position so the fire would consume them where they fell. One or the other kept trotting off to some new, well-intended chore. Finally, Al-Rabiah had come up behind them where they sat in the stubble, resting after purging and sterilizing the cistern, and shot them, one-two, below the occiput. He had immediately regretted the act, for now they had to be dragged, bleeding like pigs, first one and then the other, thirty meters back to the cottage, to be levered into the flames.

Then, because the cistern was empty, Al-Rabiah had only a trickle from the spring to wash the brain and blood off his hands. He tossed his gory raincoat and mask and goggles into the flames, but when he took the wheel of the green Focus he still looked like a working butcher, pursued by flies.

Still, a late supper with his family remained a possibility. The M4 was lovely, the Focus galloping along among the faster cars. Al-Rabiah's spirit lifted like a swallow, he forgot the blood, the flies blew away in the slipstream, the traffic moved like a mighty river of metal, no snarls in sight.

But as he turned southeastward on the M25, everything suddenly congealed. It took him two hours to reach the M20 for Dover, and by then his head was ready to explode. He felt as if he'd been holding his breath since yesterday.

The sun was almost finished when he surfaced in Calais, with all of France to be traversed in darkness. Tormented by the rude horns and flashing lights of overtaking Mercedes and BMWs, mad cars with mad drivers, Al-Rabiah stubbornly occupied the middle lane, keeping just below the speed limit. They could blow their wretched horns until doomsday and he would stay where he was. One did not play God in the morning and timid driver in the afternoon.

He stopped at an aire along the autoroute, fueled the car and, locking himself in the men's lavatory, washed away what remained of the day's sticky residue, although he could not rid himself entirely of its meaty scent. He put on a clean white shirt and bought a ploughman's sandwich and bottle of sweet tea for the final leg to Lake Léman.

The prospect of even a very late supper at the hotel had by now vanished utterly, like a lump of sugar dropped into the sea. He weighed calling his wife at the hotel, but decided against it. He was worn out, and, to tell the truth, that familiar, northern voice banging away on the telephone was the last thing he wanted to hear.

He cleared Lausanne just before midnight, running down the nearly empty A9 toward Montreux, the long, narrow blade of water shimmering off to his right, the serration of the Alpine wall beyond, blacker than the sky. He pulled off on the Route de Caux, climbing the steep hillside in a series of switchbacks that brought him to the hotel's gravel parking area.

He slid the Focus into one of the remaining spaces and got out, stretching. God, how tired he was, and how he needed to urinate! The building had gone to sleep, its lights subdued, its windows like closed eyes beneath their orange lids. He cocked his head, listening. A faint sound, something moving behind the bordering trees. Then a ginger cat appeared, pretending not to see the human as it crossed the gravel.

Al-Rabiah nearly fainted with relief. But there was nothing to fear. No one knew where he was. No one knew what he had done today. And, he added, unbuttoning his flies, no one would know that he'd peed into the gravel. His body shivered as he emptied his bladder into the night. A ray of ecstasy shot through him; he was squirting his troubles away.

Out of nowhere, a powerful arm encircled his throat, jostling him so that a cascade of urine soaked his trousers. A big hand searched him until it found the silenced pistol, which it removed. Then it spun him around and whacked him with the barrel, very hard, across the nose, which cracked audibly.

Al-Rabiah stumbled back and dropped to his knees, holding his ruptured mask together with cupped hands. He had never felt anything so unyielding, so refractory, as the cold barrel of that pistol. He uttered a silent prayer that this unknown enemy would not hit him with it again.

The gravel rattled as the intruder moved in for another blow. "Where is Anna Nieman?" asked a gruff voice Al-Rabiah had never heard before. "Quickly." A hard slap with the palm of what felt like an iron glove.

"I don't know." Al-Rabiah clutched at his face; he thought it might be melting.

"Liar." Another slap with the flat hand.

But through the pain, Al-Rabiah saw a glimmer of hope. What we have here, his mind lectured carefully, is a case of mistaken identity. Al-Rabiah had not seen Anna since the day in the hospital. He had not seen Vienna in a fortnight. So who could this fellow be? He raised his eyes to take a look. "I know you," he said to the big Russian looming over him. "Svetlana's Uncle Viktor."

"Where's Anna?"

"Really, really, I don't know." He held his hands up in front of his face, which streamed blood.

"You tried to kill her in the hospital."

"But I *failed*. I left Vienna. Forever."

"Then your people took her."

"I have no people." Al-Rabiah thought: I've just fired my last two employees. He gave his head a violent shake. No, not fired, what was he thinking? Let go. He let them go. Fear was making him giddy. "When did I supposedly do this?"

"This afternoon."

"I was driving."

"From?"

"England." He pulled out his Chunnel ticket. "See? Look at the time."

"But you arranged it."

"That's my point. I couldn't. I didn't."

Whack! The pistol was back in play.

And then, his head surrounded with orbits of brightly colored stars, Al-Rabiah had a kind of epiphany. Of course he knew where Anna had gone. "Wait," he said, holding up a hand. "Wait."

"Tell me."

"She's with Peter Gayle."

"What?"

But Al-Rabiah sensed he'd captured Uncle Viktor's attention. "He left England last night. I saw him go. So this has nothing to do with me." Now playing the injured party, Al-Rabiah stood up and brushed at his filthy costume, offended by the acrid smell of his urine, ashamed of stinking like an incontinent geezer. A bit of courage bubbled up from his discomfort. "If she's with him you can forget her. She is dead."

"Gayle wouldn't kill her."

"Gayle cannot help killing people. He is a chalice of death, although he doesn't know it."

For a time, the Russian was quiet. Al-Rabiah could almost hear him thinking, working it all out. Then, "What was in the syringe?"

"Syringe?"

Whack! with the flat of a hand. Al-Rabiah's memory of pain revived, his courage fled.

"What did Anna put into Peter Gayle?"

"A solvent."

"Why?" A long silence, punctuated by another blow with the pistol. "Why?"

Al-Rabiah was back on his knees, holding his broken face, rocking like a grieving wife. "To begin destroying microcapsules."

"Microcapsules containing what?"

"A virus."

"What virus?"

"Variola. The Aralsk-I strain."

"Anna was arming a bomb."

Al-Rabiah nodded.

"Did she know it?"

"No, she knows nothing."

"Then why try to kill her?"

"I have asked myself the same thing."

Uncle Viktor growled something in Russian and stepped forward. "Now tell me everything, and quickly. If I sense you holding back, I have a way," and he hefted the pistol, "to get you going again."

So Al-Rabiah, in the wild hope that cooperating might buy him a crucial increment of time, began slowly turning up his cards. The microencapsulation project. The cave……..

"I've been to your cave."

"I saw you on television."

"Like everybody." Uncle Viktor took him under the arm. "Come, let's walk a little."

They strolled like two policemen in an operetta, arm in arm, down the sloping lawn of the hotel to a gravel walk, from which the ground dropped to the next street, and from there to the next, and finally to the rocky edge of the lake. And as they walked, Al-Rabiah told Uncle Viktor about the microscopic vessels, the casings, the viruses. "Of course, if you work in a cave, there are going to be mistakes. Accidents. Quality control is quite difficult."

"Of course. What about the April Ten?

"They were abused in prison. We patched them up."

"And put something into their bodies."

"Yes, they became chalices for our little vessels."

"And in these chalices your little vessels stayed, all these years?"

"More or less. We watched the Ten, and when one of them showed signs of leaking, we…well, we got rid of it."

"You got rid of it."

"Exactly." Al-Rabiah had almost forgotten to be afraid of this Uncle Viktor person. The Russian had such a good grasp of everything, and, when not hammering on you, exhibited a gratifying interest in the work. He understood the magnitude of Al-Rabiah's accomplishment. "We destroyed everything by fire. A kind of thermobaric mix."

"The kind you used in the cave."

"Yes. Primitive, but hot enough. We didn't want any of the virus to be found."

"Why not?"

"Because once people detected the virus, they would take steps to neutralize it."

"But you finally decided to go ahead."

Al-Rabiah nodded. "My leader was gone. My country was ruined. And I was down to my last chalice."

"Poor thing."

"But he had to be activated. So I arranged for a pretty nurse to do it."

"You had Sophie kidnapped to secure Anna."

"Yes."

"And then you had Sophie killed."

"The Americans killed her."

"Ah, I forgot. Then you gave Anna the syringe."

"Yes, to degrade the inert casings."

"And restore variola to the world."

They'd walked farther than Al-Rabiah realized. The hotel stood behind them now, and the hillside tilted more steeply toward the lake. There were vegetable gardens here, and black stands of trees, a few darked-out structures down below, and after that the lake, deep as the sea.

"Solvents, casings, vessels. You make it sound easy," said Uncle Viktor. "Something your neighborhood chemist could do."

Al-Rabiah tried to smile, but his face no longer worked the way it should. "I doubt that. The casings were my invention. I formulated the solvent. The idea is uniquely mine. I am like the Oppenheimer in this."

"But your helpers… "

"I told them only what they needed to know. Besides, they are all in heaven now."

"So you alone possess the secret formula, so to say."

Al-Rabiah nodded happily. "I alone, yes."

"And when you die, it dies with you."

At first, it sounded like a compliment. But then, upon reflection…. "I didn't mean…anyway, no one can stop it now."

"I can try." The Russian gave Al-Rabiah a melancholy look. "You know what people used to say of me?

"No."

"That I dropped people out of windows for a living."

"Everybody needs to make a living," whispered Al-Rabiah, closing his eyes. But he was pumping up his courage, hoping to die with a sneer on his plump lips, like the hanged man. He squared his shoulders, raised his chin. Gazing back at the dark hotel, he said, "Goodbye, my darling Silfer. Goodbye, my angels. I shall wait for you in heaven. God is great." Then he looked Krylov in the eye and said, "You see, Uncle Viktor, I am not afraid of dying."

"Good for you." Krylov brought up the silenced pistol with the muzzle an inch from Al-Rabiah's right temple and squeezed the trigger. Al-Rabiah dropped with the unnatural velocity of the suddenly dead, the speed of a hanged man falling to the end of his rope. Krylov wrapped the pistol in Al-Rabiah's right hand, already losing its warmth, then raised the body to its feet and launched it into the darkness, toward the lake.

He listened as the corpse crashed down and down, listened until he heard only silence. In the morning someone would discover... what? A dead Oppenheimer? No such luck, thought Krylov. They would find another nameless dead Iraqi in a world inured to Iraqi deaths. Maybe the police would work up an identity, maybe not. More likely they would just accept the illusion of suicide and move on.

But Krylov was not quite ready to leave. He was troubled that his decision to kill Al-Rabiah had met no internal resistance. Was that because it was murder in a just cause, or because Krylov had reverted to type? Was he at heart someone who dropped people out of windows for a living? To the darkness and its newest ghost, he said in Russian, "We can argue the point in Hell."

Then Krylov turned back toward the parking area. The Hotel Victoria slept upon its hillside. He thought he might like to come here again, to eat well and play a little tennis and spend some time in the swimming pool.

But first things first. The epidemic Al-Rabiah set in motion had to be stopped, and Krylov was only halfway there. Now it remained for him to find Anna and Peter Gayle before Emerson did, and place the poor Englishman beyond the reach of mortals.

XVIII

That first morning, Anna awoke refreshed and happy, and not at all surprised when the distorting bathroom mirror showed roses in her cheeks. Standing in the hot stream of the shower she felt her fatigue and apprehension dissolve, leaving just a pretty woman whose heart ached with joy she knew was irrational and probably shortlived.

The prospect of going to Peter, of returning herself to him, had at first seemed so risky that she thought she couldn't do it. What if she reached out and found him cold to her touch? What if he grinned and took her in his arms, made love to her, lay with her, then laughed and walked away? Why would he *not* reject her?

On the other hand, Anna reasoned, this might be her last chance to recover the man who had charmed her, and whom she had betrayed and lost. What had she to lose, really? So Anna leapt like a young woman diving naked into the night from a high bridge, her clothing left neatly folded by the railing, the long fall toward black water terrifying and exhilarating in about equal proportions.

She had leapt. Peter Gayle had caught her. Now, for the first time since leaving him at the Hotel Victoria, she felt intact. It no longer mattered whether they were together for a day or forever, or that they were on the run from God knew whom or what, to God knew where; she was whole again.

But Peter was not. He had fallen into a deep, exhausted slumber as they lay like spoons on Herr Trauber's pine bed. For a time he was so quiet that she checked his pulse, as parents sometimes do a sleeping child's. Within the hour, though, she'd felt his sleep begin to shoal. His limbs moved like a dreaming dog's, and with the slightest sharp sound—a creak of the chalet in the wind, the cry of a night bird—Peter was awake. He could not find the repose in her arms that she had found in his. He's waiting for something, she thought, and it isn't me.

Anna dressed in the street clothes from her backpack, then stowed the neatly folded mauve knit dress. It was cold in the hut, chilled by the icy rain that still fell through the trees outside. She squeezed her arms across her breasts and gave a great shiver, then wrapped herself in the shearling coat and went to check on Peter.

He sprawled in a dingy tangle of old duvet, gripping the pillow like a man afraid of drowning. Anna lay down next to him, ran her fingers up his spine. His body was hot and humid to the touch, his pulse revving. She could hear his labored breathing, and, now and then, a cough. Continuing upward, her fingers gently traced a faint red stipple that ran beneath his jaw and over his shoulders, like a pointillist shawl. A little flu, she thought. Of course he's not relaxed. Of course he's having bad dreams. She smoothed the duvet over him. She could handle flu.

"Peter," she said, moving her fingers gently along his back and shoulders. "I'm going to Wiener Neustadt to shop for us. If someone comes you say you are here with Franz Trauber's niece. Tell them in English. You are my Englischmann." She gave his hot neck a kiss. "It is about nine, I am back before noon. Okay?"

"Okay," was the murmured reply from some hidden corner of dreamland.

Anna had not been alone in a car in a decade, and found it exciting to have Gayle's Viggen entirely to herself, flying down past Molzegg to the Sudautobahn, and turning north for Wiener Neustadt. The night before it had seemed a journey of many leagues, stretched by darkness and rain and the uncertainty of their destination. Now it was just a quick hop through the morning drizzle and into the caravan of lorries and service vans slowing for the Wiener Neustadt exit.

At this hour, the Mercur shopping center off the Sudautobahn was quiet and almost empty, the merchants just opening their stores, the transparent mosaic of the roof grey and puddled with rain. Anna went through the place systematically, like, she thought, a nurse in the Intensiv.

At the pharmacy she found aspirin and cough medicine for Peter's flu, soap, shampoo, toothpaste and brushes. A boutique provided her with a week's fresh underwear and a couple of cheap blouses. The sports shop was good for another sweat shirt and what she thought was a rather expensive Patagonia shell and liner, in black and midnight blue. At another place she bought five meters of light chain and a padlock to string across the entrance to Herr Trauber's drive, and, in another store, a bottle of Russian vodka. Then she went to the post office and wrote a card for Sveta:

All is good, grandmother still needs me, back soon, please tell hospital...

She hesitated a moment, then grinned and added:

I am happy, happy, happy.

In the Mercur grocery store she loaded her trolley for what she thought of as The Siege. She had no idea how long they would be in the ski-hut, or where they would go from there, and so she shoveled in canned meats and vegetables, lots of soups (for Peter's flu), eggs, apples and oranges and limes for the vodka, loaves of bread and semmels, a Linzertorte from the bakery, cheeses, milk, coffee, orange juice. From the butcher she bought a London broil, some brats, and two rather nice Schnitzels, which she would lovingly cook for Peter in their purloined nest.

When Anna thought she had enough to feed a small army for a week, she trundled her laden trolley to the cashier and paid with her Visa card, which she'd used for all the purchases. Then, aided by a thin boy from the store, she marched to the Viggen and stowed everything in the boot. Seeing the boy studying the British number plate, she handed over a ten-euro tip for his help, hoping he might keep silent out of gratitude.

The road back was nearly empty of traffic once Anna left the Sudautobahn, the two-lane tarmac surface slick and shining in the rain. She turned off into Herr Trauber's hidden driveway and stopped, took out the length of chain, and wound it around two stout-looking spruce saplings flanking the track, then locked it shut. The chain wasn't much of a barrier, but it might deter the odd hiker and perhaps even confound Herr Trauber, should he come to check on his property.

Peter was up and showering again when she arrived. Anna heard the water and his voice, a nice baritone that could carry a tune, more or less. She hadn't known he sang. She cocked her head, listening. The tune she could remember hearing as a little girl, but she'd never heard the English words before. Something very sweet about the throwing of bouquets, a rose and a glove, what people would say. Another lovely mystery, like the touch and goes. There was so much to learn about him.

The shower was quiet when Anna finished her last trip from the Saab, but the nice baritone was still working on the familiar song about people suspecting things. Then Peter emerged from the bathroom wearing khakis and a grey cashmere jumper over a light blue shirt.

"Spanking clean!" he proclaimed, "I found the electrical main so we have light and heat. "So I've been a busy bee. What's for breakfast?"

"You mean lunch." She laughed. "I'm glad you feel better."

"Better than what? I feel grand."

"When I left you had a little flu."

Gayle's face darkened. "I did not."

"Well, that's the way with flu, now you see it, now you don't." Anna gave a shrug. "But I'm glad it's gone."

"I don't have flu. I don't have anything."

She turned to him. "Peter, this morning you had a fever, a cough, a prickly heat across your neck and shoulders. Now, after rest and a hot shower, you're okay again. I can stop playing nurse."

But Gayle seemed not to listen. He sank down on the edge of the bed and put his face in his hands. "I don't have the fucking flu," he murmured. When he looked up at her, she saw despair in his face.

"It's gone, Peter. It's not a problem." But Anna felt a percolation of dread. The magnitude of his distress scared her, for it seemed to have come out of nowhere and to be about nothing. It was irrational, it was insane. It cracked the door for some horrible new development to enter their lives, something worse than having him laugh and walk away. But what could that be? What could be worse?

Heart pounding, Anna sat down next to her troubled man, intending to wrap him in her arms, her wings, and make the intruder slink away. He let her hold him, but his body was tense as a hunted rabbit's, poised to flee.

After awhile he said, "I thought the thing had died."

Anna felt her flesh move with apprehension. The new horror was some kind of *creature*. She remembered: *Dragging dead boys*. "Who were the dead boys?"

"There were three of them. And their father, Harry, as in Tom, Dick, and Harry. I called them Huey, Louie, and Dewey. Young warriors, he said. Very quick to kill, they were. Surprised they didn't kill me."

"How did they die?"

"Harry shot them."

"But why?"

"They'd caught some terrible disease. Harry said I'd given it to them because they had it, but I did not. I told him he was crazy."

"He could have found treatment for them."

"They were barely alive when he finished them off. He believed the disease was somebody's creation, like a nuclear bomb, and it had to be stopped out there on the Downs to prevent an epidemic. So he had me drag the boys into the kitchen and sit them up so he could shoot them. Then we soaked the place in petrol. He tried to get us all dead and incinerated at the same time. But I got out before he torched the petrol."

Anna was quiet then, hoping to still the roaring in her brain, hoping for her vision to clear, for her heart to stop racing. She was a nurse, she had seen it all. She had seen what the human body was capable of when it applied its sense of humor, the extra hands and heads, the little hearts beating outside the little chests, the exoskeletons. She had seen what colliding automobiles could produce in the way of human wreckage. She had eased the doomed bearers of the human immune virus down the steep decline, through pneumonia and meningitis, into the afterlife, and tried to dilute the pain and hopelessness that hung like mist in cancer wards.

But she had no experience of plagues. The Black Death was ancient history to her, although she believed it still popped up among rats and prairie dogs and in the far corners of the Third World. She had never encountered Marburg or ebola, the great hemorrhagic fevers. She had read of them, looked at the disquieting color photographs in medical texts, shaken her head in disbelief at their ability to kill; but she had never actually seen them.

Of course, they occurred at a comfortable remove, the viral inhabitants of a distant continent famed for the cruel lethality of its inhabitants. The fevers belonged in a land where some children carried AK-47s and cut off other children's hands. So there was that geographic moat between her and such afflictions, and a biological one: they preferentially infected animals, and only accidentally and occasionally jumped to humans.

"What the boys had, did it have a name?"

"Harry said it was smallpox."

In all her time as a nurse in the Intensiv, Anna had never fainted, and she did not faint now, although a black shadow flickered across her vision. "Smallpox no longer exists," she whispered, more to herself than to Peter.

"I know."

"Did you believe him?"

"No."

"Had he ever seen smallpox?"

"He said he had, long ago."

"Ah."

Smallpox lay light years outside her experience. She knew the various poxes of childhood, the eczemas and pustules and dermal inflammations and fevers that everyone caught, sooner or later. She knew smallpox was an ancient scourge, once commonplace in Europe. It was not a creature of the tropical forest, but flourished at every latitude and in every climate. It shunned animals; humans were its natural host.

What else did she know? As a child she had been vaccinated against smallpox and in the late 1990s her supervisor had insisted on a booster before a hospital exchange visit to Dakar.

She had met people who'd endured and survived smallpox, who bore its pits and scars. None of them had wrung his hands over having had the illness, but treated the experience as one of those disagreeable things that sometimes overtook you.

Esther Summerson, of *Bleak House,* came to mind. When Anna read it at the English School, Esther's illness had stayed with her. Dickens had seen plenty of smallpox, and his description of it brought the disease down to size. Esther had recovered, somewhat scarred, but not so badly that her life shriveled around her. Most victims survived. Those with previous vaccinations almost always survived. Perhaps smallpox was just a kind of measles raised an octave or two.

But this didn't match the victims pictured in what everyone called the Big Red Book of Smallpox; they were gruesome beyond telling. Its measured descriptions of such accessory symptoms as nightmares, fever, nausea, despond and delirium, a certain worried look, a sepulchral odor—they were lost in the Kodachrome glare of photographed victims. These brown, naked women lay supine in splendid color, like models sitting for Gauguin. Their skin was subsumed beneath a sheath of pustules, dense as bees swarming on their keeper. Looking at these images, Anna had whispered, "Thank you, God, for taking it away." She had shivered with relief at being spared the ordeal of treating them. Well, of looking at them.

"Smallpox was declared eradicated in 1980," she said.

"That's why I didn't believe Harry. The boys died of some desert crud, nothing to do with me."

"Are you sure of that?"

"I'm sure of nothing anymore. I'm running full lean on certitude."

"What did the boys look like at the end?"

Gayle made no reply.

"You don't want to frighten me."

"No, I don't."

"Harry tells you it's smallpox and then you come straight to me. For what, to make me a laboratory rabbit?"

"I came to you because if I factor you out of my life there is no visit to the Hotel Victoria, no 'chance encounter' with Al-Rabiah, and no mystery injection. So, yes, I think whatever is in me had something to do with you and your bloody syringe. Maybe the shot was something like pulling the pin from a grenade. The thing Al-Rabiah planted in me, in the ten of us, lay dormant all these years. You woke it up."

"The monster." Anna could hardly breathe, and she could not look at Gayle. "I'm going home," she said. "Take me back to Vienna."

Gayle shook his head. "I can't."

"Because I might be infected?" Anna looked away, trying to think through the static of fear. Like a cow in a thunderstorm, she felt a rising impulse to stampede, the need of cowboy incantations and calming songs. Patience, patience. There, there.

If she returned to Vienna, they could put her in isolation, treat her, care for her until the sickness went away. But then, what about Peter? There was nothing to treat. He was just a specimen to be studied, quarantined eternally, possibly eradicated, as the disease itself had been. *He* was the laboratory rabbit. So she would wait with Peter in Herr Trauber's isolation ward until they knew whether she was infected. If she was....well, she thought, one thing at a time.

"Harry must have been wrong," Gayle was saying. "If anybody thought I was a smallpox carrier, I wouldn't have got out of England. But there's no sign of official interest. No police cordons in germ-warfare kit combing the woods for me. You go over to Wiener Neustadt in my car, British number plates, nobody says boo. I think the people who are after me are on their own."

"Emerson," she said.

"Who's Emerson?"

"An American spy. Churches worked for him. My Russian friend told me about him."

"The mother of all scorpions."

"I don't understand."

"Harry's code for America."

"Why would this Emerson want you?"

"He wouldn't want me. He'd just want somebody to dig this thing out of me and study it. Reproduce it. Put it to work in the arsenal of democracy."

"So you have to run forever?"

"No. At some point, I shall have to stop, turn, and say something heroic, like Lay on, Emerson or whoever, and deprive them of what they're after. Or the thing, whatever it is, *if* it is, may just go away. I have no idea what kind of time I have remaining." Gayle paused for a moment, then added, with a grin, "But I hope to spend it with you."

Ah, well, Anna's inner voice whispered, ah, well. It was not as if Peter had given her AIDS or syphilis or Marburg. Probably he had given her nothing at all. And, yes, there was the matter of the syringe; she, not Peter, had revived the monster, if monster there were.

Her fears receded. She was not vaccine-naïve, as they called it; a definite plus. If she contracted smallpox, she would almost certainly survive it. She must approach her condition as she approached the conditions of others. The well part of her would minister to the sick part. She would try to be brave. She would try to be Esther Summerson and face Al-Rabiah's creation with courage. She would get through it. And when she did, Peter would be waiting for her.

"I'll take care of you," he said, as if he'd read her mind.

"Will you take me back to the Hotel Victoria?"

"When I can."

"Funny, I knew you were kidding when you said we'd fall in love."

"I was."

Anna let Gayle gather her into his arms and hold her there on Herr Trauber's pine bed. She imagined they were two survivors of a sunken ship, clinging to each other in the middle of a dangerous sea.

XIX

"Just look at this, Lamont," Emerson exclaimed. "We're on a tiny island with sixty million souls and yet, from here, you don't see a single sign of human life. Not a bit of smoke. Not a structure." He cocked his head. "Listen to that silence. And it's so fucking *pretty!*"

"Personally I like the States," piped Lamont.

"Sure you do. It's your job to like the States."

The two men stood just outside a line of yellow police tape that had been strung around the charred remains of a stone cottage on the Downs. Emerson wore his customary blazer, jeans, and desert boots, Lamont a Lakers tank top and shorts, his tattooed skin radiant as an Amazon tree frog's in the autumn light.

They had been drawn to the spot by an intercept keyed to the term *PETER GAYLE* and relayed to them aboard the Gulfstream over Ukraine. Minutes later, they received GPS coordinates for a place south and east of Swindon, and the pilot turned toward England while the co-pilot began working on a place to land. Without realizing it, they had picked up Harry's trail of crumbs, laid down to lure the other scorpions into an ambush.

The Gulfstream had come down at RAF Lyneham, taxiing in among the ranked Hercules transports like an ibis among elephants, trailing the FOLLOW ME vehicle. When Emerson and Lamont stepped onto the concrete apron, the group captain commanding the base was there to welcome them, along with two RAF non-coms, both armed. The commander looked young for his rank, with happy blue eyes and a bronze cap of hair; his smile seemed to turn the wrong way at the edges, as if the universe were droll.

"Welcome to Lyneham," he said without, it seemed to Emerson, meaning it. "I'm Group Captain Elliott." He didn't introduce the non-coms.

"Thanks for letting us in," said Emerson. "We're only here for a couple hours. Gone by tea time. Is there a civilian car I can rent or borrow?" Then, into the ensuing silence, he added, "We're just going over toward Swindon. No kidnappings or bank robberies, I promise."

"I think the Lockheed-Martin rep might do," said Elliott.

"For his fellow Americans."

"Anyone else aboard?"

"Just the pilots and crew chief."

"No, um....?"

"Lads in orange PJs? Nope."

Driving away in a forest-green Land Cruiser, which the Lockheed Martin field representative had reluctantly handed into their care, Emerson had laughed at the meeting. "We're relics of a conflict everybody's trying to forget, Lamont, along with the fact that it was a great goddamned American victory. Now they take one look and say, oh, shit, the wild men are here. Are we wild men, Lamont?"

"We have our moments."

"See what this Jap Jeep can do. I'll navigate."

Emerson took them down through Chippenham and Marlborough, into the empty, beautiful land, crowding along the narrow paved lanes until they found the drive with the old For Sale sign hanging from a chain. After a check of his mobile's GPS, Lamont had turned up the rutted trail, and the Land Cruiser gnawed its way through the apple orchard and up the slope to the cluster of police vehicles gathered there, where Lamont pulled over and he and Emerson got out to contemplate the view.

Now a tall man in a Navy peacoat detached himself from a quartet of yellow-vested police and strolled to meet them. He was as tall as Lamont, but not so heavy, sixtyish, Emerson thought, teeth like a donkey.

"Detective Inspector Wickers," the man said, putting out his hand for the Americans to shake.

"My name is Emerson, and this is my associate, Mr. Lamont."

Wickers studied the pair, then eyed the Land Cruiser. He grinned and shook his head in wonder. "Good God, how you chaps like these big motorcars!" Then, leaning toward them as though confidentially, he said, "What brought you and that thing here, if I may ask?"

"We heard the place was for sale," Emerson said, his face open as a child's. "Thought we'd take a look."

"Not much of a buy now, is it."

"I don't know. Fine vista, good-sized piece of land. Not much in the way of accommodations. What happened?"

"Not sure. Forensics poring over it. Obvious there's been a hell of a fire. Beyond that….well, look here, you two aren't journalists, are you?"

Emerson shook his head. "God no." Lamont made a bitter face.

"Well, I think it is probably another propane blast."

"Another?"

"We had one down toward Lyme Regis just the other day. Propane the culprit there. Damned volatile stuff, burns hot as Hades, you get a regular crematorium going in a building once it ignites."

"Could it have been a bomb?"

"Oh, I doubt that."

"Or a bomb factory gone sour?"

"Well, we shall look into that, of course. But we haven't found a lot of chemicals, ammonium nitrate, hydrogen peroxide, that kind of thing."

"But no lives lost."

"Couldn't say that. Some human remains inside, difficult to tell how many individuals. Naturally that will be the subject of an inquest." Wickers showed his huge teeth in a grimace of concern. "What worries me is what the press will make of it. Some sort of Downs Pyromaniac thing. The Propane Perpetrator."

"I take your meaning," said Emerson.

"Someone has done a good deal of driving around here," Wickers said, peering at the cross-hatch of tire tracks outside the gate. "And there is the matter of that bus. What do you make of that?"

For the first time, Emerson saw the stern of a Volkswagen bus protruding from a charred crumble of stone wall. "Looks like it dropped from a great height."

"Yes, doesn't it. I thought the same thing. Of course, it couldn't fly here, so it must have been driven into the cottage with some force."

"So the whole thing could be a bizarre traffic incident."

"Mr. Emerson, I think you have it. You take a crash, add propane, and…"

"Bob's your uncle?"

"Exactly."

Emerson put out his hand. "Well, we won't take up more of your time, Mr. Wickers." He uttered a short, faux chuckle. "I don't believe we'll be buying the crime scene."

"Some lovely places for sale down toward Lyme Regis," said the detective.

"Good, we'll take a look."

The man from Lockheed-Martin nearly wept with relief when they restored the Land Cruiser to him, dirty and on fumes but intact. He gave them a lift to the Gulfstream, which was hooked up to an auxiliary power unit to keep its systems going.

They boarded and Emerson took his seat on the port side, which would be in the shade headed back to Austria. A sheaf of e-mail printouts waited for him on the tray table, but he wasn't quite ready for them. For a time he just watched the C-130s trundle around Lyneham's taxiways, then watched the lovely quilt of England fall away beneath the Gulfstream on the climb toward forty thousand feet.

Emerson supposed the human remains were the Iraqis who'd held Churches, and then took Peter Gayle, and that it was their Volkswagen in the rubble. Had Gayle died with them, or had he escaped? Had he been freed by some third party? If freed, where would he go?

"Lamont, if you were Peter Gayle, where would you go?"

But Lamont, seated across the aisle, was writhing to something on his iPod, eyes closed.

"What a useless sack of shit you are."

"You say something?" The big man took off his ear piece. "Huh?"

Emerson shook his head. Christ, this was like working with a Doberman pinscher. He turned to the sheaf of messages. Signs of Gayle, so he'd survived the cottage, he was moving, heading east across the continent. Stopped at two money machines, one outside Brussels, one near Bonn, where he refueled. Predator picked up his Saab convert east of Frankfurt, tracked it to Austrian frontier. NATO unwilling to go farther, citing squawks about air-space intrusions, and retrieved Predator. Request in for satellite coverage. No further information.

"What, he vanished into thin air? Austria doesn't *have* any thin fucking air."

Lamont lifted his earpiece. "Everything okay?"

Emerson growled at him.

Ah, the promised stuff on one Anna Nieman. Nurse at the Allgemeines Krankenhaus Intensivstation in Vienna. Solid citizen. Thirties. And what was this? Identical twin of Sophie Nieman,

Austrian TV journalist kidnapped in Baghdad, accidentally killed by friendly fire during release. Emerson grinned. Somebody takes Sophie to get Anna to do something, then drives Sophie into American guns. For what? The silence of the grave. It was about as subtle as a video game. But who were the kidnappers? What did they want from Anna? "Ms. Nieman, we must have a chat."

Emerson read on. Anna shared a flat on Sternwartestrasse with Svetlana Maximovna Trulova, researcher at Centre for Analytic Studies. Russian national. Father former KGB colonel, terminated with extreme prejudice 1983. Viktor Krylov, also former KGB, now nuclear safeguards inspector, long-time friend of family. "And my old Sov chum."

Yes, and on one of those other messages, wasn't there a call yesterday afternoon to this Svetlana person from a public phone? A woman saying she was all right, hurrying to be with her dying grandmother in Klagenfurt? A call too brief to trace?

And where was Anna Nieman now? Nobody knew. Not at the hospital, not at home. Could she be racing to her grandmother's side? Had she even known her grandmother?

Back to Peter Gayle. RAF squadron leader, Tornado pilot. Shot down during Desert Storm. POW for a couple of months. Repatriated with the so-called April Ten. Dropped from flight status. Left service on a medical. Flat in Brighton. Contract work for Jane's. Recent trips to Toulouse, an overnight in Glion at the Hotel Victoria with a pretty woman, then Bern, then home to Brighton.

Had the pretty woman been Anna Nieman?

And here, a follow-up on the hotel in Glion. An Iraqi named Mohammad Al-Rabiah, aka Muckeltee, shot himself there last night. Wife and daughters in Hotel Victoria. Body a bit roughed up. Blood on clothing not all his. Police think he was beaten and killed himself out of shame. Emerson emitted a snort. "Somebody held the fucker's hand." Al-Rabiah had lived in Vienna, visiting scholar at the Centre for Analytic Studies, where the Russian woman worked. "Where we've been tapping phones since the seventies."

He put aside the messages and leaned back in his seat. What a daisy chain! Al-Rabiah and Peter Gayle and this hotel and maybe Anna the nurse and poor Sophie and Svetlana the Russian and the dead guys at the cottage, Churches, Krylov. "And me. Very definitely, me. Peas in a fucking pod. Joined at the hips."

XX

Oldenburg stopped by late in the afternoon, giving the door a peremptory rap and pushing past it. "Good God, Viktor," said the Dane, looking the Russian up and down. "You look like a dead man. What've you been up to?" Then, glancing at Krylov's purple knuckles, he said, "I see. You've been beating people up. It's 1938 again."

"What do you want, Klaus?" Krylov growled, indicating he was in no mood for bullshit.

"We're trying to find Churches' documents. I thought you might have them, since you...."

"The Embassy has his British passport. Other than that," Krylov shrugged, "sorry, wrong number."

"We'll keep looking."

"Is that all?" Krylov picked up a sheaf of papers and pretended to read.

"One thing more. I had Churches down for the snap inspection at Leningrad-II. With him gone, I'm giving it to you."

"Shit. When?"

"In a month. Be ready. And don't think you can run to Juan Carlos about this. If you want to work here, you have to *work* here. Clear?"

"Goodbye, Klaus. Close the door."

Left alone, Krylov leaned back in his chair and watched the curtain of rain that reduced the far shore of the Danube to an ashy shadow. He thought he must weigh a ton; all his limbs felt as if they'd died overnight. A plant deprived of water, he thought, would feel like this. The round trip to Glion had left him utterly exhausted, urgently wanting to shower and shave and clean his teeth. All that kept him awake was his anger, which bubbled and frothed like liquid steel as he heaped blame upon himself.

Going after Al-Rabiah, *knowing* without any real evidence that he had taken Anna, was the kind of mad impulse that had killed Maxim Trulov, Krylov's old friend. Max had followed false trails, driven by angry instinct. He had wound up with his head blown apart in the snowy Hauptallee beneath the Wheel. An idea had got hold of him the way rabies gets hold of dogs, with death waiting at the end. Krylov had resolved long ago that it would never happen to him. He would always think before he leapt.

Yet, with almost no information, he had galloped off to rescue Anna and eliminate the self-styled Oppenheimer of bioweaponry. The Iraqi had been erased, and Krylov felt no particular regret beyond the niggling fear that one did such work too easily. But his wild ride had not rescued Anna. She was with somebody else, somebody a good deal more dangerous than the little chemist had been.

"So, Maxim," he asked the empty room, "where do we go from here?"

As if in reply, his telephone rang. Itchy with superstition, half expecting Maxim to be on the line, he picked it up. "Krylov."

"Uncle Viktor, why didn't you call? I've been up all night waiting. I've worried myself sick."

"Sorry, Sveta, I've only just got back."

"Anna called. She's with her friend."

"That's what Muckeltee said."

"You talked to him?"

"Briefly."

"And then, what, he fell out a window?"

"You know, Sveta, your father has a lot to answer for, starting that stuff about windows."

"Tell me about Muckeltee."

"Not on the telephone."

"Come over tonight. I'll make pelmini."

Krylov's mouth watered. "Well…"

"I have vodka."

"Well…"

"Blinchiki with honey afterward."

"Ah."

"Even better, come get me after work."

"I've just been eighteen hours on the road."

"In that case, another hour or two shouldn't make any difference."

As always, Krylov's heart gave a happy jump when he saw Svetlana appear at the entrance to the Centre for Analytic Studies, peer through the mist of rain until she found his old Mercedes. She was so much Maxim Trulov's daughter, tall and well-formed, not beautiful so much as strikingly crafted, the pale moon of a face wrapped in its onyx braid. But beautiful was the only way to describe her heart, for she'd received none of her father's dark side, none of that latent madness, none of the violence waiting like a shark in the shallows.

In the old days Krylov had sometimes wondered if his heart leapt for her or for some combination of her and his good memories of Max. But, no, Maxim Trulov was in the afterlife—Greater Siberia, as he'd called it. Viktor Krylov was moved solely by Svetlana. He had never tired of experiencing that first glimpse of her, of having her head lift, her eyes light with recognition. It was almost like being in love. Except, he cautioned himself, this is just fatigue. It isn't Vitzya, it's Uncle Viktor.

Sveta climbed into the passenger seat and carefully arranged her string bag between her feet. She'd evidently been shopping since his call, for the bag strained like a fishing net with supplies. She swept back a scarf she'd put over her braid, and brushed a drop or two of moisture from her hair. "Were you waiting long?"

"Only a minute or two."

"Good." But she was studying him in her peculiarly intense way. "You look terrible."

"A lot of driving."

She touched his hand where it gripped the wheel. "You've been dragging your knuckles again."

Krylov laughed. "Reverting to form. Soon I'll be digging for termites with a sharp stick." He started the Mercedes and pulled out into the slow eddy of traffic in the town square.

"And look at this." Svetlana ran her hand along his arm, then showed him her palm. "Blood."

"Or rust, grease. It could be anything."

"No, it's blood. First, dragging your knuckles and now, blood on your good suit."

Krylov smiled. "I usually change when I go out to play. But this time..." and he shrugged.

"You didn't get blood on your good suit and bruised knuckles from driving."

"No. I got them from talking things over with Muckeltee."

"I see, you took him aside and he just began telling you things."

"Something like that."

"What did he say about Anna?"

"That she was with the Englishman."

"And what else?"

"What he'd done to Peter Gayle, how the thing works."

"The thing. What thing?"

"Something I have to stop."

"I don't understand."

"I don't mean for you to."

Svetlana turned away, glaring out the window. "And then?"

"He shot himself."

"Shot himself? Why would he do such a thing?"

"Remorse."

She laughed. "Was he sitting on the windowsill when the remorse attack began?"

"Come on."

"So he is gone. That means Anna is safe."

"From him, yes."

"But she's out of danger. She's happy."

"How do you know that?"

"When she called she told me she was going to see her grandmother in Klagenfurt. It's our special code."

"What, a grandmother in Klagenfurt means she's happy?"

"It means she's off on a dirty weekend and doesn't want to say too much about it."

"Hmm. So where is *your* grandmother, Sveta?"

"Kotlyakovskoye cemetery."

"No code for you, then."

She looked away from him, pretending to concentrate on the blur of villages and traffic and trees going by her window. Then she said, giving him a strong look, "I have nothing to hide." But her voice said she led a lonely life and was not very happy about it.

"Your heart is too vast for dirty weekends. And you are too beautiful to waste on some little Austrian spiv."

Out of the corner of his eye he saw her blush. "Anyway," she went on after a long pause, "she's with her grandmother in Klagenfurt. Her Englishman."

"It doesn't mean she's out of danger."

"He would never hurt her."

"He can't choose whom he hurts."

Svetlana was quiet for a time, watching the traffic, Krylov thought, in order not to look at him. Finally she asked, "What did Muckeltee do to the Englishman?"

"He turned him into a monster."

"Does he know?"

Krylov shrugged. "Maybe. We don't know anything about Peter Gayle, how he thinks. Anna betrayed him. He may hate her. He may have come to Vienna to kill her. Or then again, maybe he fell in love."

"Anna is not afraid of him. She would have let me know."

"So let's say he doesn't know what he is."

"And what is he?"

"Ah, Sveta. A terrible kind of bomb. A walking virus."

"What virus?" asked Svetlana, eyes closed.

"Ospa." Smallpox. "Chiornaya ospa." Black smallpox.

Svetlana recoiled as if he'd given her a slap. "Ospa," she whispered, still not opening her eyes. "Ospa is gone."

"It was."

A long silence in which Krylov imagined Svetlana going through a thick deck of possibilities, card by card. Finally she said, "Anna is a nurse. She must have had a vaccination."

"We can hope."

"Anna is a nurse," Sveta repeated, as if she fingered a rosary. "A nurse can work it out."

"The Americans are looking for Gayle. If she seeks treatment, they will have him."

Svetlana shook her head. "So she will stay and endure what comes."

"Even if it kills her."

"Even then." Svetlana was quiet for a moment, then turned earnestly toward Krylov. "Will I see Anna again?"

"I don't know."

She gave him a long look. "What happens if you find the Englishman first?"

"The virus has to be destroyed."

"That will break poor Anna's heart."

"By then Anna's heart will be past breaking."

They drove in silence back into the maelstrom of the Gürtel, the sun grazing the low ridges off to the southwest, night creeping in from the Ukraine like the black crows of winter. Krylov watched Sveta out of the corner of his eye, wondering when she would shed a tear for her doomed friend.

One day, he thought, she would break, she would become a regular Niobe, an Iguazu of grief. But until then all the troubles in the world were somehow accommodated in her secret heart, a place as commodious as the Cathedral of Christ the Savior, without a tear in sight.

He was lucky, finding a parking space not far from Sveta's flat. The Cobra guard across the way watched impassively as she opened the iron gate. Inside the flat, she switched on some lights against the descending night and checked the telephone for messages. "Nothing."

` "The grandmother must still be okay."

"I hope." She headed for the kitchen.

"What can I do?"

"You can get the vodka out of the freezer and give us each a tall glass of it. With half a lemon."

Krylov fetched the icy bottle from the fridge, cut a lemon and put a half in each tumbler, then poured out two good portions of vodka, which, cooled well below freezing, had the viscosity of motor oil. "Here," he said, passing Sveta her glass, already covered like an Arctic window with a film of ice.

She took it and briefly looked him in the eye. "To villains falling out of windows."

"To Anna," countered Krylov.

"Yes, especially, to Anna." Their glasses chimed like bells when they touched them. "Now, you go to the sitting room and have your vodka. And I go to work."

SVETLANA COOKED LIKE A BUSY BLACKSMITH, SINGLE-MINDEDLY, AND always a step ahead of whatever was glowing in the fire. Ordinarily, when she cooked she made no mess at all. With pelmini it was possible—for Anna, inevitable—to become covered in flour and egg yolk and grease, onion and garlic skins floating like motes upon the air. But not Svetlana.

Tonight, however, she could not quite free her mind of the awful term: chiornaya ospa. Good God. She took a long draft of her vodka, closing her eyes as it percolated down and down through her system. She imagined it must light things up inside, like a barium tracer. The horror receded. Anna was a nurse. She would be immune. She would know what to do. Oh, Annushka. Oh my God.

Sveta shed her sweater and rolled up her blouse sleeves, removed her wristwatch and a bracelet of amber and dark gold inherited from her mother, and took another long sip of vodka. Then she set to work, kneading the dough into a ghostly lump that she let sit while she lightly braised the meat and onions and garlic in a frying pan and put a large pot of water on to boil. Without thinking about it, she began unwinding her braid, the black, luminous hair fanning out in a silken cloud. She tossed back what remained in her frosted glass and poured herself another.

Long ago, Sveta's mother had brought home a pelmenitsa, a round piece of metal with perhaps twenty circular cut-outs where the pelmini dough was placed. Maxim had taken one look and thrown this thing, as he called it, into the rubbish bin.

"The beauty of pelmini," he told Svetlana later, after he had soothed his poor wife, "is that it was not intended to be mass-produced. It must be made by the hands one loves." And with that he had given Svetlana's fingers a kiss. It was among her good memories, even though she'd suspected at the time that Papa was just being colorful and didn't really give a damn whose hands touched his pelmini, so long as it arrived in his bowl, swimming in sour cream or beef broth, and there was vodka to wash it down.

Svetlana rolled out the dough and cut out little circles, which she filled with meat and covered with a second thin layer of dough. Then she swept the infant dumplings, pale and unfinished, into the boiling water, where they sank like the damned into the volcanic depths.

While they cooked she cleaned up the kitchen, put out two bowls and a fresh crock of sour cream and spoons. She wiped her hands on her skirt, leaving streaks of flour and grease, and left another pale smudge where she wiped her nose. Onion and garlic skins clung to her, like the beginnings of a fairy costume.

The last time she'd seen her father he'd worn a costume. It had been during Fasching, when there were fancy dress parties everywhere. Papa had been missing for weeks and then he'd stepped out of a blizzard into their Vienna flat, a helmeted apparition in a motocross outfit, dragging an unknown Russian woman dressed as a rag doll. He had hugged his wife and lifted Svetlana, "my little glowing moonface," into the air until she lost her fear and smiled for him. She remembered thinking her heart would break with happiness.

Moments later he and the woman were gone, hurrying down the snowbound street. They paused in a cone of light from a streetlamp, like figures in an antique snow globe paperweight. The giant motocross apparition turned, raised an arm, saluting her, saying goodbye. Saying goodbye forever. Then they were lost in the darkness, the winter hush filling in behind them.

Svetlana bit her lip, took a long pull at her vodka, and poured in a little more. Someday, she thought, she would start smoking opium. She could see herself lying in the close atmosphere of an Oriental den, old Chinamen everywhere around her in the strata of intoxicating smoke, and she herself reclined, pulling at her pipe as memory turned into dream, and dream turned into nothing much at all.

The Americans had come to the flat earlier that evening, urging Vera and Svetlana to tell them where to find Maxim Trulov. They said they could save him from the KGB. He could defect. The three of them would go to the United States, they would live in Wyoming and own horses. This was his only chance, they said.

Vera had wrung her hands, smelling doom all around her, but she had also detected something dead in the promise and said nothing. But Svetlana had believed them. She told the Americans where to find Papa, and so they had gone to the Hauptallee and shot him down like a deer in the snow.

The pelmini began popping to the top of the boiling water, little white souls escaping from Purgatory. She turned off the burner and herded the dumplings, several at a time, into a mesh cup, let them drain, and dropped them onto a layer of paper towels she'd spread across the counter. Then she refilled her glass with not quite frozen vodka, smoothed her blouse and skirt with greasy hands, and took the bottle with her into the sitting room.

Krylov sat crumpled in the corner of the sofa, his breath rumbling softly, like a hibernating bear's. He'd drunk his vodka, probably in one great gulp, and sunk into exhausted slumber.

Svetlana knelt on the floor and removed his shoes and socks, then pivoted him so that he lay supine. She got him out of the jacket with blood on its sleeve and removed his tie and put his arms on his chest, like a dead man's in a coffin. His breathing revved briefly, as he tried to rise toward the light, but she saw him give it up. Soon he was hibernating again.

Papa had often come home like this, worn out, not smelling very sweet, some blood, his or somebody else's, in a faint spray across a sleeve or trouser leg. Sometimes he brought home a bit of lipstick on his collar, a memory of someone's perfume, carnal scents. But that had been different from the man before her now.

She'd loved Maxim, but she had also feared him, aware of something terrible caged within. She had read his sexual escapades in her mother's eyes, in which the last faint light of happiness had finally winked out. But Sveta had never for an instant been afraid of Krylov. She would have trusted Uncle Viktor with her life.

Yes, and with her love, for she had handed over her heart back in the Moscow days, when she was a child and he a young officer in the KGB. She still had his letters from Afghanistan, those fables he used to write about the two bears, him and Maxim, and their adventures, redacted to take out the blood and cruelty.

"Ah, Vitzya, Vitzya," she murmured, leaning her head against the sofa, her hair just brushing his chest. She took in his smell and touched the hard, bristly line of his jaw with her fingertips and smoothed the black and grey mane of hair that spilled over his forehead. She thought she might be a little drunk, and didn't care.

"Once upon a time, Vitzya," she said in a voice too low to wake him, "there was a girl who would wander into the taiga forest hoping that a certain thing would happen to her. She met ermines and foxes and wolves and ravens and lynxes, but she would go with none of them. She had in mind being carried off by one bear in particular.

"She told herself again and again that it was only a matter of time. One day her grand old bear would lift his nostrils into the air and detect what was going on. And at last, Vitzya, my dear bear, he would understand. He would come and pick up that girl in his powerful arms and take her away to the Place of Bears, where she would make him pelmini for all the rest of her days."

Svetlana curled up against the couch, her head against Krylov's ribcage, his heart thumping like a distant drum, his sleep so deep as to draw her in as well. She sipped at her vodka and looked at her bare wrist, where her watch usually could be found, but which now bore just streaks of flour. What time was it? The great sleeping creature next to her made it seem very late at night.

She would just rest here a moment, she decided, then wake him and feed him pelmini, and send him home as Uncle Viktor. "Oh, Vitzya," she whispered, "I am so tired of saying Uncle Viktor." Then

Svetlana closed her eyes. Soon she was walking in the taiga, hoping to be found by one bear in particular.

VIKTOR KRYLOV WAS IN A DIFFERENT QUADRANT OF DREAMLAND, ARM in arm with Mohammad Al-Rabiah near the hotel in Glion, the long lake shimmering off to the south, a chill in the night air. They walked in silence for a time. Then, toward the end of the gravel track, the Iraqi stopped and turned toward Krylov.

Here, he said, handing over a small semiautomatic pistol.

Krylov thought it was the old Makarov nine-millimeter he'd carried in Afghanistan. *Thank you,* he said, studying the weapon.

When he looked up, the Iraqi was still there, watching him expectantly, but the lake had vanished. Instead there was the sparkling curve of a desert river, flanked by a green fringe of reeds and palms between the water and the barren land that climbed toward a horizon of lavender mountains.

I know this place, said Krylov.

The Iraqi said, *My cave is nearby.*

Krylov nodded. *I know your cave.*

You know what I did there.

You made bombs.

Out of men.

You deserve something for that.

I have always thought so, said the Iraqi.

Well then.

Krylov raised the pistol, aiming at a point above Al-Rabiah's left eye, and began the long squeeze required to fire the first round in the Makarov's magazine. The pistol recoiled but made no report. In silence, the Iraqi's head exploded like a balloon full of blood.

Job tvosu matj!

For a terrible moment, Krylov felt himself soaked in the stuff, dripping with it, and wiped anxiously at his clothing, trying to clear the gore away. But he made no sound, his body did not move. He tried to separate the dream from memory, the balloon of blood from the neat hole near the Iraqi's left eye that he remembered, and then the launching of the body into the night...

Krylov looked down at his shirt. No blood.

The balloon had been a dream.

But where could he be?

He lay on a sofa in a dimly lighted room. His shoes and socks were gone, along with his tie and jacket. Had he passed out somewhere? An accident? Was he a prisoner? Was he still in Switzerland?

Now Krylov noticed that a woman was tucked up under his right arm, her cloud of loose black hair spread like a dark wing against his torso. His right hand lay on bare, velvet skin where her blouse had pulled up, his fingers able to trace the long concavity between the lowest ribs and the rise of hip. He felt the blood thump down the transverse artery beneath her ribcage.

The soft underside of a breast touched the back of his hand, a warm pear wrapped in that same sweet skin, unencumbered by a brassiere. He ran his fingers along its curve. Just this tentative contact was electric, like a young man's first wonderful possession of a breast. Krylov trembled, excited as a boy, and grinned. What had he been up to? And who could this delicious person be?

But even as he reached down to lift her face so he could see it, Krylov knew where the electricity had come from. His mind caught up with his hand, which had known immediately that the warm contour of waist and hip, the breast, could only be forbidden fruit. A man of Krylov's experience did not become giddy from merely touching a female.

"Oh, Sveta," he murmured, careful not to wake her as he removed his hand. "I was so far away. I'm sorry." He got up without disturbing her, then stood looking down at this pretty, disheveled version of his wise, usually collected, young friend. But his hand could not forget that brushing, agitating contact, and he could not force himself to turn away, not yet.

After a moment, Krylov stooped and lifted her gently in his arms, causing her to utter a dreamer's startled moan, but she did not wake up. He carried her into her bedroom and laid her down upon the duvet, then sat beside her, touching her long fingers, her slender neck, fingering the soft shower of her hair.

He saw her breasts, just the faint pink tips of them, beneath the white cloth of her blouse, and longed to touch them, cup them, bring them to his lips. But he left them alone. Instead, he took off her shoes, rolled down and removed her knee stockings. Lovely feet, with long toes that were still straight. He cupped each foot in both hands, and gave each foot a kiss. He could hardly breathe, so urgently did he desire this young woman.

Still holding her feet, Krylov studied his sleeping girl, the dreamer who had begun to fidget as she picked up the trail back to the world.

"My dear Sveta," he said too quietly to wake her, "you mustn't put yourself in harm's way like this. Don't hand me your vast, loving heart. Christ, I am supposed to keep you safe from people like me, people like Maxim, men who are not too bad most of the time, but who can do terrible things without thinking much about it, who can be absolute pigs when it comes to the treatment of women. Right now I am burning to ruin you, to rip away your clothes and devour you. Devour. That is the problem. Men like me don't make those fine distinctions between loving a woman and eating her alive.

"So this is a very confusing moment for me. I want you, I am on fire. But I know that when we are finished, there will be your father and Uncle Viktor and Clio herself lying in the bed between us." Krylov released the lovely feet and spread the duvet across Svetlana, concealing her breasts, "I will have to do some thinking. If I can figure a way to have you without hurting you, you will be the first to know."

Krylov stood up, then leaned down to kiss her on the forehead. He put on his shoes and socks and the jacket with its spatter of old blood, crammed his tie into one of his pockets, and started to leave.

But, wait, what was that odor?

He lifted his nose like a dog in the south of France, smelling some delicious scent drifting down from Finland.

Sveta's pelmini.

One might walk away from Svetlana, for her own good, but not from her pelmini. Krylov went into the kitchen, scooped a dozen dumplings into a bowl and covered them with sour cream. He found what remained of her vodka and sat down to eat.

For perhaps an hour, Krylov realized, his mind had been free of all the encircling complications of the true world. Perhaps he could keep the death of Muckeltee-Al-Rabiah, known to the dreamer as the Iraqi balloon of blood, at arm's length for a while. Perhaps he could stow Emerson and Peter Gayle and Anna and chiornaya ospa in their respective boxes. Then, unencumbered by memory and anxiety, he would linger over Svetlana Maximovna Trulova's little dumplings, made with her own long fingers just for him.

Just for him. The idea made Krylov's heart ache, and he could not suppress a smile, remembering how it had been to wake up with her tucked up beneath his arm. Trouble swirled like a cyclone around them, and still one's heart could move in a youthful way. "Even at Stalingrad," said Krylov to the empty room, "people fell in love."

XXI

Anna and Peter lived comfortably enough, but with the jittery patience of small prey, always aware that, at any moment, the terrible thing might happen. The hawk would make her stoop, the constrictor coil into their burrow.

Gayle waited for the poor weather to lift and leave them exposed. He thought Herr Trauber would be inclined to take a last look at his property before winter moved in. With that in mind, Peter had driven the Saab off the property and left it hidden on a vacant lot a kilometer down the road, the British number plates smeared with mud. He carefully picked up after himself and Anna, so that there was no obvious sign of their presence in the hut. Theoretically, Herr Trauber could march in and look around and see nothing, while they hid among the trees. Gayle saw that as Plan A.

But they were not waiting for Herr Trauber, not really. They waited for the Austrian police to stop by, drawn by reports of smoke and light. They waited for the Americans to find them, or the Russians, or the bloody World Health Organization. Mostly, though, they waited for that other intruder, the unspeakable one that had struck down Harry and his lads.

If Anna stayed well, Gayle thought Plan A had a chance. He could imagine their slipping away from their web of troubles. They could flee like remnant hippies and roar off in the Viggen, and that would be the end of it.

Ah, but if Anna sickened, the chalet became a plague ship and Plan A became a fallen house of cards. Then it would be off to Plans B, C, and D, depending on how sick she became, and whether they had visitors. Each scheme was more complicated than the one before, until they clumped into a knot no human could untie. The choices became those articulated by Harry at the end.

You can go live in isolation until the thing they have grown in you dies.

You can run until the mother of all scorpions overtakes you.

Gayle thought of the three boys. If Anna sickened as they had, she would almost certainly die. And what would one do then, head out, trailing a wake of death? What would one do if Herr Trauber or some unlucky tramper showed up and had to be held in quarantine, or killed?

Poor thing, said Harry's ghost. He'd known what he was talking about: his choices really had been simpler than Gayle's.

You are welcome to join us in the fire.

Plan Zed was the worst case, the heroic moment Gayle had predicted, when the doomed man has no choice but to turn and fight, to do what he can with no hope of surviving the encounter. The adversary wasn't just another bloke, either. It was a microscopic infantry several million strong, invisible, lethal, probably immortal. By the time one arrived at Plan Zed, the only strategy left was the one improvised by Harry at the cottage on the Downs: first the coup de grâce, then the fire.

Gayle said nothing to Anna about Plans A through Z, and he took pains not to show he brooded upon their future, such as it was.

But now and then she would come upon him suddenly, before he could shed the stricken mask he now wore in repose, thinking about what lay ahead. Sometimes he came upon Anna, her eyes gleaming, her mouth set, and knew she had seen the Fates fiddling with their scales.

They talked all the time, but always about something else. Gayle told Anna stories about his mother, how they had come to be regulars at the Hotel Victoria. "Nothing especially Freudian, I didn't paint 'Enola Gay' on my kite or anything like that. We were mainly good chums. We liked each other so we got on."

Anna had laughed. "The cigar is just a cigar?"

"What else?"

He described the flat in Brighton, and Avery, the stuffed colobus who was no doubt anxious to meet Anna once all this was over. He told her how he had gone to Oxford and about his years in the RAF, and how he and Mouse had roared off into the desert night in the Tornado. He told her about being brought down and his Captivity, with some of the rough edges smoothed. When all this was over, he promised, he'd take her aloft, show her how to fly.

"We'll touch and go?"

"Of course."

"When all this is over."

Anna told Gayle about Molly and Oscar and the English School with Svetlana. She described Maxim Trulov and his friend Krylov, Sveta's Uncle Viktor. She explained how she had come to nursing, of life in the Intensiv, of Oscar's last days there, and Churches'.

When she talked about Sophie, the twin she would have died for but could not love, she mimicked what she called that "vey, vey *English* English of hers." Sometimes she parodied Sophie's inability to care about anyone else. "I em trepped, *trepped*, ectually, one *cahnt* simply *drawp* an essignment of this *impawtence*. Good-*bah* and *adieu*. The wuld is calling." Gallows humor, thought Anna, but it could get a smile out of Peter.

Gayle found Herr Trauber's chess set and they played a few desultory matches, neither able to concentrate fully, although, even distracted, Anna played the better game.

"Harry taught me everything I know," Peter said as her forces surrounded his lonely king. "Is this the end?"

"I fear it is." For a moment both looked away, afraid of what their eyes might reveal.

They said very little about being in love, or about other lovers, beyond an occasional tangential reference in which the blank silhouette of a nameless companion could be discerned. Such omissions aside, they strove to make themselves visible to each other. Every stanza of their constant talk ended with the same refrain: *when all of this is over.*

Now and then they were able to make love, but mostly they lay like stored spoons upon Herr Trauber's IKEA bed. They held hands when strolling in the forest. "Babes in the wood," said Gayle, inadvertently evoking little bodies in a shallow grave of leaves. "Sorry."

Once they drove out to Wiener Neustadt in the rain to replenish their supplies. Anna shopped at the Mercur. Gayle bought three new petrol cans and filled them at a service station. "You never know," he said. Although she did.

Anna spent an hour at the town library, pretending to look for an old spy novel set in Vienna. Peter knew she'd been scanning the medical niches of the Web. She took Peter to the treed hectare of land where she and Svetlana had scattered Oscar's ashes; nothing was said about scattering their own.

So they lived comfortably enough, and talked about everything except what was always on their minds. They talked, thought Gayle, like Scheherazade dealing out stories to keep the razor-sharp blade always one more dawn away. Time dilated around them, and often froze. "Tick," said Gayle. "Tock at eleven." Anna laughed, but her face was full of worry.

Then the dreams began.

ANNA THOUGHT SHE MUST BE BACK IN THE HOTEL VICTORIA, OR perhaps she'd never left. She stood in the dark room looking down at the naked man sprawled beside the pale duvet. His breathing accelerated and faded, his eyes beat like avian hearts behind their lids. *Bad dreams*, thought Anna, wondering who this man could be, then thinking, *Of course, it's Peter Gayle.*

She held a small syringe up to the light, shook its cylinder of clear fluid, and depressed the plunger to purge the chamber of air, releasing a pair of tiny drops. Kneeling by the supine figure, she gently moved her fingertips along his groin until they felt the artery, then inserted the needle into his streaming blood.

She thought she would wait, make sure she hadn't hurt him. But what was this? The man wasn't Peter Gayle after all. He was a stranger or perhaps a man known long ago, and from the tiny perforation in his groin there flowed a vapor of wild images, like fluid tattoos. Bright green vines climbed across his body, bearing crimson fruit and leaves the color of moss; the vines turned into serpents....

"Anna, Anna," someone said.

The dreamer wailed and cried aloud, but all Anna could say was, *"Ah!"* Then, slowly, she revived enough to understand that she was enfolded by Peter's arms, that he stroked her as he might a frightened horse or child. "There," he was saying, "just bad dreams. They go away." She closed her eyes and let herself drop into his care.

But the dream would not go away. It persisted through the day less as a dream remembered than as a memory of real events. Now and then it would intrude into her thoughts like a powerful radio transmission and she would once again *experience* the vines, the snakes—things she knew had not really happened.

Troubled by this leakage from wherever dreams were stored into the reservoir of active memory, Anna consulted her inner nurse.

Don't make too much of it. You worry because you've read that nightmares are precursory to smallpox. They are. But look at your situation. Enough anxiety there to light a city. Of course you have bad dreams. How could you not?

Anna didn't mention the odd mnemonic episode to Peter, but carried on in feigned good spirits. They talked about what they would do when all of this was over. Peter read her unease, she knew, but determinedly went along, offering comfort, cleaning up after them, insisting that she rest. Whenever Anna looked up, however, there he was, watching, stricken, wanting to help but also paralyzed by the diminution of hope. He was, she thought, a real heartbreaker.

"Bad dreams again last night?" he asked one morning.

She nodded. "Did I levitate?"

Peter laughed for her. "Not quite. More like a touch and go."

"I remember a crash."

"But here you are."

"Yes, here I am."

"The thing is, dreams are just electricity. Undigested chops."

"I know."

"As a matter of fact," he added, theatrically, "bad dreams are my *speciality*."

She managed a tired smile. "I know. You say, 'We're fucked, Mouse, out we go.'"

"Working the same problem, over and over. Maybe that's why we dream, to work things out."

"Maybe this is my Captivity."

"A few bad weeks."

"Then Christmas."

"What do you want for Christmas?"

"I want to be alive."

The inner nurse thought that might be possible. The patient was not so sure.

The dreams returned whenever Anna slept, the carnival of dread rolling in each night, always with some new freak, some new horror, to exhibit. She saw herself lying like the brown women in the Big

Red Book of Smallpox, modeling for a man she thought might be Paul Gauguin. And as he painted, what seemed at first a multitude of bees swarmed over Anna, but then rooted themselves in place, subsuming her. Feeling herself begin to disappear, she started awake.

"My poor girl," said Peter. "My poor girl."

Some nights restored Anna to the Intensiv, which had unaccountably filled with dying patients aswarm with pox, and as she made her rounds, more infected people arrived, streaming blood, shedding flesh like serpents casting skins.

Clever virus, whispered the inner nurse. *First it makes you lose your mind. Then it kills you.*

What did you say?

Nothing.

On quiet nights she felt the clever virus falling like snow inside her body, beautiful until it landed and sprang to evil life.

Now Anna approached sleep as she would have the brink of a high cliff, where she poised as long as she could before, exhausted and depressed, she surrendered to gravity and fell down and down, to where the nightly carnival was waiting.

"Just dreams," said Peter, holding her, his worry like a protective magnetic field around them.

This won't last long, counseled the inner nurse. *A few days at the most.*

What happens then?

We have to wait and see.

But the dreams persisted, distorting who and what and where she thought she was. She now and then discerned a furtive madness creeping like a feral cat among the shadows of her mind. She read its presence as an asthmatic reads the first faint throttling of breath; her mind was running out of reason the way a lung ran out of air. She longed to flee into the cold night, into the forest, and, if mad, to die wrapped in a veil of snow.

One morning she awoke with what seemed the beginnings of a mild head cold. *I can do sniffles and a low fever,* she told herself, although the symptoms filled her with dread.

Not to worry, said the inner nurse. *Yes, I know a mild flu is sometimes a precursor to something worse. But anybody would catch cold in this place. Even with the heat going, it's always freezing.*

Why say 'something worse?' Why not name the thing?

I don't want to upset you.

Anna silently recited her mantra: *the well part of me will minister to the sick part.*

But what would happen if she lost contact with the well part? What if the well part ceased to exist?

Poor Peter, as Anna thought of him, struggled to give aid and comfort, wanting desperately to help while trapped in helplessness. She willed herself to lie quietly, even to offer up a smile of pleasure, as he sponged her with a flannel, or tried to stroke her, or held her and rocked her like a child as he described what they would do when all of this was over. He gave her smiles, but, when unguarded, his face was stony with despair.

For a time she joined him at the small table, although she had lost all interest in food and he ate very little. They would sit in candlelight, she would sip the soup or chocolate he made for her, take desultory bites of buttered bread, swallow, with some difficulty, a fragment of boiled egg. She thought his grip must be all that kept her from falling. But they could both feel her slipping free of him; they both saw her tumbling away like a parachutist.

One morning, Anna awoke in a panic. The invader had come galloping after her on his pale horse. She thought he was Death, but, no, he was a mounted Cossack and she a doomed Jew, running in knee-deep snow. The horse easily overtook her, the Cossack flayed her with his blade, and left the dreamer lying in the snow where it pooled red with her blood....

"Cossacks, Cossacks!"

"Another dream," said Peter, holding her. Then, "Christ, you're on fire!"

The bed was soaked in perspiration, the sheets now clammy and cold. Anna shivered with a sudden chill. The Cossack's sword must have cleft her skull, for she could still feel the blade embedded in her head, which screamed with pain. Her stomach hurt enough that she wondered if she might be in labor, then remembered they had been at Herr Trauber's chalet not much more than a fortnight, so it couldn't be birth, and yet there was such activity, such rumbling within....

She flung the sheets aside and hurried to the bathroom, where she ejected a foul slurry, and then another, and another, until she ached with emptiness, and wondered who she was, and where, and why.

Peter had found clean sheets and had shaken out the duvet by the time she returned. She settled into Herr Trauber's pine bed like a weary spirit into its sepulcher. She wanted to tell Peter goodbye. She wanted her life to fade to nothing, to a black screen, to zero.

All her mind heard now was a cataract roar of pain inside her skull. Her skin was hot to her own touch, and she tried to think what that might mean, in medical terms, and what treatment might be in order. *Come on,* she urged the inner nurse, *give me something.*

The nurse's voice was barely audible. *I don't know what to do.*

Exhausted beyond the possibility of fear, Anna dropped into the cauldron of affliction, with neither hope nor the desire to return. The inner nurse was no longer with her, and Peter had become a mere shadow, a modulation of ambient light that moved constantly around her, whose voice seemed to come from a great distance. She was aware, more or less, of his efforts to soothe her, to keep her clean, to abate her fever, to feed and water her, yet she felt utterly alone, a solitary being adrift in a universe of fever, nausea, and pain.

Soon she sensed the first battalions of tiny lumps beginning to muster on her tongue, then deploy across the roof of her mouth, bringing pain and a kind of self-disgust as they grew and hardened and began to leak. It was as if she'd eaten them, like grapes. Day by day, as the weak autumnal light grew and faded, the rash marched across her body.

Fresh regiments of pustules assembled on her face, on her hands, along her forearms, up her legs. She felt the hot pellets of infection grow within her secret places, and upon her eyelids and lips. They continued their advance, spreading over her torso, her breasts, over every part of her. They felt like fire. When she touched them they rolled around like marbles under her skin.

She thought she must look like the women in the Big Red Book, naked, supine, covered with moist bees. She longed to scratch herself to bits, but lacked the energy; she could only lie upon Herr Trauber's fetid bed like a Polynesian girl awaiting Paul Gauguin, and let the battle take its course.

If victory went to the viral invaders, she would die. If her defenses held, she would live. So simple, thought Anna, and so trivial. She no longer cared how the fight turned out. This thing she had awakened had destroyed Anna Nieman as surely as the American guns had destroyed her twin. Everything was over, except the pain. It went on and on, like eternity, like God, like Death.

WATCHING HER, PETER GAYLE thought she must be sleeping, for she lay very still. But then he noticed, as he had often done before, a flicker of alert intelligence between her swollen eyelids. Beneath its dark crust of pox, her face had frozen into a mask of apprehension; but the eyes behind that mask watched like a cunning animal in hiding.

"Time to clean you up a bit, my girl," he said, trying to keep it light. "Get something into you. Don't want those organs walking off the job."

She hadn't moved in days, except when he lifted her up and tried to rinse away the meager waste her body still produced, the blood and sera seeping from the dark kernels that now nearly covered her body, head to toe, each black mound nearly touching its neighbor. Looking at her, he felt his heart crack, but couldn't have said if it cracked for love or pity. There was, he decided, room for both.

A messy sodding affliction, he thought, holding her as he had Huey, Dewey, and Louie, a real fucking gift from God, this thing.

When Gayle had done what he could, he would embrace her, hoping the hot outer layer of skin, which had begun to separate from the underlying stratum, would not slip off the bone. She was light as a feather, light as one of poor Harry's lads. Gayle could feel her heart buzzing like a sparrow's and hear her breath, steam rattling through ancient plumbing. Her breath stank, the chalet filled with the odor of disintegrating flesh.

At night Gayle made himself lie down beside her, to calm her, to let them both know that he was here to stay, and, perhaps, to challenge what seemed his absolute immunity to the disease. But, lying there, he dreaded sleep. When he dreamed of his Captivity now he started awake, believing he lay beneath a pile of decaying dead.

She would not, or could not, eat, but still swallowed the water he offered. "We don't want your kidneys to quit on you, Anna. We want you healthy and strong, for when all of this is over. For Christmas. Let's get you well for Christmas."

The secret animal watched him with interest, but in silence.

When Gayle left her sleeping, or seeming to sleep, he fled to a far end of the room, or stepped into the cold world outside the hut, and wiped away some of the accumulated mess of nursing. You look like you've been out murdering people, he told himself, brushing impatiently and ineffectually at the stains. You look like a sodding geek.

During these intervals, alone and worn out, he experienced despair of a magnitude he had not imagined possible, not even in the worst moments of his Captivity. He saw nothing but futility in what he did; he strove like a lorry sinking in quicksand, its wheels spinning madly but without effect. If that was what life was going to be like, it wasn't worth the bloody candle; time to put that Iraqi pistol back to work.

But then a muted cry from Anna would remind him that he was not alone, and he would shake away the paralysis and return to her side, bringing his dwindling supply of aid and comfort.

When he was able to dodge despair long enough to focus his thoughts, Gayle puzzled over the detailed mechanics of Plan Zed, the only future he could discern. Herr Trauber's chalet, and the plague with which they had saturated it, must be destroyed by fire. But how to distribute the petrol, and when? When to flood the place with propane?

The petrol and propane were the easy part. The hard part was what to do with Anna. If the disease did not take her quickly, he would have to devise some way of killing her without that sensitive inner animal picking up the scent of death impending.

Gayle thought he'd read somewhere that the maximum speed of nerve impulses was less than 250 knots, a fraction of a bullet's velocity. Death would arrive at Mach 1 or better; fear of it would follow seconds later, if he could somehow avoid those eyes.

Could he kill Anna?

Of course not.

Could he kill Anna to keep her from being burned alive? Yes, he thought he could do that.

And what about himself, the famous vector?

If he was quick, he could do himself before some unexpected tremor of intent, traveling at a mere 250 knots, arrived to break his will.

He thought of Harry, standing among his three dead sons in an explosive mix of petrol and air. He'd had to kill the dying boys before laying down the petrol, otherwise his first shot, into Louie, would have blown up the cottage. So he had shot Louie and the other two and *then* he and Peter had brought in the petrol.

But Harry had still got things wrong. By firing at Gayle, and igniting the fumes, he'd dropped himself, alive, into the fire. So one had to think straight when choreographing Plan Zed.

Gayle would have to kill Anna first. Then, with her lifeless body lying like the dead Ophelia upon the pine bed, he would spread the explosive cloud through the chalet, douse them both with petrol, and, finally, set the whole thing off with a bullet into his heart.

No, into his brain. It put less distance between the act and his awareness of it. By the time pain could register its complaint, the brain department would be closed, and he and Anna would lie in their fire with no more sensation than two dry sticks.

That sounded about right to Gayle, although there might still be some glitch he wasn't seeing. He might have it all wrong. Backwards. Upside down.

With Anna lying dead in a mist of flammable vapor, what did one do about an unexpected visitor?

If the disease killed her today, tomorrow, the day after, would he have the nerve to complete Plan Zed, or would he flee, trailing his plume of death?

Back to square one, then, back over Plan Zed, one move at a time....

A low moan from the pine bed stopped him. She was calling him, or someone, or something. Plan Zed would have to wait.

Each time he went to her, it seemed to Gayle she had slipped further away from him. He was like a swimmer trying to overtake a drifting boat, which the current kept always just beyond his reach. Anna looked as Harry's boys had done at the end, victims of a fire consuming them. Sometimes he thought he could hear one of her organs shut itself off with a muffled *click!* But the wise, brute eyes still watched him through slits in their encrusted lids; her intelligence remained sharp and ambient in the narrow room.

Because, one way or another, their time was short, Gayle began to prepare her. Holding her in his arms as he wiped away the leakage and filth, he talked about what lay ahead. "We may be coming to the end of this. We shall have a quick goodbye. Then….off we go, my darling girl."

The eyes, now yellow and inscrutable as a wolf's, watched him closely, but gave no sign.

How to do the awful thing?

Gayle thought he would lie supine beside her, holding her close with his left arm. Then, as she relaxed against him, as those eyes closed against his chest, he would bring up his right hand with the pistol and shoot her through the left temple. Death would be immediate, but if somehow her brain kept going, he would have to fire again. She would never know. And he…Christ, he would be driven crazy.

Then he would lay her out as gently as he could and set the propane flowing into the room. He would bring in his cans of petrol and soak the bed, the room, himself. Then, chilled by the evaporating fuel, he would sit down by his poor dead girl, facing away so as not to frighten her lingering spirit, and bring the pistol's muzzle up behind his madly fluttering right eye, squeeze the trigger, perhaps hear the sound and feel some pressure, with pain following the bullet at less than 250 knots.

And mind you don't miss and blow half your head away. We're not just erasing some piano lessons here. I shall be very upset with you if you miss.

But not for very long. The shot would ignite the ambient vapor, and Herr Trauber's chalet would go up like a volcano. Anna and Peter and Al-Rabiah's evil creation would be reduced to ash. Gayle shook his head in melancholy wonderment. They had traveled a long way to end up as ashes. "We're fucked, Mouse," he murmured to the quiet girl, to the room, to the still darkness. "Out we go."

SOMETHING DRAGGED GAYLE OUT OF SLEEP. AT FIRST HE THOUGHT IT must be one of his intolerable dreams, the usual Captivity stuff. He raised his head from the thin pillow, trying to get his bearings. The room was grey with a cold dawn. Familiar, but not his own. Ah, he was in Herr Trauber's ski hut. And next to him lay Anna, still as death but breathing. Breathing well, and in a calm, deep sleep. Touching her he found the skin less febrile and not so moist.

There it came again, a metallic sound, as sharp and alien in their silent mountain kingdom as a gunshot. A car door clicking shut. Their landlord come to inspect his property? The Americans, the Russians, the God knew whos?

Gayle slid out of bed and into his trousers, put on shoes and a jumper and his bomber jacket, with the Tariq like an anvil in one pocket. He poised near the entrance door, his ear against it, straining to catch the faintest sound, but there was nothing. He stepped silently into the aqueous light.

The trees stood as thin shadows that rose from a pale invisibility of stratus the night had poured into the forest. A light nocturnal rain had frozen, glazing the ground and hanging the limbs of nearby trees with beads of ice. Beyond that, the world lay hidden and mysterious beneath its shroud. Nothing moved. All was silent, but for the occasional shedding of a sheath of ice by a high branch.

He moved as quietly as he could down the driveway, keeping low behind a long keel of granite. The trees seemed to jump out of the fog at him as he advanced. When the man materialized ahead of him Gayle thought at first he was just another tree made suddenly visible; then the shape clarified.

The stranger stood just on the far side of the wire Anna had strung across the driveway, a big, powerful-looking chap with a tiny, pear-shaped head. Gayle reckoned the scalp was shaved and shining beneath the black woolen watch cap, and that the eyes behind the mirrored Ray Bans were small and piggy.

He wore a sky-blue down-filled vest over a scarlet polo shirt, which let him display his Popeye forearms and their tapestry of illustrations. His hands were as small as a girl's, wrapped in deerskin driving gloves. He wore a pair of white trainers on little gentleman's feet. A cord connected an ear bud to an iPod in the vest's pocket. Gayle could just detect a faint, tinny voice issuing from it, to whose rhythms the big man swayed and nodded. An elephant run by an ant.

Not Herr Trauber, thought Gayle. The man looked like one of those private-contract security blokes except for the absence of a gigantic automatic weapon. He was too big to be former SAS, but about right for the American special forces, which liked giants. He was the kind of apparition one would expect almost anywhere in the east, but not out here, not in thin air. As far as most Americans were concerned, this part of Austria didn't exist, yet here this fellow was.

Still nodding to the iPod music, the man looked around briefly, then whipped out his cock for a long piss into the snow, smiling like a dog writing its scent. Then he put it all away and neatened himself up. For a moment, he poised there, peering into the fog, his face settling into an expression that said he might want to take a look at the world beyond the wire.

Gayle backtracked through the cloud and into the chalet, silently closing the door behind him. The muted *clack* when he locked it sounded like a bomb going off. He took the pistol out of his jacket pocket and made sure it had a round in the chamber. Then he waited, listening to the approaching footsteps and the faint clanging of the iPod.

Leaning against the door, the pistol held close against his chest, Gayle tried to recall what he knew about firing the damned thing. He hadn't been much good with the service Browning nine-millimeter on the RAF firing range. Mickey Williams, as comfortable with his sidearm as an American cowboy, had joshed him about it. "I were you, Boss, I'd think about trading that thing for a sling and some round stones."

The crunch of footsteps had ceased, the iPod had gone silent. When he held his breath, Gayle could hear the intruder breathing heavily just outside the door. They must be standing shoulder to shoulder, he thought, ear to bloody ear, with only the thin door between them. He lowered the Tariq, ready to fire through the wood where he thought the American must be.

He jumped when one of those little gloved hands hammered on the door. "Hey," the intruder called in a boy's tenor, "anybody home?" Another rap that shook the door. "Hello?"

This wouldn't be like trying to hit a small circle twenty meters away. This was point blank. It would be hard to miss the American. Was there any inner squeamishness about shooting him? Gayle smiled at the notion that a bit more blood and brain would make a groat's worth of difference.

"Hey, open up," piped the intruder. "I've got car trouble. I need Telefonen, man. Come on." But as he spoke his voice moved away from the door. Gayle heard his footsteps recede; the faint thumping of the iPod resumed. Now, from a few meters' distance, the reedy southern voice again. "Hey, Ralph, it's me. Yeah, I'm out in the neighborhood. I checked the whole fucking mountain. There's just nobody here. I don't blame them, all this snow and shit. So this wild goose is calling off the chase, man. I'm coming in."

Listening to the footfalls, Gayle imagined the man vanishing, ghostlike, into the mist. But he still waited with his ear against the door. He heard the click of a car door, well away, then the sudden roar of a big engine, probably one of those black behemoths the Americans favored.

After the engine noise faded to silence, Gayle waited another minute or two, then cracked the door. Nothing. With the pistol held at the ready, he stepped into the cold light and walked toward the road, still wary, keeping low, and saw where the American had parked his car, the spray of slush where he had driven it away. The trees sighed in a light breeze that stirred the fog and caused a distant rattling cascade of ice. That was the only sound to be heard in the silent forest.

ANNA WATCHED PETER emerge from the cloud and approach the entrance, his face flushed and anxious, and that pistol in his hand. She stood by the window wrapped in Herr Trauber's duvet, propped against the sill to keep from falling. She had never felt so weak, so empty, and yet her situation had definitely improved. Here she was, standing. She no longer ached; the bell of pain had ceased its constant clanging. Her eyes were open, although her vision was not quite clear. She thought she would be able to speak. She even felt a pang of hunger.

Last night Anna had dreamed she descended through the deep ocean, impenetrably black except for the occasional tendril of fluorescence, some impossible creature inhabiting these depths. Her bare feet touched bottom, the soft sediments flowed between her toes. Then her legs flexed and she pushed off, rising toward the light.

The long, airless climb had awakened her, and she had gasped for breath when she surfaced in the grey dawn of the cabin. Pustules still covered her body, but the bumps seemed to have hardened and ceased their leaking. Black scabs littered the bedclothes.

Your bees are dying, said the inner nurse, her voice audible once again. *You're dropping scabs.*

The door opened, spraying light into the room. Peter entered like a shadow. For a moment he didn't see her, but stood puzzling over the empty bed. Then he turned and there she was. "You're up."

"I wondered where you'd gone."

"There was a man outside. An American. A big bloke covered with tattoos."

"I know the one you mean. I saw him too." Then she shook her head. "No, I dreamed him."

Good for you, said the nurse. *There are dreams and there are memories, and now you can tell the difference.*

"He didn't see me," said Gayle. "I don't think he did."

"If he saw you…"

Gayle made an impatient gesture. "If he saw me, he saw me. I want to look at you. You're standing up. You can see. You can speak."

"My bees are dying."

"Your bees?"

"These things." She pulled the duvet aside and waved a hand at her naked body, shuddering. "These horrible things."

Gayle lifted her into his arms. "You're coming back."

"What's left of me."

"I'll clean you up, we'll take a look."

"I'm very hungry."

"I'll make breakfast."

"First call Svetlana. Tell her it's over."

XXII

"We got 'em," Lamont was telling Emerson, seated across the small, barren office they shared at Embassy-Vienna. "I stopped to take a leak and, bingo, here comes our guy. The poor son of a bitch comes out of his hidey hole leaving tracks a blind *woman* could follow. He's got this little nine-mill Iraqi automatic that I generally just walk up and take away from people. So he hunkers down behind some rocks not ten meters away, like he was invisible or something. He takes a look at me and hurries back into the fog. I follow him and here's this A-frame you can't see from the road, no wonder I missed it before. I walk over to the door, knock a couple times, ask for help. Nothing. But I feel him on the other side. And I'm like: What're you gonna do, shoot me through the door? I don't think so.

"So I make a fake call to you saying I didn't have shit and was coming in, and walked away, knowing the guy'll come tiptoeing after me. I went off and parked the car, then doubled back and watched through the trees with binocks. The Limey doesn't look sick. Worn out, maybe, but not sick. No sign of the girl."

Lamont thought Emerson should do a joyful back flip or something to show he appreciated the good work. But that wasn't Emerson's way.

A fortnight earlier, Emerson had come in, all smiles, and said a Saab convertible with British plates had been spotted by Austrian police in Wiener Neustadt.

"A man and a woman," he'd said, "the guy buying gas by the can, like he's going to burn down the Ratthaus. When word of this percolates up the Austrian chain of command, on lines we've tapped since nineteen forty-five, the embassy calms the Wieners down and we get the ball." Emerson had leaned toward Lamont, a canine grin playing on those mean lips. "So what do we ask ourselves now?"

All this "we," meaning "I," wore Lamont out. "You got me. What?"

"Why are these people still so close to Vienna?"

"And what do *we* come up with?"

"They didn't want to travel. They wanted isolation. Quarantine."

"They're sick?"

"And how. They're a pandemic waiting to happen."

Lamont had shut his eyes, imagining a circus ring with those cute black and white bears on beach balls and unicycles under a big banner in scarlet Barnum ultrabold: THE PANDEMIC.

"So, old son, we have to go beat some bushes."

We, thought Lamont, meaning *me.*

Grumbling that he didn't have a whole hell of a lot to go on, and thinking that *we* hadn't really located anything or anybody, Lamont had obediently driven down past Wiener Neustadt in the Suburban. "This is going to give us zilch, Ralph. Zilch," he complained, thundering down the Sudautobahn. And zilch was what he'd come up with, at first.

Then Emerson, ever the magician, had pulled out another card. "Anna Nieman's papa once bought a hectare of mountain land down past Molzegg…"

"Mole's egg?" Lamont giggled. "Mole's….egg?"

"Molzegg. I think she's made a sentimental choice. Always a mistake, Lamont. Never follow your heart." Emerson had given his minion a long look. "Well," he added in that disappointed voice of his, "I guess that goes without saying."

And so Lamont had driven back into the mountains of Lower Austria and rented a room from a jittery old couple in Ternitz. They'd been unable to take their eyes off this exotic, dangerous-looking American. Lamont thought they saw him like he was a visiting X-Man or something. Then he'd begun working his way through the ski-huts and fancy vacation homes in the surrounding mountains.

There had followed a week of empty structures and cabins inhabited by Austrians who didn't speak English. "This isn't giving us shit, Ralph," Lamont would grumble, pushing the Suburban along the winding mountain lanes. "Not shit." Well, that was then, right? Because, due to a pit stop and a little carelessness on the part of a certain Limey, he'd found them.

"We've got to be damned careful the way we handle this," said Emerson, on his feet now, pacing the room.

"Like a jar of nitro, yes?"

"Two jars. Can we get a chopper in?"

"There's a cleared lot a klick down the road. Ingress and egress, no problemo." Lamont grinned; he liked talking military.

"So we go in. Get him, get her too, if she's still alive, put them into some kind of germ-proof wrapper. Bug suits, body bags, whatever. We get them out on the chopper and ferry them to the Gulfstream at Schwechat. Eight hours later they're in Fort Dietrich's level-four containment and Bob's…"

"Your uncle?"

"You got it." Emerson studied Lamont for a moment, then shook his head and grabbed the young man by both shoulders, giving them a painful but affectionate squeeze. "Shit hot, Lamont!"

Lamont beamed and blushed. Coming from an old soldier like Emerson, "shit hot" was about as good as it got.

But Emerson was already back at work. "We extract them and destroy that ski-hut with fire."-

"I can handle that, Ralph." Lamont had a fondness for setting fires.

"Of course. Hell, the way I feel about you today, Lamont, I'd give you a ten year old girl if you asked for one."

"Well," and Lamont looked bashfully away, "maybe later."

XXIII

For weeks, Krylov had twisted and turned like a bear in a net, buying time as he waited for some signal from Anna. He had to be there to retrieve her, or what remained of her, and to do what had to be done with Peter Gayle.

Sensing that Krylov had personal reasons for staying in Vienna, Klaus Oldenburg turned the inspection screw a bit harder. "I think it is finally cold enough in Russia for you to do Leningrad II," he'd drawled with the usual sneer.

The Dane, as Juan Carlos Imler kept reminding Krylov, was only doing his job, and, yes, he seemed to do his job with a vengeance where Krylov was concerned. "But he's within his responsibilities, Viktor. So I guess it's St. Petersburg for you."

"Who's coming with me?" Krylov asked Oldenburg.

"Churches would have done. But, well…" A tired shrug. "Anyway, you're a big, smart fellow, you speak a little Russian. You can do it alone."

"Isn't it against the rules to send an unescorted Russian to look at a Russian reactor?"

"I send whom I want to send."

"What if I miss something? Russia could get the Bomb."

"Very funny."

Near the end of a fortnight's desultory preparation, Krylov had told Imler and Oldenburg of a death in his family. He hoped the lie would not bring a curse down upon his children. "There's rather a mess. I need to take a week's leave to clean it up."

"In Russia?" Oldenburg asked. "You could do Leningrad II on your way back."

"Spain," said Krylov, improvising wildly. "An old man in, um, Toledo."

"How old?" Imler's eyes gleamed with interest. "Was he in the Guerra Civil?" The Spanish Civil War was his favorite.

Krylov nodded. "At Teruel. The Ebro."

"What a man!"

"Indeed."

Having no relatives, living or dead, in Spain, Krylov spent the week hiding in his flat. Svetlana brought him food and drink, and took him on the occasional clandestine outing to forage in parts of Vienna most Agency employees avoided.

Krylov thought Anna's silence was the silence of the grave, but said nothing to Svetlana, who still spoke of how they would bring Anna home and solve everybody's problems. They never spoke of what to do about the Englishman.

"Ah," Oldenburg had exclaimed with mock enthusiasm when Krylov returned to work, "bienvenido a Vienna, as your late relative would say. But you've no color at all. I thought Madrid was having a hot autumn."

"I was indoors most of the time."

"I'll bet you were."

"Now I do Leningrad II."

"Marvelous! We get to keep you on."

"Lucky you."

Oldenburg stomped away.

Austrian Airline tickets to St. Petersburg had been purchased, two aluminum instrument cases hauled into Krylov's office, along with the Leningrad II documentation. On the eve of his departure, however, Krylov had spent an hour in the lavatory, from which he returned pale and jittery. "Spanish food," he murmured. "All that olive oil."

"In your late relative's army," said Oldenburg, cheeks burning, "they shot malingerers."

"Malingerers?" Krylov looked at the Dane with suffering red eyes, a tremor in his big hands. Then he hurried back to the lavatory.

Krylov took a week's sick leave, causing consternation among the human resources people, as he had never before lost a day to illness.

"A week of sick leave every twenty years sounds about right to me," Imler told the Dane.

"Malingering is malingering."

"Try proving it, but not now, and not with me."

Imler had stopped by Krylov's office, entering with the deliberate step of a wading heron, a Marlboro held between thumb and index finger. He coiled his long frame into the visitor's chair. "Viktor, we need to talk."

"Then talk." Krylov glared at him, for he was always angry now—angry at Oldenburg for remaining steadfastly his irritating self, at Imler for not helping, at Anna for her silence, at Peter Gayle for being a chalice of death, at God for everything.

"Dragging your feet doesn't do any good. It's like weight training for Klaus, it makes him stronger by the day. He can make a case for dropping you."

"Let him," snarled Krylov.

Imler lit a new cigarette off the old one, which he mashed out in the glass ashtray Krylov kept for him. "Why is it so important that you stay in Vienna?"

Krylov looked into the wise, grey eyes behind the Dr. Strangelove glasses. For a moment, he felt the urge to share his problem with his old Argentine friend, to have someone else carry some of the burden of the risky business he was in.

I need to stay in Vienna, because if I don't there will be a smallpox pandemic. If I stay I can stop it. Well, I think I can stop it. I hope I can stop it. Maybe I can stop it. There is a slim chance I can stop it. Unless, of course, it can't be stopped....

Christ, thought Krylov, he spiraled down like a shot bird. He grinned, imagining his feathered carcass falling to earth with a great *plop!*

"What's funny?" asked Imler.

"Sorry," said Krylov. "You're right, I need to stay in town. But I can't tell you why."

If I tell you, you will want to bring in the authorities and the weapon that Al-Rabiah created will go into somebody's arsenal.

"It involves others. You see how that is."

"You're a hard man to help, Viktor." Imler got up. His feelings had been hurt; now, Krylov knew, he would not lift a finger to help. "Haven't you learned the net always defeats the bear?"

"I know, I know."

"Just do the week at Leningrad II and come home. Then it's over." He stubbed out his cigarette and left.

Although Imler had not said as much, it had clearly come down to a choice. Krylov could continue in Safeguards, nursing his moribund belief that he still might do some good, or he could go to a desk in Administration or Logistics or, God forbid, Human Resources, and wait for Anna's signal, which might never come.

It had been a month, give or take, since Anna had gone off with the Englishman. There had been a single call, then the *happy, happy, happy* card to Sveta, then weeks of nothing. She must be dead. So must the Englishman.

Or they could be on the move.

They could be forty thousand feet above the Atlantic with three hundred others, sowing viral seeds their fellow-travelers would disperse across the world. Krylov imagined the passengers fanning out, leaving in their wake vast fields of black flowers. Did it matter where he was when he learned that the tiny Aralsk-I creatures had won their secret war? Not in the least. Imler was right. The net always won. He would go to fucking Leningrad II.

KRYLOV WAS IN THE PARKING GARAGE, STOWING THE INSTRUMENTS and the Agency briefcase in the boot of his Mercedes when Oldenburg caught up with him.

"Are you *driving* to St. Petersburg?"

"Just to the airport, Klaus."

Oldenburg studied Krylov's outfit, the leather coat, khakis, walking shoes. "No suit, no tie?"

Krylov shrugged and turned to his cases.

"I can't believe you're actually going."

"Then don't believe it."

"To tell the truth, I'm a little disappointed. I thought we might finally chuck you out."

"Hard luck."

"Next time."

"Goodbye, Klaus." Krylov adjusted the instrument cases against his leather bag and closed the hatch, then took a quick inventory of his own documents: Austrian Air ticket, United Nations passport, Russian passport, and here, what was this…? Another UN passport. Krylov opened it and there was poor Churches, the fair-haired British boy. Well, Churches would be with him after all. Krylov put it back in his pocket, rather pleased to have his treacherous old chum along.

"What's funny, Viktor?"

Krylov shook his head, grinning. "Nothing to do with you, Klaus." A faint buzz sounded and Krylov pulled out his mobile. "I have a call."

"Another dying relative in, where, Peru?"

Krylov put a big hand over the telephone. "I wouldn't taunt me where no one can see us, Klaus. Now, I have a call."

"Just a matter of time," Oldenburg said, but he was retreating. "You're finished."

Krylov watched him recede and finally vanish through an exit. Then he put the telephone to his ear.

"Uncle Viktor." Svetlana's sweet, familiar voice came faint and filled with static, like calls from Moscow in the old days. "She's alive. She needs our help."

"I'll pick you up."

He put the mobile in his pocket. Until now he hadn't realized how completely he had written Anna off. Christ, he'd had her dead and buried. And now, here she was, back among the living. Like a freeze-frame released, their narrative would proceed. They would go to Anna; Svetlana's wings would enfold her. Krylov would eradicate the Englishman, saving the world but breaking poor Anna's heart. And when he returned to the Agency from this lethal escapade, Oldenburg, like an avenging angel, would cast him out.

But, driving to the southern suburbs to get Svetlana, Krylov wasn't thinking about Oldenburg, or Anna, but about Peter Gayle, the man he would murder later on this chill, gloomy day. He had no idea how he would go about it, no mental picture of the Englishman, whom he had never seen. He might use the old Makarov in the glove box of the Mercedes. It had been Maxim Trulov's, a gift from Svetlana, which Krylov had accepted diffidently, aware that the pistol hadn't done Max a great lot of good at the end. Well, there was always a way to murder someone, if that was what one had to do.

Still, it bothered Krylov that God or, more likely, the Devil had anointed *him* for the job. It was one thing to kill an Al-Rabiah, someone who'd tried to murder him and Anna, who would have come after Svetlana, and who had, without the faintest tremor of intent, lit the fuze of a terrible pandemic. Killing Al-Rabiah had been like pulling up a poisonous plant—more or less.

Peter Gayle was different. Krylov knew Gayle had been a military pilot, so he wasn't a coward; he had to be pretty hard to survive an Iraqi prison. But he must also be something of a romantic. Only a romantic would lure a strange girl to a fine hotel in Switzerland, make love to her, but do her no harm. As far as Krylov knew, Anna had never given her heart to anyone, but here she'd handed it over to this stranger. Did that make him a good man or just a clever one?

Mainly, the trouble with destroying Gayle was that he had not caused any of this. He was just an instrument fashioned by Al-Rabiah, Muckeltee, whoever.

Ah, but what if Gayle *knew* he was such an instrument and still moved through society, risking the spread of what he carried? If he were so strong and brave, why had he not set himself on fire when he learned he was a monster?

Because he'd needed to come to Vienna to find out what had happened in his brief time with Anna. But then why go into hiding with her? Why not seek treatment, quarantine? Because, thought Krylov, he needed to keep clear of Emerson, clear of those Russian thugs the embassy had sent over to the crematorium, clear of any agents of any government or cause.

This meant that Krylov and Gayle understood the situation in somewhat the same way. The people who wanted Anna and Peter Gayle weren't interested in preventing a plague. If they were, they'd have brought in the authorities, regiments of specialists in biowarfare suits. Instead, they were pursuing Gayle and Anna on their own. They were only interested in getting them on morgue tables where their dangerous biology could be studied and replicated and put to work. They wanted to see how Al-Rabiah had worked the weaponizing problem.

"So, Englishman, we may be kindred souls," Krylov said into the roar of southbound traffic. Yet here one went, off to the kill.

SVETLANA WAS WAITING FOR HIM OUTSIDE THE MAIN ENTRANCE TO the Centre for Analytic Studies, looking very end-of-the-century Viennese in a long green sheepskin coat and soft leather boots, with the French vanilla palace behind her. Krylov's heart gave its happy little jump when she climbed in, causing him to smile at his foolishness and look away, careful not to spook her with some glow of affection.

Waiting for Anna's signal, they had spent much of their free time together, and he had found her prettier each day. Except, he thought, looking at her now, pretty was the wrong word. Striking, beautiful in a very Russian way; one could see Siberia and the east in that luminous round face.

"Anna called," she began, breathless and excited. "She said, 'My bees are dying. Come get me.'"

"Bees?"

A shrug. "Who knows? But she's alive."

"Is it far?"

Svetlana shook her head. "Below Molzegg."

"Did she say that on the telephone? The Americans have tapped the Centre for decades. Also the Russians."

"She was careful. She said, 'I'll see you at Oscar's.' Oscar was her father. We scattered his ashes on a piece of mountain land down there. I think I can still find it."

"And then?"

"We bring her back with us."

"Is she sick?"

"She didn't say."

"Did she mention the Englishman?"

"No." She was silent for a moment, watching Krylov. Then, "Are you going to break her heart?"

Krylov ignored the question. In silence they got back on the Sudautobahn, where he pushed the aging machine up past a hundred fifty. "How long was she on the telephone?"

"A minute? Two? No longer."

"Did you say you would go to her?"

"I said something like, 'Sure, see you at Oscar's.' Nothing for the listeners in that."

"Enough for them to follow us."

"If they do, you have to lose them. Shake them off your tail."

"You sound like a Chicago gangster. Where do you pick up that stuff?"

"Movies."

"I thought you spent your evenings reading Tolstoy and Turgenev in Russian."

"I spend my evenings waiting to hear from my dear Uncle Viktor and when nothing comes I look at a movie."

Their eyes met for an instant; both looked quickly away. "How is your arm?"

"My arm?"

"The vaccination."

"The nurse didn't use my arm. That would leave one of those big round scars. Nobody does that anymore."

"Wherever she put it…"

"My left buttock."

Krylov laughed. "So, madam, may I ask how your left buttock is doing?"

"Still a little itchy. But the scab formed and fell off."

"Fell off?"

"Yes, like a dead fly."

"Like a dead bee."

"*Ospa!*"

"Christ."

Below Wiener Neustadt they turned off into the low hills and wound their way up and up, until snow appeared along the shoulders of the narrow road, until they climbed almost to the base of grey stratus that curtained the high forest. Svetlana leaned toward the windscreen, squinting through the pale swirl of droplets, now and then issuing a steering command. It felt to Krylov as if they drove in circles, and he was about to say as much when she said, "Here," and relaxed against her seat.

Krylov stopped the Mercedes and set the brake, but kept the engine running. He reached across her to the glove box and took out the Makarov. "Be careful with this thing," he told Svetlana. "It's loaded. Just point and pull the trigger. Like the movies. When I get out, move into the driver's seat and lock the doors." Then he stepped warily into the cold mist.

At first he could see nothing but the pine trunks, ranked like sentinels, rising to a shadowed invisibility in the cloud, with here and there a fall of old trees, granite boulders, thin patches of grey snow. It took a moment for his eyes to pick out the fog-colored body of the Saab, parked not ten meters away, its engine idling. A man leaned against the driver's door. Krylov stopped where he was. "Grüss Gott," he said.

"Grüss Gott," the man replied.

The stranger was about as tall as Krylov, but very thin, with a shock of nearly white hair above a fine-boned, aristocratic face full of troubles—the face, thought Krylov, of a political prisoner. He wore khaki trousers and a leather flight jacket, and stood with his ankles crossed and arms folded, as if utterly relaxed, although Krylov thought he might hold a weapon in his concealed hand. Still, there seemed nothing dangerous about him. Even at this distance, Krylov could sense the man's exhaustion and something it took a moment to recognize: the faint sweet stench of the abattoir.

The pair studied one another for a time, neither moving closer, neither speaking. Is it you I've come to kill? wondered Krylov.

Something in the man's pale eyes seemed to respond to the silent question, for he smiled slightly. "I've seen you before," he said in English. "On television."

"A lot of people did."

Krylov heard the Mercedes door click open behind him, heard Svetlana's steps.

"You're Peter Gayle," she said, moving past Krylov with her hand extended. "I am Svetlana Trulova. Anna's good friend. And this," and she turned to the Russian, "is Viktor Krylov."

"Uncle Viktor?"

"The same." It sounded friendly, but neither man moved to shake hands. Krylov thought the Englishman had recognized his executioner.

"Well, now we go to Anna," said Svetlana.

"Yes, follow me." Gayle got into the Saab and started up the one-lane road, the Mercedes trailing a few car lengths behind.

"Sveta, where's the pistol?" Krylov wanted to know.

"Back in the glove box." She gave him a sharp look.

They wound through the forest for several kilometers before the Saab turned off into an alcove among the trees and boulders. Gayle got out and came over to Krylov's window. "Our place," and he smiled. "Well, Herr Trauber's place, is about a kilometer farther on, on the right. A red A-frame. Anna is eager to see you. I'll be along in a bit."

Krylov eased the Mercedes forward. "Why is he having us go ahead? Will he run?"

Svetlana laughed. "He's just letting us meet Anna on our own. You only have to look into his eyes to see he's beyond running."

"I don't know what I see in his eyes." Both knew he meant: I don't want to look into his eyes.

They turned into the drive and up to Herr Trauber's chalet. Krylov whipped the Mercedes around, facing outward, and shut it down. He listened for a moment, head tilted like a dog's, then got out. Svetlana joined him and for a moment they hesitated, preparing themselves for what might await them inside the hut.

Then the front door opened. A thin and haggard woman of indeterminate age stood there, dressed in a wrinkled navy sweat shirt and blue jeans, torn and forever stained with purple and brown free forms. He wondered for a second who she might be. But Svetlana didn't lose a beat. "Anna," she cried, and ran to her, gathering her old friend into her arms, her wings, as Krylov thought of them. "Oh, Anna."

Anna's hair was frazzled and nearly white, her face blurred, like an impressionist painting; the pale surface was pitted and rough with a kind of dermal gauze, as if the skin were not secured and might at any moment flake off and sail away like cotton seeds, leaving only a skull. Remnant pink freeforms seemed to drift beneath the skin, a kind of fossil pox that would soon go away. She was terribly thin, and too weak to stand for very long.

Without speaking, she led them inside. Krylov shut the door behind them. Anna sat on the bed, with Svetlana next to her, and he took one of the chairs at the kitchen table. The place stank of sickness and dead flesh.

"I think I am going to be all right," Anna began, "although never pretty," and she released a tiny laugh. "It will be better than death, at least. And think of the immunity!" Then, suddenly distraught, "Where's Peter?"

"He's coming," said Svetlana. "He had to park his car."

Anna calmed immediately. "They turned him into a monster." She said this as she might have told them he had a tan, or a head cold.

"And the monster brought you this." Krylov made an angry gesture with a hand, unable to say the awful word.

"He didn't mean to. He wasn't sure. Well, now it's over. We have to think of what to do next.

"Next we take you back to Vienna."

"But people are looking for us."

"After today, it's over."

"But we had an American here yesterday."

"What did he look like?"

"A big man with a lot of tattoos. We don't think he knew we were here."

"Sveta, get her ready to travel."

"What's wrong?" asked Anna.

"The man you saw is Emerson's hound. They know you're here. We have to move quickly."

"What about Peter?"

"What about him?"

"Is it over for him too?"

"Yes."

"And he will be safe?"

"The Americans won't get him."

"That wasn't the question."

"He will be out of danger."

Anna stared at Krylov, her tattered face contorted as she began to understand him. "Where, in Heaven?"

"Peter is the carrier, Anna."

"In Heaven?" Anna clutched at her chest, her eyes wild and gleaming with tears. From somewhere deep within there came a heart-rending cry. Svetlana put an arm around her, held her close, but Anna could not take her eyes off Krylov, and her body trembled like a sparrow's.

"You don't know what this is like," she said, her voice barely controlled. "You can't imagine what Peter has had to do to keep me from dropping into the land of the dead. You can't imagine the filth, the fleshy awfulness of this disease, a person reduced to poisonous dead meat, burning up, covered with running pustules and scabs, like swarms of bees. You think your body will just burn away, leaving an empty shell of scabs, a crust of dried serum and blood. You pray that it will. But then you realize death is not even nearby, not even in the same room as you, and this thing, this horrible, filthy thing will go on and on and on...."

"Anna," whispered Svetlana. "Anna."

Krylov got up and moved about the room. He imagined how it had been for Gayle, keeping her clean, uninfected, hydrated, alive. A man who could do that would be able to look death in the eye and smile. "Ah," said Krylov then, seeing the filled petrol cans stacked along one wall, reading the Englishman's intentions.

Gayle had already made his arrangements with death. He wasn't going to leave this place alone. Had Anna died, he would have destroyed her remains, the fallen bees, the chalet, and himself, and burned everything out of existence. Not knowing Al-Rabiah was dead, he meant to rid the world of the good doctor's last remaining chalice.

"I'm going out," he said.

"Don't, Viktor. I love Peter. I can't imagine life without him. Please let him be, please, I beg you."

"I'm back in a minute or two."

"If you kill him," Anna whispered, "I will kill you."

Krylov turned on her. "Anna, I don't care what you think of doing to me. But I know Peter Gayle does not want to carry smallpox into the world. He hopes someone, something, will stop him."

"No, he thinks we've come through. He thinks we're safe."

"As Sveta would say, look into his eyes. They will tell you how wrong you are."

"We'll go away, far away, where no one lives."

"What, to the Arctic ice? The Sahara?"

"If you kill Peter, I shall kill myself."

"Then he has put himself through hell for nothing." He turned to Svetlana, "Get her ready. We're out of time."

Outside, he leaned against the entrance door, adjusting himself. Gayle was not the only one Al-Rabiah had turned into a monster. Only a monster would walk away from Anna's broken-hearted cries, which he still heard, faintly, through the door.

After a moment he went to the Mercedes, where he took the Makarov out of the glove box and checked its load. He dropped it into his coat pocket and started down the drive, hoping to intercept the Englishman.

They would meet, Krylov had decided, exchange pleasantries, walk along together, chat a little. Gayle would be allowed to get a pace or two ahead. Krylov would shoot him quickly from behind. The time-honored Russian execution, like being struck by lightning, like an act of God. As what, Krylov asked himself now, was not?

And at that moment, as he mused about God's lethal surprises, someone struck him with such force that he went sprawling, prone on the muddy ground, and then a club or possibly a hardened foot flicked at the back of his head like a blackjack, causing his vision to flicker and fade to darkness sparkling with stars. Another kick to the back of his head, and another.

Clinging to consciousness, clinging to the planet with his fingernails dug into the mud, Krylov thought it must be the fucking Englishman, and if it was one couldn't blame him. But Gayle had made a fatal mistake, for, any minute now, the big Russian would turn like a bear and sweep the attacker away, go for the Makarov in his coat pocket...

But the bear was having trouble moving, trouble focusing his thoughts. Krylov imagined he smelled candy, perhaps licorice, or perhaps a sweet, shitty infant odor. So his assailant wasn't Gayle. Gayle smelled of death, and the Englishman had nothing like the strength of these blows. The foot kicked again and Krylov's neck went numb, electricity dancing up and down his spine like St. Elmo's fire as the body sent its frantic signals of impending failure. Christ, thought Krylov, drifting in and out of darkness. Christ.

Hands grabbed his coat and gave him a shake, as though to flatten him out like a duvet, and dropped him face down in the muck. As feeling began to flow back into his body and he tried to move, the hard foot hit him again in the neck; he couldn't make a fist, he couldn't think...

The cold snout of a pistol briefly touched his nape, and the awful foot settled itself against the base of his spine.

"Gotcha!" piped a voice Krylov thought he recognized. "You smart-ass Sov son of a bitch, I gotcha."

Lamont.

Krylov shut his eyes. Perhaps if he lay very still the voice would go away, as bad dreams always do. Perhaps if he lay very still his body would recover enough to get back into the fight. Perhaps....

"Lampshade? *Lampshade?* I may be as stupid as I look, motherfucker, but I just put you in the shit. Now I like read you your rights. You move, you wiggle a pinkie, I blow your head off. Lie quiet-like, you get a moment's peace."

Lamont brayed his shrill, boy's laugh.

"Then I kick your spine a couple inches north and you're the new poster boy for paralyzing injury. We load up your English pal and his girl and that big Russian pussy and off we go. Eventually somebody'll find you lying here, probably still alive. You're a big guy. Big guys are hard to kill…"

The shot boomed in the forest, Krylov heard birds start up, a general rustling among the trees, and thought he must be dead although he'd felt nothing. Maybe that's how it was, you felt nothing, you barely had time to hear the detonation. But, no, somebody was screaming and he didn't think it was he. No, by God, it was Lamont yelling, "*Sumbitch, sumbitch!*"

A second shot. "*Motherfuck!*" More screaming, someone lumbering away at speed, crashing through the undergrowth. A third shot, and a fourth, that screamed off boulders into the misted trees.

Hands gripped Krylov under the arms and he thought, Christ, Lamont's come back.

"Can you move?" It was the Englishman.

"In a moment."

"I hit him. Didn't bring him down, though."

"Big men are hard to kill."

"That's what he said."

"He'll come back. Won't be alone."

"Can you get up?"

"What happened?" Svetlana was suddenly beside him. "Viktor, what happened?"

"Here, help me up."

Slowly, Peter and Svetlana raised Krylov to his feet, and let him stand while his damaged nerves revived. He looked at Gayle, the man he'd come to murder. Sharing the joke, Gayle smiled.

"Thank you, Peter," said Krylov. "Anna will be worried. Go show her you're all right."

Gayle hurried to the house. Svetlana put herself under one of Krylov's arms, providing him a human crutch, and they started toward the chalet. "Did he break anything?" she asked.

Krylov shook his head. "He wanted me a quadriplegic. So I guess he pulled some of those punches, although," and he tried to grin for her, "not nearly enough."

"Peter saved your life."

"Yes, my dear."

"Did he save his as well?"

Krylov nodded.

"So, what now?"

"We do plan B."

"And what is that?"

"I'm working on it."

A distant, rhythmic thumping came to them, then, interrupted by terrain and trees, so that it rose and fell and sometimes faded to nothing. "Rotor," said Krylov. "A kilometer or so away, inbound." It sounded like one of the Mi-8s that had carried him all over Afghanistan, and into Iraq, the cave, and this universe of adversity. It would be another Hip, this one with some sort of Cyrillic markings. Perhaps the same crew, what's his name, Panov, in the left seat. The rotor slap was steady. The chopper must be in hover, touching down.

"How is Plan B coming along?"

Krylov heard a note of fear in Sveta's voice, something he hadn't thought possible. But, in fact, something like a plan had begun to coalesce down in his deep interior, where old instincts still lived like canny priests and magicians, improvising outlandish schemes for his salvation. "It's nearly finished."

XXIV

Emerson had hoped to keep the assault quiet, just him and Lamont, four contractor people, three islanders, and the usual Bulgarian pilots for the Hip. No joint-service-lightweight bug suits, although Emerson had made damned sure everybody was vaccinated. They all carried 7.62-mm SCARs and radiated an evil kind of joy at the prospect of putting the rifles to work.

He'd sent Lamont down earlier in the Suburban to scout the area and get in position to guide the Hip to a landing. Then they would make a quick strike, roar up the driveway in the truck, bust into the house, everybody prone on the floor at gunpoint. A tranquilizing needle for the Englishman and the girl, a bullet for anybody else. Stuff them into body bags and get out in the chopper. Lamont would clean up after them, burn the chalet, and take the truck back to Embassy-Vienna. Textbook simple. Easy as pie.

But then he'd seen Lamont standing in the mist, a burning flare in his right hand. The other arm dangled like a dead thing from his big, sloping shoulder and he bled like the Lamb of God. Emerson's heart sank into his desert boots; he sent up a silent prayer that next time somebody shot at his giant child they'd kill him.

When the helicopter touched down, Emerson leapt to the ground and hurried to Lamont, who leaned against a boulder, his tattoos vivid upon a pallid canvas of skin.

"The fuck…?"

"Sorry, Ralph. Sorry."

"That Viktor's there, isn't he?"

Lamont nodded miserably.

"And you just couldn't resist. You went for him."

"I did."

"And he took away your weapon and shot the shit out of you."

"No." Lamont shook his head vigorously, like a dog shedding water. "No, I nailed him. He was finished. But then that Limey sumbitch comes up behind me…"

One of Gayle's shots had shattered Lamont's left clavicle and excavated an exit wound rimmed with bone and gristle. Another had creased Lamont's tiny bald skull, carving a shallow groove that was the source of most of the blood.

"He damn near got you, Lamont." *Better luck next time.*

"Yeah, I know. Well, and I don't feel any too good right now, either."

"You know what you did?"

"I got shot?"

"You didn't just get shot."

"Lost my gun?"

"No, not that either. You put our element of surprise right down the toilet. Down the fucking toilet, Lamont. Goddammit."

"Sorry, Ralph. Honest to God."

The pilot stayed in the cockpit as the helicopter idled on the ground, the five rotor blades swinging ponderously, beating out the time. The contractors and islanders stepped off the aircraft, but kept their distance. The Fijians fiddled with their gear, slipping black body bags over their shoulders like serapes; they pretended not to see Lamont. Panov came over with a first-aid kit.

"Patch him up enough that we can do our thing," said Emerson.

"He needs doctor."

"He gets doctor afterward."

When the copilot just stared at the wounds, Emerson yanked the first-aid kit away from him. "Stop bleeding, protect wound, prevent shock. Jesus, Panov, don't you have Boy Scouts in Bulgaria?" He jerked his chin at one of the contractors. "Conroy, give us a hand."

Conroy was one of those black Americans who still looked like he'd stepped out of the African bush that afternoon. He wasn't a giant, but he was big enough and strong as a lion and integrated, as if he'd been carved from a single block of ebony. He was with Emerson after twenty years in the Corps.

He poured disinfectant on both wounds and dried them with sterile gauze. A wad of gauze pads to the head wound, tightly held in place with adhesive tape, some antiseptic ointment swabbed around the messy crater in the shoulder, another bandage. Then he administered a shot of morphine. "There you go, boss." Conroy rarely spoke above a murmur.

"Thanks. Okay, Lamont, we're going to put you in the chopper. First Officer Panov here can take your place."

"Oh, no, I am pilot. Only pilot. Or maybe engineer."

"If you want to be aboard when we fly out of here, my friend, you will join us in the infantry. Yes?"

On a signal from Emerson, the contractors came over and hoisted their fallen comrade onto their shoulders like a slain boar and marched him to the helicopter. The pilot had opened the rear clam-shell hatch and put down a tarpaulin to protect the metal deck. He didn't want his aircraft full of blood.

The contractors lay Lamont on the tarp gently, as if he were a sleeping princess, perhaps hoping he would do the same for them. The pilot put some flotation cushions under the wounded man's head to keep it elevated.

"Where's the truck?" asked Emerson.

Lamont was looking at something very far away. His voice was barely audible. "In amongst the trees."

With the wounded soldier stowed, Emerson could think more clearly about the operation. The people in the chalet knew he was coming, they were armed and waiting, maybe in ambush. Gayle wouldn't know what to do; aviators were as awkward as birds on the ground. But the Russian had been everywhere and done everything and could be a world of trouble, even for this talented squad of rowdies.

Emerson decided they'd best approach on foot. He led Panov, now uncomfortably armed with a spare SCAR, and the others down the road for half a kilometer, then waved them out into the trees, where they became shadows drifting through the forest.

The red A-frame came into view like a ship in fog, its prow suddenly visible twenty meters away. Emerson crouched behind a boulder, studying the place through his field glasses, his troops kneeling behind him. The air was wet and cold as the grave.

Okay, there were at least three people in that building, one of them adept, two of them amateurs. At least one armed, maybe two. He turned to Conroy. "I want you over by the woodpile. We'll cover you."

Conroy nodded calmly, but said nothing. He put his head down and burst out of their cover, galloped across the open space and threw himself flat behind the stacked firewood, rolling over, ready to fire.

The house was silent, dark, no lights…

Then it exploded in a tower of flame. Nearby treetops flared, showering Emerson and his team with glowing needles and twigs. They danced around, stomping on the embers, brushing frantically at hot ash on their clothing. The waning day was suddenly bright as a dying star, the conflagration warm upon their faces. The walls toppled inward, sending a spiral of sparks into the mist.

Sudden and disturbing as a burst of automatic-rifle fire, an engine cranked. "They're on the road!" Emerson yelled. "They're on the road!" He sprinted for the driveway.

The distant engine revved, tires skittered on the wet tarmac. As Emerson reached the narrow lane a Saab convertible shot past them and vanished in the mist. For a moment he stood on the road, briefly paralyzed by failure. Behind him the chalet crashed in upon itself, spewing a fresh cloud of bright particles.

Emerson gave himself a powerful mental shake. The islanders would take the truck, he told them, he and the contractors would take the chopper. "Go, go, go," he barked at them as they ran down the road, looking for the parked Suburban. His heart drummed with the effort, singing its sad refrain: *Too old for this, too old for this, too old for this…*

By the time they came upon the black mass of the Chevrolet, Emerson was nearly blown. He toddled up to the car, leaned his back against it, bowed his head and put his hands on his knees, trying to breathe. "Let's go, let's go," he panted.

"I don't think so." The contractor named Conroy pointed his rifle at the Suburban, which listed like a sinking ship. Somebody had slashed both tires on the driver's side, no doubt that fucking Sov, ghosting through the woods. Emerson turned to the nearest islander. "Fix it."

"How we fix, boss?" one of the islanders wanted to know.

"Just drive it someplace and fix it. Conroy, you boys are with me in the chopper. Get the body bags."

Emerson led Panov and the contractors down the road toward the thump of the idling rotor. He wanted to sprint, but could not. He thought his heart might explode in his chest before he reached his window seat and could breathe again. The abandoned Fijians watched them go, glad to be out of it, whatever *it* was.

The Mi-8 stood like a spectral insect in the clearing, its rotor spinning vortices of mist, the trees beyond a faint, grey serration. "Let's go," yelled Emerson, hauling himself into the fuselage.

From his right-hand seat, the pilot watched Emerson warily through the oval hatch behind the cockpit. The copilot squeezed through the opening and plopped down in the left seat. He made the crazy sign, rotating an index finger next to his ear. The pilot nodded. "I take us back to Wien."

"No way." Emerson had just about recovered his wind.

"We lift out of here, okay," said the pilot. "But then instrument approach to Schwechat."

"No, we get under this stuff and find that Saab."

"Under cloud?" The pilot laughed and rolled his eyes for the copilot.

"On the flats we'll have a couple hundred feet."

"Not enough. Not legal."

"Fuck legal."

"Not safe."

"This isn't United bloody Airlines, chum. You were hired to fly low, slow, and dirty. That's what we need today. Now let's go."

Muttering in Bulgarian, the pilot slipped on his headset and turned to his controls. He brought up the power; the big ship trembled as the rotor yanked it off the ground. Its nose lowered, the Hip prowled slowly westward just above the veiled treetops, following the descending terrain toward the motorway.

Emerson stepped through the hatch and took the jump seat behind Panov. At first, he could see nothing but a grey infinitude through the droplets streaming across the windscreen. Then, as they emerged from the cloud base a gloomy vista of ashen fields and black trees opened ahead of them. Off to the north Ternitz glittered like a fire dying in the rain, with the coals of Wiener Neustadt barely visible in the distance, the towns linked by the Autobahn's twin rivers of light. Emerson put on the spare headset.

"North, south?" Panov asked on the intercom.

"South," said Emerson. The Englishman wouldn't return to Vienna. "Yeah, it's south. But put on some speed. That Saab can do two hundred."

"So can we," Panov replied, "with tailwind."

"I need your chart."

Panov passed him an obsolete ICAO Luftfahrkarte that had been folded and refolded almost to destruction. Emerson opened it on his lap and studied the veins and arteries of lower Austria. He put his finger on the yellow freeform denoting Graz. That would be the decision point for Gayle. From there his choices bloomed like a daisy. He could go on down toward Klagenfurt, or northwest to Salzburg, Munich, and the rest of Europe. He could cross into Serbia, or go east into Hungary.

Emerson looked out the window on his side of the helicopter. There was the Sudautobahn below them, and tendrils of moving light spewing from both sides, like sparks blowing through the night. They were looking for a particular spark, one ash in a vast plume of them scattering across that field of dark meadows and clustered village lights. One of many moving needles in this black haystack. "Shit."

Now, above the hiss and beat of the helicopter, Emerson heard a faint keening, which it took him a moment to realize wasn't part of the mechanical clatter of the Hip, but a song of pain. An annoying distraction. "I'm going back to Lamont," he told the pilots. He took off his headset and stalked aft to check on his wounded boy.

"Lamont?" he yelled over the noise.

"I'm really hurting."

"Say again?" Emerson leaned in to hear.

"I said *really hurting.*"

"We're going to finish this within the hour, son," yelled Emerson. "Then it's hospitals for *you.*"

Emerson looked him over. The head wound had finally stopped bleeding; the bandage had become a stiff roan beret. The shoulder was as okay as it was going to get before he saw a doctor. No red vines branching under the skin. "So far so good."

"What?"

"SO FAR SO GOOD."

Emerson rummaged in the first-aid box and brought out another vial of morphine. "One more for the road. By the time it wears off you'll be surrounded by pretty nurses and white muslin."

"But I'm a Christian, boss."

"Here, take your morphine."

He returned to his jump seat and put on the headset. "Anything?"

Panov just shook his head.

If they'd lost Peter Gayle, thought Emerson, they'd lost the war. The plague would now be truly loose in the world; it would be finished as a weapon in the clandestine war on terror. The bio-containment guys would take over, get things under control at some cost in human life, and put Gayle on ice, living or dead.

Then some suit in the Eisenhower building would thank Emerson, maybe arrange a Medal of Freedom, and suggest it might be the moment to find a little place out by the Shenandoah. Give the war on terror a break. Put on those bib overalls, let the white beard sprout. Get a dog. Find a woman. Emerson felt like a dying Apache, turning his face to the tepee wall. He shuddered. All that traffic thundering over his grave.

"Look," Panov called. "Ten o'clock."

Emerson turned and at first saw only a flickering against the wrinkled land off to the southeast. A pillar of flame shot skyward, as if from a crack in the earth.

"Christ," muttered the pilot.

"You want to look?" asked Panov.

"Why not?" A tingle of dread touched Emerson on his lower spine, his heart thumped. Closer now, he could see it was a vehicle burning furiously in the middle of an open field. Emerson leaned forward. "Take us down."

"You want to land?"

"I want to see the car."

The pilot flew a low circle around the fire, looking for the wind, then gingerly put the helicopter down on the black loam fifty meters away. Emerson could smell the fire now, and thought he could feel its heat.

He stepped back into the cabin, cracked the hatch, took a deep breath, and dropped to the soft ground, Conroy close behind him. They stood watching the fire, their faces and clothing singed by the heat. Emerson shielded his eyes with both hands and peered into the glare.

A Saab convertible, no question about it. Emerson could discern the low-slung jaw of the air dam, the broad hips, the soft top burning like a sheet of parchment, eaten by its fiery rim. The cockpit was a pool of fire. The steel skeleton shimmered at red heat, the metal skin glowed where it was not molten or ripped away. Moving to one side he saw the boot just beginning to redden, and, below, the British number plate.

Emerson thought it was all rather stately, the Viggen upright and on its own feet, so to speak, as it dissolved in fire. Somebody had driven the car out into this field, soaked it in gasoline, and waited for the Hip's strobes to appear in the distance. Then a match or a Zippo into the front seat and there was a flicker, followed by the fountain of flames. Everything deliberate, calculated. It reminded Emerson of Buddhist monks immolating themselves for the waiting cameras.

He leaned closer to the blaze, looking for some sign of life, or death, a face burned into a silver mask, blackened fingers spread in agony—something. But there was nothing.

"Nobody home?" said Conroy.

"Just that wild goose."

Emerson studied the wreck a moment longer, then he and Conroy walked back toward the helicopter. Some cars had stopped along the fence line and a platoon of passers-by stood along the wire, their faces orange ovals in the firelight. He could feel their consternation even at this distance, seeing the burning car, the Russian helicopter, a black man and a white one in the middle of an Austrian field.

"Best we go," said Emerson, pulling himself through the hatch. "Okay," he called to the pilots, "that'll do."

The big insect fluttered up into the night, with that host of orange faces watching. The pilot came on the intercom. "So, anyway, we are finding it after all."

But Emerson wasn't listening. He was thinking it had been a couple of hours since the Saab had bolted from the forest, two hours since he had taken the bait and gone after a fucking *decoy,* two hours in which that goddamned Sov could spirit Peter Gayle and his girl away to....where? By now they could be three hundred kilometers away, in any direction. That is to say, *anywhere.* Emerson was so angry that his head hurt.

"Back to Vienna," he said on the intercom. "Tell Embassy we've got wounded aboard."

Emerson took off his head set and rubbed his eyes, which burned with fatigue. Then he leaned against the window, watching the fire recede until it was just an ember among the nebular village lights, then nothing at all.

FROM THE FAR EDGE OF THE FIELD, SVETLANA MAXIMOVNA TRULOVA had watched the helicopter advance on the burning Saab, circle it like a moth drawn warily to the flame. The machine landed, its engines idling with a soft hiss, the drooping rotors turning not much faster than a carousel.

Two men got out and walked over to the fire, took a long look at it, and returned to the helicopter. A moment later, with a great spume of dust and mechanical clatter, off it went, turning north, the strobe lights winking smaller and smaller until they were finally out of sight. People were still arriving on the road and she could hear the bleating of the approaching fire brigade.

"Head for Graz," Viktor had told her. "But a few kilometers north of town, get on the country roads to the east. At night they are darker than Bulgaria. Then I want two things to happen. I want the car burnt where they can see it. And I want you safely back in Vienna."

"In that order?"

"Not exactly."

Sveta had thought it might be scary, but, in fact, it had been wonderful. She hadn't driven a car in a year and suddenly here she was, going like the wind in a truly fast car. She could go two hundred kilometers in an hour in this car.

As she fled down the Sudautobahn she saw the helicopter pick up the scent and follow, its anti-collision lights sparking in the rear-view mirror, the pale flutter of the rotary wing. Her heart pounded with excitement. This was like being one of those grey-caped Russian crows soaring over birch forests and fields of snow. It was like being chased by the Headless Horseman.

The helicopter was still behind her when she turned off into the gently undulating farmland that went off into the Hungarian night, and hurried through one tiny village after another, and past the isolated lights of farms. When the strobes were about even with her, but still well to the west, over the motorway, Svetlana had turned off the Saab's headlamps and driven into the center of an open field, where she could see no lights. Then she'd soaked the interior with petrol from the can Viktor had given her.

Off to the west, the strobes started back toward the north; the helicopter was turning toward her. She dropped a lighted match onto the driver's seat and ran for her life, feeling the hot shock wave spreading from the detonation behind her. When she reached the trees at a far corner of the field, she turned to study the awful thing she'd created and feel its warm touch upon her face.

Now, as she walked past the parked cars, Svetlana noticed the tall Russian girl reflected in their dark windows. She hardly recognized herself. Oh, she had the same old moon face, the same wreath of sable hair, somewhat tousled tonight; the same suggestion of the Siberian east. But the girl in the car windows was exotic, even beautiful. Her cheeks burned with high color, her dark eyes gleamed, she smiled like a woman trying not to laugh aloud and reveal her pleasure.

Had she not known better, Sveta would have said the girl had spent the day in the arms of a wonderful man. Both she and her reflection chuckled at that; what they'd been doing was better than sex.

She would find a ride with someone back toward Graz, catch the train for Vienna. By midnight she would be in her flat on Sternwartestrasse. And Viktor and the others, where would they be? "Where will you go?" she'd asked Krylov in the forest.

"Home," he replied.

XXV

North of Warsaw it began to snow, the big, wet flakes spinning past the Mercedes headlamps like white moths to crash against the windscreen and be swept away by the relentless wiper blade. Peter Gayle didn't mind the snow; he welcomed any distraction on this long tunneling through Eastern Europe's black night.

Krylov was having a troubled nap in the passenger seat beside him. The big Russian sat with his legs drawn up in an awkward cross, arms folded across his chest as if holding his torso together. The hair at the nape of his neck was stiff with dried blood, the flesh swollen. Gayle thought it would hurt like hell when he woke up. But Krylov's only outward sign of discomfort was the occasional jerk of an arm or leg, the spasms of an anxious dreamer.

Gayle saw Anna's reflection in the rear-view mirror and found her looking back at him, her pale eyes luminous as a cat's. He smiled for her. "Okay?"

She nodded and huddled more tightly in her corner. Having caught Peter's eye, she closed her own.

They had burst out of the forest near Molzegg minutes after Svetlana was southbound on the Autobahn, and turned north toward Vienna, Krylov using the whip on the old Mercedes. He had offered to take Anna home, but she vehemently declined. Peter needed her, she said. She was immune now. She was a nurse, she could help him. And, although she didn't say so, she was terrified of being separated from him. Her calm nurse voice told Krylov, "Whatever you have in mind, Peter and I will do it together." But one could also hear the undertone: *Part us and I will die.*

"Done," said Krylov.

During the first hours of their journey Gayle had rested in the back seat, Anna leaning against him, wrapped in his arms, weak and still, except for a faint burring sound as she breathed. Believing himself awake, Gayle had dozed off for an hour, awakened, and then dropped back into sleep for an hour more. He traveled like a dog, for whom a long trip is a series of short naps.

Whenever he opened his eyes, there was Krylov, driving like an angry cop past the melancholy line of lorries that shuffled down the highway. With Anna relaxed into his arms, deep in the exhausted sleep of convalescence, he told Krylov, "She was afraid you'd drop her and kill me somewhere up the line. Makes sense."

"It made sense before. Now we are in, what, Plan B?"

"At the chalet I was working Plan Zed."

"I saw how you prepared the hut. You seemed to know what you were doing."

"Bags of experience. What's Plan B?"

"Later. First we *shake* Emerson and his *boys*." Krylov laughed softly. "We *lose* them, as Svetlana would say."

"Where is she now?"

"She went south and east. I don't know how far."

"You're not worried about her."

"At the moment I don't have time to worry."

Gayle thought he heard some worry in the Russian's voice. "She went southeast. What then?"

"She lit a beacon to draw the helicopter."

"You mean she set fire to my car."

"It had to be destroyed. Like the chalet."

"Like me."

"Right now, you're another department."

Just beyond Krakow they'd stopped to refuel. Krylov brought some bottled water and shrink-wrapped cheese sandwiches in which the lettuce had turned to green paper. "It's all there was in the cooler."

"I have to…" Anna began, raising herself and opening her door.

Gayle moved to help, but Krylov intervened. "I'll take her. You have to stay away from public places."

"I'll look for a tree."

When they returned and were eating, Krylov said, "I'm beginning to see things that aren't there. Barriers. Elephants. Can you drive awhile?"

"No problem."

Krylov had fumbled in the glove box and brought out a tattered road map of Poland, which he folded to show where they were. "We're here," he said, putting a fingertip north of Krakow. "Tell me when we get here." The finger moved to the Lithuanian border.

They had slipped past Warsaw after midnight, across the metal ribbon of the Vistula, past the grove of modest skyscrapers draped with strings of lighted windows. Gayle followed the ring road around to the northwest and picked up the S8, which ran in a series of long, straight lines north and east to the horizon.

Snow was accumulating along the edges of the highway, paling the dark fields beyond. The land was as featureless as a calm sea, on which scattered lakes floated like shards of glass amid islands of black trees. Gayle smiled, recalling his silent wish that Europe were larger. Well, he thought, here we are, a thousand miles in a day. The old place was bigger than she looked.

The fuel needle settled toward empty, but Gayle pushed on. Now and then a village would drift past, a few lights suspended in the snow. He took another look at the fuel gauge. "Find us a tanker, Mouse."

"What?" It was Krylov, returning from the dead, rearranging his cramped legs, gingerly touching his injured neck with his fingertips. "Where are we?"

"Towns ending in *ki*. Must be Poland."

"You were talking to someone."

"My old backseater. Now deceased."

"Maybe you should take a break." Krylov rubbed his eyes. "Soon we come to the Budzisko border-crossing. It used to be complicated. Now it's just a sign with an EU flag saying that suddenly you are in Lithuania. Like suddenly you are in New Jersey."

A few lights, faint and nebulous in the snow, appeared ahead of them. Gayle could make out a low skyline, lines of trees. A long concertina of lorries dilated and compressed along the right side of the road. Off to his left Gayle saw a smear of red and white, which resolved into an ORLEN service station sign. "Nick o' time," he said, tapping the fuel gauge with an index finger. He slowed the Mercedes, fishtailed off the road, and stopped by the scarlet pumps.

"Good," said Krylov. "One, we do petrol. Two, we find something to eat. Three, we talk about Plan B."

WHILE GAYLE FILLED THE MERCEDES, KRYLOV KNELT AND PICKED UP handfuls of snow, which he rubbed against his nape and over his face, hoping to scare away his body's painful memory of Lamont's assault. He stood up, stretching, gave a leonine yawn, and rubbed another handful of snow on his face.

More himself now, Krylov opened the hatch and rummaged in his bag, coming out with a freshly laundered sky-blue shirt in a plastic sleeve. He went to the office door and pushed it open.

A stout, dark-haired woman sat behind what looked like an elementary-school desk, reading a magazine flattened in a small pool of lamplight. She wore blue coveralls with the sleeves rolled up, like those muscled factory women in Soviet posters.

"Excuse me," he said in Polish, "we are looking for breakfast."

She glanced at him and seemed to smile with sharp green teeth. Her face was pale and pitted, with powder crusted like frost in the larger craters. He thought her dark eyes looked ferocious. Perhaps she was crazy. Her voice had a keening note that went right to one's bones. "You won't find anything like in Vienna. Oh, yes, I saw your number plate. But there is always a food wagon down the line. Lorry drivers flock to it like flies." She studied him a moment. "Ah, what a bad boy. You've been fighting. How does the other one look?"

"I don't know."

"You don't know?"

"Last time I saw him he was falling out a window."

"Ah, one of those. A throwback." She cackled. "You people never stop."

"Does the lavatory work?"

"Where do you think you are, Russia? Of course it works. Help yourself." She waved a pointing thumb to show him the way.

Krylov found the cubicle and pulled the light string, actuating a small, pale bulb that hung from the ceiling. There was a chipped, nicotine-colored sink, and a French crapper with two footholds. A good many people had missed the hole, and no one had cleaned up the mess. "Talk about throwbacks," he muttered.

A warped metal mirror showed him a strangely elongated man he barely recognized, his collar brown with old blood, his hair matted, his neck raw and puffy where he'd been kicked. He looked as if he hadn't slept in years. His jacket and shirtfront were smeared with mud. He felt like cutting off his head.

He took off his leather coat and wiped at the mud with the thin, much-used green rag that served as a communal towel. Then he pulled off the soiled shirt, which he wet and used as a sponge on his neck and torso and dried himself with the tail, then put on the fresh one. He splashed his face with water and patted it dry, pushed back his hair with his fingers. Not beautiful, but it would have to do.

As he went out, the woman looked up from her magazine. "Very nice."

Back at the Mercedes, Krylov told Anna, "There's a lavatory, but it's very dirty."

"Where's Peter?" Her eyes opened wide with worry.

"Looking for a tree."

Anna went into the office to find the lavatory. Krylov went inside to pay.

The woman looked at a read-out from their pump. "You have zlotys?"

Krylov shook his head. "Euros."

"Lucky me."

While she worked out the price in euros, Anna returned. "Phew! Ech! I see what you mean," she said, and went out the door.

"What's she talking about?"

"All that shit on the floor."

"People should clean up their own shit."

"Of course. You're a democracy now."

"Your girl's been sick."

"She's better now."

"I know what she had. I had it once myself."

"Ah." Krylov studied the woman, wondering whether she was someone he would now be forced to silence. He could hear her chatting to a comrade about a girl from Vienna just getting over *smallpox,* and the comrade telling the wife of someone in authority that this banished disease had returned to the world right here in Budzisko, and one thing leading to another....

Something must have shown in his face, for she turned back to her magazine. "It doesn't matter. When it's gone, it's gone."

"Like love."

"I wouldn't know. Good night, handsome."

Gayle was waiting at the car. "Found my tree," he said, forcing a smile. He'd washed his face with snow and smoothed down his shock of blonde hair. But, to Krylov, the eyes still looked dead. The Englishman could banter happily enough, he thought, but, in fact, he had given up. He waited, helpless as a lost animal, for the next calamity. That would be a recurrence of a mild flu, signaling he was once again a viral bomb.

THE FOOD WAGON WAS AN ANCIENT ZUK MAIL VAN, STILL WEARING the dull orange livery of the Poczta Polska, with a big window opening upward on the driver's side. A plump, bald man in a tee-shirt and black down-filled vest stood wreathed in steam, whistling one of those tunes everyone remembers but nobody can name. Krylov bought boiled eggs and bread and coffee, then got back into the Mercedes and drove down the line of lorries past the EU sign that said they were now in Lithuania.

They stopped to eat in a small lay-by about twenty kilometers on. The snow had thinned enough that the bright intrusions of the dawn could be seen in the southeastern sky. Krylov parked the Mercedes in the lee of a large oak, which muffled the roar and rattle of vehicles charging past on the road. "Now," he declared, "we have breakfast."

Krylov watched his two passengers, who sat in the back seat, their flanks touching. They ate like orphans left on their own, quietly intent, the future utterly obscure. Anna was weak and worn out, with no color beyond the mauve scars of her illness. She picked at her food. When she faltered, Gayle handed her a morsel, and another. He ate bit by bit, scrap by scrap, as a prisoner would, using the meal as a way to murder time.

They had been all the way to Hell, these two, and there was more, perhaps a good deal more, to come. Krylov's fondness for Anna, pretty Anna of the scarred face and bottomless fatigue, had seated itself long before this. But he had also quickly warmed to Peter Gayle. Well, it would be hard not to like this Englishman. He seemed immune to panic, and brave. He could look Death in the eye without blinking, and, as the petrol cans in the chalet had shown, he was capable of doing the necessary. Krylov shut his eyes against a sudden vision of that final scene, the death, the immolation. Yes, these two were heartbreakers, all right.

"As for Plan B," Krylov began when the food was gone and they were sipping tepid coffee from Styrofoam cups, "Svetlana has bought us some time. So has the weather. The EU borders are still open, which means no one knows officially what we are carrying. But we have some challenges ahead. At the Ubylinka crossing into Russia they will give us a close look." He fumbled in his coat pocket and pulled out two passports, handing the blue one to Gayle. "Peter, you are now my colleague, an English Safeguards inspector named Churches."

"I hope we do better than poor Churches," murmured Anna.

"Amen," added Gayle.

"As far as anyone is concerned we are making a snap inspection of the Leningrad II reactor. That means they don't officially know when we are coming. How do you feel?"

"If you mean do I feel contagious, no."

"Good. We don't want to leave souvenirs. Now, Anna, here is yours," and he passed her the dark red passport. "You are now Svetlana Maximovna Trulova."

"She can't travel as Svetlana," Gayle protested. "They look nothing alike. She doesn't look Russian. Do you speak it at all?"

Anna shook her head.

Krylov said, "Right now Anna doesn't resemble anybody, to be frank. Of course we need to make her more like Sveta. We also need to hide signs of her illness. At the petrol station I was reminded that in Russia everyone of a certain age has seen smallpox. They know its mark."

Anna touched her cheeks with her fingertips; her hand leapt away, as if independently repulsed.

"I know," Krylov said, "it doesn't feel like the real you. But it will get better. For now, we will have to do some camouflaging. When we cross, we keep you completely silent. I will spin some sort of frightening lie."

"Why Russia?" asked Gayle, who didn't sound convinced.

"Because the Americans can't follow you there."

"Rubbish. They always find a way."

"Not this time. I am taking you to a lonely dacha no one has lived in since Soviet times. No telephone, no hot water except what you boil on the stove. A rough shower outside. An outhouse. No picturesque village, no anything, except an old fellow named Axel."

"Your trusted retainer?"

Krylov smiled. "Please, don't be snide. I have known Axel all my life. I shall tell him you are working on a book and need absolute quiet and isolation to finish your great work. Democracy has mixed him up a little, but he is as reliable as a Russian volkodav, a wolf killer. He will protect you and keep you in food and water and firewood."

"A Russian winter with the girl of my dreams in an abandoned dacha. I wouldn't miss it for the world. What's second prize?"

"Two winters in the dacha."

"Or until the Americans arrive," said Anna.

"Russia isn't quite *such* a pushover. Besides, we don't need decades. We need a few weeks. Before Emerson finds his way to where you are, you'll be gone."

"This time to the Moon?"

"I don't know where to, Peter."

"Maybe to have a natter with the chap who created this horror."

"That chap is dead."

"With some help from a friend?" Anna gave Krylov a long look.

"Maybe a little. Even at the end he was proud of his creation, what he called his ten chalices of death. But he knew they were fragile, he'd seen them fail over the years, one by one. He had no idea how long Peter would carry the virus, whether it would be for a month or all eternity. He had no idea how to switch it off once it was activated."

"Meaning I'm fucked." Gayle said this without recrimination, as he would have said he was a few minutes late, or a little hungry.

"Meaning we don't yet know what you are. I believe the creature he put into you will finally go away. I am betting my Motherland on it and taking you to Russia, to my home, where you can wait for it to die."

"And if it doesn't?"

"You will have to choose."

Gayle was quiet for a time. Then, "I can take any horse I wish, provided it's the one nearest the stable door." He made a sad grin. "Hobson's choice, as we say."

"I am not leaving you," said Anna, watching Gayle warily. "I will not."

"Yes you will. If your beloved monster believes he is going to be a monster forever, you'll have to go away. I'll call Viktor to come for you. And then I'll take that horse nearest the door."

"And what if I say no?"

"Then it all ends here, right now. Chalice number ten walks out into the snow with a can of petrol and a gun."

"You'd do that?"

"Can you imagine anything I wouldn't do?"

She turned away from him. "This thing has made you crazy."

"No, it's made me serious. Look, Viktor is giving us a little time, a chance…"

"A chance. What you said, this Hobson thing."

"Something is always better than nothing."

"I used to think that." Anna put her face in her hands. "Now, I'm not so sure."

"Still, promise."

"Promise what?"

"To survive me."

After a moment, she said, "I promise to survive you."

"Is that good enough, Viktor?"

"Yes, it's good enough." Krylov thought it was a vow Anna would keep not much longer than a day, once Gayle was gone.

Gayle leaned forward. "There, the old girls have spun and measured. My destiny's set."

Krylov thought he heard a troubling wild note in Peter's voice. Well, and why not? A complicated future had been suddenly reduced to just two possibilities, like an ON-OFF toggle switch labeled LIVE-DIE. But simple might be better. He thought he detected a faint light in Peter's formerly empty eyes.

THEY HAD CROSSED LITHUANIA with the sun rising like a silver coin behind them, the snowflakes swirling out of nowhere beneath a low stratum of leaden clouds. Krylov drove, but without his former ferocity. Somewhat to his surprise, he found himself precisely where he would have wished to be, with these two people he liked so well. He imagined how, with a bit of luck, the four of them would meet on the far side of all this, like a little family, he and they and Sveta, and roll their eyes at the magnitude of their adventure.

He glanced at Anna in the mirror, where she reclined across the back seat, fitfully asleep. She did not look much like anyone he knew. After they'd entered Latvia, Krylov had driven them into Daugavpils, through the outer grids of low factories and pall of smoke, to find a chemist's shop.

When they stopped to refuel the Mercedes at a Statoil station on the far edge of town, Krylov had taken Anna to the lavatory. He dyed the fine blonde hair an uneven black and padded over the tattered skin with foundation and an olive-tinged powder. A touch of lipstick broadened the mouth.

Anna turned her new face this way and that, in a parody of primping before the mirror. "What a hag. Peter will run for his life." She put a hand on Krylov's arm. "You may have a future in make-up for scary films. But Svetlana would be horrified to learn you thought this thing looks like her."

"It's not meant to. It's meant to resemble a sick woman who wants to breathe Russian air for the last time."

"Your frightening lie?"

"Part of it."

THE MERCEDES SLID PAST THE HERD OF LORRIES, SCORES OF THEM now, slowly advancing toward the border crossing at Grebnevo. The short November day was nearly gone, the sun just an amorphous light behind a curtain of snow. The countryside around them stood bleak and empty, its low relief pocked with ragged ponds. It was the no-man's land along a border that, as though suddenly, had become the boundary between Russia and all of Europe.

Joining a line of smaller vehicles, they crept up to the illuminated stalls of the Latvian check point. Krylov handed their passports to the uniformed young man in the booth, hoping Klaus Oldenburg hadn't called in Churches' as missing. But the guard swiped the documents through the computer, took a quick look at the people in the Mercedes, and stamped them out of Latvia, Europe, and the Western World.

Then they were on their way into Russia, part of a long queue of cars creeping past cargo carriers idling on the side of the road, veiled in diesel exhaust. There were hundreds of them; some, Krylov knew, would be there for days. The fenced, well-lighted road narrowed like the net of a weir, guiding traffic toward a string of spotlights marking the Ubylinka portal.

Armed Border Guards in green berets and battle dress watched the arriving vehicles from the sidelines. The cars sidled up to the lighted booths, where a couple of uniformed guards waited, while a third passed a wheeled mirror under the vehicles. "Looking for Mexicans," said Krylov, giving his companions an encouraging grin. He stopped the car next to a booth and the two guards came over. Krylov got out and greeted them in Russian.

One of them grunted something neutral in return. He was young and fit, his junior-sergeant's uniform not quite settled on his middle-sized frame. His skin was as white as soap, his hair and eyes the flat black of slate. Youth, thought Krylov, without the blood. The other guard was also a junior sergeant, fatter and quite a bit older, white-haired and red-eyed, with a good many stainless steel teeth and an unkempt look, like Russia herself. Krylov thought they might have some shared memories of Afghanistan.

"Austrian number plates? Where are you coming from?"

The younger guard's voice, like the rest of him, had not quite settled into place.

"Vienna," said Krylov.

"You must enjoy driving."

"We had stops to make in Poland, and from here we go to Finland for another project."

"Vienna must be twenty hours from here."

Krylov shrugged. "At least."

He studied Krylov for a moment. "Were you in a fight?"

Another shrug. "Some car trouble on the way."

"Passports?" The young guard held out a gloved hand. He studied the United Nations documents, flipping their pages, then peered into the car at Gayle, who said, "Cheerio."

The older guard took a look at the passports, then grinned at Krylov. "Ah, the atomic watchdogs. What are you dogs watching in Russia?"

Krylov puffed himself up a little. "We inspect the Leningrad II reactor. Mr. Churches and I."

"St. Petersburg, you mean," said the younger guard, lifting his chin.

His colleague said, "The reactors are still Leningrad. Like Pulkovo Airport is still LEN."

Krylov said, "I grew up around here, so it is always going to be Leningrad."

The old boy laughed. "No new tricks, right?"

Krylov nodded.

The young one retrieved the passports and pulled out Svetlana's, like an ace from a pack of playing cards. "Is she also a watchdog?"

Krylov moved between the young man and the car, and lowered his voice. The older guard leaned in to hear. "Miss Trulova is an analyst in our Vienna laboratory. There was an accident. It was like a little Chernobyl. A big flash. Radiation everywhere. She suffered horrible burns. It left her deaf and mute. When she learned we were driving up here on mission, she begged us to bring her along. We couldn't say no."

"How could a mute beg?" The older guard wore a puzzled frown.

Shit! thought Krylov. "She wrote a note."

"But why make such a journey, being so sick?"

"To stand on Russian soil and breathe Russian air."

"Has she come for medical treatment?"

"My boy," said the older guard, "you don't come to Russia for the medicine, you come to Russia to die."

The young guard ignored the jibe. "Has she family here?"

"No," said Krylov. "She has no one anywhere. She is the last of her line, and she is dying."

"Let's see what you have in back."

Krylov opened the boot and pushed the luggage aside, showing the aluminum instrument cases. From one of them he extracted a sheaf of documents identifying them as Agency property.

The young guard thumbed through the papers, nodding as if he understood the purpose of the devices they described. As he turned back toward Anna, Krylov said in a voice too low for her to hear, "Sergeant, she is sensitive about her appearance. You will see why."

The guard took out his torch and flicked the bright beam of light on Anna's face. She peered into the glare like a trapped animal, eyes wide and stony with apprehension, a hand hiding her mouth. In the garish illumination, her heavily made-up face was a tattered, pitted mask, the eyes a little mad. The young man leaned into the window, comparing her to the photograph in her passport, and quickly turned away, shaken by what he'd seen and by the scent of old flesh. "Fuck your mother!" he whispered to the descending night. He took a moment to collect himself.

The older guard took a brief look as well, then withdrew, shaking his head. "Christ." He plucked the passports from his colleague's hand and took them into the booth and stamped them. When he gave them back to Krylov he said, "If she wants to take that breath of Russian air you talked about, best you hurry."

Past the Ubylinka control point and its grove of lights, Anna could see no signs of civilian life whatever. The highway was strongly fenced on either side. Border guards and soldiers minded the road where it went through the sparsely illuminated village of Gavry. Then the Mercedes was back in darkness, the low, saturated land stretching out to invisibility on either side, with a suggestion that somewhere artillery and armor were dug in, waiting for NATO.

"Without Anna, we'd be stuck back there like some of those poor sods they pulled aside." Anna smiled; she loved hearing Gayle's voice.

"Yes, trying to figure out whom to bribe."

"I nearly turned those poor guards to stone," she said.

Gayle looked back at her. "It's just the makeup. I'll give you a good scrubbing when we get where we're going."

"Meanwhile I can keep the crows out of the corn."

Anna thought it odd that a sad girl who felt dead inside could joke about keeping the crows out of the corn and turning guards to stone, and being, as a poor facsimile of Svetlana, quite the hag. Why was she not wrapped in sorrow and silence? How could she speak?

"We are in a mysterious place, like the Bermuda Triangle." Anna heard in Krylov's voice the hope that, as their cheerful tour guide, he could steer them clear of melancholy. "Latvia says Russia refused entry to two thousand cargo vehicles. Russia says no, it was ten thousand. Eight thousand lorries are, what, out in the swamps?"

"Sounds like the point of no return," said Gayle.

That sounded about right to Anna.

"Soon we come to Ostrov."

"Ostrov."

Anna leaned forward, eager to hear more about Peter's earlier life.

"Mickey Williams and I stood nuke alerts at RAF Brüggen, up by the Dutch border. Ostrov was one of our secondaries. It had a bomber base shaped like a tilted letter B. The stem of the B was the runway. The two loops were taxiways sprouting revetments."

"Good memory," Krylov said.

"We memorized everything. Once launched you're too low and fast to read charts. Our first look at the target would've been when we popped up to lob our nuke."

Krylov made a face. "Would you have done it?"

Gayle watched the Russian for a moment. "Why not? The assumption was we wouldn't be going in at all if you lot hadn't already nuked Trafalgar Square."

"Those were the days."

Outside Ostrov, Krylov stopped the car at a checkpoint and a pair of GAI highway patrol police took quick looks at the three passports. When one of them peered into the Mercedes, Anna averted her face. Nothing was said. She thought some money might have changed hands.

Anna lay back and watched Russia wheel past her window. She envisioned Peter waiting with his friend, Mouse, in some sort of airplane with a nuclear bomb hung under its wing. Then the word coming over the radio: *Attention all aircraft, attention all aircraft. Attack the Soviet aerodrome shaped like the letter B. I repeat…*

What would the Englishmen have said? Jolly good? Tally-ho? But then off he and Mouse would have gone, following the flat terrain at great speed, to drop their bomb on poor Ostrov aerodrome, and then to be destroyed by anti-aircraft fire or run out of fuel and crash. She closed her eyes against the images of the Russian town consumed by fire, and Peter's aircraft exploding like a New Year's rocket.

Would you have done it?

Can you imagine anything I wouldn't do?

I can imagine a lot of things. I can imagine you taking off my clothes and vomiting at what you see.

I can imagine my cleaving to you like a hideous mermaid and taking you down and down and down...

Ah, Christ, she was crying! The disease had left her not just ugly, but contemptible as well. Christ!

What she had to keep in mind, Anna told herself, wiping at a slurry of powder and tears, was that Peter knew everything there was to know about her appearance and anatomy and bodily functions; he knew more than she did about what the disease had done to her. He had not once flinched from handling, caressing, cleaning, feeding the thing she had become. He had put no distance between them.

Had he radiated the faintest signal of revulsion, she would have detected it, and she had detected nothing. Had she died, he would have followed. They were like Siamese twins, joined at the heart. This brought a little smile to Anna's improvised face.

"Viktor, when do I get to take off my hag disguise?"

"After we get you settled."

Settled where? In an unused dacha north of St. Petersburg, just as the Russian winter began to take herself seriously. The authorities would discover their frozen bodies in the spring. Or perhaps it would be the Americans, who would arrive in their helicopter or Sports Utility Vehicle, or on snowmobiles. She imagined a combat formation of tattooed men with weapons that looked like Martian ray guns. But they would be too late. The monster they wanted would have vanished without a trace, lost to Mother Russia's terrible winter.

Another airport went by on their left. An airplane climbed into the weather and disappeared. The runway lights winked out, two by two.

"Pskov," said Krylov. "Falling apart for centuries. In Leningrad we say there is nothing there but Pushkin's coin collection."

"Peter, do you know this aerodrome?" asked Anna.

Gayle shook his head. "Pushkin's coins weren't targeted."

Anna smiled at this man she could no longer live without and curled up in her corner. She gave Russia a last, fond look and put her head against the seat. Soon she was back in her abyssal sleep, dreaming of the terra-cotta army of men she'd turned to stone.

GAYLE LOOKED AT THE ROAD MAP OF NORTHWESTERN RUSSIA KRYLOV had given him, tracing their route with an index finger. They had picked up the M20 at Ostrov, and followed its long, straight course northward, now and then turning a few degrees to a new heading and then another long, straight line. They might have been on a bomb run, so untroubled was their path by terrain; the place was all marshes and lakes and winding rivers on their way to freezing. The usual caravan of lorries toiled down the verge.

He glanced at the big Russian, who leaned into the steering wheel as if to push the Mercedes along that bit faster. Krylov's attraction to his Motherland was almost palpable in the close confines of the car; he was as helpless to resist her gravitation as an iron filing summoned by a magnet.

Gayle smiled, wondering whether Britain held such attraction for him. He supposed she did not, although, thinking back, he could remember flying home from the States and having his heart lift at the sight of the Scilly Isles, those little rocks awash in the sea.

Ahead of them, a dome of light paled the night sky and he could discern a horizon of low, rounded hills thinly capped with black trees. The illumination would be St. Petersburg. It meant their long journey was nearly over and that their ordeal by dacha would soon begin.

Gayle wondered whether he was up to it. Back in Herr Trauber's chalet, Plan Zed had made sense to him, and he had been confident of carrying it out with a steady hand. Now, as this new, more isolated exile became real, he felt that confidence wane. Why and how had he become so accepting of misery and death? Had the thread of his life really been spun and measured, and now merely waited for the shears? Would chalice number ten really have walked into the snow with a can of petrol and a gun?

Why would a man destroy himself to prevent the spread of a disease that, as Anna proved, was survivable? The world would not end if he remained loose and contagious in it. It was a dangerous old world anyway. Those nuke alerts with Mouse, ready to raze entire cities for Queen, country, and market democracy—nobody thought *that* especially monstrous. Maybe this dangerous old world didn't need him as its goat. He might just go forward with his life, and when the mild flu returned, keep to himself, as he was doing now.

Ah, but how could he keep to himself and look after poor Anna, coiled there asleep in the back seat? They were bound. They had to make some sort of life together, one without this self-imposed quarantine. In that life, when he met a pretty girl at a press conference there'd be no more Hotel Victoria, just a tip of his hat, and back he would go to Anna.

Would he miss those pretty girls?

Right now, he missed them very much, although he knew that what he regretted was not so much the women as his memory of their clean beauty, their sweet-scented clothes, the odors flowing off their healthy bodies. He shut his eyes, recalling Anna as she'd been on their first day, so exactly what he'd wanted for that Friday afternoon.

What do we do between eating and drinking in your favorite place on earth?

We fall in love.

Gayle recalled the exchange with amused wonder. He rather missed the chap who could sweep pretty strangers off to dirty weekends with such ease, that good-looking former squadron leader, old Whitey Gayle. Cool as liquid nitrogen, that one was, clean and shaved, no flesh or blood or dead bees under the fingernails, none of this fucking stench that would never quite go away. They said it was only in tanks you couldn't smell your own shit. Well, they didn't know about Herr Trauber's little hellhole in the forest.

But, if he thought of the chalet, of all that had happened there, of his final hours with Huey, Dewey, and Louie, the idea of carrying such a nightmare to even one other person was repugnant; spreading it to hundreds, thousands....Gayle shuddered. His nerve, which he realized had begun to fail, recovered.

One might be a monster, but one needn't think or act like one. Before, when he'd had a nuclear weapon under his wing, he would have used it. He was no longer capable of razing cities full of innocent strangers. Now, with another kind of weapon ticking away inside him, he knew he would keep it contained, one way or another. He would remain Jekyll and it could be Hyde, slinking around within, dying of neglect as its viral tritium decayed to nothing.

So, yes, chalice number ten *would* walk out with a can of petrol and a gun. He *would* destroy himself to keep the monster in check. It was not Clotho spinning and Lachesis reckoning the length of his existence, but him and this girl with whom he had fallen in love. Atropos could bloody well keep her scissors until they called her.

A Russian winter with the girl of my dreams in an abandoned dacha. I wouldn't miss it for the world.

Beyond the nearest line of hills an airport beacon pulsed its green and white welcome. "Pulkovo," Krylov said. "Was Leningrad also one of yours?"

"They kept that one for the submarines."

"A miracle we got through those times."

"Back then it made a weird sort of sense."

"It was a real plague. Everybody was sick with it. You were, I was. Children believed it would happen at any moment. A real epidemic of the mind."

"Well that one is over."

Krylov shook his head. "No it's not. I used to think I, we, could stop it. Now I think we may have delayed it a few decades." He glanced at Gayle. "I hope to do better with this one."

"Mine, you mean?"

"Ours."

They were silent for another few kilometers, then Krylov said, "We need to get you ready for winter. By the airport we have an O'Key, what we call a Hypermarket. Everything is there. So we put petrol in the car, I buy food and maybe some clothing and kerosene. Vodka. Warm coats. Wellies. Whatever I can think of. And I get some rubles out of the machine for you."

"Let me write you a check."

"You can be sure Emerson is watching your money. All he has to do is march into your bank and whisper *War on Terror* and everyone begins kissing his feet. We need to keep you invisible a while longer." Krylov held up his palm to still further argument. "Look, I am well paid. I spend hardly anything. Besides," and he smiled mischievously, "I owe you a car."

It was as if the Motherland had opened her arms to him. By the time Krylov had stowed the mountain of supplies from the O'Key in the Mercedes the stratus deck had lifted and begun to fissure, so that the illumination from a rising gibbous moon dripped like mercury upon the afternoon's snow. It was so beautiful that he was tempted to take Anna and Peter into the lovely heart of St. Petersburg. Ah, well, another time.

When they were beyond the city's glare, the stars popped out to greet them. Krylov craned his neck as he drove, picking out the Big Bear, and then its little brother, or was it the child, with the Pole Star a bright jewel in its tail. Because the two bears were almost overhead at this latitude, Krylov had the dizzying sensation of standing in the center of the universe as it carouseled around him.

"If I were a greater man," he said, waving a hand toward the horizon, "I would have a nice dacha over there in Solovyavka. I would be in the Ozero cooperative with Putin. Fly there in my business jet. But the Krylovs were not intended for greatness. My parents were such good communists, there was never a kopeck to spare."

Krylov followed the main road northward for an hour, then turned off on a narrow track that wound through wetlands sliced by finger lakes. They had been created, he was told as a boy, when the Big Bear reached down and raked the narrow isthmus with his claws. In another few weeks they would all be sealed in ice.

Krylov had come to the dacha in every season, even in the dead of winter, when it was like living in an ice cube and there were fresh wolf tracks every morning near their door. He had skated for kilometers on the frozen lakes and flown across the buried land on waxed wooden skis.

In the spring thaws, he had ruined countless boots and nearly sunk the family Lada in the bogs. He had trekked through golden grasses and flowers and legions of humming, biting insects in the hot summer, his skin going brown as an Inuit's with the sun. His family had grown currants and apples and cabbages and carrots, hunted wild berries and mushrooms in the woods. Why, he wondered now, had he given up coming here? He resolved to do better, once all this was over.

As though conjured by his reverie, the dacha came into view through the stands of birch and stunted firs. The driftwood-colored structure was half-hidden among evergreens and feral fruit trees on the far side of a broad lake, where fragile panes of ice had formed. Krylov eased the Mercedes along the rutted track that circled for almost a kilometer westward around the lake to a causeway barely wide enough for a car, leading to a gravel space near the dacha.

It could barely be called a cottage, just the single floor of three rooms beneath a sagging shingle roof, fronted by a fence of wooden boards leaning every which-way. The house was put together like a rude toy, never painted, and as rough as a pine fruit-box, as if the builder had gone into the forest with an axe and come out with this rudimentary structure. On one side was a porch that had always been dangerously frail, with an improvised shower enclosure at the back, and in the shadows behind the place, an outhouse.

The only finishing touches were someone's attempt to scallop a line of wooden sea waves over the entrance door and a small pentagram cut in the shutters by the single narrow window, which stared blindly at the world. A rusted iron weather vane dithered on the shingle roof, searching for the wind.

They stopped and got out into the silence.

Anna said. "It's just what my father wanted for his piece of forest land."

"I have no idea how my parents managed it. They were such believers. They gave everything and got very little and died young. So much for the idea of from each according to his abilities, et cetera."

Anna looked around them. "It's very still. In winter it must be amazing." She shivered involuntarily.

"Amazing isn't the word for it. But the cottage is pretty tight, and quite private, as you see. Seventy kilometers from Finland, the same from St. Petersburg. Not even Google knows it is here. When I was a boy I called it The Middle of Nowhere."

Gayle laughed.

"What's funny?"

"We called the chalet Thin Air. So now we've gone from Thin Air to the Middle of Nowhere."

As they spoke the door opened and a man appeared, poised on the upper step. In the moonlight he seemed not merely old, but dead, his large face creased and pitted as a barren planet, held together by a scruffy grey tangle of beard and a shock of short white hair that looked as if he cut it himself. He had the thorax and shoulders of an Altiplano Indian, balanced on spindly legs; he seemed to carry an invisible piano on his back. His tight, dark suit barely covered his collarless white shirt, and his freshly shined boots were rimmed with mud. His hands were the size of wicket-keeping gloves. He took a moment to study the Mercedes and the people.

"Here is Axel," Krylov cried in Russian.

The old man stopped, tilted his head like a dog trying to work a puzzle, then exposed huge yellow dentures in a broad grin and cupped his cheeks in his big hands. "Master Viktor, is that really you?"

"None other." Krylov strode over to his old comrade and embraced him, with a kiss on both cheeks, and started to lift him in the air.

"Oh, Master, please don't pick me up. I can't abide being off the ground."

Krylov released him. "It's wonderful to see you, Axel. Why has it been so long?"

"I wondered the same thing. I wondered would I see you again."

"You will always see me again. Here, meet my friends, Peter and Anna."

Axel stepped forward, put his heels together, and made a short bow.

"No, no, no, like this." Krylov extended Axel's hand for his companions to shake. "Democracy, democracy."

The old man let his hand be clasped, but took a step back from the newcomers when this ordeal by equality was over. Democracy was for those who could afford it.

"Axel, Peter is English. He is working on a novel."

"A novel?"

"Yes, like *Anna Karenina.*"

"I've seen that book. It must weigh a kilo."

"Peter's novel will come in at two kilos, at least."

"That's a prodigy of a book, sir."

"He needs a quiet place to work."

"Well, there is nowhere quieter than here, not this side of the grave."

"Anna is from Vienna."

"And what is the matter with her?" Axel asked, staring at the rough, powdered face.

"She has had *ospa.*"

"Ospa! Merciful God, see what it has done to her."

Anna turned to Krylov. "Tell him I am merely ugly, not dangerous."

"What is she saying?" Axel leaned toward the meaningless sound of English, his head cocked to listen.

"She says she isn't dangerous."

"I never thought she was. It's just a shock to see what ospa can do to a pretty girl. But I don't fear it. Everybody had it in the old days. Sometimes it would come in, stay awhile, and leave, with little to remind us of its visit. But it could be terrible. One of my sisters died of it. It just ate her alive. So we must see that Mistress Anna gets plenty of food and rest. That's the way you get through the pox."

"Did you have it?"

Axel nodded. "All the boys in my family did. But none of us died. God was saving us for the war."

"But here you are."

"Yes, I got past ospa *and* the Germans. I alone. A miracle."

"May I leave these two in your care?"

"I'm glad to try, although I can barely care for myself."

"I will see that you have money. Have you a car?"

"The Lada you nearly lost in the mud."

"It's still running?"

"If I can keep running, it can keep running."

"Then you can drive into town."

"If I must."

"So now and then you can go to Kuznechny Market and find something special for the three of you. Anna can drive in with you. But not Peter. Peter has to write."

"I'm glad to do that, but I shall eat in my cabin."

"If they invite you, why not join them here?"

"Because I know my place."

"Your place, my friend, is where you can look after these two people." Krylov took Axel's two big hands in his and studied them. "I think you can still swing an axe with these great paws of yours. You can teach Peter how much wood a dachniki needs to cut in winter and how he gets water after the well freezes."

Axel laughed like a crow. Then, "How is their Russian?"

"Almost as good as your English."

"Ah, well, we shall all learn something from this."

"Tell no one they are here."

"That's easy enough. There's no one to tell."

"Tonight, make them feel at home. Show them how to lay the fire and heat water for the shower and use the lamps. See that they have plenty of wood. Stay with them for dinner, have a glass or two of vodka, so you are old friends already when you return in the morning. If you need me, take Anna into town and she can call."

"But aren't you staying?" Axel's old grey eyes gleamed. "I had hoped…."

"I have to work." He clapped Axel on his powerful back. "But we'll have other times."

"You promise?"

"I promise." Putting an arm around the old man's shoulders Krylov guided him over to the Mercedes. "Do you have a gun?"

"Of course. Everyone hereabouts has a gun."

"A true gun, a hunting rifle?"

"No, I just keep a small shotgun for doves when they come around. I used to have a proper rifle and went after wolves and deer and bear. Now I'd rather eat meat from a tin than shoot such creatures."

Krylov reached into the car and picked the Makarov pistol out of the glove box. "Do you remember this?"

Axel beamed. "An officer's pistol!"

"This one belonged to Maxim Trulov. You know, my friend from the old days."

"Oh, I remember. Very fine you both were, too, dressed up like regular field marshals. I thought at the time, 'This is like a folk tale with two dangerous bears in it.'" He leaned toward the pistol. "And you say this was his?"

"Yes."

"But doesn't he need it?"

"Maxim died some years back. His daughter gave it to me. If I give it to you, will you be able to use it?"

"I wasn't an officer. I was barely a grown man."

"That wasn't the question."

"You and your friend, you could hit anything with a pistol. I remember. But I could bring down a dove with a rock before I could hit one with this."

"I'm not worried about doves. What about men?"

"Men are another matter. I'd have no trouble bringing down a man." He made himself taller. "With a pistol or a rock, for that matter."

"Then it's yours."

Axel hefted the gun, which looked like a toy in his huge hand. He frowned. "How shall I know what man to shoot?"

"The one who wants to harm your new friends."

"And how shall I recognize him?"

"He is an American not quite as old as you, with bodyguards tattooed like convicted murderers."

"He sounds like someone to be avoided." Axel tucked the pistol into his jacket pocket, then peered at Krylov, reaching a hand up to touch the swollen nape. "Did one of those bodyguards do this? Did you grab him by the throat and shake him like a rat?"

Krylov shook his head. "I had a fall. Now let's unload the car."

XXVI

Commander Elizabeth Mabrey moved among the American ambassador's Thanksgiving guests in a kind of counter-eddy, keeping to the fringes. She had been in Vienna not quite two months and knew hardly anyone. But she enjoyed her anonymity. A uniform, like a mask, made one easy to spot, but difficult to identify. She liked to think that all she wore on her sleeve were three stripes.

She also liked the way she looked in Dinner Dress blues, small and trim in the waist-length cutaway jacket, the starched white shirt imparting a fine, strong curve to the chest without suggesting breasts. Her strawberry hair was freshly trimmed and brushed smoothly back, like a Dickens boy's, and she wore no make-up; she'd been born lightly freckled, with red lips and roses in her cheeks. She stood erect without stiffness and sipped her champagne, adrift among the promenading strangers.

But as she precessed around the room, seeming to study the art and furnishings of the residence, her attention remained fixed upon one figure at its center. The woman was nearly six feet tall and wore a cream-colored suit of raw silk. Her face, framed in a thick blonde wreath, was heart-shaped and intelligent, with none of the vacancy sometimes seen in the very pretty; her dark eyes seemed never to be idle, but always moving, always feeding.

Liz Mabrey had brought Sandy to the dinner dance, which Embassy-Vienna called The Turkey Day Buffet, to show her off without seeming to make any claims upon her. She had released Sandy into the room as she might have a macaw into an aviary of ravens and crows. At intervals Sandy would look up and scan the room until her eye caught Liz's, and both women smiled, reviving the spell that linked them.

Even such faint contact caused Liz's heart to melt and deepened the roses in her cheeks. Soon she and Sandy would have to break apart, again. "Too bad," Sandy told her, "you just fell in love with the wrong gender. It could happen to anyone."

Because they tried to keep their love a secret, their life together had been like crossing the Sahara, a parched eternity of separation punctuated by brief, clandestine pauses in oases along the way. Vienna was the oasis of the moment.

"The daughter of the regiment!"

Liz's heart sank. She shut her eyes briefly, composing herself, then turned toward the familiar voice. "Hello, Ralph."

"Hi, Liz," said Emerson, giving a slight bow. "Happy Thanksgiving." He wore a dark suit with an indigo shirt and a scarlet cravat tied like a shoelace.

"Nice tie, Ralph. Oscar Wilde?"

"Stefano Ricci. But you look fab'lous. Dinner Dress blue. My favorite. Makes me want to join the Navy." He nodded toward Sandy, who watched them from across the room. "Who's the knockout?"

"She's my cousin. From the States."

"Over for a visit."

"Yep."

"Is she a Mabrey?"

"She's a Marshall."

"Your mother's side?"

Liz nodded. "Her name's Sandra. But I fear she's already taken, Ralph. A nice boy back home. Bad luck."

Emerson laughed. "I can *see* she's taken."

Liz heard the sneer, felt the threat. She looked across at Sandy, who raised her head like a wary deer in an open field, sensing *something...*

"Let's walk over by the window where we can talk."

"Whoa. Everybody already thinks I'm your Thing. I don't want to encourage that."

"Not everybody. Just old Viktor. How is he, anyway?"

"I haven't seen him."

"But you work on the same floor."

"We avoid each other because he believes I'm the new Churches. I see to it that our paths don't cross."

"So you wouldn't know where our Russian pal is on this fine Thursday in November?"

Liz shrugged, relieved to be talking about Krylov instead of Sandy. "Inspecting the Leningrad II reactor."

"Really?"

"He got there last Tuesday morning. He called Oldenburg."

"And Oldenburg told you?"

"He told everybody he met. Viktor drove up there, wasting an airline ticket, and he got there a day late. Klaus wants to fire him. I don't think he can."

"Where is Viktor from?"

"No idea."

Liz became aware that Emerson was gradually edging her out of the crowd. "I think I'll be going," she said, starting to push past him.

"Not yet." He gripped her upper arm. "Stay a bit longer."

"Hands off, Ralph."

Emerson released her. "I need a little help on Viktor."

"Talk to Oldenburg."

"No, I'm talking to my old associate, Commander Elizabeth Mabrey."

"Old as in former. Send in Lamont."

"Lamont is too stupid. Also, he's temporarily indisposed."

"I'm going, Ralph."

"Commander, one thing I know about you is you really love the Navy. You're forty-two and up for captain. I could be looking at the first female CNO. But here's the thing…"

Liz tensed, as if to flee, but didn't move. She knew what was coming and the knowledge paralyzed her. She'd seen cattle freeze that way on the ramp when they smelled death waiting for them.

"Liz, I'm fighting a war on terror. Right now my ability to fight that war depends on my finding out where Krylov has been the past few days."

"With your resources, it should be a piece of cake."

"We thought that too. Conroy and I bluffed our way past Viktor's landlady and went through every damned thing in his flat. We found nothing. He lives like an orchid."

"I can't help you." Christ, her voice shook. Show some conviction, Commander.

"Sure you can. You work at the Agency, on the same floor. You can get into his office." Liz was shaking her head, but Emerson paid no attention. "Churches said Viktor's office was a world-class mess. But I bet it's messy in an organized kind of way, like a garage where the tools are piled all over the place, except the mechanic knows exactly where everything is. I think the office is where Krylov keeps his little secrets. With your informed eye, I bet you could winkle out where Viktor went on his way to Leningrad II."

"Why do you care?"

"I care because he didn't go alone. He's hidden some people I, meaning the United States of America, want to talk to. It's important, Liz."

"For the war on terror." Almost a whisper.

"You got it."

Liz paused, gathering herself, willing her cheeks to pale, her heart to wind down. She felt as she had at age seven, trembling on the high platform, the blue water of the pool impossibly far below. She shut her eyes and leapt. "I won't help you, Ralph. I can't be your new whore. Sorry." She looked into his eyes, then quickly looked away, frightened by the menace there.

Emerson waited several beats, letting her soak up the threat he posed. "You know what the man said, give me a lever and tell me where to stand and I will move the world? Well, I will damn sure move yours, Liz." He looked at Sandra Marshall and waved. "A nice boy back home. What a crock."

He leaned closer to Liz, his breath moist and wine-scented against her face. "You've heard of don't ask, don't tell?"

"That's over, Ralph." Her face must glow like a brake light now, she thought.

"Sure it is. And unless you fucking ask I will fucking tell and you'll be doing whatever girls do as a disgraced civilian. No fourth stripe. No admiral's star. Maybe no Sandra either. Why would pussy of that quality want a failed *ex*-person?"

"That's enough, Ralph."

Emerson fashioned an evil, hungry grin. "I don't let my people keep secrets, Liz. I know all about your trysts, in the States, in Japan, in Kuwait, in Vienna. You two have redefined 'kissin' cousins.' You've made it hot."

"The Navy doesn't care."

"It doesn't care what you are. But it sure God cares what you do. The camera doesn't lie, that's what they used to say. Of course it lies all the time. But ours is the real deal. I don't care what the Navy thinks. We'll let your Sandy tell the Navy all about it under oath. We'll let her shuffle through our deck of dirty pictures. How long do you think it'll take to break that beauty? A minute? Two?"

Liz's deep blue eyes gleamed, the room distorted in a lens of tears, which she angrily wiped away. Emerson was bluffing, she insisted to herself. Don't ask don't tell was over. It didn't matter if he outed her, although she knew it did. Well, then she would out him, reveal the lunatic within. They would end like the Gingham Dog and the Calico Cat. Okay, she thought. Okay, I can do that.

But she couldn't shake the image of Sandy being dismantled in a courtroom. Liz looked up. Sandy was watching her, the lovely face a pallid, frightened mask. Liz gave her a teary smile that said: *You know what's happening, we've been here before. It's how we have to live, one ugly bargain at a time.*

"There, there, Commander. Haven't you heard? Boys don't cry."

XXVII

Years earlier, when he was recovering from his Bolivian adventure and post-Soviet funk, Krylov had told Svetlana, "Not to worry, the bear is back on his unicycle." She had closed her eyes and imagined Uncle Viktor in the squalid ring of a Russian circus, pedaling round and round in shackles before the nearly empty stands, his fangs bared in a grin of hatred. Now, she thought, the bear is off the unicycle, which, in her mind's eye, lay in the sawdust, a crumpled knot of rubber and red metal.

Why, Sveta wondered, would Krylov return from St. Petersburg so wary and preoccupied? Al-Rabiah was gone. The Americans had been thwarted. Anna and Peter had been spirited away to "the dacha" and the care of "Axel."

In a way, Svetlana was annoyed by his distraction. They had been running close to something romantic, and now he'd veered away, into this preoccupation with Anna and Peter and the bloody Americans. It was a shame, because Vienna was having the kind of winter that brought joy to the Russian heart and caused couples to put on their fur coats and ushankas and walk close together, as if conjoined.

The snows had begun in earnest during the first week in December, and they were frequent and deep. Warnings of falling cornices of ice adorned the pavement. The Autobahn suffered the usual multi-vehicle wrecks in the winter fogs off the Danube. The city lay desolate and empty and beautiful, the boulevards without traffic, and over everything, a wonderful hush.

Vienna's large population of giant figures wrought in marble and stone stoically accepted the Arctic cold. Wearing little or nothing, they stood on their plinths and on rooftops among television dishes and cables. Snow crusted on their hair, beards, helmets, swords and shields, and icicles drooped from their finely chiseled noses and chins.

The tiny huts of the Christkindlmarkt clustered around the Rathaus, transformed by thousands of white bulbs into a luminous spaceship recently landed on the snowbound square. Svetlana and Viktor walked among the huts, sampling this and that, stopping for a Glühwein, then strolling off into the crowd, sipping the hot, sweet concoction. It made her dreamy, to be walking in this intimate way with her favorite man.

"Have you heard anything?" He always asked.

"Only the one card." She always gave the same reply. A fortnight before Christmas, she'd received a postcard showing the Hermitage at night, above the mirror of the Neva. *Happy Xmas* was written on the back.

"They might have said a little more," Krylov complained.

"Not with everybody watching."

Krylov had returned from St. Petersburg and the Leningrad II inspection worn out, his bloodshot eyes set in dark hollows. His Mercedes looked as if it had been through the Great Patriotic War. Of course, Oldenburg had been waiting eagerly to tell Krylov he had finally gone too far, wasting an expensive airline ticket and arriving at his post a day late.

"He said, 'You're finished, and good riddance,'" Krylov told Svetlana afterward. "I was taking this in, when in comes Juan Carlos Imler. 'Good news,' says he. I would have to repay the Agency the cost of the ticket. But they would give me mileage because I hadn't had to rent a car in St. Petersburg. As for being a day late, Juan Carlos said he'd heard from the reactor managers at Sosnovy Bor. How clever I'd been to arrive a day later than they'd suspected. A real surprise for a change."

"You saved the world without losing your job. What a man."

"Yes, exactly. For the moment work is all right."

"But...?"

"Emerson came to my flat while I was up there."

"How do you know that?"

"I could tell I'd had visitors. That's just something I do. But Frau Steiner told me. They gave her some story and she let them in. I told her that was not a very Austrian way to behave."

"What did they find?"

"Only what I keep there: Nothing." His voice, which had grown friendly and warm telling his Imler-to-the-rescue story, turned to metal.

Svetlana made herself always available to him. She would meet him at UN City for lunch in the cafeteria, then go to the commissary to load up with red champagne from Russia, vodka, Johnny Walker, gin, and the stuff of further pelminis. She shepherded him to the Burgkino for their *nth* viewing of *The Third Man,* and to the State Opera for *Eugene Onegin.*

They walked everywhere, arm in arm like a young couple, the snow fluttering around them. They bought frankfurters from a Würstel stand in the old Jewish quarter and strolled through the snow and steam along the Danube canal. She went with him to sit on a wooden bench in Türkenschanzpark with a bag of corn to feed the big crows from Ukraine, who strutted and hopped around them in the whispered fall of snow.

"How is it," Krylov wondered aloud, "they are all black, while crows in Moscow and Leningrad have grey capes?"

"Trotskyites?"

"Of course."

At such moments, Svetlana hoped that he was finally thinking of something besides their hidden friends and the Americans. But, no, when they were once again in motion she could feel the tension in his body return. He might have been a soldier on patrol. It was as if he found the very atmosphere in Vienna smoky with menace, and expected any minute that his adversary would…what?

"What are you waiting for?"

"I'm not sure. I feel something is out there. I'm waiting to see what it is."

"Would Emerson attack you?"

Krylov shrugged. "I can see where he might decide I'm too much in his way. I think of poor Maxim, picked off by a sniper from the Wheel."

Picked off. Sveta shuddered, seeing Papa prone in the reddening snow of the Hauptallee.

"But it's not just Emerson. Sometimes I see us as being like those chocolate rabbits at Easter, except we haven't been dipped in chocolate, we've been dipped in blood. In death. I told everyone good bye up there, hugs, kisses, a few tears. Peter followed me out to the car. He said he wanted to thank me for keeping them safe. But then he said an odd thing. He said, 'First time I saw you, back in the forest, I thought: *Joe Black.*'

"'Joe Black?' I asked. 'Who's Joe Black?'

"'Death in human form. From a film,' he said. Then he grinned like a cancer victim and said, 'If things go wrong and my nerve fails, you have to help me, Joe.'"

Krylov gave Sveta an anguished look. "I am trying to believe that if we wait awhile Peter will be free, the ospa will evaporate or die or whatever it does at the end, and the Americans will lose interest. But

I also think of what it means if ospa decides to stay, and Peter's nerve cracks, and I must become this Joe Black person for him. Death in human form. Christ."

"No wonder the bear jumped off his unicycle."

Krylov laughed. "You remember the unicycle."

"My dear Uncle Viktor, there is nothing about you I don't remember." For a moment, looking into his eyes, which were suddenly attentive, Sveta expected to be swept into his arms, to be lifted into the air by a big, contented man. To be kissed.

But then he cocked his head, listening like prey to the silent park, to the chatter of the Ukrainian crows. "Oh, Viktor," she murmured. But he didn't hear her. He was, as usual, thinking of something else.

SVETLANA REFUSED TO SETTLE for a perfunctory Christmas. Although Krylov was often with her and Anna at this time of year, Sveta secretly regarded this Christmas as their first together. They would, by God, celebrate.

She insisted that Krylov come with her to buy a small tree and some new handmade ornaments in the Rathausplatz market, and new lights, they had to have new lights for the tree. On Christmas Eve she made Viktor dress up in one of his fine old KGB-abroad suits and take her to a late lunch at the Palais Schwarzenberg. He looked quite grand, and, for the moment, almost happy.

Svetlana thought she'd come out looking rather pretty. She wore an embroidered suit of charcoal wool, a scarlet cashmere scarf, black sheepskin boots, and a fur newsboy cap that had been two sizes too big when Maxim gave it to her on her twelfth birthday. She thought of it as a gift from an unfortunate Arctic fox. "In that cap," Krylov told her, "you look like a girl."

"I am a girl."

"I mean a very young girl."

"Like I used to be."

"Exactly."

Later, at her flat, Sveta handed him a large flat box wrapped in silver paper and a blue ribbon. She imagined his troubles flying away like startled sparrows. When she went to the kitchen to pour two vodkas, she heard him opening the paper with the diffident care of someone unaccustomed to receiving gifts, then slowly refolding the paper and coiling the ribbon. Tears came to her eyes. She wiped them away and brought in the glasses.

"Sveta, it's beautiful." Krylov held up a black cashmere turtleneck and turned it this way and that. Then he gave her a serious look. "But, really, you can't spend so much on me."

She lifted her chin like a Kirov ballerina. "I can do whatever I wish." Her eyes glinted with pleasure. "Try it on. It may be too small."

Krylov stood up and wriggled into the pullover, which fit him with some comfortable room to spare. "I've never had one of these before."

"It makes you look dangerous."

"It's wonderful." Krylov pulled her into his arms for an Uncle Viktor hug, careful to keep some space between them. But Svetlana melted against him and kissed him on the lips, then quickly moved away, blushing furiously.

"Sorry," she said.

"Don't be," said Krylov, coming to her and tucking her back inside his cashmere-clad arms for a moment. "But," he went on, releasing her, "I did not come exactly empty-handed." He found his coat and fumbled through its pockets, then brought out an oblong box, wrapped in turquoise paper with a yellow ribbon. "Here I was, in Russia again without you, so, well, I made a detour."

Svetlana unwrapped her gift and opened the box. She lifted out a necklace of glowing amber beads in several strands, each bead isolated by tiny golden grommets. "Oh, Viktor."

"Try it on. It may be too small."

She lifted the necklace and studied it for a moment. "It looks almost alive."

"I came through Pushkin on my way back and thought, I must get a piece of Russia for my dear girl back home. I remembered your mother's amber bracelet. So I went to Tsarskoye Selo and did some shopping."

"But it must have cost a fortune."

Krylov shook his head and changed the subject. "Let me help you." He moved behind her and, while she held up her thick black hair, draped the necklace around her neck, which, he saw now, was long and the color of ivory, without even a freckle. "Amazing," he murmured. Sveta held her breath.

He snapped the catch together and settled it around her neck. Then he leaned down and kissed her nape and put his arms once more around her. They stood that way for what seemed a long time, but was just a minute or two, unmoving and quiet as statues. Finally Krylov said, "Speaking of dangerous," and let her go.

Svetlana fingered her amber beads, as if she hadn't heard him. Her cheeks burned, desire stoked a delightful fire within. At last, she thought, we're getting somewhere. But then, looking at him, she saw he had already begun to drift again. He sank into his corner of the sofa and took a long pull at his vodka.

"As I was driving away from the dacha," he began, like a man telling himself a story, "I looked back. The oil lamps were lit, reflecting on the lake outside, and on the snow. The window was golden with light. I could see figures moving inside. It was beautiful. Beautiful and sad."

As the weeks went by, Svetlana did her best to keep her distracted bear occupied. Krylov cooperated as best he could. He allowed her to drag him to Stephansdom for Epiphany mass, although neither of them believed in much of anything, and to the Volksoper's *Der Fledermaus*, despite his horror of operettas. They took the odd meal at the Bürgerhof on Währingerstrasse, or went out for Chinese near Stephansdom or had venison or pheasant at a rustic Gasthaus just off the Gürtel. Some evenings they settled for a bowl of nuts and pickles in the fine bars at the Sacher, the Bristol, the König von Ungarn.

450

A few vodkas usually weakened Krylov's grip on his preoccupations, dropping him back into Sveta's presence, at least for a little while. But on this late-January evening, when he and Sveta were having a second drink in the Blue Bar, Krylov would not, or could not, relax. He remained tightly coiled and tense.

"What's the matter?"

"Someone's been going through my stuff at work."

Svetlana laughed, relieved; he was merely going crazy. "I've seen your office. How can you tell?"

"Trust me, I can tell. So finally I set out a few hairs to see if anything disturbed them. After that, it stopped."

"He saw the hairs."

"No, he found what he was after."

THE NIGHT LAY FREEZING COLD AND CLEAR OVER THE CITY'S BLANKET of old snow, and quiet, except for a distant clang of traffic and the happy exclamations of masked Austrians headed home from fancy-dress parties. They streamed along the pavement, through pools of light from the streetlamps, toward Peter Jordanstrasse and the Gürtel to find a tram or taxi. There were faux diplomats with scarlet sashes, pretty girls dressed as black cats under their fur coats, Arabs, kings, queens, cowboys, Indians; they appeared suddenly in the spheres of light, then vanished into darkness, like people in a dream.

Everyone was a little tipsy, but no one was honest-to-God drunk. Like vampires, they would spend tomorrow hidden in their quotidian lives, waiting for another night of wine and fancy dress to relieve them of identity and inhibition. As the year decelerated toward Ash Wednesday and forty bracing days of Lent, they danced faster and faster.

Watching them, Liz Mabrey felt a pang of envy, for her own personal Ash Wednesday had arrived earlier that afternoon, when she watched Sandy cross the security barrier at Schwechat and vanish into the shops and cafés of the boarding area. So long, gaiety.

She huddled in the shadows near a stone house that stood as though abandoned among its ancient trees, one narrow window on the ground floor dimly lighted, not a sound beyond the occasional yapping of a small dog somewhere within. A Freudian impulse, Liz supposed, had put her into the nautical mufti—the pea coat, watch cap, and black turtleneck—of an ordinary seaman. She smiled into the darkness. Very ordinary. Everybody was in costume tonight.

A figure appeared farther up the road, a big man in silhouette, approaching at a brisk walk. As he crossed a pool of lamplight she saw it was Krylov, and for a moment felt her nerve go soft with apprehension. He slowed, then stopped on the pavement. She thought he'd seen her. Putting on something like a smile, Liz stepped out of the shadows to greet him. "Viktor?"

Krylov waited a moment to reply. "What do you want?" He came a few steps closer, came within range, and she saw his face was dark with rage, his fists knotted for a fight. Her heart thumped. Then, realizing that he hadn't recognized her, she pulled off her watch cap and shook loose the strawberry hair. "It's me, Viktor."

"Commander Liz." His face cleared a little. He slowly opened his fists and took a deep breath. "We meet in the oddest places."

"I need to talk to you."

"Did Emerson send you?"

"Nobody sent me."

"Well, talk."

"Walk with me?" She put her watch cap back on. "Please?"

They strolled up the hill into Türkenschanzpark, snowbound and desolate except for the odd pack of costumed figures crossing pools of light along the pavement. Liz was aware that Krylov studied her; but when her eye caught his she saw no trace of the comradely affection they'd discovered at the cave. The rage had faded; there was just a pale contempt. What could she say?

I'm sorry I betrayed you?

I thought I had no choice?

The devil made me do it?

Krylov steered them to a wooden bench and brushed the snow away. They sat down. "So, now we talk."

Liz wished he would simply read her mind. "You're right to think I'm not quite my own person. I wanted to be. I tried to be." Her voice trailed off. Where was she going, anyway?

"But, what, God had something else in mind?" Krylov uttered a hard laugh. "Let me speed up this confession. Emerson asked you to do something you didn't like. You told him no. He threatened you. He would do X unless you did what he wanted."

"Yes, he would do X."

"X usually means we reveal somebody's dark secret."

She nodded. "I would have braved it out, but someone else was involved. That paralyzed me. So I've fouled myself. Next I burn my boats…"

Krylov held up his palm for quiet. "This thing Emerson got you to do was about me?"

"Yes."

"You were searching my office?"

"You knew."

"Everybody leaves a few tracks. But you stopped. You must have found what Emerson wanted. What was that?"

"He wanted to know where you went on the way to Leningrad II."

"Did he say why?"

"He said you had some people he needed to talk to. He said it was part of the war on terror."

"Like everything. But there was nothing to find."

"I kept telling that to Emerson, but he just turned the screw, saying there had to be *something.*" Liz rummaged in her pea coat pocket and brought out a folded sheet of paper. "Then I found this."

Krylov took it and spread it flat. It was a photocopy of an envelope addressed to a post box in Michurinskoye. "Shit," he said.

"It was lying on your desk."

"I meant to post it to Axel."

"Who is Axel?"

"An old friend. He helps me. I send him money."

"Usually when I showed anything to Emerson he'd just look at it and tell me to try harder."

"But not this time."

"No, this time he gave me a big smile and said, 'Bingo!'"

"When was this?"

"Three days ago."

"And finally you decide to tell me about it?"

"It took me this long to get brave enough to act. To send my friend back to the States. To decide to leave the Navy. I was afraid to tell you…"

"Afraid of me?"

"I'm so ashamed."

"You should be. You may have killed three good people. This envelope," and he waved the photocopy, "tells Emerson where Axel gets his mail. So next he finds the Krylov property. Then he and his boys go in."

"But why?"

"Because he thinks they can help America create another of those weapons everyone is afraid to use." Krylov leaned forward, his elbows on his knees, his body slack and without energy. Liz thought of an old father seeing his dead son. Finally Krylov said, "I will go to them." But his voice held not a trace of hope. He stood up awkwardly, as though in the grip of a Jovian gravity.

"Can I help?"

Krylov looked at her for a time, as if he'd forgotten she was there. "Thanks, but, no." Then he asked, "Is your friend boy or girl?"

"Girl."

"Ah."

"You know, don't ask, don't tell?"

"Yes. Nobody gets it right."

Liz gave him a sad smile. "So much for our winding up in each other's arms."

"Good bye."

"Good bye."

But when she was a few meters away, he called, "Commander Liz!"

She stopped and looked back. Krylov still stood by the park bench, hands in pockets. But the slackness she had seen earlier was gone. He seemed to have shed his grief and prepared himself for battle. He was grinning like a wolf.

"What?"

"We'll always have the cave."

Liz smiled and waved a hand at him. Then, costumed as a small and very ordinary seaman, she went off through the empty night, the frozen city blurred by tears, her good heart broken.

XXVIII

Three days. What could Emerson do in three days? Krylov thought it would take a day or two to turn up the dacha property records. But even if Emerson knew where it was, there was no way for him to get a Russian visa that quickly. That meant he and his boys would be sneaking in. From the Gulf of Finland in Zodiacs? Krylov thought not. They'd make a dash into Russia with that old Mi-8, and dash out with Anna and Peter. Dead or alive.

For a moment, Krylov's mind went blank with sorrow and guilt: he had absent-mindedly left the envelope where Liz could find it; he had failed people he'd promised to protect; he had handed victory to the Americans and something terrible to the world. Then his mind cleared. Perhaps he and Emerson were still synchronized, moving contrapuntally, like two parts of a duet.

The dacha was a long way to take the old helicopter without something giving out. So add a day or two to fix that. Would it have the same Bulgarian crew? He pictured Panov, who served as copilot, navigator, and engineer, working like a cartoon octopus to keep the machine flying. Krylov thought that, if he hurried, he could be there ahead of Emerson.

The morning after seeing Liz, Krylov took his seat on Air Austria's ten-fifteen flight to Pulkovo. Emerson, he thought, would just be boarding the unbranded Gulfstream, they would fly almost in formation toward....where? Lithuania. No, Finland. But not to Vantaa, to Lappeenranta, just thirty kilometers from the Russian line but big enough to take the Gulfstream. Twenty minutes to the dacha, the helicopter flying among the trees. Twenty minutes out. As he had a hundred times that morning, Krylov checked his watch.

The Pulkovo terminal's receiving area was packed with travelers, all waiting to pass through the filter of passport control. Only one booth was occupied, and the crowd would not queue, but eddied and jostled, with some weary nomads dropping off along the walls to wait out the ordeal. Here and there men were circling one another, ready to fight over a place in the amorphous line. Children wailed. The room smelled of soiled babies, vodka, cigarettes, anger, and despair.

Emerson would debark at Lappeenranta without such delays. He was just another foreign national loose in the European Union, like the Bulgarians waiting for him in the Mi-8.

A pretty blonde in the uniform of a Border Guards sergeant took Krylov's United Nations passport, paused over it a moment, and asked why he was coming back to Russia so soon. "You were here already in November."

"I can't leave her alone."

She smiled, the hard, sergeant face softened for just a moment, and she stamped his passport. Krylov crossed into the Motherland, took a deep breath, and looked at the sky outside the terminal. Only about an hour of grey light remained in the short winter day.

Soon Krylov was hurrying through the dying afternoon in a Nissan Pajero four-wheeler from Hertz. He thought the helicopter must be just lifting off in Finland, the nose lowered like a preying insect's as it fluttered toward the darkness rising in the east. He pushed the Pajero northward, ignoring the dance the tires were doing on the slick tarmac. He wanted to get to the dacha before the Americans did. He wanted to save Peter and Anna, or die with them in the Russian winter. He was afraid of finding them already dead.

But as he drove, it occurred to Krylov that he might have got everything wrong. Emerson wouldn't have bothered with property records. He would have gone straight for Axel, tortured what he needed out of him, and then taken Anna and Peter. The American could have made his move yesterday, or the day before. Krylov cursed himself, and Liz, and God.

Night had fallen by the time he reached the turnoff into the northern forest. He steered the Pajero along the narrow track and switched off its lights, then crept forward at an idle. Expecting to come upon more death, he was surprised when, through a screen of spruce, he heard, then saw, the Mi-8.

The helicopter was just visible in the faint light, a great insect squatting tail-low on an uneven meadow of snow, the five rotor blades whushing quietly in idle, the turbine a low hiss. They'd taken time to repaint the machine in winter white, with Russian markings.

Krylov felt momentarily weak with relief. He was not that far behind Emerson after all. He set the interior light switch for darkness and got out, leaving the engine to idle. The cold bit him immediately. He wished he'd worn something warmer than a leather jacket, khakis, and the black turtleneck Sveta had given him, which he had brought with him less for comfort than for luck.

The near shore of the lake lay about half a kilometer farther on. Krylov headed for it at a run, then stopped and lay prone behind a tangle of fallen birch, letting his breathing settle down. The lake was frozen hard, the evergreens bowed with their burden of snow. Across the strip of ice, the dacha looked like a wrecked ship sinking in dunes of white sand, but oddly festive with a garland of icicles around the eaves. A faint ochre light showed through the single window, but he saw no movement within.

Axel lay a few meters from the near shore, curled fetally at the end of a long carpet of his own blood, frozen now, like everything. He looked no bigger than a child, his oversized hands grasping at his thorax. Krylov crawled over and pulled him gently to the shore, then up behind a berm of snow. He felt for a pulse and found only a febrile whir, like the heartbeat of a dying sparrow.

The old man had not been shot; the blood came from his torso cracking open, as if he'd fallen out of the sky. They hadn't tortured him in any obvious way. They hadn't even bothered to take the Makarov, which was still tucked in his belt. Krylov removed it, wiped it with snow to clean off the blood, checked that it was loaded, and slipped it into his leather jacket.

Now the old eyes opened. "Master Viktor," Axel whispered, bringing a bloody bubble to his lips, "I waited for you." His dentures were out on the ice somewhere, and his words came slurred and barely audible, so that Krylov had to lean close to hear him.

"I went to my post box today."

"Don't talk." Krylov held some snow to the bloody lips, wiped the tangled beard.

"An American met me. He says to me, in very bad Russian, 'Show me the Krylov dacha, I wish to buy it.'"

"Tell me in the hospital."

Axel tried to laugh and brought up more blood. His breath whistled, his pulse revved crazily. "God has been after me all day, Master. I can't keep him waiting much longer. So I tell you now or never."

"Then tell me."

"'We can go in my helicopter,' says the man. My heart nearly stopped."

Krylov dabbed at the pink froth spreading through the beard. Axel, who hated being lifted even a centimeter off Mother Earth, would have protested, but the Emerson bullshit would have brought him around. Being a little feeble-minded makes one easy to trick.

"I stepped into the machine. It took off. And then," and here Axel's eyes widened with remembered fear, "I saw a tattooed man and recalled what you told me." Axel was silent for a time; his shattered little body shivered with memory and cold. "I tried to misdirect them. The American smelt it. He had the tattooed one hang me out the door. We were above the trees and going like the wind." Tears streamed down his ruined cheeks. "My nerve failed. I showed them your place."

"And then he let you fall."

"Like an egg to the pavement."

"Be quiet now."

"I failed Anna and Peter. I am so afraid for them now."

"And I failed you, my friend. I should not have brought them here."

Axel nodded, then his eyes closed and he seemed to drift off to sleep. Krylov slid the small figure, still curled around a terrible pain, into a declivity in the snow, and patted an insulating white wall around him. He felt again for a pulse. His fingertips sensed only a faint buzz; then, suddenly, as if a switch had thrown, nothing at all. One could only keep God waiting so long.

Krylov knelt in the snow beside the old man, his heart like an anvil in his chest, his rage guttering in a sea of grief. He thought he might stay just as he was and freeze, to be discovered, to thaw, in the spring. Then, remembering the others, he felt his rage rekindle. He gave himself a shake and crawled to a spot where he could see across the lake.

Although there was no moon, Krylov could make out the Americans. One dark figure crouched on the far shore of the lake, not quite aligned with the lighted window, but off to the right by a few meters. A second figure was prone, dressed in winter white like a proper Russian soldier, fifty meters to the left. Another hundred meters on, a third man in white lay prone with a long-barreled rifle. The sniper, if all else failed.

The first, thought Krylov, had to be Emerson, moving in to work his magic on the people inside the dacha. And one of the other two would be Lamont. Krylov thought he would like to find Lamont.

"Peter Gayle!" The call rose like an evangelist's howl of prayer. It was Emerson, his hands cupped around his mouth to form a megaphone. "Peter Gayle!"

The light in the window dimmed and went out.

"Peter, I'm not the enemy. You've nothing to fear from me. Viktor sold you to the Russians. I've come to take you out of here. You and the woman. Will you let me come inside?" Emerson stood up in plain sight of the window. "See?" He waved his arms in the air to show he had no weapon. "See?" The evangelical quaver gave the word several extra syllables.

Krylov backed away from the lake and, bent low, ran back to the Pajero. He got in and eased the vehicle into gear. The Hip was a couple of hundred meters away, with its nose slightly elevated and facing him. The idling rotor blades drooped listlessly, the tail rotor spun lazily at the end of a long upswept boom.

He studied the aircraft for a time, then set out toward it at the gallop, crossing the hummocks and frozen puddles and stands of withered marsh grass like a charging Cossack. The Pajero bucked and rocked, yawing crazily as its four wheels chewed at the earth and snow, the vehicle pitching and rolling nearly to its tipping points before somehow righting itself.

Fifty meters from the helicopter Krylov switched on his high beams and saw for an instant the startled faces of the pilot and, yes, it *was* Panov, in the greenhouse cockpit. At the last instant, Krylov spun the wheel to the left, sending the Pajero into a long skid. The right flank of the car struck the helicopter's starboard main gear, shedding steel and plastic shrapnel as the fender and side panels ripped away. The aircraft's wheel wobbled off into the darkness. The undercarriage buckled and the great machine listed to the right, slowly, like a doomed ship taking on water.

Krylov charged on, then spun the car around and headed back, crouched low beside the steering wheel, aiming at the flailing blades of the tail rotor, each a good meter and a half long. There was a great clatter as the blades struck and chewed their way through the Pajero's roof. Krylov felt their passage just above his spine, felt a tip whip through his leather jacket below the shoulder, but somehow not ripping him open. Then he was past them, in the clear. Krylov switched off his lights and pushed the tattered car onward, into the woods on the far side of the field, where he shut it down and got out to watch.

Spinning with mad eccentricity, the twisted blades of the tail rotor tore themselves apart, flinging spears of aluminum into the night. As the tail rotor disintegrated, the main rotor tips tore at the earth. The big craft writhed in mechanical agony as the blades beat themselves to pieces in a shower of soil and snow.

Krylov smiled, thinking of Panov and the pilot furiously trying to shut the thing down as it jerked them around like dolls. Once the turbines were stopped, the craft ceased its frenetic dance and lay broken on the snowfield. Krylov could see tiny figures dancing around the wreckage, and hear snatches of what sounded like Bulgarian. Nobody was going to be dropped out of that Hip anytime soon.

He circled away from the helicopter, back into the birches and pines, into the greater darkness. From the direction of the lake he could hear Emerson.

"*The fuck's going on?*" Then, "*Conroy, go find out the fuck's going on!*"

The nearer figure rose from the snow and jogged off toward the helicopter, his special forces rifle cradled like a football in one arm.

Krylov moved closer. The third man was still in position, the long barrel of his rifle still lay along a rise of snow. Emerson had retreated to the rim of the lake. "Peter Gayle? Gayle?" The evangelist had evidently lost some of his belief. "Peter?"

The third man, the sniper, was now ten meters ahead of Krylov, no doubt distracted by the Conroy fellow's leaving the field. A sweet, infantile odor, something between candy and baby oil and shit, drifted on the night. Krylov recognized it. Very quietly, he wriggled forward over the snow, the cocked Makarov in his right hand.

Lamont lay in his winter camouflage, his entire attention focused on what Emerson was doing. He held a Dragunov SVD sniper rifle against his cheek, with the sling wrapped around one arm to steady the weapon. He moved the barrel slightly to watch Emerson, then back to cover the dacha entrance, then back to Emerson, humming something and tapping his left foot. Then, sensing the intruder, Lamont flipped over and brought up the rifle. "Whozit? Conroy?"

Krylov kicked the rifle barrel aside. As Lamont tried to gain his feet, Krylov kicked the man's jaw with all his strength. Lamont fell back, momentarily stunned. Before he could recover Krylov put the Makarov against the man's left knee and fired. Muffled by the trouser cloth, the shot was a soft *pop!*

"Ah, Jeez, shit, Christ," cried Lamont, falling to one side.

"Be quiet." Krylov pressed the Makarov against the other knee, and fired. *Pop!* Lamont screamed, his hands gripping both thighs. "Be quiet." Krylov put the muzzle of the Makarov under Lamont's chin, which twitched uncontrollably. "Quiet."

Emerson stood, head cocked, listening. "Lamont? You okay? Lamont?"

"Quiet," said Krylov. With his free hand he worked the sling off Lamont's arm and put the rifle to one side in the snow. "Now, go wait for Emerson in the helicopter."

"I can't, you fucking destroyed my legs."

"You can crawl."

"Druther be dead."

"I know." Krylov moved the Makarov down to Lamont's crotch and pressed the muzzle against something soft and small.

"Please don't shoot me there."

"Then go."

Lamont put out his powerful arms and dragged himself out into the open, leaving a glaze of blood on the snow behind him. Krylov watched him make his painful way to the near shore of the frozen lake and sprawl on the ice, exhausted. After a moment, Lamont looked back at Krylov, nodded his head as if to say, *I know, to the helicopter.* Then he pulled himself out across the frozen lake into the growing darkness.

Krylov stretched out prone with the Dragunov, and took a look at Emerson through the sight. The American had aged since Krylov had last seen him; perhaps he'd grown old this afternoon. But he didn't look afraid of anything. Even when his eye caught the movement of Lamont's labored crawl onto the lake ice, he didn't look afraid, just angry, ready as always to blow up the world.

Go on, it's an easy shot from here. Go on, take him. Go for the heart or the head. But do it. Viktor, you won't get another chance like this one.

Poor Sasha, the young Spesnaz sergeant of yore, had been right the first time Krylov had seen Emerson, and he was right this time. Krylov settled himself into the snow, centered the sight on Emerson's nose. As deer sometimes did, Emerson seemed to hear the stealthy approach of his death. He looked up, as if peering back at Krylov through the telescopic sight. He didn't flinch. Krylov fired.

The round took away Emerson's left ear, and he grabbed for the stump, his hand dark with blood, and looked wildly at the source of the shot. But he did not run. Krylov took more careful aim, inhaled, let out half his air…

A pistol shot, from the dacha, made him release the trigger. Krylov held his breath. There, a second shot. Seconds later, the place went up in flames, the antique, tinder-dry pine boards feeding a tornado of fire into the night.

Krylov lay his head against the snow. "Christ," he moaned. "Oh, Christ." Why? He was so close to saving them. Why do it now? He thought they, poor Peter, poor Anna, had read the situation wrong, had given up, had gone to fucking Plan Z. "Ah, Christ, ah, Christ."

Emerson hadn't moved. He stood outside the dacha, bathed in the hot yellow light of the fire, blood streaming from his wound. Krylov picked up the Dragunov and put Emerson back into the sight, this time with his right eye at the center. The telescope placed Emerson in the plane of the fire, as if he were rising from, or being consumed by, the flames.

"Is that you, Viktor?"

Krylov didn't answer.

"Did you do this?" The magnified man in the sight jumped around, as if he were running in place, with a handkerchief held against the wound like a mobile telephone. "Did you do this to me?" Krylov looked past the sight. Emerson was running at him, his free hand brandishing a pistol. *Did you fucking do this to me?"*

Krylov returned to the sight and put Emerson's right eye back in the center. He breathed in, breathed out, steadied. This was the man, he thought, who'd opened the cavern from which pestilence and death had fluttered into the world like a cloud of bats. This was the man who'd wanted to use Al-Rabiah's creation in his endless war. It was Emerson who'd let Axel be dropped from the sky, the egg to the pavement. Emerson had caused Anna and Peter to abandon hope and set themselves on fire.

With the ghost of Sasha and all the other dead lying beside him, Viktor Krylov squeezed the trigger, and saw Emerson's head explode.

Krylov lay there for what seemed to him a long time, the snow around him slowly melting in the hot light from the dacha. Trying to think what to do next, he kept stumbling against a vision of Peter readying the dacha for the torch, shooting Anna, shooting himself as the flames leapt skyward. "Ah, Christ."

"Nice shot." The black American named Conroy stood behind him, his assault rifle hanging from its sling, the muzzle pointed in Krylov's general direction. "Right betwixt the eyes, I mean, a very nice shot."

Krylov rolled over, leaning on his elbows. He thought this was about the right way for him to end up, blown apart by this black stranger. An American. But then it occurred to him that he had other work to do. He got slowly to his feet, brushing off the snow, and picked up the Dragunov. Ignoring Conroy, he walked slowly down to the lake. He followed the dark smear across the ice to where Lamont lay. Conroy came up and knelt by his colleague, trying with one ungloved hand to find a pulse.

"I thought he'd get farther than this," said Krylov.

"Me too," Conroy replied. "He was kinda crazy but, you know, brave, strong as could be." He studied the remains. "Course, you dinged him up pretty good here."

But Krylov wasn't listening. He kept going to where he'd left Axel, slung the rifle across his back, and picked up the frozen, broken boy of eighty-something. Then he turned and carried his old friend back across the lake to the dacha. There, leaning into the furnace heat of the fire, he laid Axel on a neat stack of chopped birch logs and put the dead man's hands upon his huge, cracked chest, making sure the rheumy eyes were closed. Surprised at what one remembered from childhood, Krylov made a small sign of the cross on Axel's forehead, and waited while the flames began their march up through the wood. He felt a powerful impulse to join his friends in the fire.

"Best come out of there," said Conroy. He took Krylov by the arm and led him gently toward the lake. Looking at what remained of Emerson, he asked, "We gonna put Ralph in the fire?"

Krylov looked at the surrounding trees. The large birds, black with grey capes, had begun to gather. "Let the crows have him."

For a time the two men watched the fire. Then Conroy said, "I'll tell you something, my man. I am a rough kind of person, you know, pretty dangerous, loyal as some dog. But old Emerson just wore me out with that crazy smallpox shit, like we need something worse than what we already got. Then dropping some scared old guy from a helicopter flat leaned out my allegiance. What I'm saying, I don't care what you did to Emerson and that mean boy of his or even to that old chopper. I intend you no harm at all. But I will have your car keys."

Krylov fished the Pajero keys out of his pocket and tossed them over to Conroy. "Good luck."

He turned back to the fire, and squatted down in the snow to watch the only property ever owned by the family Krylov and the remains of lost friends decline to nothing. Some distance away he heard the Pajero start up. Now and then an anguished sentence would drift over from the wrecked Mi-8. But mostly he sat in silence, except for the steady voice of the fire and a faint wind stirring the trees. One hates to leave a grave.

Toward dawn, when the dacha and its burden of dead were a smoldering mound of ash and stone, Krylov slung the Dragonuv over his shoulder and began walking cross-country toward Michurinskoya, a bit over ten kilometers away. Axel had got his mail there, and would have left his ancient Lada there when Emerson picked him up.

Krylov marched off through the frozen marshes and ponds, his heart in fragments. He thought he would never recover from this. Maxim had liked to tell him, *Only the end of the world is the end of the world.* Well, maybe this was it. Maybe this was the end of the world.

XXIX

If Krylov had been preoccupied before, he was haunted now. Peter and Anna followed him everywhere. When he slept they flowed into his dreams. He found himself kneeling in a rowboat floating on a dark sea, his hands gripping theirs, although the dreamer knew they must slip away into the black water. Then they were gone and Krylov was awake in a varnish of sweat, for a moment uncertain where or who he was.

They did not always sink into the sea, but the dreams always put them at risk, and he was always unable to help them. Their hands just slipped out of his and down they went. Krylov slept less and less, although, perversely, he was not ready for his ghosts to leave him alone.

During the day, he toiled as listlessly as a mule on a barge canal. His aura was so diminished that Klaus Oldenburg left him alone, as if he were no longer worth trying to bully. Juan Carlos Imler fluttered around, offering conversation, lunch, dinner, a play, anything to get the rusted Russian machinery going again. Krylov barely noticed, so busy was he reconstructing the final moments in the dacha.

He had no trouble imagining how the scene had opened. Peter and Anna would have heard the beat of the Mi-8 rotor, and seen Emerson and his helpers move into position. Gayle would have gone immediately to Plan Zed. They had no petrol, but the place was dry as reeds; kerosene and a single match would send it up to heaven. And then? Two shots. It was on the second shot that Krylov's scenario stalled.

Why two? The bargain they'd struck was that she would survive him. So why two shots?

Because, Krylov reasoned, Gayle knew Emerson's only interest was to capture or kill him. Anna was just someone to be silenced. Perhaps they'd talked it over. Perhaps she had preferred to die by Peter's hand. Perhaps they amended their bargain, embraced, prepared themselves as best they could for the end.

But how had Peter brought himself to kill poor Anna? A surprise from behind, like a Russian execution? Had he then laid her on the bed and put her hands together on her abdomen and kissed the fading warmth of her pale lips? Had he then flicked a flaring match into a pool of kerosene, felt the rising furnace heat, and brought the pistol to his temple, or his mouth, or his heart….?

"I'm like a fussy director trying to fix a play I don't understand," Krylov told Svetlana. "It's worse than the dreams."

Svetlana urged him to let Anna and Peter and Axel go. She told him he looked terrible, and, peering into her dark, eastern eyes, Krylov could see her heart was breaking. His behavior signaled that she was insufficient, that it was not in her power to cure him. He feared that she, like the others, would slip away. And he was no help at all. Krylov felt as constrained as a corpse sewn into a canvas sack for burial at sea. Poor Sveta could barely stand to look at him, but, of course, she said nothing. She let him do the talking, while her heart crumbled within.

"The strange part," Krylov explained to her, "is that I have been everywhere and seen everything. I have done terrible things and slept like a baby afterward. Yet here I am, trapped in the dacha, endlessly replaying a story I should have put to rest. Ordinarily, I would have closed this book and put it back on the shelf with all the other books of terrible things."

"But you did nothing terrible. You tried to save them. You stopped the ospa from spreading." A long, sad look at him. "Anna and Peter, and Axel too, would beg you to let it go. To let them go. It's not your business how they worked things out at the end."

"But I'm Russian, you see. And what does a Russian do when things don't make sense? He goes mad."

VIENNA WAS HAVING ONE OF THOSE PERFECT SPRINGS THAT DANCE in on the heels of serious winters. Birds sang their little hearts out in every tree, in every Hof; after dark, the nightingales took over. The entire city bloomed as flower-stalls bursting with color appeared everywhere. The sky was blue with barely a drop of the usual milkiness. Even the pewter Danube looked a bit blue. The air streamed crisp and cool, but not so cool one could not take a table outside at the Konzert Café Schwarzenberg.

Krylov found a table in a corner next to the Hapsburg-yellow wall, from which he could see the Ring and most approaches, and waited for Ivan Silmov, who had asked for a meeting. It seemed years since they had met and Silmov had handed him the envelope containing details on the April Ten. Al-Rabiah's ten chalices of death, all shattered now.

Silmov had arrived minutes later, sleek, well turned-out as usual in a raw silk suit of a midnight blue, a tie the color of arterial blood, a slate-colored shirt, shoes shiny as mirrors. He looked like the wealthy mayor of an American city. He was a long way from the charred young fellow Krylov had dragged from the Mi-8 wreckage in Afghanistan. One couldn't imagine this immaculate chap breaking a fingernail or letting his steel-grey hair go unattended for more than ten days at a time. Simlov had left his ostrich attaché case at home. Other than that, he was the same; his eyes were still empty of light, he was still a broken comrade. Krylov stood up and gave a slight bow, which Silmov returned, but neither offered to shake hands.

"Well, Viktor Viktorivich," Silmov began when he was seated, "here we are again."

"I thought we were finished."

"So did I. But then I thought, maybe not." Silmov studied him for a time, while a young man in a tuxedo took their order, a couple of mélanges and Linzertortes. "Are you all right, Viktor?"

"I am, how shall I say, a little run down."

"On the move, eh?"

Krylov nodded.

"More trips to Russia?"

"The usual amount." Krylov felt a chill of apprehension. Where was Simlov going?

"The reason I asked to meet, Viktor, I wanted to tell you about a bizarre incident up in your neck of the woods."

"My neck of the woods?"

"Leningrad Oblast."

"Nothing to do with me, I hope."

Silmov adjusted himself in his chair, then leaned toward Krylov, elbows on the little table. "It evidently occurred some weeks ago, but everything had been covered by snow, preserved like a popsicle until the thaw. Then some hikers made a horrible discovery."

Krylov looked away, watched the trams clanging and sparking on the Ring, listened to the din of traffic. The waiter brought their order.

"A dacha was burned to the ground, along with part of the surrounding forest."

"Dessicated wood loves fire."

"It loves kerosene too." Silmov grinned and, for an instant, Krylov thought he detected a glimmer of light in the dead eyes.

"Human remains were found in the ashes. So far we have, what, arson? Murder?"

Krylov fiddled with his coffee.

"But, wait, there's more. Outside the dacha was a man with his head blown apart. The crows had been at him before he was buried in snow. An American. A second body was in the nearby lake, another American. Someone had shot out his knees."

"Ugh."

Silmov took a moment to break off a chunk of torte and chew it carefully with his incisors, like a rodent, then wash it down with a sip of mélange. "Not two kilometers away from the dacha was a wrecked Mi-8 helicopter. Well, we know that machine pretty well, don't we?"

Krylov nodded.

"This one had Russian markings. It was deserted. A real mystery for them."

"'Them' being…?"

"The St. Petersburg and Leningrad Oblast Department of Special Affairs."

"And how did they resolve this mystery?"

"It had all the earmarks of a mafia operation gone astray. Drugs, weapons, laundered money. Who knows? The helicopter was seen earlier at Lappeenranta, just across the line in Finland. A mysterious Gulfstream flew out just hours before the Finnish police visited the aerodrome. That was the reason for involving us. Otherwise we would not have known about it."

"We the FSB?"

"We my little corner of the government."

"Did the people from Leningrad Oblast reach any conclusions?"

"In the end they applied Ockham's Razor. Things are generally what they seem. A bunch of bad guys shooting each other to death over something valuable. The dead men were Americans. The helicopter crew was Bulgarian, or so the Finns at Lappeenranta told us. We are giving them a little squeeze to get a better picture of what happened, and then we will send what's left of them home. And the burned remains in the dacha? Nobody knows."

"Why tell me about it?"

Silmov laughed aloud. "Why, because the dacha is your property."

"I'm not sure you'd call it 'property' if you saw the place. I'm surprised it lasted until now. It was abandoned long ago."

"You know, Viktor Viktorivich, we had about lost interest in you. But then here I was, skimming a report of this strange incident from Leningrad Oblast and suddenly, *boom!*, I see your name. Viktor Viktorivich Krylov, property owner. What a tiny world, I say to myself. Then I recall that you were in Russia back in November…"

"Inspecting the Leningrad II reactor."

"Yes, so I saw. Aided by your British colleague, Mr. Churches."

"Yes."

"And by your good friend, Svetlana Trulova."

"She hadn't been home in a while."

"The dacha. Completely abandoned?"

"I have an old fellow who looks after it." Krylov thought of the tiny, broken body lying on the ice. It was like remembering nothing about poor Yorick but the skull.

"A reliable old fellow?"

"I would trust him with anything."

"Would he have been involved in the mafia?"

Krylov made himself laugh. "Axel? He's more than eighty years old. He's feeble-minded."

"Sometimes feeble minds run deeper than you think. Sometimes the idiot is the wise man."

"Dostoyevsky would have us think so."

"I think he may have died in the fire. Axel, I mean."

"I doubt it. I will write to him."

"How did Mr. Churches perform at Leningrad II?"

"He was not able to finish the work with me."

"And where is he now?"

Krylov shrugged. "I am not his keeper."

"Then I'll tell you. His ashes are feeding his mother's roses in Suffolk."

"Devon."

"He accompanied you posthumously."

Krylov said nothing.

"And how did Ms. Trulova like Russia, considering she never left Vienna?"

Krylov scanned the traffic again and this time found what he was looking for. Simlov's pair of goons loafed across the Opernring, reading a tabloid, occasionally looking up to see how things were going.

"They are here in case you grab me by the throat."

"I will try not to."

"What took you back to St. Petersburg?"

"When?"

"The last time, in February."

"Probably more Leningrad II."

"No, you went to see this posthumous version of Mr. Churches and this fake Trulova woman. They were at the dacha. You drove out to see them in a Pajero all-wheeler from Hertz." Simlov wasn't looking at Krylov, but into the coffee, which he stirred slowly, round and round, with a spoon. "You are not a drugs or money or weapons kind of person, Viktor. So what were you up to?"

"I took two friends to the dacha. The Americans wanted them. I went to see how they were coping."

"But the Americans were there ahead of you."

Krylov nodded.

"You know," Simlov said, grinning with genuine warmth, "the police found your rental car."

"Good. I reported the theft to Hertz."

"Yes, you said you parked it while dining at Restaurant 1913 and when you came out it was gone. But, in fact, it was driven away from the dacha."

How long had it been since he'd eaten at 1913, Krylov wondered. He couldn't recall the food, but there had been three beautiful women with long dark hair, dressed in furs and boots, one playing the cello, another the violin, the third singing in a clear soprano. Krylov smiled, remembering.

"Are you listening?"

"Sorry. The car was insured. I had what they call a Self-Protection Policy."

"They found it up by the Finnish border, in terrible condition."

"Thieves never take care of what they steal."

"Something had cut the roof to pieces, torn off the front right wing and trim. They must have run it into a wheat combine. Or maybe a big helicopter."

Krylov thought about Conroy with the Pajero, dumping it near the boundary and nipping across. When the Gulfstream took off from Lappeenranta he must have been aboard. "Too bad. It was a pretty nice car."

"Out of curiosity, how did you get back to St. Petersburg?"

Krylov couldn't help but smile. "The hard way."

There'd been no Lada waiting for him in Michruinskoya after all. Axel had apparently parked it somewhere else.

"You walked?"

"I found a ride."

Krylov had started down the road with the Dragunov cradled in his right arm. When he heard the sound of a motor behind him, he turned and held up a palm, and a Japanese pickup slid to a halt. He got in and told the small, middle-aged fellow at the wheel that he needed to get to Pulkovo. The driver had looked at the sky. Then he told Krylov to get in, adding that something weird was always happening out here. But he admired the rifle and said he didn't mind taking Krylov to the airport, despite the cost of fuel. When Krylov got out at Pulkovo, he gave the Dragunov to the driver.

"Leningrad Oblast also found an antique Lada registered to you."

"Really? Where?"

"In St. Petersburg."

"I have no idea." Krylov wondered how he would incorporate the Lada into his scenario. Why would Axel leave his car in the city?

"I think the human remains in the dacha are your friends. Do you know how they died?"

"I am still trying to figure it out."

"The Americans killed them."

"Maybe. The Americans killed Axel."

"And you killed them."

Krylov looked at the traffic.

Simlov finished his mélange, brushed his jacket and trousers with a quick flick of his hand, and stood up.

"What now?" asked Krylov.

"Well, you could be sent home and tried for murder, traveling on false papers, arson, car theft, all sorts of things."

Ordinarily, Krylov would by now have worked out a defensive maneuver that his old comrade in arms might not have survived. But today he was numb to dire possibilities; what happened, happened. "I could wind up covered with tattoos and eating stone soup."

"You could. You probably will. But not because of me. I agree with Leningrad Oblast. The incident is just what it seems. Now the matter evaporates."

"That's good of you."

"You saved me, Viktor. Now I've saved you. We are back to square one, as they say." Simlov looked into Krylov's eyes. "You're not getting any younger. Stop making trouble for yourself. Get a hobby. A dog. Fall in love." He grinned, and for a moment Krylov saw the young Alfa Group officer of long ago. "Otherwise you'll end up looking like me."

"You look like a million euros, Ivan."

"I meant on the inside." Silmov put out his hand and Krylov took it.

Then Krylov asked, "The Lada, where was it in St. Petersburg?"

"Oh, on the street. Near the Finland Station."

Then he strode off into the eddying Opernring crowd, his two goons moving into position twenty meters behind him.

NEXT DAY KRYLOV WAS IN HIS OFFICE, head down, towing barges as usual, when Lou Bell stopped by. The little reporter tapped on the door, then stepped in, closing it behind him. Even dressed for the lovely Vienna spring in light jacket and paisley tie, Bell looked as if he'd lost his ship and washed up on the banks of the Danube. His exhausted blue eyes retained their former wildness, their evocation of having looked too often upon the unspeakable. Bell gave Krylov a lunatic grin and stuck out his hand for shaking. "Viktor, hallo."

"Hello, Lou," said Krylov, taking the proffered hand, both men putting something extra into the squeeze. To Krylov's surprise, he felt real pleasure at seeing Bell.

"I was in the area and thought I might pop in. Buy you lunch or something."

"Have a seat." Krylov waved at what he thought of as Imler's chair.

Bell sat down, studying Krylov closely, like a mental patient taking the measure of his psychiatrist. "Actually, this isn't entirely a social call."

Krylov laughed. "Have you made an entirely social call in your life?"

"I must stop wearing my notebook on my sleeve. But, no, I guess I haven't. I've been thinking about the cave."

The cave, thought Krylov, where all of this began. "A long time ago now."

"Barely half a year. Not very long at all. The thing is, when I walk out into the desert people talk to me. They may be afraid not to. Piercing blue eyes, certifiably mad to be out there at all. But they tell me things. The last few weeks I was up in what will one day be

Kurdistan. A lot of mythology with the cave at its center. People disappearing. People dying mysteriously. They even tell a tale of a man and his three sons going away to discover the Secret of the Cave, and never returning."

"The elusive Grail."

Bell nodded. "So, as I was in Vienna I thought I might give Emerson a squeeze, see if he'd share with me. But the embassy says he's not in town. Off the record, they don't have a clue where he's got to. Then our man in Moscow tells me the authorities found one of those tableaux that belong in the Mexican desert, only it was north of St. Petersburg. Crashed Russian helicopter. Two American bodies. Maybe because of the Russian chopper, I immediately thought of Emerson."

"You thought it was time to give me one of those squeezes."

"Exactly."

"I don't see any great mystery. Of course people who went into the cavern came down with radiation sickness, which, if you don't know the source, can seem like black magic. I don't know about the father and sons. And Emerson being Emerson, he's often absent. I wouldn't try to connect those dots."

"What was really in the cave?"

"What we told you at the time. Cesium isotope. Signs of a very hot fire. Some debris. Some human ash."

"But no dirty-bomb factory."

"No."

"So what was it? You promised to tell me."

Krylov waited, framing his reply. "A laboratory."

The stubby pencil and narrow notepad came out.

"But that was a long time ago. The Iraqis shut it down after the first Gulf war."

"Why shut it down?"

"Because it was a failure."

"How a failure?"

"It was like the Nazi Bomb, years of marching up a blind canyon. The things they were building didn't work. So, in the end, the Iraqis destroyed the lab and masked the ruins with fire and radiation."

"What were they building?"

"Monsters."

"Monsters?"

"Yes."

For a time the two men sat in silence, Bell peering at Krylov, the Russian studying some invisibility on the wall. Finally Bell shook his head and put his pencil and notebook away. "That's it, isn't it?"

"Yes, Lou, that's it."

"I'm withdrawing my offer of lunch."

"I understand."

"I think I'll go see Sophie Nieman's pretty sister. Maybe she'll join me for dinner."

"She's....away."

"Away where?"

Krylov shrugged. "I think she went to visit her grandmother in Klagenfurt."

Bell laughed aloud. "Code for you don't know? She's probably run off with Emerson." He got up to go. "Christ, what an outfit!"

KRYLOV SAT IN THE DIM, AQUEOUS LIGHT OF THE SACHER'S BLUE BAR, nuts and pickles on the low marble table, a glass of sub-zero Russian vodka condensing moisture out of the air. The room was quiet as an azure grotto under the sea.

It was coming on Easter, Svetlana had told him, they should go out, somewhere nice so they could dress up. He could wear one of those linen-silk KGB suits of his. She would come in on the bus from the Centre and meet him at the Sacher bar, and they would work out the rest of the evening from there.

Things were better between them. After his talk with Simlov, he'd told her, "The police found our old Lada by the Finland Station. Why would Axel leave it there?"

"Maybe it died on him. You know, like an old horse."

. "I wonder how he got home?"

"We'll never know."

And there, for the first time, Krylov had really heard the fatigue in her voice, which said, *Please, please, please, I am so tired of this.* Her exhaustion was so deep and so visible that he promised himself to take better care of this beloved and irreplaceable woman. He had given up talking about the dacha, the lost people, the dreams, the two shots. Indeed, he began to think he might be healing, becoming his old self. For her, the bear might even do a few laps on his unicycle.

Svetlana appeared at the entrance to the bar, what Maxim had called her little glowing moonface in its dark wreath of a braid. She waved at him, he gave her a salute, and then she hurried across the floor and sat down on the loveseat next to his chair. "Sorry to be late, the traffic was terrible."

Sveta took off her light raincoat and carefully laid it on the cushion next to her. She wore a light, canary cardigan and a spring dress that was like a spiral of climbing flowers, and the amber necklace from the shop at Tsarskoye Selo. Krylov thought she had never looked more beautiful, and something in his expression must have signaled it, for she turned away and even blushed.

Krylov gestured to the waiter, who came over and took an order for two more vodkas and a snacks menu.

"That would be wonderful, I'm starving," she said. "But I almost forgot. Look here." She rummaged in her raincoat and handed him a red and yellow envelope. "This came for you today. Sent care of me at the Centre."

"What is it?"

"How would I know? It was for you."

Krylov hefted the packet. The label said it had been sent overnight from Lausanne. He held it to his ear and up to the light of the chandelier. "I don't want to spoil our evening by having my hand blown off."

"Who's it from?"

"It says 'Piers Ploughman.' No one I know."

"We read *Piers Ploughman* in school, but I don't remember what it was about. Open it."

Krylov found a thumbhold and ripped open the envelope. He extracted what looked like small booklets, wrapped in white paper with an elastic band around them. Svetlana leaned toward him as he undid the band. Krylov found his heart drumming like a bird's, and Sveta's cheeks were flushed and rosy. They glanced at each other; he pulled away the paper.

There were two passports. One was the color of old blood, embossed with the double-headed eagle of imperial Russia. The other was dark blue bearing the insignia of the United Nations. Krylov's hands trembled, he had difficulty breathing.

He opened the Russian passport, issued to Svetlana Maximovna Trulova. The other bore the surname Churches. Both had been stamped out of Russia at Svetugorsk and stamped into Finland at Imatra.

Krylov's eyes filled with tears. Two shots fired into the air. The empty dacha up in flames. Axel's Lada waiting at Michurinskoye, then abandoned at the Finland Station. He felt as if his heart had begun to beat again after a long silence.

"There's something else," said Sveta.

She held up a postal card on which a white hotel poised against its mountain, golden awnings set like sails, and, along the roof, in large yellow capitals,

VICTORIA.

On the back was written: *No more monsters. Wish you were here.*

"Will you take me there?"

Krylov nodded, unable to speak.

###

Carl A. Posey is the author of eight published novels, a number of non-fiction books, and dozens of magazine articles, many of them involving science and, because he is a licensed pilot, aviation. He lives with his British wife and Norwegian elkhound in Alexandria, Virginia.

carlposeyworks.com